Rose's

By
A.L. Stephens

Rock Creek Press

Rock Creek Press

First Edition. Printed in the United States of America.

Books may be purchased in quantity by contacting: alstephensbooks@gmail.com or Rock Creek Press at 541-580-4717

PB ISBN: (pbk.) 978-1-946353-11-5
PB ISBN: (EPUB) 978-1-946353-10-8

Books written by the author:

Emma Hart and the Demi gods (Book 1)

Emma Hart and the Werewolves (Book 2)

Along Came You

Rose Bud's (Sequel to Rose's)

CONTENTS

CHAPTER 1

I look up from my book and glance around Central Park for what feels like the tenth time. I've been sitting here reading and drinking my coffee for— I glance at my watch — 45 minutes already. I pull my phone out and see I have no missed calls or texts.

He should be here soon, I think to myself. For the last year we've met at this spot to celebrate certain things. This time, it's my birthday.

I can't believe it's been over a year already, I think to myself again.

I look back down at my book and think back to when my life changed last year.

My family owns Rose's, an elegant restaurant in New York City. Last year my parents, Stephen and Viki Rose, approached me about their retirement and having me buy out their shares. But I couldn't, and still can't afford to. I'm still paying on my culinary education loans. Along with the ones I took out to go to school in Italy and travel.

I went to the Institute of Culinary Education, also known as ICE, in New York City. When I finished there, I traveled to Italy and went to a school there called the Italian Chef Academy. After finishing there, I spent one year traveling around different countries, learning from different chefs.

Rose's started focusing more on Italian foods because of my schooling in Italy. I found I enjoyed cooking mostly Italian by the end of my time abroad. We made the transition almost three years ago, when I got home from my time away. I also love baking, which is why I have my own little bakery and coffee shop called Rose Bud's. Because of my love for baking, the dessert menu at Rose's has a wide variety of delicious treats. Not only do we do Italian food, but we also have a couple steak and seafood options on the menu.

So, my parents want to retire. I can't buy them out yet, so they have spread the word that they are looking for a partner to buy them out. There is a clause in the contract that states once I am able to buy the partner out, they can't contest it. I'm not too excited about that option, but I can't really see another way, so I reluctantly agree.

About a year had gone by since they announced they wanted to retire and there still weren't any signs of anyone who was interested. I was closer to paying off my loans but I'm still a few years out. I had contemplated on taking out more loans or selling Rose Bud's, even though it was doing so well. Just thinking of it made me want to cry. But it might be the only way to buy Mom and Dad out.

I talked to my parents about that option at one of our

family dinners and they told me absolutely not. They said they can wait until they find someone or until I can do it without a loan, and they told me I am definitely not to sell Rose Bud's. So, we've waited.

It's been three months since that conversation. But, as I'm about to board my connecting flight, I get a call from my mom saying they have an interested purchaser, and I won't believe who it is. My parents say they won't make any decisions until I'm back and can meet the interested party. They refuse to tell me who it is, or give any hints.

I send a text to my boyfriend, Jason, that I'm boarding my last flight and should be home shortly. I've been out of town for the weekend, at my best friends, Kayla and Peter's house in Wichita, Kansas. Peter called me a couple weeks ago and said that he was going to propose and wanted me and Jason there. However, Jason couldn't make it because of work. The four of us have been friends since high school. So, I flew out to Kansas, watched as he got down on one knee, and proposed.

The last stretch of the flight goes by in a flash and before I know it, the plane touches down and we're taxiing on the runway. I pull my phone out and send a text to Jason, to let him know I made it back. I don't have to go to baggage claim, since I was only away for two days, my carry on is all that I need to grab.

When I get through the airport, I call my mom to let them know I've landed and heading home. She, however, tells me to get to the restaurant, the interested party is there looking it over now.

"Mom, I can't come right now," I protest. "I'm still in

traveling clothes."

"Abbigail, he won't mind, just get over here," she insists.

"Okay, fine, I'll be right there," I tell her. Then I stick my hand out and holler, "Taxi!"

I still haven't received a message or call from Jason by the time a Taxi pulls up. I tell the driver where I need to go and we zip out into traffic quickly. As we make our way to Rose's, I try to clean myself up the best I can. Luckily, I'm wearing black jogger type leggings and a black t-shirt, so I'm not dressed too bad. I fix my makeup, which only ever consists of mascara and eyeliner, and throw my hair into a messy bun, behind my ear. There's not much I can do with it sitting in the car.

Looking in the little mirror from my travel bag, I notice my dad's hazel green eyes and smile. Out of my parents looks, his eyes are the only things I got. Both my parents, and my older siblings, Patty and Spencer, are all blonde. My mom, brother, and sister all have blue eyes. My dad and Spencer are in the 6-foot range and my mom is around that 5'8-5'10 height zone. My sister, who's the oldest, has Down-Syndrome, and is an inch shorter than I am but when she wears the right shoes, she is taller and likes to boast about it. I'm 5'4", brown hair with natural honey highlights, and I have a nice sun kissed tan color to my skin year-round. And as a baker and chef, I'm pretty curvy.

We pull up to the restaurant thirty minutes later and it's packed, as per usual. I've trained my Sous Chef perfectly. Which he didn't take much training since we went to school together in Italy. His name is Royce Romano.

Patty meets me at the door and she's giddy.

"What's up, Sis?" I ask.

"I can't tell. Mom says I can't tell anyone," Patty says, bouncing.

"Tell anyone what?" I ask.

"Who's here," Patty answers, she starts biting her fingernails, her sign she's nervous and excited.

"Why are you so nervous?" I ask, rubbing her arm, trying to calm her down.

"Because I want to tell you, but I don't want Mom mad at me. She says it's a surprise."

"Okay, you don't have to tell me. I'll go find out," I say, kissing Patty on the head.

I can't think of anyone who would make my family act this crazy. We're used to famous people coming into Rose's all the time. As I walk through the restaurant, I greet customers as I go, and I eyeball the food on the tables. Everything looks top notch, and I think to myself, *Way to go Royce.*

When I get back to the kitchen, I tell the staff they're doing an amazing job, and to keep it up.

Royce stops me, "Do you know who's here?"

"No," I say.

Before he can elaborate, my mom, sticks her head out of the office door and comes out to Royce and me.

She points to her ear and says, "Patricia said you were here. Come on, come on. He's a patient man but he's also very busy."

"Who?" I ask again.

Mom doesn't say anything and just smiles. We walk into the large office that my parents and I share. There are three desks in different corners and a larger table in the middle that seats eight people comfortably.

I skid to a stop. Sitting with my dad at his desk is none other than Kallon Keller. Kallon Keller the mega popular actor. Not to mention the best-looking man I have ever seen. He was/is my celebrity crush.

Kallon is well over 6 feet tall. Dark, almost black hair. Blue eyes. Right now, he's rocking a little scruffy beard, but the jaw line and chin are looking stronger than ever. Even wearing slacks and a button up shirt, I can see his sculpted muscles straining against his clothes.

Mom loops her arm in mine and pulls me towards Dad and Kallon. I have to remind my legs they know how to work. In a nano second, I have a quick moment to think there is no way Kallon Keller is interested in Rose's. Another nano second, I decide I need to treat him like anyone else, with respect. But I need answers if he really is interested. Just because he's Kallon mother-lovin'-Keller, doesn't mean I should act like a crazy, lovesick fan. I put my game face on and walk more confidently into the room.

"Oh, here she is," my dad says.

Kallon turns and smiles at me as my mom and I get closer. Both he and my dad stand. Mom gestures for me to sit next to Kallon, while she walks around to the other side and sits next to my dad.

"Mr. Keller, this is our daughter, Abbigail Rose," my dad says. He and Mom are the only ones who call me by my full name, unless they call me by my family nickname, which is Buds. "Abbigail, this is Mr. Kallon Keller."

"Please, Mr. Rose, as I've said before, call me Kallon,"

Kallon says to Dad. He turns to me and offers me his hand. "It's nice to finally meet you, Miss Rose."

"It's nice to meet you as well, Mr. Keller," I say taking his very large hand and giving it a soft but firm shake. Dad always said just because I'm a girl doesn't mean my handshake should feel like a noodle.

Kallon squeezes my hand back gently and smiles an earth stopping grin and says, "Please, all of you, call me Kallon." He smiles at all of us.

We all take a seat and sit in silence for a moment. I look at my parents and they nod at me to take charge. Interviews and leading a meeting aren't new to me. As the Head Chef and restaurant assistant manager, I've had to run so many meetings I've lost count.

I clear my throat and say, "So, I take it you're the one who is interested in Rose's, Mr.—" I start to say but change it to, "—Kallon."

"I am, Miss Rose," Kallon says.

"Abby, please," I suggest.

Kallon smiles and nods, "Okay, Abby—" another smile "—I am definitely interested in Rose's."

"Do you know much about our restaurant? What all have my parents told you?" I ask.

"I know the food is fantastic, as I've eaten here almost every time I have a free moment. As far as what your parents have said? Not much. Other than they're looking for someone to buy their shares so they can retire. I presume you are their other partner?"

"I am and I'm the Head Chef," I say. Still surprised Kallon has eaten here. I don't remember ever being told he was here. Although we tell our staff to treat all customers the same, I still would have thought I'd been told about him. "Although, my sister holds a small portion of the shares as well."

"You're Head Chef?" he asks, looking a little surprised.

"I am," I say, proudly.

"I'm impressed," Kallon says, smiling at me.

I blush and as I tell him about Rose's, he pulls a small notepad from his pocket and starts to take notes.

"Rose's is open Tuesday through Saturday, 4pm to midnight. There are three stories to the building. A bar and the kitchen are on the main floor. There are 75 tables that seat four to each, totalling 300 seats. The main floor dining area can seat 100 people. The remaining 200 seats are on the 2nd floor, which has it's own bar. The second-floor bar is a wrap around and is located in the middle of the floor. There are 21 additional seats at that bar itself, as well. There is a laundry room on the second floor."

"The third story is for events like weddings, parties, and meetings. It's big enough for 200 people or it can be portioned off for different meetings or functions that need to take place at the same time for smaller number of attendees. We also have a suite available for bridal parties or other people to use if they want the premium package."

"Kitchen staff gets here at 3pm to prepare for the day and stops cooking at 10 o'clock PM. Kitchen staff works from 3pm-11:30pm. They have an hour for prep and an hour and a half for clean-up. Servers arrive at 3:30pm. They must have tables cleared by midnight if all customers have left. We won't push people out if they are still drinking and having a good time, but they can't stay past 1 AM. I'm the one that stays if there is a table or two that is still here after midnight," I take a minute to think about what else to tell him.

"Umm, we have a cleaning crew that comes in the mornings and vacuums and washes windows. They also do the laundry. We have 15 people for our kitchen staff, 16 if you count me. There are 18 servers for the restaurant, six for the main floor and twelve for the second floor. There are three hostesses on the first floor and two on the second floor. There are three bartenders and three servers for the bar areas. There are nine additional tables in the main floor bar for patrons to wait to be seated in the restaurant, but they can choose to stay in the bar. There are 10 more seats at the bar, as well. We have nine bussers, three for the main floor and the remaining six for the second."

"Everyone gets a 30-minute lunch break and breaks when they need it throughout the evening. All employees are on a salary, plus benefits, and time off. We… well, I, cover the time off, but it has to be reasonable and there can't be multiple people gone at the same time or during our busiest time of the year. Mom and Dad found that if they created a family like working environment that pays well and offers benefits, our turnover rate is practically nonexistent, they all want to stay. We do ask that our employees don't smoke, as no one likes their server or the kitchen crew to smell like cigarette smoke. For the most part, we haven't had a problem asking this of our staff."

I lean back and look to my parents, raising my eyebrows, in a gesture to ask if I've left anything out. They smile at me and then look at Kallon.

"Well, it sounds like a wonderful place to work and as I stated before, the food is incredible," Kallon says with a wink. I blush again. "So, talk to me about the contract side of things."

My dad clears his throat and says, "We have a few contingencies for the contract. Now that Abbigail is here, we can go over what we would like to see happen."

"Okay," Kallon says, leaning back, getting comfy in his seat. He flips another page in his notepad and looks ready to take more notes. He smiles and says, "I'm listening."

"The most important thing is that when Abbigail is ready and able, she can buy you out of the contract. The part you buy is from us. She can buy it back from you when she's ready. You basically get your money back," Dad says.

Kallon looks deep in thought, writes a note, but nods for Dad to keep going.

"Staff stays as is, as does the way the restaurant is run. You run things by Abbigail if you see that improvements can be made or have any suggestions," Dad says.

Again, Kallon doesn't say anything but nods for him to go on and writes another note. Dad looks at Mom.

She says, "Our other daughter, Patricia—" Mom pauses "—Well, we'd like for her to stay on as long as she would like to. There aren't a lot of job opportunities for people with Down-Syndrome and she has been working here since we opened. She does a great job and loves what she does. We believe she creates a happy, fun atmosphere for patrons when they walk through the doors. She remembers our most loyal customers and knows where they prefer to sit, and which servers they like best."

Mom stops and looks nervous, but Kallon still nods her on and once again, takes a note.

"Stephen and I would like to stop in occasionally, just to visit with customers and check on the place. This place was our dream come true; we'd like to still be a part of it when we're here in town. We plan to travel and enjoy retirement, so don't worry about us being here all the time," Mom says with her nervous laugh.

Kallon nods again and writes something down.

Mom looks at Dad and raises her eyebrows.

"Oh, the shares. We understand we are asking a lot, but we'd like for you and Abbigail to split the shares, 45 to 45, equal partners," Dad says.

"And I take it Patricia has the other 10 shares?" Kallon asks, pen at the ready.

"Yes," I answer this one before my parents can reply. Some of their contingencies make me feel like they think I'm just going to kick my family to the curb after they sell their shares.

"I see… Okay," Kallon says. "Anything else?"

"This sale and contract only apply to Rose's. Rose Bud's Bakery is Abbigail's, and hers' alone," Dad says, sternly.

"I'm sorry?" Kallon asks in surprise.

"Rose Bud's Bakery is my bakery over across from Central Park," I say. "I work there in the mornings and the days that Rose's is closed."

"That's your bakery?" Kallon asks in disbelief.

"It is," I say, nodding my head.

"You have the best—" he shakes his head "—well, everything. My assistant brings me coffee and breakfast from there every day while we're in New York."

"Oh, well, thank you," I say, smiling.

Kallon laughs a little and then says to my parents, "Okay, is that everything?"

My parents look at each other for a moment and then look at Kallon.

Dad nods and says, "Yes, we think so."

"Let me see if I got everything," Kallon says, pulling his notepad closer to himself. "You'd like Abby to pay me back when she's able, giving her the majority of the shares. In the meantime, you'd like for her and me to have equal shares, 45 to 45, with Patricia keeping her 10. Patricia keeps her job, as does everyone else. The restaurant stays as is unless I have a good idea. You two would like to come by when you're in town, for a visit. Abby's bakery stays hers'. I paraphrased but did I forget anything?"

"Sounds about right," Dad says, Mom nods.

"I have no problem with any of that. I have bought many well-established businesses and kept them running as is. Why mess with what's been working? However, I feel like with this deal, I'm more of a silent partner, which I have no problem with but with how much money I'm willing to pay, I do have one stipulation of my own," Kallon says, as he puts his notepad down.

I sit up straight in my seat and look between him and my parents.

"And that is?" my dad asks.

"There needs to be a time limit for Abby to come up with the funds. It can't be an open-ended contingency," he states.

Mom and Dad look at me.

"What do you propose?" I ask. I don't want to mess this deal up for my parents but if his suggestion on a time frame is outrages, I either deny and we wait for another buyer or risk having him as a business partner for life. Which honestly, wouldn't be a bad thing, if he does have some successful businesses.

"Three years?" Kallon suggests.

My heart drops. I'm scheduled to be done paying off my loans by then. I could take out another loan and figure some other options out but before I can say anything, my dad talks.

"Five years," he counters.

Kallon looks at me and then back to my dad.

"Five years would be better for me," I say.

Kallon looks at the table, rubbing his chin as he thinks.

"Okay, five years. But, if after the five-year mark, you haven't bought back the shares or you decide having me as a business partner isn't so bad, I get to keep my shares," Kallon says with a smile.

"What happens if in ten years, you decide you want out of the restaurant industry?" I ask.

"You get first dibs to buy me out," he states.

I look at my parents, they're smiling. They like how this meeting is going.

But I have a couple questions of my own.

"Why do you want to buy into Rose's?" I ask.

"It's a great business opportunity," Kallon says.

"And you have no problem with being, to use your term, a silent partner?" I ask.

"No problem at all. Why would I mess with something,

mess with a restaurant, that is booked out for weeks on end? You all run this very well, I see nothing that needs to change."

"How often are you in New York?"

"Pretty often. My last movie was filmed here and my current one is being filmed here also."

"When you're not here, where do you call home?"

"Well, I have a couple homes. One here, although it's a penthouse. I have a house on some acres in Montana. A suite in Seattle. And a penthouse in LA. Oh, and a condo in Hawaii," he says, looking sheepish for some reason.

"You call all of those place's home?" I ask.

"Home is wherever I'm at and the happiest," he smiles, and I see his dimples under his facial hair. "Sometimes that's in Hawaii and sometimes that's in Montana."

"Not in Seattle or LA?" I ask, intrigued. I can see my mom looking at me in a way that says I need to stop asking personal questions. But, if this man is to be my business partner, I need to get to know the real him and not what I've read in magazines. Which haven't been bad things, but still, I want to hear things about him, from him personally.

"Seattle and LA are more for when I'm working, like here in New York," he says. "I have a couple businesses in both Seattle and LA but also have shot movies in both cities as well. It's nice having a place to go to instead of living in the trailers the studios provide."

"That makes sense," I say.

Mom cuts in and says, "Unless there's anything else business wise you have to ask Kallon, he probably needs to get back to set or back with his lawyers to make this deal final."

"Oh right, sorry. No, I don't have any more questions pertaining to business, not right now anyways," I say, embarrassed.

"Don't be sorry. I don't mind. I feel like we should get to know each other better, especially if we're going to be partners."

"I agree," I say, smiling at him and then looking pointedly at my mom.

"Oh, I do have one more stipulation," Kallon says, getting our attention.

"What's that?" I ask.

"I would like for my partnership to be kept a secret. You'd be surprised how many people try to take advantage of a 'deal' they might be able to get because they think we're friends or because we've worked on a movie. Or they're friends of a friend. I had to learn the hard way when I bought my first hotel chain. So, if you'd like to keep making a profit and not piss off celebrities or other people who think they are entitled to free stuff because of who they are or who they know, it would be best to keep my name out of the public knowledge part of the business," he says.

"That can be arranged. Only on the contract will your name be listed, and we can make that confidential. Is there a name you'd like to use as code?" Dad asks.

"Charles Webb," Kallon says laughing. "Charlotte's Web was, is, my favorite book from my childhood."

I can't help but laugh. What an unexpected thing to say, it's my favorite childhood book too.

"Charles Webb it is," Dad says. He turns to me and adds, "See sweety, you two have more in common than you probably knew."

Mom and Dad stand and shake Kallon's hand.

"We'll have our lawyers draw up the contract and get it sent over to you, then we can negotiate the price," Dad says as he and Mom walk out.

"Sounds good, sir," Kallon says.

I stand and make my way to the door.

"Tomorrow is Sunday," Kallon says as I get to him.

I yawn and nod. My long day of travel is catching up to me.

"Are you working at your bakery in the morning?"

"I am," I say.

"I'll stop by, and we can chat. Get to know each other better?" he says it like a question.

"Sounds good," I say, smiling.

"I take it you aren't working today?" he asks as we walk through the kitchen.

"No, I took the weekend off. My best friend, Kayla, got engaged yesterday—" I point to myself "—I'm her oldest and best friend. Her fiancé, Peter, who's also an old friend of mine, wanted me there for the proposal."

As we walk through the kitchen, I tell the kitchen staff to keep up the good work. I look at the clock and see it's 7:15pm. Four more hours and I'll have been up for 24 hours, the downside to the red eye flights with a layover. I couldn't sleep on the planes or in the airport either, too many people and too much noise.

I look around and see everyone staring at Kallon.

"Hey," I say, as I walk us out of the kitchen. "What do we tell the staff? I feel like we can trust them, but they are human and might get excited and tell someone. It's hard not to brag if you're one of the bosses."

Kallon laughs, "Well, I do a gag order. If they want to stay working here, they sign it stating they won't tell anyone who the new owner is unless they want to be fired and fined a certain amount of money. I've done this with my other businesses when my anonymity couldn't be kept quiet from staff, and it's worked so far."

"That's a good idea. I wouldn't feel right lying to my staff. I wasn't kidding when I said they're more like family than employees," I say.

We get to the front where my parents are talking to Patty, she sees us coming.

"Were you surprised?" she asks.

"Yes, I was," I say, smiling at her.

"Your boyfriend is here to see you," she says clapping her hands.

"Oh, Patty, Kallon isn't my boyfriend," I say as my face turns bright red from embarrassment.

"But you have his poster in your room at Mom and Dad's. He's younger in it, but it is him," Patty says, scrutinizing Kallon.

My eyes go big, and I feel what was my red face, drain of all color. Leave it to my sister to remember the one poster I had hanging up from my teenage years. I put my hands over my face and shake my head. I can hear Kallon and my parents laughing.

I put my hands down and say, "And on that note, I'm going to say goodbye."

"Did I say something bad?" Patty asks with concern.

"No, Sis, you're okay. I'll see you tomorrow for lunch?" I ask her, not looking at Kallon.

"Like every Sunday," she says with her little sassy tone.

"Okay, see you tomorrow," I hug her. "Bye Mom, bye Dad."

"Bye Abbigail," they say with too much humor in their tones as they hug me.

"Bye, Kallon... It was nice meeting you," I say, not looking him in the eyes, but extending my hand out to him to shake.

"You as well, Abby. See you tomorrow," he says, shaking my hand. Then he adds. "I have a few more questions for you."

I look up in shock and he winks and then starts to quietly laugh. I turn and rush out the doors, embarrassed.

CHAPTER 2

I wake up early and make my way downstairs to get my bakery up and running for the day. Betty Brown, my right-hand gal here at Rose Bud's, came in yesterday and prepped all the things for today. She won't be in until 8am but I need to thank her again for all her hard work.

Betty is about ten years older than me. She's about 5'8", gold blonde hair that she keeps in a tight bun at the nape of her neck, and kind green eyes. She loves baking as much as I do, and I was lucky to find her a year ago when I realized I needed some help in the bakery. I had only had my ad out for 'HELP NEEDED' for one morning, when she stopped in, and filled out an application. She was working in a grocery store bakery department at the time and the hours weren't conducive to her home life.

Betty's a single mother of a pre-teen, Maggie —who is the spitting image of her mom— and needed to be home in the mornings to get her daughter off to school and be home when she got home from school. My hours I was needing someone, fit her needs, surprisingly, perfectly. I even told Betty that if Maggie needed to come to the bakery before or after school, or even on days she didn't have school, she was more than welcome to come. An additional bonus was that Maggie's school was within walking distance of the bakery. I also offered my condo upstairs as a place for Maggie to hangout in if the bakery got too busy or boring. It's worked out great so far.

Betty is great at her job and never shies away when I need her. But, right now, I'd love for the distraction of prepping cinnamon rolls or scones or something. But I have no distractions this morning, nothing to keep my mind off yesterday.

How embarrassing! He must think I'm crazy for having his poster, I think to myself.

But in all fairness, I haven't lived at home in 7 years. And I haven't been in my room in that amount of time either. I always assumed Mom changed it into something else once I got back from traveling and turned the second story of the bakery building into my home. The third story is just for storage for now. I haven't decided what I'll do with it... if anything.

As I slide the tray of cinnamon rolls out of the cooler and into the proofer, I grab a tray of cinnamon scones and put them in the oven. I look at my watch and see it's just after 4am.

I pull out my phone and see I still haven't heard from Jason yet. It's not completely unheard of that I haven't received a text or call from him but seeing as I was away all weekend, I would have thought he would have at least called me back last night.

I pull out some of the pastries Betty baked yesterday and put them in the display case. I walk around straightening the bookshelves and putting chairs down. Once the cinnamon rolls and scones are done baking, I pull them out and put them on a cooling rack. I fill the regular coffee makers with fresh water and put in a fresh coffee filter and coffee grounds. I turn on the espresso machine and let it warm up. Once the cinnamon rolls and scones have cooled a little, I scoop them out, and put them on paper, and then put them in my hot case that keeps them nice and warm.

I grab another rag and wipe down all the surfaces. Betty did it last night, but it's something for me to do to keep me from completely obsessing over Kallon. As I wipe down the tables, I turn my lights on as I go. I look at my watch again and see it's a quarter to 5.

I decide to unlock my door and turn my open sign on early. My early birds will enjoy that, Frank, Bill, and Henry. They are always my earliest and first customers on Sundays and Mondays. They come in right at 5, get a carafe of black coffee, three cinnamon rolls, and then shoot the breeze for about three hours. Sundays, they leave right at 8 o'clock to go to church with their wives. Mondays, they hangout a little longer.

Their wives, Bessy, Dorothy, and Anita, come in after they get home from church and have their own gossip time. They usually have tea and a variety of pastries. Mondays, they usually come in just as their husbands are leaving.

The two groups are my favorite part of having the bakery. I have businesses that have a standing order. Those are mainly on Mondays-Fridays, but I have four on Sundays as well. As I wait for my gentlemen trio to come in, I start to bag up the goodies for the four business that will be sending someone over to pick their stuff up by 7:45am.

I pull a tray of blueberry scones out of the cooler and pop them in the oven. I flip through the paperwork under the register while I wait for the scones to finish baking. When there's a minute left for them to bake, I pull out my homemade frosting and heat it up so that it's ready when the scones get done. The timer goes off for the scones, so I pull them out of the oven and put the tray on the counter. I take my frosting and drizzle it over the top of them. I let them sit for a minute and go pull the jugs of juice out of the big walk-in cooler in the kitchen and take them up front to my small fridge.

After putting the juice away, I scoop the blueberry scones out and put them in the hot case with the cinnamon rolls and cinnamon scones. I go back to the kitchen and grab a new quart of milk and a bowl of strawberries that Betty washed yesterday and bring them back up to the front. I put the milk in the fridge and start to cut up the strawberries for any smoothies anyone might want or for the fresh fruit bowls I offer.

As I hear my large wall clock chime 5 o'clock, I hear the bell on the front door ding. I stand up and I'm about to welcome my trio, when I see Kallon standing just inside the door, looking around.

Today he's wearing jeans, a t-shirt, and a baseball cap. And he makes it look good! My throat closes and I can feel my face turning red.

Get a grip! It was a poster from a long time ago and I'm sure he finds out girls have, or had, his poster all the time, I mentally chastise myself.

I can feel myself calming back down by the time Kallon makes eye contact with me. He smiles a warm and happy smile. I can't help but smile back.

"Good morning," I say. "Welcome to Rose Bud's."

"Thank you and good morning to you too," he says. He points around, "This looks great."

"Thanks, it's a library meets bakery, meets coffee shop with extras," I say laughing as I look around at the shelves that have books upon books on them, and smile.

"I like it," his smile grows wider. He walks up to the counter and looks up at the menu.

"Thanks," I say again. "What can I get for you? If your assistant was with you, I'd probably know just by seeing him."

Kallon laughs and says, "Probably, I have him stop in every day."

"What's your usual?" I ask.

"Medium black coffee and two of your blueberry scones. I can smell them now," he says, closing his eyes and breathing deeply through his nose.

"Does your assistant order himself a cinnamon dulce triple espresso, raspberry turnover, large black coffee, and banana muffin?" I ask, thinking now I do know his assistant.

"Possibly, I don't usually see him with anything by the time he gets back to me," Kallon says, looking thoughtful.

I think about the guy and the name he uses on his order, "Is his name Randy?"

"It is!" Kallon exclaims.

I laugh, "I do know him! He's very nice and always courteous."

"That's good to know," Kallon says smiling.

I hand him his coffee and grab two scones for him.

"Can you join me?" he asks, just as my bell chimes from the front door again.

"Grab a table and I'll be there in a second," I say as my gentlemen trio walk in.

Kallon nods at them and moves out of the way and grabs a table close to the counter.

"Good morning, Bill, Frank, and Henry," I say, smiling at them individually. "A little late this morning, huh? Did we have a lay in?"

Bill grunts, "The wife miss placed the house keys. Took us a minute to find them."

Frank chuckles and says, "We helped them look."

Henry leans on the counter and says, "They're all blind. The keys were in the key bowl right by the door."

"Hogwash!" Bill shouts. "Apologies Abby-dear, but I looked in that bowl twice. The missus must have been playing a joke this morning."

"Well, I'm happy you made it," I smile at them. They remind me so much of my grandpa. "The usual, fellas?"

"Creatures of habit, my dear, we're creatures of habit," Henry says, patting my arm.

"Sounds good," I say. "Why don't you go get your table and I'll bring your order out."

"Thanks doll," Bill says.

I watch as they shuffle over to their table, the furthest from the counter and closest to the window. It's the best way to people watch and talk about the neighborhood.

I grab their cups; they prefer real coffee cups. I usually

give people to-go cups, but these guys get the real ones. I take their mugs and carafe of coffee and place it on their table. Then I get the cinnamon rolls and put them on plates, and grab forks. When I get back to their table, they're already on to a subject of who in the neighborhood broke what rules yesterday. I smile and walk away.

When I pass the table Kallon is sitting at, I say, "I'll make my coffee and be right over."

He nods and smiles.

After making my coffee and grabbing a cinnamon and sugar scone for myself, I walk over to Kallon.

"I figured this was a good table in case you need to help a customer or take something out of the oven," he says as he stands and pulls my chair out for me.

"Thank you," I say shyly. I've never had a guy do that before. "And yeah, this table's perfect."

"So, what's your order?" he asks, looking at my plate and coffee. I use one of my personal travel mugs.

"Caramel macchiato, double espresso today, and a cinnamon and sugar scone. It changes day to day though. I don't usually do double shots, normally just one in a large cup."

"Needing the extra kick this morning?"

"Yeah, yesterday was a long day. I was able to go right to sleep when I got home though. Which surprised me."

"Why's that?"

Crap! I didn't want to get into this right off the bat but, better get it over with at the beginning.

I say in a rush, "Because I couldn't stop thinking all the way home, how you must think I'm crazy to still have a poster of you up at my parents' house. In my defense, I haven't lived there in 7 years, and I got the poster when I was 14. It was the only thing I had, or apparently, have, on my walls that wasn't food, cooking, baking, or travel related."

"Don't worry about it. I thought it was funny and quite the coincidence that you've been a fan for so long, and then your reaction to your sister outing you," he laughs. I cover my face. "No really, Abby, don't worry about it. I'm not, I'm flattered."

Shaking my head, I pull my head up and look him in the eyes, they are so blue.

"So, tell me about this place," he says, waving his hand around us.

Welcoming the change of subject, I say, "The building was a compromise. I wouldn't let my grandparents pay for my schooling and travel, so they insisted on gifting me something once I got home. I didn't realize it was going to be an entire building. I tried refusing but they insisted and told me a deal was a deal and they already paid for it. They picked this one because it was a deli before, so converting it to a bakery was really simple. I look for books to fill the shelves everywhere I go—" I'm about to continue but Kallon politely interrupts.

"I'm sorry, they gifted you this entire building?" he asks.

"Yes," I answer with a laugh. "The main floor is the bakery. The elevator goes down into the basement where I keep most of my inventory. The rest of the building, the next floor up, is my condo, and the third floor is for storage right now. It was my grandpa's idea to remodel and make it my home. I tried to argue that wasn't part of our deal and they needed to let me pay them back for it. But they counter argued that they could do what they wanted with the building as it was theirs until I signed the deed. Which I did without looking over the whole place. They were sneaky, and only showed me this floor, and the basement. They mumbled something about the top two floors could be a nice home if I chose to remodel later. It wasn't until they handed me the keys, that they confessed to what they had done, and showed me my new home. My grandparents are hard to beat in an argument."

"They sound like amazing grandparents, and they obviously love you," he says, smiling.

"They're the best," I smile back.

"You said when you got home, like back from somewhere? Where did you go?" he asks.

"I went to ICE, which is Institute of Culinary Education, for a little over two years. Then I applied and got into the Italian Chef Academy in Italy, where I spent a year focusing on Italian cuisine and baking. After that, I spent a year traveling around, mentoring with about six different chefs in different countries. Trying different techniques and cuisines, trying to find what I enjoyed most and what would fit at Rose's the best. I kept going back to Italian foods and took a little of each baking experience and made up my favorites in my head. I've been home now for three years and absolutely love what I do," I say, as a huge smile crosses my face.

"How old are you, Abby?" Kallon asks, seriously.

I immediately feel like I shouldn't be so happy about

what I do, it's not such a prestigious carrier, or so I've been told.

I reluctantly answer, "I'm almost 25, why?"

"I think it's amazing that you found your true calling at such a young age," he says, smiling encouragingly.

"Oh."

"Why do you sound surprised?"

"Other than family and my best friend, I've had people tell me that being a chef and baker isn't really a lifelong carrier."

"That's ridiculous!" Kallon says slightly angrily. "Who said that? Have they tasted your cooking and baking?"

"They have," I say sheepishly.

"Who said that? I'd like to have a word with them!"

"My boyfriend, Jason," I say, reluctantly.

"Your..." he shakes his head. After taking a deep breath, "Your boyfriend said that?"

"Yes. He feels I should be out in front, managing from the front of the restaurant. And he thinks Patty should retire with my parents. He's got all sorts of ideas for Rose's, but I've told him nothing will change. He also has had a relator come look at this building—" I point to the ceiling "—to tell me what I could get for it if I were to sell."

"You're kidding, right?"

"Nope. I told him I'm not selling now, or anytime soon, if at all. And Patty stays."

"How long have you been with this guy? He doesn't sound like he knows you at all. Hell, we just met, and I feel like I understand you better than he does."

"We've been together since I was 16, so 8 years," I say.

Kallon just shakes his head.

To change the subject, I ask him, "Did you always want to be an actor?"

"Yeah, I think so, but I never thought I'd make it. I was in drama in middle school and high school. I really enjoyed all the different roles I got to portray. I also played sports, football, basketball, and baseball. I had a pretty busy schedule. I was cast to play in a movie when I was 16—" I think to myself, *That's the poster I have of him in my room.* "—but decided I wanted to finish high school before I did anything else or decide what I really wanted to do. Once senior year came along, I had some decisions to make. I could have gone to any D1 school to play sports, on a full ride. But my heart wasn't in sports. I wanted to act. So, I applied to Juilliard and got accepted. My parents, Jimmy and Pam, were… are, both teachers, so they couldn't afford to send me. So, I reached out to a friend who said she could get me a modeling job to pay for school. I modeled in my free time and went to school all the rest of the time. My second paid acting job was for a commercial. Then I got another commercial, then a lead role on TV, and then the movie deals started coming in! I did finish school, it was my goal for myself. No matter what, I was finishing what I started. Which I did while I was doing my second movie. I don't think I have ever been that exhausted in my life. I think I was averaging three hours of sleep a night that last year of school!"

"Oh, man! That's rough," I say.

"Worth it though," he says. "I decided to go back to school when I was 25 to get my business degree."

"No way?" I ask, shocked.

"I needed to start investing my money so that I wouldn't spend it all on stuff I didn't need. And that's how I started buying businesses, mostly hotel chains all over the US. Some apartment complexes. Various other businesses. When a friend told me Rose's was looking for a buyer, I was intrigued. Like I said yesterday, I love the... YOUR food... and the atmosphere of the restaurant," Kallon says, smiling.

"So, what do you love more?" I ask. "Business or acting?"

After thinking for a minute, he says, "I'm not really sure. Maybe still acting? I still enjoy all the different roles I play, but I know it won't last forever. Which is where my investments come in."

"That makes sense."

"I don't think I have the passion for anything like you do for cooking and baking though," he smiles.

"How old are you?" I ask, realizing he never did say, although I never asked and have never searched him on the internet. But if he did his first movie when he was 16 and I was 14, then that would make him 28.

"I'll be 28 on my next birthday," he laughs, confirming my mental math skills.

"Which is?"

"What kind of fan are you? Don't even know my birthday?" he asks, teasingly.

"I'm a fan, not a stalker," I answer, while laughing too.

"Touché," he laughs out. "My birthday is June 13th."

"That's next month," I obviously state. "You went back to school about three years ago and you've already gotten your degree and already invested in so many businesses?"

"Yes. When's your birthday?" he asks, answering my questions with the shortest answer possible.

"May 24th," I reply quickly. I ask again, "You got your degree in less than three years, invested in businesses, and you're working on your 3rd movie in the last four years. How? Where do you find the time?"

"You really are a fan," he smiles and winks.

"Seriously, Kallon, how?"

"I don't know. I guess I've always had the mentality of making time for what's important."

"So, what happens if we become partners and I call you up with an emergency but you're at a fancy party for a movie, or for a colleague? Which is more important?"

Without hesitation or a second thought, he says, "The restaurant emergency."

"Really? You'd leave your movie premier if I called and said there was an emergency at Rose's?"

"Yes."

"Okay, why?" I ask, not totally believing him.

"Because there's nothing more I can do once the movie is made. If I'm already at the premier when you call, I've already made my appearance."

"And if the premier hasn't started?"

"Then I'll be fashionably late. As long as I make an appearance, nobody cares."

"Oookaaay," I say reluctantly.

"Did I pass the test?" he asks laughing.

"Well, what if you're clear across the country?"

"If it's a big enough emergency that you need me here, I have a private jet. I could be here in a few hours."

"A big enough emergency?"

"Yes," he states. "If we're partners, I'm going to trust you 110% to run the restaurant. Whatever decisions you need to make, I'll support."

"What would constitute as a big emergency?"

"Hmmm… If you decide to expand, as in do a second location somewhere, I'd like to be a part of that discussion. I'd like to help make some of the decisions and be a part of that process."

"I don't think that would ever happen."

"Abby, I've had your food and I've seen a snippet of how you run your kitchen. What you expect of, not only your kitchen staff but the entire restaurant crew. You could definitely open another Rose's and it would be just as successful."

"I could never franchise Rose's."

"I'm not talking about a franchise. I mean a second location. Rose's could be just as successful in Seattle or L.A., or anywhere else you would choose."

"I've never even thought about it," I say.

"I'm not saying it needs to happen but that's what I'd be good at, helping make decisions to move Rose's further up the success ladder."

"Hmmm," is all I can say. I take a sip of my coffee and think for a minute. He's not wrong, he does have an intriguing idea.

I look up and see my trio looking over at us.

"Excuse me a second, I need to check on my guys," I say as I stand. I glance at the clock and see it's already a quarter after 6.

Kallon nods and stands as I walk away.

"You guys okay? Ready for carafe number two?" I ask as I step up to the guys' table.

"That'd be great, doll," Bill says.

I take the carafe and go re-fill it. Somedays they only get through two carafes, somedays three. Today is looking like a two-carafe day. They must have too much to catch up on, to drink coffee. I take their coffee back to them and as I set it down, they all lean in, and Henry grabs my hand gently.

"Abby, the young man you're talking to? That's not your usual gentleman caller," Henry whispers.

"No, he's a new friend," I answer.

"If I'm not mistaken, that's that actor fellow who played in that one movie with the actress playing his mother who starred in the movie that was popular when we were younger," Bill says.

With that very obscure description of Kallon's movie, I smile and say, "Yes, that's him."

"Kaycee or Kelly or something like that?" Bill asks, still in a whisper.

"Kallon Keller," I correct.

"That's the one!" Henry whisper shouts.

"How'd you meet him?" Frank asks, glancing Kallon's way.

"His assistant has been coming in a lot and I guess he decided to stop in himself," I've never been good at lying but this technically isn't a lie.

"He a nice fellow?" Frank asks.

"Very nice, so far," I say.

"Think he might be taking what's his names role as

your leading man?" Bill asks.

"Oh no! It's not like that at all," I stammer out.

"Okay," Bill says with a wink.

"Bill!" I say in surprise. "It's really not."

"Well don't let us keep you. We'll be good for a while now," Frank says, patting my arm.

They chuckle but then start talking about Mrs. Pearl and something about her husband number five. I make sure to always walk away when they start gossiping. I grab a pot of coffee and bring it to mine and Kallon's table. I top his coffee off and sit down.

"Thank," he says, smiling as he takes a sip. "This really is the best coffee I've ever had and I'm not just saying that. It really is the best."

"Thank you," I say. I don't argue, he does seem genuine. I ask, "So tell me more about yourself. Where did you grow up? Family?"

"I grew up in Northern California. My parents are high school sweethearts and were lucky enough to both get jobs for the school district they went to. My mom is an elementary teacher and my dad is the high school history teacher. I have an older brother, Chris. He's also a teacher but lives and teaches in Colorado. He and his wife, Kara, have twin eight-year-old girls, Haddie and Hailee. They are two of my most favorite people in the world. If they need Uncle Kal, for anything, I'm on the plane, heading their way."

"Aww, that's sweet," I say, smiling. "Do you have any plans to have a family of your own?"

"If I meet the right girl, it's a possibility."

"Are you dating anyone now?" I try to ask as naturally

as possible. I hope he doesn't think I'm asking because I'm interested.

"I am, her name is Tina Shell," he says.

"The model?" I ask in surprise. Which I shouldn't be too surprised, actors date models all the time.

"Yeah," he says, smiling.

"And she's not the right girl to start a family with?"

"She's not ready to have kids and as of right now, I guess I'm not either. What about you and Jason?"

"He says he wants to marry me and have a family. But he hasn't purposed yet, which is okay because I'm not ready for any of that right now."

"When you were at school and then abroad for school and traveling, were you guys still together?"

"Yeah, it was tough, but we made it through," I say, sighing. Kallon has a look on his face for a second but then he changes it to a smile. But the look has me asking, "What?"

"What do you mean?"

"That look? What was that for?"

"Nothing, just a fleeting thought but it's not important."

"What did you think?"

"It's not my place and we've known each other for—" he looks at his watch and laughs, "—about twelve hours."

"That's okay, I'd still like to know. Your look was a little skeptical."

With a sigh and a scrutinizing look, Kallon says, "You were going to ICE for about two years and abroad for another two years. Every long-distance couple I know, didn't make it, and most of them were only a couple states away."

"Well, he was going to NYU while I was at ICE, so we got to see each other a little bit. Not as much as in high school but we both understood that once our schooling was done, we'd have more time for us."

"And what about when you were in Italy and traveling?"

"We talked, but it was hard to talk as much as we would have liked. We emailed more often than talked on the phone but with the time difference and our schedules, that was more convenient."

"And how often have you seen each other in the last three years, since you've been home?"

I glare at him and look at my coffee.

"Not that often?" he asks.

"What's often?" I ask back. Then actually answer with, "We see each other at least once a week unless we have an event or party that we would like the other to go to. We're both busy with work and he likes having his own space, his own home."

"What does Jason do for living?" Kallon asks.

"He works for an investment and financial advisor company."

"I can see how that would be time consuming. And you working two jobs, essentially running two restaurants. It doesn't leave much time for a personal life."

"We make it work," I say. "We love each other, and we know that right now is the best time to focus on work. Family can come later."

"Is that what you think or what Jason has said?"

I glare again. Jason has said it a couple of times

whenever we've talked about where our relationship is heading. Until now, I've never really thought about it being strange.

"Jason's idea, but I understand. I'm not ready to have kids either and I honestly don't know if I want any."

"Does Jason?"

"He's not sure either."

"Have you guys ever broken up in the almost eight years of being together?"

"Once," I say grudgingly. "Last year. After a fight, we had a conversation about where our relationship was going and it got even more heated. He wasn't sure if he wanted to be in a relationship, so we broke up, but it only lasted a month. He apologized and said life without me was definitely not what he wanted. We decided we'd make a standing date to see each other every Sunday. Which we've kept unless something important comes up or an emergency."

"So, he'll be here today?" Kallon asks.

"Well, yeah. He comes here shortly after I lock up and then we usually go for a walk in the park and then go to dinner."

"That sounds nice," Kallon says, sincerely.

"It is. So, like I said, we don't have one of those 'have to see each other every day or spend every waking free moment together' relationship, but we have history and love, and with that, we can build on."

"That's true. Some of my relationships only lasted for a week because there wasn't anything substantial to it," Kallon confesses. Then, I'm guessing to change the subject again, he asks, "So is Patty your only sibling?"

Welcoming the new subject, I answer cheerfully, "I have an older brother too, Spencer. He and his wife, Mary, live in Seattle. They have a son, Max, he's four, and a daughter, Annie, she just turned one. And like you, my nephew and niece are two of my favorite people. Spencer is a relator and Mary works from home."

"Are you the youngest?"

"I am. Patty is the oldest, then Spencer, and then me."

"Were you guys raised here in New York or did you live somewhere else?"

"We are born and raised New Yorkers. My dad moved here from Nebraska after he graduated high school. Mom is from Maine. They met through mutual friends at a college party their junior year, they've been together ever since. They saved and bought a beautiful old Victorian home over in Brooklyn. The three of us kids were all raised there. Patty and my parents still live there today."

"Rose's has been open for how long?"

"It'll be 20 years this fall."

"What did your parents do before that?"

"Mom waitressed and bartended while she was in college. She became the manager of the restaurant she worked at and changed her degree to business management. Dad went to ICE as well and got hired on as a Sous Chef at one of the big hotels with a restaurant on the top floor and roof top. He became Head Chef when the other guy moved back to France. They both stayed at their jobs until they realized they wanted to open their own restaurant. The Universe was all for it because the building Rose's is in finished getting built the month they got their business plan put together and had enough money saved for a down payment."

"So, Rose's is the only business to be in that building?"

"Yes, and with its location, I can't see why they... or we, if you sign on... would ever leave or sell it."

"I can't imagine that either. It's an amazing location. Just like this one," Kallon says, waving his hand to indicate my little bakery.

I glance at the clock and see it's 7:36am.

"Shoot, time has flown. Excuse me for a minute. I need to get some orders finished. They'll be here in less than 10 minutes."

"Can I help?" Kallon asks and stands as I do.

"Umm, well if you'd like to box up the baked goods that I have wrapped up, I can get their drink orders. But you don't have to, I can get it."

"I don't mind," he says, following me behind the counter.

"Okay, ummm, well... each business has wrapped goodies, I've put their initials on each bag. If you want to put them in a box and initial each box, that'd be great."

"Will do," Kallon says. Before I ask him to wash his hands, he's already turning on the faucet and getting his hands wet.

I get the coffees and teas made for the first business and get them in their drink carriers. The second batch are all coffees. Third is coffees, teas, and one hot coco. And the last order is three smoothies and the rest coffees.

"I didn't know you make smoothies too?" Kallon says, excitedly.

"Yeah, I only offer two flavors so that it doesn't

become too complicated. I do a strawberry banana with spinach and a mixed berry one that's full of antioxidants."

"They both sound really good."

"You should try one sometime."

"I definitely will," he says as he goes and sits back down at our table, having gotten all the goodies boxed and labeled quickly.

The first gal comes in, followed by the three guys from the other businesses. They are always so gracious and thankful that I have their orders ready for them. They give off the vibe that their bosses expect them to never be late, even on Sunday.

Just as I'm about to sit down, Bill, Frank, and Henry saunter up to the counter.

"We better head off, would hate to make the wives angry by being late for church. Thanks a lot, Abby, everything was top notch as usual," Henry says, paying for their stuff.

"Thanks, doll," Bill says, smiling.

"See you," Frank adds.

"Thanks, guys," I say, waving at them as they leave.

I sit down and I'm about to take a drink of my coffee when I hear my cell phone go off by the register.

"Excuse me, let me check who that's from."

"No problem," Kallon says.

I walk back behind the counter and grab my phone and see I have a new text from Jason.

Jason: *Hey babe, I have a meeting this afternoon at the office. I'm going to have to catch you next time. Unless you want to grab a quick dinner* *tonight, might be late.*

Shaking my head and thinking about what Kallon was hinting at earlier, I reply quickly.

Me: You've cancelled 2 weeks in a row.

Jason: Well, I can come over later tonight when my meeting gets over. ;)

Me: No, that's okay. I have to get up and be down in the bakery @4am.

Jason: I hate missing our date but I have a meeting.

Me: It's fine. I'm kind of having a meeting right now.

Jason: Your parents are there?

Me: No, someone who might be interested in Rose's. I told you my parents were looking for a potential buyer.

Jason: Who is it?

Me: I can't say, they want to stay anonymous.

Jason: I won't tell.

Me: Sorry, but I can't say.

Jason: Fine. Maybe I'll see you later.

Me: Yeah, okay.

I put my phone down and walk over to our table.

"Everything okay?" Kallon asks.

"Yeah, it's fine. It was just Jason... he's got a work thing this afternoon so he's going to miss our date."

"I'm sorry," Kallon says sincerely.

"It's alright. I have an early morning and a long day tomorrow, so it'll be nice to have an early to bed night for me," I say turning my coffee cup in my hand. "Do you want more?"

"I'm okay," he smiles.

We sit in silence for a few minutes. And then Kallon asks, "So of all the places you traveled, where was your favorite?"

"Oh man, I loved them all so much. From a chef standpoint, they all had something amazing to offer but I kept going back to Italy. Everywhere I went, I always compared the food to what I learned and ate in Italy."

"And from your personal view?"

"I still can't pick just one. Italy and Greece were beautiful, and the people were very nice. France was a fun experience. The U.K. was a lot of fun. And Scotland... it's definitely a top three favorite."

"Would you ever like to go back?"

"Oh yeah, definitely!" I say, excitedly. "Have you gotten to travel much for movies?"

"Yeah, quite a bit, actually. For the Viking movie, we shot a lot of the big fight scene in Iceland, we spent about three months there. For King of Hearts, that as in Sweden for a good portion of the outside shots, and we spent four months there. Also have spent a lot of time in Hawaii and Alaska."

"Oh, that sounds fun."

"Yeah, it is. I do enjoy it more when we do the movie in the States, though."

"How come?"

"Don't get me wrong, I love traveling and seeing new countries and places. But, being there for work, and being on a time schedule, it doesn't leave much free time to really enjoy the places. I'd like to go back to everywhere I've worked and see it from a tourist's viewpoint."

"I can see how working all the time would take the fun out of it."

I hear my side door open and look over, and see Betty and Maggie walking in.

"Morning, Betty," I say, happily. "Hi, Maggie."

"Good morning, Abb—" Betty starts to say and then skids to a stop, staring at Kallon. Maggie keeps walking, waves but doesn't look up from her book. She heads to the back to go up to my condo.

"Betty, this is Kallon Keller. Kallon, this is Betty Brown and that was her daughter Maggie."

"It's nice to meet you," Kallon says as he stands and walks over to Betty, extending his hand to shake hers. She's still speechless but extends her hand out as well and shakes Kallon's hand.

She clears her throat and says with a squeaky voice, "It's... it's nice to meet you too." She glances at me and then back at Kallon for a quick second before looking at me again. "Sorry I'm a little late. There was an accident in the tunnel."

"It's okay, it's been pretty slow. Kallon and I have just been visiting," I say.

"That's... nice," she chokes out.

"I better get back to baking," I say as I start to walk towards the kitchen.

"No!" Betty hollers. Then she clears her throat and says, "No, you stay and visit with Kal... Kallon and I'll get things going."

"Okay," I say. "I'll be back there soon."

I turn and sit back down just as Kallon's phone rings.

"Excuse me for a second," Kallon says. I nod as walks

out front. I watch him pace and nod every few seconds.

"Abby!" Betty says rushing over to the table. "How do you know Kallon Keller?"

I can't tell her about the Rose's side of how I know him, but I can tell her the Rose Bud's side.

"Do you remember Randy who comes in?" I ask.

"Yes," she replies, looking from me to Kallon quickly.

"Apparently, he's Kallon's assistant and he's been having Randy come in for his morning coffee and breakfast whenever he's here in New York. He decided today he'd come in himself," I say.

"That's amazing," she says. She adds quietly as if Kallon can hear from outside, "He's very handsome and so polite."

"Yes, he is," I say in agreement.

"Ooop, here he comes," Betty says and hurries back towards the kitchen.

The doorbell jingles again as Kallon opens the door and walks in. He's got a huge, devastatingly handsome, smile on his face.

Kallon sits, leans forward, and says, "That was my attorney. The papers are a go, and we can sign tomorrow, if you'd like?"

"Whoa! That was fast," I exclaim. "Are you sure?"

"Like I said, I know a good investment when I see one."

"Even with all the stipulations?"

"Your parents requests aren't the most outlandish ones I've heard. Keeping the family a part of the restaurant makes sense. Your family is the restaurant and people know that and enjoy that about Rose's."

"This is so quick," I stammer.

"Is there something on your end that you are hesitant to welcome me to the team?"

"No, not at all. I just thought it would take a lot longer to either convince you to sign or maybe you'd want to spend a month or so around the restaurant to see if it's a good fit."

"I already know it's a good fit. Talking with your parents the last few days and meeting you, I know I'm making the right choice. I saw how the restaurant was ran yesterday and I've eaten there enough times to know the food. Don't worry, I'm not rushing into this as much as you think I am."

"Okay," I say.

"Do you think it would be possible to have a staff meeting tomorrow? I know it's their day off, but I was hoping to get the gag orders signed soon after I get the contract signed with your parents."

"Yeah, I can send out a message that there will be a 20-minute meeting tomorrow. What time do you think?"

"Let's say 11am, so that way it doesn't interfere with plans in the afternoon. My attorneys are calling your parents to see if a 10am meeting will work for them, will that work for you?"

"I can see if Betty can cover here for a couple of hours. What does your gag order usually say?"

"Something along the lines of, 'If you tell anyone the real identity of the owner, you will be fined $10,000 and fired.' If we have people sign one who don't work for Rose's, then it will just say fined the 10k."

"That's a lot of money," I say, shocked.

"I set it high so that it scares people to keep my anonymity. I have yet to have to enforce it. It also states that it's lifelong or as long as I own the business. So, if someone quits, they can't go around telling people and think they don't have any consequences just because they don't work for me, or us, anymore."

"I guess I can see how that would work."

The doorbell jingles again and when I look up, I see Jason walking in. He stops suddenly and stares at Kallon with his mouth open widely, gaping in disbelief.

"What the—" I start to say. "Jason?"

When Jason starts walking again, he looks like he puffs his chest out a little bit and struts. This is the walk I've come to know as his 'intimidation' walk.

Oh great...

"Thought I'd swing by for a coffee," Jason says when he gets to our table. Kallon stands, he's at least six inches taller than Jason. Jason has opposite coloring than Kallon. Jason's light brown hair and hazel brown eyes look as if they've dimmed a little, as he stands next to Kallon. "Betty, I'll take a Vanilla Latte, no foam, almond milk, extra shot of espresso."

After spending the morning with Kallon and his manners, I start to see how little manners Jason has.

"Please?" I suggest.

"Yeah," he says, ignoring me. "So, who's this?"

Trying not to sigh because I know he knows who Kallon is but, I say, "Jason, this is Kallon Keller. Kallon, this is my boyfriend, Jason Phillips."

Kallon extends his hand to shake Jason's. Jason looks down with a confused look on his face at first and then shakes Kallon's hand.

"It's nice to meet you," Kallon says, politely.

"You the guy interested in Rose's?" Jason blurts out.

"No," I say without thinking. I know Jason and he'll go blabbing to everyone if he knew Kallon was buying into Rose's. I am going to need to get a gag order for him, as soon as possible. Kallon sits back down in his seat, letting me take on Jason's inquiry. "Kallon has been having his assistant come in here for quite some time and decided he'd come check out Rose Bud's for himself today."

"Hmmm… isn't that… nice," Jason says with a tone of cockiness.

"Here's your coffee, Jason," Betty says, handing Jason a to-go cup.

He nods at her, again, not saying thank you or anything.

"Didn't you say the buyer was here?" Jason asks, turning to look at me.

"I did," I say.

"So where is he?" he asks.

"I didn't say it was a 'he'," I answer.

"Why are you being so secretive about it?" he asks snarkily.

"Because they have asked to stay anonymous, as I told you in the text message," I answer sternly. "Is that the only reason you came down here? To try to see who was interested in Rose's?"

Kallon stares at his cup, turning it around in his hands, acting like this conversation has nothing to do with him.

"Of course not," Jason says, trying to kiss me. I move away and put my hands on my hips and raise my eyebrows at him. "What? I can't come down and get a coffee from my girl?"

"You never have before," I say.

"I felt bad I cancelled on our date this evening. So, I thought I'd come get my coffee from you this morning. I was on my way into the office, and I was running a few minutes early, so I stopped in," he says trying to sound convincing. Then his tone turns to accusing when he says, "Why are you defensive? Am I interrupting something here that I should know about?"

"Umm, no, Kallon and I are just visiting," I say, starting to get annoyed now.

Jason's tone changes quickly as I'm sure he can tell my tone has changed as well, "Oh okay, I was just asking. I trust you."

"Can I get you anything else, Jason?" Betty asks from behind the counter.

"No, this is all I need," he says. He turns to Kallon, "It was nice to meet you. I'm a big fan."

Kallon looks up at him and nods, "Mmm, nice to meet you too."

Jason looks at me and says, "So later tonight?"

"No, I told you. I need be up early. So, if it's after 7, I'll be in bed."

"You're 25, not 75, you know that right?" he grumbles.

I roll my eyes and say, "Yeah, well, this 25-year-old has to be up no later than 4 in the morning."

"Come on, just one night out with me?" Jason pleads.

"Sorry, no. Not tonight," I say. "I'm still tired from traveling."

"Okay, well, then I'll see you later then," Jason says, nonchalantly.

"Okay," I say.

Jason bends down and kisses me. I open my eyes, about to pull away, because our kisses never last very long. But I see him peak out from under his eye lashes and looks down towards where Kallon is sitting. Then he closes his eyes and hurriedly makes our kiss deeper. It's messy and feels forced.

A second later he pulls away and says, "Bye, babe... Kallon."

Kallon looks up, nods, and waves, not saying anything. Jason leaves and I sit back down in my seat.

"Sorry about him," I say. "He's not usually like that."

"Umph," I hear Betty say from behind the counter. I look over at her and she just shrugs. She walks through the doors leading back to the kitchen.

"That's okay," Kallon says.

"I'm going to need a gag order for him. He's definitely one that will try to use your name to get in with people at work. He's not the newest employee but still tries really hard to get in with the higher-ups. I won't let him use you or Rose's to move up the ladder. His work and work ethic can do that for him."

"I'll have a couple extra made up for people we, or you, think of later," he says. He nods towards where Betty had disappeared and said, "Probably should have Betty sign one too, just in case you and I have meetings here. Then we won't have to worry about her overhearing."

I just nod. I want to tell him we don't have to worry about Betty blabbing to anyone but decide it's better to have everyone sign one than chance someone getting overly excited and accidently tell. The gag order definitely makes you think about not saying anything to anyone.

"I should probably go. I've got a few things to do before tomorrow. Here I'll give you my personal number," he waits for me to run over to my phone. I sit back down and open it to enter a new contact. He continues with, "Okay, it's 555-525-5665. Text or call me when you've let the staff know about the meeting and if 11am works for all of them."

After I enter Kallon's number and save it, I call him.

He looks down at his phone, back up at me, and says, "515-222-9767, is that you?"

"It is," I say, smiling.

"Perfect," he smiles back. He taps on his phone quickly and then puts it away. "Alright, we can talk more tomorrow but I should really get going and let you get back to work."

"Sounds good. Thanks, Kallon," I say as we stand. I extend my hand and he takes it gently but with a firm grip.

"I enjoyed our visit, hopefully we can catch up more tomorrow," he says.

"So did I and I'd like that."

"Betty," he says a little louder, walking over to the counter. Betty quickly pokes her head out from the kitchen. "It was nice meeting you. I'm sure I'll see you again soon."

"Oh," Betty stammers. "Yeah, it was... nice meeting you too."

He pulls out his wallet and waits for me to tell him how

much he owes.

"Today is on the house," I say with a smile.

"I insist, Abby," he says, holding out his card.

Shaking my head, I ring up his order and run his card.

As he takes his card and receipt, and says, "See you tomorrow."

"Yeah, see you tomorrow," I say with a wave.

He gets to the door and turns around, and waves once more. He pulls sunglasses out of his pocket and puts them on before disappearing down the sidewalk.

"I could get used to seeing him around here," Betty says. I look back over at her and she's fanning herself.

"Are you sure about that?" I ask, laughing.

"Might take a couple visits but, yeah, I think I'd get used to him," she says with a straight face.

We stare at each other for a good couple of seconds before we both burst out laughing. We spend the rest of the morning talking about the movies Kallon has played in and starred in throughout his career. We also talked about the women he's dated, at least the ones the magazines Betty read, reported him dating or had been seen out with in public. Betty carried the conversation since I hadn't really picked up a magazine in a couple of years.

CHAPTER 3

"Earth to Abby…" I hear Betty say from beside me. I glance over at her and she waves her hand in front of my face.

"Sorry, deep in thought," I say, shaking my head.

"Big meeting this morning?" she asks, smiling, trying to prompt me into telling her about it. She had asked yesterday afternoon when we closed up shop, if I wanted to go have dinner with her and Maggie since Jason had cancelled on me. I declined politely and explained that I had a meeting in the morning, so I needed to get down here earlier than usual to get some things going so I wasn't leaving her with it all to do, again. She had asked what it was about, but I told her my parents found a buyer, but I couldn't say who, not yet. She let it drop but I could tell she wanted to know.

"Yeah, and I promise to tell you all about it after," I say. And in my head, I add, *Once I get you to sign a gag order.*

"Well, like I said yesterday, I have no problem doing all of this, if you want to cut out early," Betty says.

"No, I can't do that to you again. I truly appreciate all your help and I completely trust you can take care of everything, but I don't want to over work you and then lose you because I'm taking you away from your daughter too much," I say, expressing a fear I have that if I over work Betty, she might quit. The job description when I hired her was for a part-time position, but in the last couple of months, it's turned more into a full-time job.

"You know I love working here for you and unless something catastrophic happens, I have no plans on leaving, even if you leave me to run the bakery for days on end," she says, smiling a teasing smile, touching my arm. "For goodness sake, what other employer would let their employee bring their kid to work with them and not only feed them for free but offer their apartment for them to hangout in?"

"An employer who keeps changing her employees shift times?" I reply as a question.

Betty gives me a disbelieving look and says, "You asked me to come in an hour early this morning, that's not a ridiculous request when you have a meeting mid-morning. Plus, you're allowing me to work and have my kid with me, I wouldn't be able to find that anywhere else, let alone love where and who I work with on a daily basis."

"That's just today, but I had you open and close for me all weekend while I was at Kayla's. And covering while I'm at my meeting and that could last the rest of the day."

"Abby, you deserve some downtime. You work yourself to the bone, both for Rose's, and Rose Bud's. If I can help give you some time off, I will. Please don't beat yourself up over that. Did I have a problem with it at the store I worked at before here? Yes, but only because I had nowhere for Maggie to go and they never gave me time to figure it out. At the time, Maggie wasn't close to being old enough to stay home by herself, as much as she thought she was, so she ended up having to stay with our next-door neighbor. Ms. Lee is a nice enough lady but she's in her 80's, and as much as Maggie enjoyed her time with her, it wasn't the best fit. Maggie is a little older now and soon she'll be old enough to be at our home by herself without me completely worrying about her. But the fact you opened up the bakery and your home to not only me, but my daughter as well—" she shakes her head "—no, I'm not going anywhere."

"I hope you know how much I appreciate you," I say, whole heartedly.

"I do," she says, patting my back.

We get back to rolling out the berry rolls. They're like cinnamon rolls but made with a berry jam rather than cinnamon and sugar mixture. Once we get those done, we switch to actual cinnamon rolls. Then the scones and the other pastries we'd run out of yesterday.

As I wash out the mixing bowl I was using, I glance at my watch.

"Oh no!" I shout. It's 8:52am. "I need to get upstairs and get cleaned up. I'll have to take a quick shower and rush over to Rose's. Are you sure you're okay with me leaving?"

"Yes, go," Betty says. "Don't worry about me."

"Thank you so much!" I exclaim as I dry my hands off.

"Good luck," she says. "Or is that not the right sentiment?"

"No, that works," I say, while laughing. "I'll text you when we're done. If you're still here, I'll tell you all about it when I get back."

"Sounds good," Betty says.

I run past her and up to my condo using the back stairs that are in the back of the bakery's kitchen that leads up to my kitchen. I don't let just anyone use this entrance into my home. Only Betty, Maggie, and I use it while we're at work. Everyone else uses my front door, which is on the side of the building.

I get up to my apartment and say a quick hello to Maggie. Then hurry to my room and bathroom and shower in record time. I change into a nice pair of dark jeans and a burgundy blouse. I don't have anything more business attire than this, so, jeans and a blouse will have to do. I don't have time to do anything with my hair so I just through half of it into a barrette and throw my eye makeup on, the only makeup I ever wear.

I put my cute black boots on, grab my phone and bag, and race out the front door. I hear the automatic lock click as I run down the stairs. I burst out of the building door and hear it lock behind me as well. Both doors auto-locking were my grandpa's idea. I smile at the thought of his overprotectiveness for me.

I get to the street and throw my hand up for a taxi. I only have to wait a couple of seconds before one is screeching to a stop in front of me. I jump in and tell him the address to Rose's and we're off in a hurry. The Universe must really like me today because we didn't hit one red light. We make it to Rose's by 9:45am. I pay the driver and hurriedly get out.

I test the door to see if it's unlocked, it's not. As I'm entering the passcode into the keypad, I hear a car door open and close behind me. I turn and see Kallon standing in a nice pair of black dress pants and a white button-down dress shirt. No tie or jacket but he looks like he's ready for business. His sleeves are rolled about halfway up his forearm. He looks good. Shaking my head and turning my attention away from him, I watch as the black, sleek, sedan pulls away from behind him.

"Good morning, Abby," Kallon says, smiling, pulling my attention back to him.

"Good morning to you too, Kallon," I say, smiling back.

"You look nice," he says as his eyes travel from my face down to my feet and back up again.

"As do you," I say as politely and nonchalantly as I can. I think to myself, *It's okay to think he's good looking. Anyone in their right mind would think that, but don't make a fool out of yourself. He's just another person and he's potentially going to be your business partner. Reel it in Abby!*

"Let me get that," Kallon says, reaching for the door as I get the numbers entered into the keypad, and start to open the door.

"Oh, thank you," I say, surprised again by his act of chivalry.

"No problem," he says, smiling and nodding at me.

"I'm going to do a quick walk through if you'd like to join me. Or you can head back to the office, my parents should already be in there. My dad is meticulous about being early for any meeting. And with how important this one is for them, I'm guessing they've been here since 9am," I say, laughing.

"I'll walk with you," he says, putting one hand behind his back and the other gesturing me to go ahead. When I start walking, he steps next to me, and walks along with me. I see him put his other hand behind his back.

The restaurant is dimly lit but it's my favorite time to be in here. It's so quiet. I look at the hostess counter and see that it's clean and organized, as expected. I walk over to the bar area and peek behind the bar. Clean, organized, and ready for tomorrow. I run my hand over the bar and it's soft and smooth, a clear indication it's clean. No sticky left over booze or anything like that. Walking through the restaurant, I check every other table, and see they are clean as well. The vases we put fresh roses in once a week, are cleaned and ready for their new flowers and water tomorrow. When we get to the kitchen, I check the dishwashers. They're all emptied and cleaned out. Garbage's are empty as well. I can hear quiet talking the closer we get to the office. When we walk in, Mom and Dad are sitting with Mr. Dallas, our attorney, and a man I don't recognize.

"Miss Rose," Mr. Dallas says, standing and extending his hand out to me. "Good morning."

"Good morning, Mr. Dallas," I say, shaking his hand. "Hi, Mom. Hi, Dad."

"Good morning, Abbigail," Mom says, coming and giving me a hug. "Cutting it close, aren't you?"

I look at the clock and see it's 9:58am.

"I might have slowed her down," Kallon says. My mom's eyes go a little wide. "She was doing her walk through and I insisted on walking with her. I have a feeling she was going slow for my benefit."

I laugh, "Not at all, I always go through slowly."

"That's my girl," my dad says, hugging me.

I see Kallon walk over to the other man and they shake

hands.

"Abby, this is Jack Jennings, my lead attorney," Kallon says. "Mr. Jennings this is Abbigail Rose."

"It's nice to meet you, Miss Rose, I've heard a lot about you," Mr. Jennings says, looking at Kallon and then back to me. "I got here a little early and had the pleasure of visiting with your parents and Mr. Dallas for a good little bit."

"It's nice to meet you too, Mr. Jennings," I say, shaking his hand.

"Shall we get started?" Mr. Dallas asks, motioning for us to take seats around the table. Mr. Jennings and Kallon go around to the side Mr. Jennings was sitting on when we walked in. Dad holds out a chair for me, while Mr. Dallas holds one out for my mom. I'm sitting across from Kallon, he smiles at me, and I can't help but smile back.

"Here are the contracts, once the price of purchase has been agreed on, we'll write it in," Mr. Jennings says, handing the contracts over to Mr. Dallas.

"What's your starting offer?" Mr. Dallas asks.

Mr. Jennings is about to say something, but Kallon touches his arm and says, "Ten million."

My mouth falls open and my eyes must be bulging out of my face. I have enough sense in my stunned brained to see Mr. Jennings look at Kallon with a look that says something like, 'We don't start at that high of a number right out of the gate.'

"Ten—" my mom stammers out "—Ten million dollars?"

"Are you joking?" Mr. Dallas asks, he looks just as shocked as I feel.

"Not at all, Mr. Dallas. This restaurant is amazing and has a lot of potential. This is fair market value for a business and building of this caliber and location in New York City," Kallon says, interlocking his fingers and placing them on the table.

"That price kind of negates the negotiation process," I hear Mr. Jennings try to whisper to Kallon. But his whisper isn't so much a whisper as it's a little quieter than his normal volume.

Not trying to lower his voice, Kallon says, "I'm not into negotiations right now. This is what I'm willing to pay and I'm not interested in going back and forth. Mr. and Mrs. Rose, what do you say?"

We all look at my dad and mom. They look at each other and then at me.

"Can we have a minute to talk?" my dad asks.

"Absolutely," Kallon says, just as his phone starts to buzz in his pocket. "We'll step out into the kitchen, and I'll take this."

I see Mr. Jennings shaking his head in disbelief but he stands and follows Kallon out.

"What do you think?" Mr. Dallas asks, he looks absolutely thrilled.

"I think it's a dream come true," Mom says.

"Too good to be true," Dad corrects.

"He wouldn't make the offer if he didn't mean it," Mr. Dallas says.

"What do you think?" Dad asks me.

I take a minute to get my thoughts collected. My first reaction was my parents could live their second dream life and travel like they've always wanted. But, my second reaction is, "I'll never be able to pay back ten million dollars in five years, but this is life changing for you two."

"Oh sweety," Mom says, taking my hand.

"Would it be so bad to have Mr. Keller as a business partner?" Mr. Dallas asks.

"I don't think so but..." I pause. I'm not sure why I feel hesitant. Kallon is a smart businessman, so he'd definitely be a priceless addition. I just can't imagine why he'd offer such a high price to begin with, right at the beginning. "What's the lowest you would have sold for?"

Mom and Dad look at each other and Dad says, "Well, probably anywhere between three and five million."

"Exactly, so why didn't he negotiate?" I ask.

"Thinking from his point of view," Mr. Dallas says. "If he knew he was willing to go as high as ten million but also knew your parents would be okay with half that, but also figured I'd try to get them as much as possible, he just cut out the back-and-forth numbers game and started with what he thought the price would end up being once it was all said and done."

"But by not negotiating, he could have saved himself a couple million dollars," I say.

"Are you more worried about not being able to pay the ten million or that he didn't save himself money by negotiating?" Mr. Dallas asks.

"Both, I guess," I answer honestly. "I don't want him to end up feeling like he messed up and then regrets buying in to Rose's and then be a horrible business partner. There's no way I'm going to be able to pay that back in five years, so he'll be my business partner for life or for as long as Rose's is open."

"You don't know that Abbigail," Dad says. "You'll be getting a substantial pay raise by becoming part owner with Kallon and full-on manager. Rose Bud's is really starting to pick up. You could very well be able to pay him back in five years."

I don't like arguing with my dad, but I don't think he truly believes I'll make ten million dollars in the next five years. But I can't stand in the way of them getting this amazing deal. We can't very well turn it down and tell him to make his offer less, that would be ridiculous and honestly, extremely selfish of me.

"You're right, Dad," I say, smiling as genuinely as I can. "Take the deal."

"Are you sure?" he asks, as Mom grabs his hand and squeezes mine a little more.

"Yes," I say. "It's mind blowing how great of a deal it is. Except, to call it a great deal is an understatement."

"Agreed," Mr. Dallas says, smiling. "I'll go get Mr. Keller and Mr. Jennings."

He walks quickly from the room and I lean back in my seat.

"Are you sure about this, sweety?" Mom asks, now she looks more concerned than relieved.

"Yes," I say. "I'll either figure it out or Kallon will be forever in our lives."

"That's not such a bad thing," Mom says, smiling.

"Mom," I say.

"What?" she asks, sheepishly. "He's a very nice man."

"We just met him," I say. "Or at least I did."

"Well, you'll get to know him a lot better soon enough, because he's about to become a big part of your life," Mr. Dallas says, hurrying back into the room.

He sits down just as Kallon and Mr. Jennings walk into the room.

"I'll call you back," Kallon says and then hangs up his phone. He's got a smile on his face.

"You guys made a decision?" Mr. Jennings asks. He doesn't look anymore thrilled than he did when they left the room, but he looks resigned to the fact his client bombed the negotiations. I have to kind of laugh at the thoughts he must be having about this meeting.

Mr. Dallas looks at my parents and they grin. He looks at Mr. Jennings and says, "We have."

Dad stands and walks over to Kallon, who stands as well. Dad extends his hand out and when Kallon takes it, Dad says, "You've bought yourself into a restaurant partnership."

Kallon smiles and says, "Wonderful news!"

Mom gets up and walks over to Kallon as well and shakes his hand and then gives him a hug. Mr. Jennings and Mr. Dallas take the contracts and write some things in them and then my parents walk over and sign, as well as Kallon.

Kallon reaches into his back pocket and pulls out a folded piece of paper. Turns and hands it to my dad. He opens it and his face looks stunned.

"You already had a check written out for ten million?" Dad asks.

"This isn't how business deals usually go, is it?" I whisper to my mom.

"No, not usually this smooth or quick," Mom whispers back.

"I wasn't going to go any more or less than that," Kallon says. "I had already made up my mind."

Mr. Jennings just shakes his head but then smiles, "Always something with you, Mr. Keller."

"I try to keep you on your toes, so you never get bored," Kallon says, patting Mr. Jennings on the shoulder.

"I could never get bored working for you, sir," Mr. Jennings laughs. He pulls a folder out of his briefcase and hands it to Kallon. "Here are the gag orders you asked for. There should be extras in there for anyone else you guys might want to have sign them."

"Thanks a bunch," Kallon says.

"I guess my job here is done for now," Mr. Jennings says. "I'll stop in tomorrow to grab those gag orders and return Friday for any that come in later. You all have a good day. Mr. and Mrs. Rose, congratulations."

"Thank you, Mr. Jennings," they say at the same time.

I step forward and grab a pen they had used to sign the contracts and I grab a gag order from the folder.

"Oh, Abby, you don't have to sign one of those," Kallon says. "You've proven to me multiple times you won't tell anyone about me being co-owner."

"If I'm going to have my staff and other people sign this, I'll sign one too," I say, signing my name quickly. I put the form back in the folder and put the pen down.

"We'll sign one as well," Dad says. He steps forward and does the same as I did, followed by Mom.

"We'll take one home for Patricia to sign, even though

she won't go against us telling her she can't tell anyone. At least this way she'll know it's 100% legal to not to tell anyone," Mom says, grabbing a blank form to take home.

"I appreciate that," Kallon says and then looks around as if realizing something. "Where is Patty?"

I like that he uses mine and Patty's preferred names and doesn't fall into using our given names like our parents. It makes him seem more like a friend.

"She's having a hard time coming to terms with us selling our part of the restaurant. She didn't want to come," Mom says. "She'll be okay when she realizes nothing will change, other than not seeing us here every day."

"Of course nothing else will change," I say. "Is that why she didn't come to lunch yesterday?"

"Yes, she stayed up in her room," Mom answers.

"I'll talk to her about it at dinner tonight," I say.

"That would probably help a lot, thanks Bud," Dad says.

Mr. Dallas and Mr. Jennings walk out of the room, talking about something that was going on in the news. Kallon is hanging back and looks at his watch. I had told him last night the staff was told to be here by 11am. I look at my watch and see we've got about 15 minutes before they should be getting here.

"Kallon?" I ask. He turns and looks at me. "For the meeting with the staff, I was thinking it would be best if I talked to them first. I can tell them they can choose to sign the contract or not. If they choose not to, that's okay but they need to leave before you, the new partner, comes in to welcome the staff? But if they stay and sign, they need to fully understand they can't tell anyone, not staff members that left, family, and friends, even strangers."

"I think that would probably be best," Kallon says.

"What if your mother and I take a few minutes at the beginning to give them our parting words? Then Abbigail, you can explain what's going on," Dad suggests.

"That sounds good," I say. I walk over to the folder and grab five forms and put them off to the side.

"Who are those for?" Mom asks.

"Jason, Betty, Maggie, Kayla, and Peter," I say. "You should probably grab some for Spencer and Mary. The kids are too young to understand anything right now."

"You think Maggie will fully understand?" Mom asks.

"She's 11 and very smart for her age, she'll understand," I say. "But I'll talk to Betty and see what she thinks. Maggie might not even associate you with Rose's unless she happens to overhear me and Betty talking."

"I'm not too worried about kids but if Betty thinks Maggie might have a problem keeping my anonymity, then we'll figure something out. I don't think making a child sign a gag order with the same repercussions as adults, is fair."

"I'll let you know," I say. His consideration for kids and not holding them to the same expectation to adults is admirable.

I hear the buzzer from the front door go off.

"Some staff must be here already," Mom says. "I'll go let them in and have everyone hangout by the tables just outside of the kitchen."

"Thanks, Mom," I say as I grab the folder of gag orders. I turn to Kallon and ask, "Ready?"

"Yup," he says nonchalantly. We leave the office and start walking through the kitchen.

"If you want to stand over here, just on this side of the kitchen entrance door, I'll introduce you when everyone has finished signing their gag orders."

"Sounds good."

I nod at him and walk through the doors. By the looks of it, everyone is already here. I wave and greet those closest to me but stay standing next to my dad. Mom walks over to us a few minutes later.

"I tried to check everyone off the employee roster but they're all mingling around. But I think they're all here," she says.

"Okay," Dad says. He clears his throat and the entire restaurant quiets. "If everyone could look around and see if you notice anyone missing, that would be great. From what we can see, everyone is here but we want to make sure before we get started, as we are starting about ten minutes early."

I glance around and see everyone else looking around as well. There's a unanimous murmur of everyone being here.

"Let me start off by saying how grateful we are that you took time out of your morning, on your day off, to come in for a meeting. We won't take up much of your time and will hopefully have you on your way shortly," Mom starts to say. She's always been the one to run the meetings. "As you all know, a year or so ago we, Mr. Rose and I, decided we would look for a partial buyer for Rose's. We are happy to announce that a couple weeks ago we were approached by someone and have just finalized the contracts."

A murmur of surprise goes across the room.

"You're really leaving us?" Sarah, one of our Station Chef's, asks. She was the Sous Chef while I was in school. But once I got back, she asked to be put back to a Station Chef position, where she preferred to be.

"Yes, but not completely gone," Mom says, looking at her kindly. "We'll come in for a visit and check in from time to time but more from a patron standpoint than as your bosses. Have no fear, we are leaving you in very capable hands. Abbigail won't be going anywhere and has become co-owner, full time manager, as well as her Head Chef position. The other co-owner, is very good at business and will make the perfect business partner for Abbigail."

"Who is it?" Paul, the Junior Chef, asks.

"Before we get to that, Abbigail has something to say," Mom says. She turns and nods for me, so I step forward.

"Thanks for being here. I'll make this quick. The new co-owner wishes to stay anonymous to the public, they don't want Rose's to be taken advantage of by people who think they might be entitled to a free meal or any other services we offer here. So, what I have here—" I raise the folder in my hand "—are gag orders. I'll read it for you all."

I grab a form out of the folder and clear my throat so I can speak even louder.

"I, you write your name, understand that if I speak out or let slip the true identity of the new co-owner of Rose's, am liable to all consequences of breaking this gag order. Which include, if employed at Rose's, immediate loss of job, and a fine of $10,000.00. If I am not employed at Rose's but I am a friend or family member that has signed this gag order,

I am legally bound to pay the $10,000.00 fine, as well. I understand this is a lifetime gag order and not a onetime fine. I sign this gag order with complete understanding of what is being asked of me and I completely understand that I agree to these terms if I break this gag order. And then you sign and date at the bottom," I say. I look around the room and it's completely silent.

"10 Grand for letting slip who the person really is?" Royce asks.

"Yes," I say. "They are very adamant on staying anonymous. They've had issues before of people finding out their new business deals and have been taken advantage of and felt pressured to give extreme deals, if not free things. They don't want that to happen to Rose's."

"And we have to sign it?" Tim, another Station Chef, asks.

"No, you don't have to sign one, but you won't be told who the co-owner is, you'll be asked to leave before we introduce them," I answer truthfully. I also add, "It would make working here easier if you did sign one though. I signed one, as well as my parents. Our entire family will be signing one. You all know we wouldn't ask you to do something, if we weren't willing to do it first."

"I'll sign," Royce states, stepping forward. His statement sets off a loud agreement of what appears to be, everyone else.

"Now would be a good time to announce if you won't be signing and we'll ask you to leave with no hard feelings and we'll see you tomorrow for work," I say. I wait silently for a count of 30 seconds. I step forward and I lay out five piles of the forms and put pens beside them all. I say excitedly, "This is great news! Get in five lines and once you've signed one, hand it to me or one of my parents. Once we've collected them all, we'll introduce the new co-owner to you all. Please read it again, carefully, to yourself before signing it. As clear as it's written, we still want everyone to fully understand what they are signing."

Royce leads the first group up, reads, and then signs. He walks over to me, smiles, winks, and hands me his form. Then goes and stands back over by a table, a short distance away from everyone else. It only takes about five minutes for everyone to get through the forms and then they're all standing back by Royce. Mom and Dad hand me the forms they were given, and I thumb through them. I grab our staff roster from Mom and mark off names quickly. Yup, sure enough, everyone is here, and everyone has signed.

I turn my head slightly over my shoulder and holler towards the kitchen, "You can come out now."

Simultaneously, when Kallon walks through the door, I hear a multitude of gasps.

"Everyone, this is the new co-owner, my new business partner, and your new boss, Mr. Kallon Keller," I say.

CHAPTER 4

Silence.

I look at Kallon, he's just smiling, and looking out at everyone. Giving them a moment to collect their thoughts before he speaks.

"Is this a joke?" Bridget, our purchasing manager, asks.

"Yeah, April Fool's Day was last month," Cammy, one of the bartenders, says.

"No, this isn't a joke," I say, laughing a little at their stunned looks, I have a feeling that's what I looked like too, when I walked into the office the first-time meeting Kallon the other day.

"Hi everyone," Kallon says, a few of the girls actually gasp. I can't blame them for that either, he does have a nice voice. "Like Miss Rose said, my name is Kallon Keller, but I'd like you all to refer to me as Charles Webb, Mr. Webb."

"An alias?" Royce asks.

"Yes, to help keep me anonymous," Kallon says. "So, if someone asks who bought out Mr. and Mrs. Rose, you can tell them Charles Webb, instead of saying, that you're not allowed to say. I have found that saying you aren't allowed to say, peaks peoples interests further than they were originally interested, which makes them dig into it more. If they had just been given a name, they would just let it drop. Hence, my alias."

"What if they look into it anyways and search you on the internet?" Sherry, our other hostess, asks.

"They'll come across a website of all my business ventures and business moto and what not, only under the name of Charles Webb, and not Kallon Keller," he says.

I look around and see everyone nodding and looking much more relaxed.

"Do you guys have any questions?" I ask.

They look around at each other, seeing who will be the bravest to ask first, if they do have any questions.

"What changes will there be to Rose's?" Royce asks. I figured he'd be one to ask.

"None," Kallon answers. But then he amends his answer by saying, "If there ARE any changes that I find need to be improved, Miss Rose will have final say. I didn't buy into Rose's to come in and change anything. I've actually been here quite a few times and have never had any complaints."

"Staff will stay the same?" MaryAnn, a server, asks.

"Yes, staff and everything pertaining to staff, will stay the same. The menu will stay the same," Kallon says, smiling warmly at her and then around to everyone else, they smile back.

It's quiet again. I look around, checking to see if anyone else has any more questions.

"If that's all the questions you have, I guess the meeting is over," I say. "Just remember, as soon as you walk out the door, you can't use Mr. Keller's name, it's Mr. Webb. And no referencing that he's a movie star or anything that could give away his true identity."

I look around the room and see everyone nodding. For the next 10-15 minutes, Kallon walks around shaking hands and meeting the staff individually. I watch as all the guys start out with puffed up chests and all trying to seem taller. But by the time they're done talking with Kallon, they're relaxed and smiling.

The girls on the other hand, they start out with giddy expressions and twinkles in their eyes. By the time they're done talking, they look as if they've fallen even more in love with him. I silently laugh at how easily Kallon has won over the staff, not just because of who he is, but because of what I'm realizing is his personality. His genuine kindness and how at ease you feel when you're around him.

"We're going to head home," Mom says startling me, walking up after talking to Bridget.

"Sounds good. Dinner at the usual time?" I ask.

"Yes," Mom says. "Dad is making fried chicken and sides."

"I'll bring a dessert," I say, as I hug her.

Dad walks up and gives me a hug as well.

"That went smoothly," he states.

"About as smoothly as the day we started this place," Mom says joyfully.

"That's because the Universe is in agreement with us again," Dad says, laughing. Mom playfully pops him on the chest.

"Love you guys, see you tonight," I say.

"Love you too," they say at the same time.

My parents follow a large group of the staff out the door. There's only a handful left hanging around talking to Kallon. I say my goodbyes and walk back to the office. I grab the gag order forms I'd set aside for the people I needed to sign them and put them in a different folder and put it in my bag. I walk over and sit at my desk and look around. The restaurant might not change but this room is going to need some changes. We won't need three desks anymore. I start to look around, trying to decide what and where we should put things.

"Hey, Abby, do you have a minute?" Kallon asks from the doorway.

"Sure," I say, scooting my chair away from my desk to stand.

"Oh no, sit... sit," Kallon says. He grabs a chair in front of my desk and sits down.

I sit back down and look at him.

"What's up?" I ask.

"I have a question to ask you," he states.

"Okay..."

"That phone call I took earlier," he starts to say. "Before we finalized the contract?"

"Yeah?"

"It was the set manager, Stephanie Steel, for the movie I'm staring in at the moment."

"Okay," I say, not sure where this is going.

"Well, apparently, the business she hired to cater breakfast, isn't working out. Something about stale food and cold coffee that's supposed to be hot. Anyways, she knows I never eat what's offered on set, at least not for breakfast. She also knows Randy brings things to me. She called to ask if I knew what bakery he goes to and if he'd be able to get her in contact with the owner," he pauses a moment to let me digest what he's staying. And if what I'm thinking he's saying is what's he's saying, this could be huge for Rose Bud's. I nod him encouragingly to go on. "I told her that I knew the owner and would talk to her, you, personally. She was thrilled."

He stops and looks at me with a huge smile on his face. But I'm not going to jump to any conclusions, he's going to have to spell it out for me.

"Okay, for what?" I ask, heart racing.

Kallon laughs and says, "Would you, would Rose Bud's, like to cater breakfast for the movie crew? Do you cater?"

My eyes about pop out of my head. *YES! That's what I was hoping he'd say!*

"Ummm, yes we've catered before, for like weddings and what not but..." I stammer out.

"Stephanie understands it's short notice, and she's been told to offer a sizeable bonus upfront if you agree to do it," he says, leaning forward.

"Do you know the details?" I ask.

"I had her text me what's needed," Kallon says as he pulls out his phone from his pocket. He swipes around and then finally clears his throat and continues, "It would be one day at first to see if it goes well and then after that, Monday through Friday. There needs to be breakfast items for 150-200 people. Drinks, both hot and cold preferably. The food and drinks are to be set up by 5am and everything packed and cleaned up by 11am. The lunch caterers are there by 11:30am to start setting up for lunch. Do you have a catering truck?"

"I do," I say. "Well, it's a van but still, it's what I use for catering events."

"Oh ok, she said they could get one for you if you needed one, but you've got that taken care of," Kallon says.

"So, if I do this, I need to have enough food for 200 people by morning?" I ask, stunned.

"Yes…"

"Is there a specific menu I'm supposed to follow, or do I have free rein on what I bring?"

"You have full control over what you want to bring," he says.

"How much did she say they'll pay?" I ask.

"$10,000 plus $15,000 for the short notice bonus," he states.

"$25,000 to cater a movie?" I ask, shocked.

"Oh, sorry, no, it's $10,000 a week, $2,000 a day, Saturday and Sunday's off," Kallon corrects. My mouth hangs open. "With not knowing how long a movie will take to shoot, they pay weekly. If we finish on a Wednesday, you'll still get paid for the full week."

"You're kidding?" I stammer out.

He laughs and says, "Not at all."

"How much is left of the movie?"

"We just started shooting six months ago, but we still have a lot left, I'd say maybe four months to a year."

"You've got to be kidding?" I half shout, half breathlessly say.

He again laughs, "I'm really not."

"That's a lot of money for food," I say.

"You know how people get when they're hungry. Now add in people who are hungry but also stressed to get to deadline. The food they get to eat first thing in the morning, can make or break how their day goes. They put food in the budget for a reason."

"I guess I could make a couple different scones, turnovers, cinnamon rolls, as well as the berry rolls. Maybe some muffins. I also have recipes for those things for people that would prefer a healthier option, although they don't taste as good as the original but still decent. I could bring in coffee and tea, both hot and cold. I've also been wanting to try out the new portable smoothie machine I have," I say, not really talking to Kallon, just thinking out loud.

"So, you'll do it?" he asks excitedly.

I take a second to think but then say, "Let me call Betty and see if she's willing to put in some extra time. Prepping for all this and the bakery itself, I'll need her more than ever. But I need to make sure she's on board before I officially accept."

"Sure, call her," Kallon says.

I grab my phone from my bag and hit Rose Bud's number. I stand and start pacing. She answers on the third ring.

"Thank you for calling Rose Bud's. This is Betty, how can I help you?"

"Hey, Betty, it's me, Abby. You busy?"

"Oh, hi Abby. Uhh, no, not busy right now. Just had our morning rush, so just cleaning tables."

"Oh good," I say.

"What's up? How was your meeting?"

"The meeting went well. The contract is signed."

"That's great news! Your parents must be thrilled."

"Yeah, they are pretty excited," I say, taking a moment. "Betty, I know I've been asking a lot from you lately and what I'm about to ask is going to be even more."

"We talked about this; I really don't mind."

"I'm glad you feel that way because I've just been offered an amazing opportunity for Rose Bud's."

"What is it?" she asks, excitedly.

"How would you feel about helping me cater breakfast for a movie set?"

"A… what?" she stammers out.

"A movie set," I say while chuckling.

"Like a for real movie set? With actors and all those kinds of people?" she asks.

"Yup, a real movie set with actors and everyone else involved in making a movie."

"When would we start catering for them?"

"In the morning."

"Holy buckets of french-fries! That's awfully soon. How many people are we needing to feed on such short notice?"

"200…"

Silence.

"Betty, I know it's a lot, but you know I wouldn't be asking if I didn't think we could do it. This first day will be a little chaotic but once we get it figured out it'll be a cake walk," Kallon snickers at my pun. I laugh at it a little too. "But, if you think it's too much, I'll refuse the offer."

"I know we can do it. I'm just shocked is all," she takes a breath. Then she says in a more serious tone, *"Is it for Kallon*

Keller's movie?"

Stunned silent for a moment, I ask, "Yes. How did you know?"

"He was here yesterday. Is that what he was doing? Checking out the bakery for catering possibilities? I didn't think an actor like him, so well known, would do that. Unless he's picky about what he eats, and he gets to decide who caters."

"I don't know about that, but the set manager asked him about Rose Bud's because of Randy coming in all the time for him and he told her he'd talk to me about it. I told him I needed to talk to you about it before I decided."

"Abby, this is your bakery, I'm your employee. If you tell me we need to have 200 plus breakfast items ready by morning, I'm going to work my tushy off to make sure we get it done."

"I know you feel that way but to me, you're more than just an employee. Your opinion means a lot to me. So, what do you think, should we do this? It'll be about four months to a year of doing this, five days a week, Monday through Friday."

"How much are they going to pay?"

"$2,000 per day, paid weekly, Saturdays and Sundays with a $15,000 upfront bonus because it's so short notice," I say.

Silence. It stays quiet for so long I feel like I might have lost connection. I look at my phone but see we're still connected.

"Betty? Are you still there?"

"Mmm hmmm," she mumbles out.

I laugh, "Are you okay?"

"Do you know how much money that is?"

"A lot," I laugh again.

"What details do you know?"

"We can talk about that when I get back from Rose's. So, what do you say?"

"I say heck yeah! Let's do it."

"Thanks Betty, I'll be back there shortly."

"See you soon."

"Bye."

"Bye," she says, and we hang up. I put my phone down and look up at Kallon and smile hugely. Kallon stands up and walks over to me.

"She's in!" I say, excitedly.

"That's awesome!" he says. "I'll let Stephanie know."

I hug him without thinking, but surprisingly, he hugs me back.

I clear my throat and step away.

"Sorry about that, I'm just excited. Thank you for thinking of me, of Rose Bud's," I say feeling my face turn red from embarrassing myself again. "This could be the thing that Rose Bud's needs to really get our name out there. Don't get me wrong, we do fine right now, but this could definitely get us more customers."

"Not just more customers but more catering jobs too," Kallon says. "Set managers are always looking for new catering businesses to use. I know you aren't a catering business, but Stephanie is someone that can get your name out there to other sets."

"I need to get back to the bakery. Betty and I have a ton of work to do," I say, walking over to my desk and grabbing my bag, I put my phone back in it. "Can we meet sometime tomorrow, and I'll get you everything you need to get into Rose's? We can also go over how you think the office should be rearranged."

"Don't worry about that right now, we can keep it the way it is for a bit," he says. "Go get things going for tomorrow. I'll be on set today from 3 o'clock until we wrap for the night, but I'll check my phone often. Please, call if you need any help."

"I won't be calling to bother you," I say. "I appreciate the offer though."

"Abby, if I find out you and Betty were struggling and didn't call me, I'll be really upset," he says, looking at me with squinted eyes.

I shrug, smile, and say, "We'll be fine."

"I'm sure you will be but in case something happens, and you need help... call... me..." he says. "We're business partners now and that doesn't just end at Rose's. Anytime you need help or something, don't hesitate to call or text."

"Okay," I say, only to placate him. I really do think Betty and I can handle this and having just met him and have only been business partners for an hour or so now, I don't think calling him for help will be an option anytime soon. I need to show him I can hold my own side of the business deal, even if Rose Bud's isn't a part of the business he signed on to.

"I'll walk out with you," he says as he pulls his phone out and types something out really quick. Then he walks towards the door and holds it open for me.

"Thank you," I say, as I walk out the door.

We're silent as we walk through the kitchen and then through the restaurant. We reach the front doors and Kallon holds the door open for me again.

"Thanks," I say again. He just smiles his heart-breaking smile.

I step to the curb and look down the street for a vacant taxi.

"You don't drive?" he asks.

"No," I say. "I mean I can, and I have a car, but I only drive it if I'm going out of town."

"Why is that?" he asks.

"I grew up here, but the traffic still terrifies me to drive in," I laugh. "I'd rather sit in the back of a taxi and be oblivious to the chaos."

"I can understand that completely," he says. "I thought L.A. traffic was bad until I tried driving here once and ended up stuck in traffic for two hours because I missed my exit."

A black car pulls up and the driver gets out and opens the back passenger door.

"And now you have a driver," I say laughing.

"Let me give you a ride to Rose Bud's," Kallon says. "Abby, this is Dax Wilson. Dax, this is Abby Rose."

"It's nice to meet you, Miss Rose," Dax says with a nod.

"Nice to meet you too," I say smiling up at the big man.

"Thanks, Dax, I've got it," Kallon says, taking the door from Dax. Dax nods and walks back around the car and gets in.

"Oh, no, that's okay," I say. I look back down the street and still don't see any available taxis.

"This is just like a taxi and Dax is the best driver there is," he says, smiling. He gestures his left hand, palm up, towards the inside of the car.

I look down the street one more time. I decide if I want to get back to Rose Bud's, this would be the quickest.

"Alright," I say in resignation. I sit down and slide over to the other side, making room for Kallon to sit.

As I put my seatbelt on, I look around the car, I can see the appeal of having a personal driver. This car is far superior to riding in a taxi. Extra bonus, it doesn't smell like cleaning supplies or air freshener trying to cover the smell of urine and puke.

"1050 5th avenue, please, Dax," Kallon says, as he puts his seatbelt on too.

"You go it, Sir," Dax says.

"So—" I say but my phone ringing interrupts me. I pull it out of my bag and see it's Jason calling. I smile apologetically to Kallon, "Excuse me for a second."

"No problem," he says. He gets his phone out of his pocket and starts doing something on it.

"Hey, Jason," I say, answering the phone.

"Hi, babe. Where you at? I tried the bakery, but Betty said you weren't there."

"I'm on my way back there now, I've been at Rose's for the last couple of hours," I say. I look at my watch and see its exactly noon.

"Oh, what were you doing there so early? Isn't it closed on Monday's?"

"Yes, it's closed on Mondays, but we had our meeting with the buyer, remember? I told you about it yesterday," I say, exasperated. Jason was a good boyfriend when he wanted to be but if he was distracted or stressed or otherwise uninterested in what was going on in my life, he wasn't very attentive.

Silence.

"Jason?" I say, even more exasperatedly.

"Sorry, I saw something. Anyways, yeah, I remember you saying something about the buyer. Who is it again?"

"Come by Rose Bud's later and I'll tell you," I say.

"How late are you going to be there today?"

"Pretty late," I say laughing.

"What's so funny? Why late? Aren't you closed by 2:30-3pm?"

"Yes, Jason we close at 2 but I have to stay late. I was offered an amazing opportunity—" I start to say but he interrupts me.

"Sorry babe, I gotta go. I'll swing by later, Bye."

Click

"Bye," I say to the dead tone.

"Everything okay?" Kallon asks, he puts his phone back in his pocket.

"I guess, Jason never said what he needed. Just that he tried calling Rose Bud's. He then got off the phone quickly. I'll send him a quick text to make sure he's okay," I say as I open our text history and send him a message.

Me: Hey, is everything okay?

I see the little dots like Jason is replying, which is awfully quick for him. He usually doesn't reply that fast, to me anyways.

Jason: Everything's fine, why?

Me: You called but never said why and then got off the phone quickly. Just making sure everything's okay.

Jason: Oh, yeah. Everything's fine. Shawn just came into my office and wanted to tell me about his weekend.

Me: Oh…

Jason: I'll try to come see you this evening. ;-)

Me: Jason, I'm going to be pulling an all-nighter down in the bakery. You can come help if you want to.

Jason: Me? Bake? Haha No.

Me: Okay…

Jason: Why are you pulling an all-nighter?

Me: Come to the bakery to find out. I'll be there in 20mins.

Jason: Just tell me.

Me: No, not over text.

Jason: Why?

Me: It's too important and too exciting. Just please, come to the bakery.

Jason: Alright… I'll try.

Me: Don't try, come. Please, this is important to me.

The three little dots are back but he doesn't reply right away. I look up at Kallon and give a half-hearted smile. I look back down and see Jason's reply.

Jason: K

I put my phone in my pocket and close my eyes. *Ugh… He can be so… self-absorbed sometimes.* I think to myself.

"I'm sorry," Kallon says.

"For?" I ask, opening my eyes and looking at him.

"That Jason can be self-absorbed," he says.

"Did I say that out loud?" I ask.

Kallon laughs and says, "Yes."

I close my eyes and lay my head back.

"Sorry, I didn't mean to say it, I thought it was in my head," I say.

"Don't be sorry for speaking your mind. You've had a big morning. You should be excited and want to tell your closest friends."

"I'm sure he's just busy with work," I lie. The fact that Jason hung-up on me so quickly because his work friend came into his office is starting to really upset me. "Anyways, I was about to tell you I like this car, when he called."

Kallon looks at me doubtfully but doesn't say anything else about Jason. Instead, he runs his left hand over the empty seat between us.

"Yeah, it's a nice car. Tina thought I should get something fancier, but I don't need anything showy. Just something comfy and smooth to ride in from the set to home and to events. If you pick the color black, it can make almost any car look fancy," Kallon says.

I laugh, "Your Lexus RX 350 makes my Honda CR-V look like a granny car. But I do have to say, my charcoal gray color does make it look really nice. It's not black, but still looks good."

"You know cars?" Kallon asks, leaning back in the seat but turning towards me.

"My grandpa is a big car guy," I say. "When I was younger, I helped rebuild a 1975 Chevy Camaro."

"No way! That's my dream car," Kallon says, eyes wide. "What color is it?"

"Rose Red, of course," I say, laughing.

"Oh, so your dad's father is the car enthusiast," he

laughs. "If... no, when, I get one, I want it to be blue."

"Is that your favorite color?" I ask.

"I don't actually have a favorite color, but I guess you could say blue is in the top three, I tend to like them all. I do go in spurts where I'll wear one certain color but then the next month, I'm over it and move on to a different color. Do you have a favorite color?"

"I guess I'm like you, I don't have one color that I favor out of them all. But blue, green, brown, and yellow are my top picks."

"Brown and yellow?" he asks with eyebrows raised.

"Yeah, sunflowers are my favorite flowers," I say. "And I love going for drives out in the country and seeing the spring green and fresh turned dirt next to the green. Blue skies and blue water, make me happy."

Kallon is looking at me in a peculiar way.

"You are fascinating," he says.

I bark out a laugh, "Fascinating? Me? Umm, no! Why do you say that?"

"Your answers always surprise me. They aren't what I usually hear from girls," he says.

"You'll come to see that I'm not like most girls," I laugh. "What do they usually say?"

"It usually has to do with something they can wear that makes them feel like they look prettier. Like pink brings out their natural blushed cheeks. Or a green or blue makes their eyes pop. Or another color makes them look tanner, it's all usually superficial. You are the first girl I've met that had a deeper reason for liking a color. It's refreshing," he says, smiling.

"Oh," is all I say. Then add, "Well, I don't usually wear clothes because of how they make me look but because of how they make me feel."

"See, another genuine answer," he laughs. "And from my experience with girls, if their last name was Rose or some other flower, that would be their favorite one. They'd make something up like, it was their given name so there for it's there given flower."

"I like roses, they just aren't my favorite," I say.

"And I think that's great. It means someone would have to get to know you, to know that. Instead of assuming it was roses because of your last name," he smiles a lopsided smile. I look out the window to distract myself from how beautiful it makes him look.

"Well, you don't act like how I thought you would either," I say with a soft laugh, to change the subject to something other than me.

His turn to bark out a laugh, "And how did you think I would be?"

"I don't want to say," I admit, embarrassingly.

"Why?" he asks.

"Because I thought the worst," I say, looking down at my hands.

"It's okay, tell me," he says. Out of the corner of my eye I see he reaches out slightly like he wanted to take my hand or something, but then he puts his hand back in his other one, in his lap.

"Arrogant. Pompous. Ostentatious. Rude. Selfish. Male chauvinist. You know, those types of things," I say quietly.

I hear Dax chuckle upfront.

"Wow," Kallon says as he takes a deep breath. "You were a fan of someone you thought was like that? Dax, do you have something to add?"

"Just that you are nothing like that, Sir," Dax says, looking at Kallon and then me, in the rearview mirror. He nods at me when our eyes lock.

"I honestly didn't know what to think. I was just making a comparison to what I do know of guys in New York and what I have read of other actors. I haven't picked up a magazine in a few years, but when I would, there wasn't a lot about you in them," I say. "But I'm happy to say that getting to know you has changed my mind. You are not at all what I mistakenly perceived you to be."

"I guess the difference between me and the other guys, is that I was raised to keep my core beliefs and morals. That just because I'm in movies, which in turn makes me famous, and makes me money, doesn't mean I can let myself turn into, to paraphrase your description, a jerk," Kallon says, shaking his head but has a smile on his face. "My mother would drive across the country in her little Toyota Camry to smack me upside the head if I ever did anything that she found to be foolish. And for the magazine thing, I don't do anything bad for them to find entertaining. My publicist, Jerry, tries to get me to do or at least pretend to do things to get in the media, but I refuse. I won't do anything that would bring negativity to my name, because it would disappoint my parents and family. From what I've seen, when actors do things that are negative, they have to do ten times the work to make things better. I don't want or need negative publicity. If my acting goes downhill so bad that Jerry says my only choice is to do negative things to get noticed again, I'll retire. I was raised to believe that your reputation is something that you build and keep but once you ruin it, it's never the same again. You can do a million and one good deeds but if you do one bad thing, you'll always be remembered for that one thing. So, I do my best to always do what's right. I keep my personal life out of the media the best I can. My girlfriends, or dates at the time, don't understand why I don't like standing and talking to reporters. I was in a magazine story once because my then girlfriend had pretended to get in a fight with me outside of a restaurant in L.A. But I just walked away. She tried to explain our publicist were just trying to get some fire going for the both of us, but when I talked to Jerry, he said he had nothing to do with it, it was all her and her publicist. I broke up with her that night. I wasn't going to have a girlfriend that would try to ambush me with fake fights, just to get in a magazine or online forum."

"Yeah, you're definitely nothing like I thought you would be," I say, smiling up at him.

"No wonder why you were so hesitant to believe I wanted to buy into Rose's for good reasons," Kallon laughs.

"I thought wrongly of you, I'm sorry," I say, sincerely.

"Thank you for that but it's not necessary. We all make assumptions about someone based on what we think we know of a group of people. Sadly, the group of people I'm associated with aren't usually the best. Granted, there are a lot of great actors, men and women, out there but the ones that either don't care about their reputation or they are just trying to stay relevant, are the loudest so they get seen a lot more than the rest of us. The media wants loud and crazy news, not the good stuff. For whatever reason, they like to push the negative more than the positive."

"That's true and I think that's why I stopped reading magazines or even watching the news. I knew there was more good, than bad, going on in the world but the media just focused on the bad and it made me feel horrible. Once I stopped and focused on my world around me, I saw goodness again, and felt better."

"Speaking of your world, Miss Rose, we're here," Dax says as he pulls up in front of Rose Bud's.

"That was quick," I say, looking around.

"Good conversation will do that," Kallon says. Dax is about to get out, but Kallon says, "I've got it, Dax. Thank you."

Kallon opens the door and stands off to the side, holding the door. When I slide over and I'm about to get out, he offers me his hand. Without thinking, I take it.

"Adding that to my new list of words to describe you," I say, laughing. I let go of his hand and step further onto the sidewalk.

"What's that?" he asks, stepping back towards the car, to get in.

"Oh nothing, I'm just making a new list of words that describes you more accurately," I say.

"And what would that list have on it?" he asks.

"I'll tell you later," I say. "I'm still compiling it."

"I'll hold you to it," he says, laughing.

"Have a good rest of your day," I say.

"You as well," he says. "Don't forget, call if you need anything."

"Okay," I say, as I walk towards the door to go into Rose

Bud's.

"I'm serious, Abby!" he hollers as I'm opening the door to go inside.

"I know," I say. I turn, smile, and wave before walking inside.

Once I'm in, I turn and watch as he shakes his head and gets back into his car and Dax pulls away.

"That was a fancy way to show up," Betty says, her eyes bulging. She asks in a hurried but quiet voice, "Was that Kallon Keller? Again? What's going on?"

"Come here," I say. Luckily the bakery is empty. I pull the folder out of my bag and grab a form. She walks over to me quickly and I hand it to her. "Read this and if you agree, I can tell you everything."

She reads it quickly and I know when she gets to the fine because her eyes go wide.

"That's a lot of money," she says. "I'm not a loud to even tell Maggie, am I?"

"No, but I have one for her to sign as well," I say.

"She's a smart kid but I don't know if she'll be able to keep it quiet."

"Then we use his alias name," I say.

"His alias name?" Betty asks.

"I can tell you everything if you sign that, but I totally understand if you don't think you can."

"No, I'll sign it," she says. "The suspense is killing me."

She signs in a hurry and puts the pen back in her apron. She hands me the form and looks at me expectantly.

"Okay, the buyer is Kallon," I say, not able to help the huge grin spread across my face.

"No stinkin' way!" she shouts.

"Yeah, but he wants to be referred to as Charles Webb when it comes to Rose's," I say.

"Why?"

"He doesn't want friends or acquaintances of his to feel like they should get special treatment if they go into Rose's. He had some bad experiences when he bought his first couple of hotels. He doesn't want Rose's to be taken advantage of," I say.

"He really is a good guy, isn't he?" she asks in shock.

"Yes, I think so," I say, smiling.

"What's with the smile?" she asks, looking at me weird.

"What? I can be happy. My parents got bought out and they can travel. My new business partner is a good guy and knows his stuff. He also got us a catering gig. I'm happy," I say. I realize that I am actually happy, genuinely happy for the first time in a long time.

"Okay, but as long as that's it," she says wearily. "You can't go getting feelings for him. That would just be a whole can of worms not worth opening."

"Oh my gosh, no!" I say and laugh at the absurdity of anything happening between Kallon and me. "Sure, he's nice and handsome but he's on a completely different planet than me. And plus, I'm with Jason. We're... happy."

I'm not sure why I stumbled over the word happy when I said it. Jason and I are happy. At least, I think we are.

"Okay, just wanting to make sure," Betty says. And then she adds, "You are closer planet wise than you realize, though."

"Oh my goodness, no we aren't," I say, laughing.

Changing the subject, I say, "Anyways, do you want to hear about the catering gig?"

"Yes!" she says excitedly.

I spend the next few minutes explaining to her about what Kallon had said was needed for the set. And then we sit down and write out a list of the pastries we want to make and get to work.

CHAPTER 5

Betty and I worked our tails off all afternoon. We closed at 2, just shortly after the last customer left. We finished the cinnamon rolls, berry rolls, blueberry muffins, and banana bread muffins. We also made gluten-free with sugar substitute of everything, as well. We're just getting the last raspberry turnovers into the oven, and about to start on the scones, when my alarm goes off on my phone.

"It's 5 o'clock already?" I ask, looking at my watch. Sure enough, it is. "Shoot, I have to go to dinner at my parents. Why don't we stop for now? I'll come back once I'm done with dinner and finish the rest."

"Maggie and I will go get something for dinner and then we'll come back and help. We can have her help as well," Betty says, walking towards the kitchen.

"Oh no, that's okay. We just have the scones to make and then we're done with the baking side of things. You worked really hard today, you should go home with her and get some sleep," I say, walking behind her as we get back into the kitchen.

"The scones will go even quicker if we help, and then we can all get a good night's sleep," Betty counters. I can't argue with her logic.

"Okay. Well then, I'll meet you guys back here between 7:30 and 8," I say. "My family will understand why I have to cut out early. Actually, they don't even know about the catering job yet."

"They're going to be so excited for you," Betty says, smiling. I smile back at her.

I rinse the mixing bows we had been using for the turnovers and put them in the dishwashers. I dry my hands and hang my apron up.

"I'm going to run upstairs and get ready to go to dinner, do you want me to send Maggie down?" I ask.

"Yeah, that would be great," Betty says as she dries her hands and then starts cleaning the counters off.

Betty and I talked to Maggie about what a gag order was and what it meant. She said she wanted to know and took the whole gag order as seriously as I thought she would. She singed and promised not to tell anyone. She said she'd call Kallon, Mr. Webb, no matter what. I promised her I'd introduce her to Kallon, Mr. Webb, as soon as he had a chance to swing by Rose Bud's.

I walk out and grab my bag. I walk back through the kitchen and head for the stairs.

"Thanks for all your help, see you in a couple of hours," I say.

"No problem, see you soon, tell you family hi for me," Betty says, as she takes a sanitized rag and wipes the counters down now that she's washed them.

"I will," I say. I get to the stairs and pull my phone out. Still no call or message from Jason. I was really hoping I'd see him to tell him my good news.

I get upstairs and find Maggie sitting on the couch, watching a movie.

"Hey, Mags, you and your mom are going to go get some dinner and then come back to help me finish up some scones. Do you want to help us with them?" I ask.

"Yeah, that'd be great!" she says excitedly. She is so much like her mom, always willing to help.

"You can leave your things here since you'll be coming back after dinner," I say as she starts to pick up a book and her bag.

"Okay, thanks Abby," she says, as she puts her book in her bag and puts her bag back down on the chair. "I'll see you later."

"See you, sweety," I say as I put my bag on the kitchen counter.

I wait to hear the door lock and then I head to my room. I pull my phone out of my back pocket and throw it on my bed. I take a quick shower. I change into jeans and a long sleeve t-shirt. I throw my hair into a side braid and put on some shoes. I grab my phone and check it. Still nothing from Jason.

As I'm walking out into my living room, I hear the buzzer for my door. I walk over to the intercom.

"Hello?"

"Hey, it's me, buzz me up," Jason's voice says.

I hit the buzzer and hear him running up the stairs. I open the door just as he's getting to it.

"Hey," he says. He pulls me into him and kisses me deeply.

I pull away and say, "Hi."

"What's wrong?" he asks. He walks in and takes his suit jacket off and hangs it on a coat hook.

"I'm about to leave," I say.

"To where?" he asks.

"It's Monday night, Jason," I say, prompting him. We've been dating for almost nine years now and for the last two years, my parents have had a family dinner at their house every Monday night. He's even came to a couple.

"I know it's Monday," he says. "But didn't you say something about a late night or early morning or something."

"It's dinner night at my parents," I say, annoyed.

"Oh, that's right," he says. "Well, let's have a quicky and we can head over to their house."

"No," I say.

"What? Why not?" he says pouting. "I haven't seen you in over a week."

"I saw you yesterday," I say.

"You know what I mean," he walks over to me and pulls me close to him, wrapping his arms around me.

"Jason, I have to go, I'm already running late. And I do have a late night and an early morning," I say.

"Why?" he asks, now he sounds annoyed. I step out of his embrace and walk over to the kitchen counter. He asks, "Where are you going?"

"I can tell you all about it after you read and sign one of these," I say as I pull out a gag order form.

"What's this?" he asks.

I read it to him and then say, "Now you read it."

Jason reads the form and as he does, I see his face get cocky.

"Who does this guy think he is? Asking people to sign a gag order?" Jason says, waving it in front of my face.

"Well, I can't tell you who it is unless you sign, but I'm not going to make you. You need to decide if you're going to sign it or not, it's your choice," I say.

"You really won't tell me?" he asks, putting on his pouty face.

"No, Jason, I won't. I signed one of those," I say, pointing to the form in his hand.

"Alright, well I'll sign then," Jason says as he pulls a pen out of my junk drawer.

"Only if you want to, you understand that if you tell anyone who it really is, you'll be fined the 10k, right?"

"Yeah, sure, sure," he mumbles as he signs the form. "There, all done. Now who is it?"

I grab the form from him and look it over. Sure enough, he's signed it. I put it back in the folder with Betty and Maggie's signed copies.

"Kallon Keller, but his alias when it comes to Rose's, is Charles Webb," I say.

"HA! I knew it," Jason says, pumping his fist in the air. "Hey, you lied to me."

"No, I told you the truth about why he was here yesterday. He actually did come to check out Rose Bud's because his assistant has been coming here for a long time for him."

"So, Sir Kallon wants people to call him by an alias? He's even more self-centered than I thought," Jason says.

"And Charles Webb? That's stupid, he could have picked a way cooler name than that, I know I would have picked better."

"Actually, Kallon is very nice and considerate," I say. "He uses an alias, so people don't take advantage of him and his businesses."

"Well, that's ridiculous, why wouldn't he want to give freebees away to people, especially if it means making new friends or contacts?"

"Jason, do you realize that if everyone Kallon knows, or they think they are friends with him, came to Rose's and asked for free dinner and/or drinks, we'd lose money. Rose's would go bankrupt. And if we refuse to give them a complimentary meal, they'd bad mouth the restaurant. That's why he uses an alias. It's one thing to give a free bottle of champagne or celebratory drinks or something like that but to give free dinners and 100's of dollars' worth in drinks? That's not good business sense. He learned that the hard way when he bought his first hotel chain," I say.

"He owns hotels? Sweet, do you think we could stay in one the next time we are out of town?"

I look at him dumbfoundedly. "Are you serious? That statement right there is exactly why he uses an alias and why he has people sign gag orders."

I knew having Jason sign an order was the right thing to do and the one person I knew I needed to have sign it. He just doesn't get it and I don't know how to make him understand.

"It's different for you though, because you're his business partner," he says, trying to make up for what he's saying.

"But there is no difference," I say. "He and I are business partners for Rose's, a restaurant, not for any of his other business. Those are completely separate, just like Rose Bud's is separate. He has no say in what I do with my bakery, and he even refused to let me give him free breakfast, he insisted on paying yesterday morning."

"Well, doesn't he sound like a saint," Jason says sourly.

"Don't act like that. I'm just saying, he knows that businesses, especially ones that rely on customers, only make money when things are paid for. It's the absolute, only way. Do you get that?"

"Of course, I do!"

"Well, then you should understand the gag order and why he has an alias attached to all his businesses."

"I do, babe, I really do. So, can we stop arguing and talking about Kallon now?" he asks, stepping closer to me, with a look in his eye that only means one thing.

His ability to switch gears has always made me a little dizzy.

"You should probably get used to calling him Charles when we're talking about Rose's," I suggest. "But yes, we can stop arguing. But I do have one more thing to tell you and it does involve Kallon."

He drops his hands to his side, exasperated. He asks, "What now?"

"He got me a catering gig!" I say excitedly.

"Who?" Jason says, sounding confused.

"Kallon…" I say in a 'duh' tone of voice.

"Kallon or Charles?" he asks. He sounds even more

confused.

"Oh, for crying out loud, Jason, Kallon. Kallon is Charles. We just went over this," I say, throwing my hands up in the air, frustrated.

"Oooh, yeah, Sorry. I got sidetracked."

"In the two seconds that's passed since I told you, you should call him Charles?"

"Did you?"

"Are you serious? Are you listening to anything I have to say?"

"Of course, I am," he says, putting his hands behind my shoulders and pulling me into him. "Tell me about this catering gig."

"It's for his movie set," I say, dejectedly.

"Really?" Jason asks. I can see the wheels in his mind turning.

"Yes," I say. "Betty and I have to make food for 200 people, all by morning."

"How much are they paying you?" he asks.

"That doesn't matter, it's a catering gig for a movie set," I say. I don't want to tell him how much I'm making. He'll try to push me into turning Rose Bud's into a strictly catering business and that's not what I want.

"What am I supposed to tell people when I tell them you're catering a movie set? They won't know Kallon is Charles," he says, annoyed.

"Jason, when it comes to anything outside of Rose's, you can call Kallon by his name. But when referring to him associated to Rose's, it needs to be Charles," I say. "So, you can tell people Kallon got me the catering job. And he got it for me because he's been eating at Rose Bud's for a year or so now, through his assistant until yesterday."

"This is going to get really confusing," he states.

"No, it's not. How do you figure?"

"Having to remembers when to call him Kallon or Charles."

"Just when you're talking about who the new co-owner is of Rose's. And honestly, how often do you talk about Rose's?"

"That's true," he says, not realizing how much of a jerk he sounds like with that statement. "I usually just tell people my girlfriend is the chef and owner. I guess that doesn't have to change."

I roll my eyes at him and start walking towards the door. I don't have any more time or energy to fight with him. I don't know why I'm just now realizing how exhausting it is talking to him about important things. Which is why we haven't really talked about anything substantial in the last few months.

"I have to head out to get to my parents, do you want to come have dinner with us?" I ask him.

"No, I should get back to the office," he says, looking at his watch. "I only stopped by for a quicky and since you're in such a hurry—"

"Only stopped by for a quicky? Seriously?"

"What? You said you were going to have a late night," he sounds like a little kid getting in trouble.

"The fact that you don't even see the issue is astounding to me right now."

"What issue?"

"I had exciting news to tell you but all you cared about or remembered was that you wanted to get laid. You didn't care about what my news was, just that there might be a chance you could get some."

"I'm sorry I made you feel that way, I didn't mean to," he says, pulling me into a hug. Only, he sounds like he's practiced those lines, instead of genuinely meaning them.

"Whatever, Jason, I really have to go. We can talk later," I say, stepping away. I grab my bag and walk towards the door. I open it and wait patiently for him.

"Okay," he says. He pulls out his phone and messes with it as he walks towards me and the door. He grabs his jacket, kisses me quickly on the head, and starts walking down the stairs.

I shut the door and it locks behind me. He gets to the door at the bottom of the stairs and he's out the door before I get down the last step. He lets the door swing shut. Shaking my head, I push it open and step out into the side alley. I start walking towards 5th Avenue to find a taxi. Jason steps up beside me, walking with me but still on his phone. We get to the street and I'm about to raise my hand for one of the vacant taxis to pull in, when a black car pulls up. Jason finally looks up from his phone.

The car parks and Dax gets out.

"Hey, Dax," I say, surprised. I look towards the back passenger door, expecting Kallon to get out but the door stays shut. "Did I forget something?"

Jason looks at me and then at Dax.

"No, Miss Rose, Mr. Keller just thought you could use a ride to your parents' house tonight for dinner. He had me drop him off at the set and come back and wait for you," Dax says, opening the back passenger door for me.

I don't remember telling Kallon about dinner. Maybe he overheard my parents and I talking about it before they left the restaurant.

"What's this?" Jason asks. "You got a new ride?"

"Oh sorry, Jason, this is Dax Wilson. Dax is Kallon's driver. Kallon gave me a ride home after our meeting at Rose's," I say. I turn to Dax and say, "Dax, this is Jason Phillips, my boyfriend."

"Nice to meet you," Dax says, extending his hand out for Jason to shake.

For a split second it looks like Jason isn't going to shake his hand but then he decides too. He probably decided that disrespecting a man of Dax's size, wasn't the best idea. He looks like he could have been a lineman for a professional football team. Dax also looks more like a bodyguard than a driver. He's a wall of muscle with a neck tattoo of what looks like angel wings that wrap around from the back to the front of his neck, and he's bald. He's wearing a black button up shirt and black slacks, and what look like black combat boots. All that would make him look tough but add that he's wearing his dark sunglass, makes him look even more tough.

"Yeah, nice to meet you too," Jason says. "So, you have a car and driver now?"

"No, this is a surprise to me," I say.

"Could you drop me off at the office?" Jason asks.

"It's in the opposite direction," I say apologetically. "Maybe Dax could take you there after dropping me off at my parents?"

"Sorry, Miss Rose, I was told to stay with you," Dax says, sternly.

"What the fu—"

Jason starts to say but I interrupt him and say, "I'll figure out what's going on, but I really do need to go."

"So, I'll just take a taxi then?" Jason asks.

"It's how you got here," Dax says, with an air of annoyance in his tone. I look up at him. He looks like he's starring Jason down. *Yeah, Dax doesn't like Jason. He just met him, but he already doesn't like him. Great.*

Jason is about to say something to Dax, but I step in between them.

"Please, Jason," I say. "I'll call you when I get home, okay. If it's not too late, maybe you can come over."

He looks down at me and says, "Yeah, okay, maybe."

He kisses me and then steps back.

"I'll call you when I get home," I say, stepping down to get into the car.

Jason just nods. Dax shuts the door and without looking at Jason, or saying another word, he walks around and gets into the car.

"What's your parents' address?" he asks. I look at him in the rearview mirror with my eyebrows raised.

"What? Kallon didn't tell you that information?"

"No, Miss, he didn't. Just that they live in Brooklyn," he chuckles.

"Dax, why are you here?"

"Tell me the address and then we can talk on the way," he states.

I roll my eyes and tell him, "870 Ocean Ave."

"Thank you," he chuckles again. He pulls out into traffic and starts making our way to Brooklyn.

"So," I prompt. Dax just drives. "Dax?"

"Yes, Miss Rose?" he replies.

"Why are you driving me to my parents?"

"Like I said, Mr. Keller thought you could use a ride."

"But you said you're to stay with me."

"To give you a ride home when you're ready to leave your parents."

"But why?"

"I don't understand the question."

"Why is Kallon doing this?"

"I can only guess it's because he didn't like the thought of you riding in a taxi."

"That's insane," I say, laughing. "I've been riding in taxis since I was old enough to go places by myself."

"He thought it would be quicker and easier for you to have me drive you places instead of being at the mercy of an empty taxi."

"I'm sorry, what?"

"What?" Dax asks, confused.

"You said to drive me places? Not just to and from my parents' house tonight?"

"Oh... I wasn't supposed to say that," Dax says, embarrassed. If a 200 plus pound man of nothing but muscle could be embarrassed.

"Well, you did, so what do you mean by that?'

"I am your driver now, this is your car," Dax says. "Mr. Keller was going to tell you tomorrow."

"You're kidding?"

"I'm don't kid," Dax says seriously.

"Why does that not surprise me?"

He chuckles.

"Okay so hypothetically, if I agree to this, who will be driving Kallon around?"

"Trevor, the other driver," Dax says nonchalantly.

"Kallon has two drivers?"

"Had," Dax corrects.

"Oh, for crying out loud! I haven't agreed to this," I say, trying not to shout.

"It would be pretty silly not to agree to it. Before a taxi could get to you, I'd be parked in front of you, door open, and ready to go. Doesn't that sound better than waiting for a ride? Isn't this car better than those stinky things?" Dax asks.

"I thought you just said you don't kid?" I ask, smirking at him through the rearview mirror.

He tilts his head just a little so that I can see his eyes from the top of his sunglasses.

"I don't kid," he states again.

"Well, I can't afford this. I can't afford you," I say.

"Mr. Keller already paid for my services for a year."

"What?" I ask. "That's pretty presumptuous of him to think I'd take the offer without even having a conversation about it."

"Sorry, I meant he had already paid for my services for himself. But now it's been transferred to you, as he's paid for Trevor to be his main driver now for the next year."

"I'm sorry you've been demoted," I say, laughing. I see him smirk.

"Not a demotion at all, Miss," he says, and I can tell he's

trying not to laugh.

"Well, I can't waste Kallon's money so I'll agree to this until I can talk to him about it. But under one condition?"

"What's that Miss Rose?" Dax asks.

"You call me Abby," I state.

"No, Miss, I can't do that."

"Yes, you can, I'm telling you, you can."

He looks at me in the mirror, sternly. I stare back at him and raise an eyebrow at him.

"Fine, when it's just us in the car, I will call you Abby. But when Mr. Keller or anyone else is around, it's Miss Rose, deal?"

Sighing I say, "I guess that'll work."

"And please don't make me drive your di—... boyfriend around," Dax says. "I can't stand guys like him."

"You just met him," I state.

"I'm a good judge of character," he says. "You talk to me like I'm your friend, even though we just met, and I work for you. Your boyfriend will talk to me like I'm his servant."

I can't argue with him. I can totally see Jason doing that.

"Tell you what, you won't have to drive him anywhere unless he's with me," I suggest.

"Well, I can't argue with that," Dax says.

BUZZ-BUZZ

"Excuse me a second," I say, as I reach for my bag where my phone is and pull it out. "It's my mom."

"No problem, Mi— Abby," he corrects last minute. "It'll

take me a couple times to get that changed."

I wink at him.

"Hi, Mom," I say as I answer the phone.

"Are you close?"

I look at my phone and see it's 6:15pm.

"Sorry, Mom, I'm still about 20 minutes out. Jason stopped by. I had him sign a form and then it started to turn into a thing," I say.

"Oh, I'm sorry, I'm sure that wasn't pleasant," she says. And then I hear her holler something to my dad about me being 20 more minutes out.

"How's Patty doing?" I ask.

"She's still sulking in her room."

"Maybe I can make her see reason."

"If anyone can, it's you."

It's true, Patty and I have a special bond. Ever since I was old enough to walk and talk, I was the only one that could get Patty to do things she didn't want to do or calm her down when she got upset about something.

"I'll try my best," I say. And then realizing something, "Shoot, Mom. I forgot the dessert."

"It's okay sweetheart, your dad made enough food to feed an entire football team. He forgets it's just us girls, unless Jason is coming too?"

I look up at Dax and say, "No, he's not but I will have an extra mouth to feed."

"What do you mean? Is Kallon with you?"

"No, but I'll explain when I get there."

"Tell me now."

"Ha! Now you're the one who has to wait to for more

information," I say, laughing.

"Abbigail Marie Rose!"

"Hey, you'll only have to wait 20 minutes. I don't want to get into it on the phone. I'll see you in a little bit, Mom. Love you."

"Abbigail!"

"Mom, please?"

"Oh, alright, see you soon. Love you, sweety."

"Love you," I say. I hang up and put my head back. The craziness of the day is starting to set in and I feel tired.

Next thing I know, I hear someone calling my name.

"Abby?" Dax's voice. "Miss Rose?"

"Abby will do Mr. Wilson," I say yawning. I look out the window and see my parents' house. Dax has pulled up and is parked in front of their garage. I look over and see my mom and dad starring out the window. Probably wondering who the heck just pulled in. I can't help but laugh.

"Fair enough, but Dax is what I prefer to be called," Dax says.

"As is Abby, for me," I counter.

He just looks at me. I smile at him and start to get my stuff, I put my phone back in my bag. Dax jumps out before I can tell him I can get my door. I look at my parents and they both look concerned. I laugh again because Dax does have a certain look. He opens my door and I slide out. I look up at my parents and now they look even more confused.

"Come on Dax, you're eating with us tonight," I say.

"Sorry, Mi— Abby, I stay with the car," he says.

"Oh, come on, you can come in and eat."

"I appreciate the invite, but I can't."

Shaking my head, I head up to the front door. My mom is opening it as I'm walking up the steps.

"What is that all about?" she asks.

"Kallon," I say. She looks at me questioningly. "Let me tell you and Dad at the same time so I don't have to repeat it. I'm tired."

She nods and ushers me in.

"Hi Buds, who's the bodyguard?" Dad asks, laughing at his joke. Although, I don't think he's too far off. The question is why Kallon thinks I need someone like Dax to drive me around.

I wonder what Trevor, the other driver, looks like? I think to myself as I take a seat on the couch. I tell them about the rest of the day after they left the restaurant. Up until Mom called me when I was on my way here.

"A catering job?" Mom asks surprised and excited. "For a movie set?"

"Yeah, starting tomorrow," I say. "Speaking of, I'm going to have to leave early tonight to finish baking everything for tomorrow. Betty is meeting me back at the bakery around 8."

"That's okay," Dad says. "Wow! What an opportunity!"

"I know. I still can't believe it," I say.

"And Kallon just gave you a driver and car?" Mom asks.

"Looks like it," I answer. "But I'm going to talk to him about it tomorrow. I can't accept this."

"Why not?" Dad asks. He was the last person I thought that would ask this question.

"Because I can't afford it," I say.

"Sounds to me like Kallon took care of it for you," he

says. "If we could have afforded it, you would have had a driver a long time ago. I've never liked you riding in taxis."

"So, you think I should accept his offer? You don't think it's too much?"

"It's definitely too much, but it's already been done. You said he's already got himself a new driver?" Dad asks.

"Yeah, a new regular driver, Trevor. It sounded like he and Dax took turns or something," I say.

"If you feel like it's too much, talk to Kallon, maybe you two can come to a compromise or something," Mom suggests.

"That's a good idea. I'll try to think of something," I say.

"And it sounds like you could afford to keep him with this one catering job. Can you imagine getting one after another?" Dad asks.

"If we can pull it off for the entire length of the making of the movie, it would be incredible to cater movie sets," I say, getting excited again. I look around and don't see Patty. "Patty still up in her room?"

"Yes," Dad says solemnly.

"I'll go talk to her," I say, as I stand up and head for the stairs.

"Thanks, Buds," Dad says.

I climb the stairs like I have since I was a little kid. I turn sideways, with my left side facing up the stairs, using my left foot first, I step up, then cross over with my right foot up on the next stair, and make my way up. I always called it my stair dance. It used to drive everyone crazy, but after a while, I got really good at it and could zoom up the stairs really fast. I make it to the top, slower than I like to admit but

I make my way to Patty's room.

I knock our secret knock.

KNOCK

Pause.

KNOCK-KNOCK-KNOCK

Pause.

KNOCK-KNOCK-KNOCK-KNOCK

"Come in, Abbigail," I hear Patty say.

I open the door and say, "Abbigail? Patricia, you aren't in a good mood, are you?"

"Don't call me Patricia," she says, pouting on her bed.

"You called me Abbigail first," I say, walking over to her and lying down on my stomach, like I used to always do when we were kids. "What's the matter, Sis?"

"Nothing," she answers.

"You can't fool me," I say, patting her foot. "Tell me what's wrong? Are you scared of something?"

She nods.

"What are you scared of?"

"Change."

"Oh, Patty," I say, sitting up. "I know change can be scary, but this is good change."

"No, it is not," she says.

"Why do you say that?"

"Mom and Dad won't be at Rose's anymore."

"That's true but I'll still be there."

"I know but you won't be able to keep him from making me retire too."

"Who?" I ask.

"Jason."

"Patty, Jason has no say, whatsoever, on what goes on at Rose's. I'm sorry you overheard that conversation. Why did you take so long to tell me you heard him say that?"

"Because Mom and Dad were still there."

"Oh, and now that they're gone, you think I'll let Jason make some changes?"

She shrugs.

"Patty, look at me," I wait until she looks up at me. "You aren't going anywhere. You work at Rose's as long as you want. But you might not want to keep working there when you start to see the fun Mom and Dad are having."

"I love working at Rose's with you and everyone else," Patty says, wiping a tear.

"Oh sweety, don't cry," I say. "We, everyone, loves you too. All of our customers love how you greet them. You don't have to worry about leaving Rose's until you are ready. You are the only one that gets to make that decision, okay?"

"What about Mr. Webb?" she asks and then winks at me. Letting me know she knows who Mr. Webb's real identity. I smile at her.

"He wants you to stay too," I answer honestly. "He's not going to change anything. I promise."

"Okay," she says. She slides off her bed and comes to me and pulls me up so I'm standing. She gives me her signature hug, which lasts about 5 minutes.

"Ready to go downstairs?" I ask.

"Yes."

"You've been scaring Mom and Dad, hiding out up here,

you know that?"

"Yeah, I'm sorry."

"It's okay. But you should tell that to Mom and Dad. We should be celebrating their retirement."

"I know. I will," Patty says as she takes my hand and we walk back down the stairs.

"Abbigail, you did it again," Mom says, coming up and giving us both a hug. "Do you feel better, Patricia?"

"Yes," Patty says matter-of-factly.

"Good," Dad says. He winks at me and then says, "Dinner's ready. Let's eat."

"Can I take a plate out to Dax?" I ask.

"Why don't you invite him in?" Mom asks, nervously.

"I already did. He said he has to stay out with the car. I think it's a load of poo but, what do I know, I've never had a driver with a car before," I chuckle.

"Who is Dax?" Patty asks.

"Why don't you fill her in and I'll take him a plate," I say to my parents, as I load a plate up for Dax.

I get outside and tap on the front passenger window. It rolls down and I reach my arm in and offer him the plate.

"Here, curbside service since you won't come inside," I say, laughing. I look at Dax and see him starring at the food and then at me. "What? It's food and an amazing chef made it."

"You?" he asks, sounding actually excited.

"No, my dad. And he's better than me."

"I've never—" he clears his throat "—I've never had anyone bring me food out before."

"What?" I ask in shock. "You're kidding?"

"I don't—" he starts to say but I finish it for him.

"Kid. Yeah, so you've said. Kallon has never brought food out for you?" I ask.

"He knows I bring my own food."

"Well, you drive for me now. Soon, you'll be sitting at the table with us. But if I have to treat you like a frightened wild animal until you trust me, then I will."

"I trust you," he states.

"Then you'll be at the table sooner than I thought. But tonight, if you're more comfortable eating out here, you can," I offer the plate to him again. "My arms aren't going to get any longer."

He takes the plate of food reluctantly, but I see his eyes shining with delight.

"Thank you," he says.

"You're welcome," I say. "I'll be back out for the plate in a little while. Or you can come in for more if you're still hungry when you finish."

"This will be plenty, thank you," he says.

I nod and head back inside.

The next hour is spent just talking to my parents about their plans now that they're retired. Sounds like a trip to Europe is at the top of the list. I gave them a list of places they have to go, places I fell in love with when I was there.

CHAPTER 6

As I'm hugging my parents and sister goodbye, there's a knock at the door. Dad opens it and Dax is standing there holding an empty plate. My parents look at me and then back at Dax. Patty peaks out from behind Mom, looking Dax up and down like she's never seen a man before. I step forward and take the plate from him.

"Mom, Dad, Patty, this is Dax Wilson. Dax, these are my parents, Stephen and Viki Rose. And this is my sister, Patty," I say, making the introductions. "Dax is Kallon's... well, he was his driver."

"And now I am your driver," Dax says to me.

"For this evening," I say. "I still haven't agreed to this arrangement."

Dax gives me an exasperated look then turns to my parents, "It's nice to meet you, Mr. and Mrs. Rose, Miss Rose," he says, nodding and smiling kindly at Patty. She ducks back behind Mom. "Thank you for dinner, Mr. and Mrs. Rose. I see where your daughter gets her cooking skills."

I look at him questioningly. I don't remember ever seeing Dax eat at Rose's or Rose Bud's, and I know I'd remember him.

Mom looks taken aback by Dax's manners, but she recovers and says, "You're welcome. Maybe next time you'll come in and join us?"

Dax looks at me and I just grin, he looks back at Mom, and says, "Maybe, Ma'am."

"Alright, we better go," I say. "I need to get back to the bakery and get things finished for tomorrow."

"Let us know if you need help," Dad says. "We can help load the van and set up, if you need it."

"I'll see how it goes and if I realize I need help, I'll have you guys help Wednesday," I say.

"Okay, but let us know," Dad says, looking at me sternly. "We know how you are and how you don't like asking for help."

I laugh and say, "I will, I promise."

I hug them again and turn to leave, Dax is holding the door for me.

"Bye, Dax," Patty says quietly from behind Mom.

He turns, smiles sweetly, and with a very kind voice, says, "Bye, Patty."

I look and see her smiling the biggest smile I've ever seen. We walk out, he shuts the door behind us, and we make our way to the car.

"You just made her year," I say laughing.

"She seems sweet," he says.

"She is," I reply. "She's the best person I know."

We get to the car and he holds the door open for me. I get in and slide to the middle and put on my seatbelt.

Once he's in, has his seatbelt on, and turns on the car, I say, "Home, Jeeves."

He looks at me in the rearview mirror and then starts to laugh.

"Oh, look at that, he does have a sense of humor and a nice laugh," I say, laughing with him.

Dax shakes his head but is still laughing as he pulls away from my parents' house. We drive in silence for a few minutes before I remember something.

"Dax, when have you tried any of my cooking?" I ask.

"Almost as much as Mr. Keller and Randy," he says.

"Are you the large black coffee and banana muffin that he orders when he comes into Rose Bud's?" I ask.

"I am," he says, smiling at me.

"Have you ever eaten at Rose's?" I ask.

"I have," he states. "When Mr. Keller goes in to have dinner, I sit in the bar area and have dinner myself."

"Oh, ok," I say. "I just had never seen you in either place, so I wasn't sure if you were just being polite to my parents or not."

"Well, yes I was being polite but that doesn't mean I wasn't telling the truth," he says. "Your food, whether baked goods or cooked food, is really good."

"Thank you."

He just nods. We slip back into silence again and the ride home is a quiet one.

We pull up to my building and find Rose Bud's is dark. I look at my watch and see it's 8:12pm.

Betty and Maggie will be getting here soon, I think to myself.

I open the car door, Dax is there, pulling it the rest of the way open for me.

"If Mr. Keller sees you opening the door before I get to it, I'll be in trouble," he says, shutting the door behind me. "Either getting in or getting out of the car. Will you let me do my job?"

I look at him with one eye squinting and my lips pursed.

"You'll have to be quicker," I jokingly say. He tilts his head to the side and glares down at me with frustration. Then I say more seriously, "I'm not used to that, it might take me a few times before I don't automatically go for the door."

"Doesn't your boyfriend get the door for you?" Dax asks.

I think for a minute and then answer truthfully, "Maybe once or twice since we've been together."

"How long has that been?"

"Coming up on nine years."

Dax is silent for a long minute. I look up at him, he's glaring down the street.

"What?" I ask.

"I'm sorry, I guess I was just raised differently than your boyfriend."

"Jason," I remind him. "And he has manners."

Dax just looks down at me with eyebrows raised.

"Manners and treating your lady nicely, are two different things. To say please and thank you to anyone is totally different from doing nice things, for the sake of making your lady feel special, loved, and appreciated, is a whole other thing."

"In his defense, I've never asked him to or expected him to do those things for me. Is it nice? Yes, but it's not something I expect, I guess."

"You shouldn't have to ask. If he was raised to treat his mom with chivalry, it would come naturally to him. Does his father not do these things for his mother?"

"I honestly don't know," I say. "I didn't really see them much when we were in high school. I have only seen them a handful of times since we graduated. They moved to Japan for his dad's job, the day after we graduated."

A look of understanding crosses Dax's face.

"You let me drive for you, you'll get used to it," he says, no other comment about Jason's lack of chivalry.

"Okay," I say. "Well, have a good night, Dax. Thanks for the ride."

"Have a good night, Miss Ro— Abby," he says shaking his head. "See you in the morning."

"That's okay, I'll be using my catering van tomorrow," I say. I wave and walk towards the side of my building.

I hear the door of the car open and close. I can hear the tires moving slowly up the road, when I get to the side of my building, I see Dax has stopped by the curb so he can see me. The front passenger window is rolled down, I can see him watching me. I get to my door and enter my code and pull the door open. I turn and wave at him, he nods, but doesn't pull away. I walk through the door and let it shut, locking automatically. I count to five and then open the door and poke my head out. The car is gone.

Shaking my head, I shut the door, hearing it lock again, and I head up my stairs. I enter my code, hear the lock click, and open the door and walk inside. I grab my phone out of my bag and toss my bag on my entryway table. I make my way to the back stairs and head down to the bakery.

When I get to the kitchen, I turn the lights on. I see everything is clean and put away but there's a note on the prep counter to the left of the doors leading into the main area.

Abby,

Maggie and I went ahead and finished the baking. We figured you'd be tired once you got home and thought it would be nice for you to get some good sleep before your big day tomorrow. I also pulled some strawberries and spinach and put them in the fridge for the strawberry banana smoothies and extra strawberries for the fresh fruit bowls. We also pre-cut some melons and pineapples. Bananas are on the counter up front. I set the smoothie maker up so it's ready for you, so you can make the smoothie mix first thing in the morning like you had wanted. I also washed the smoothie dispenser machines you'll take with you, so they're already to load in the morning as well. The icemaker is set just beside the smoothie dispensers, so we don't forget to send it with you. I'll be back at 2 to help box everything up and help load the van. If you want me to go with you to help set up, just let me know in the morning. Maggie and I are grabbing something quick for dinner and then going straight to bed when we get home, but I'll leave my phone volume turned on so if you need me, call.

Okay Sweets, see you in the morning! Get some rest!

-B

"She does too much," I say out loud to myself, with tears in my eyes. I walk back through the kitchen, turning the lights off, and heading back upstairs. When I get back into my kitchen, I lock the door, and head to my room.

I change into pajamas and crawl into bed. Pulling my phone to me, I see that it's 8:30pm. 1 o'clock is going to come quick. I plug my phone in to charge, roll over, and fall right to sleep.

My alarm wakes me up in what feels like 5 minutes. I roll over and turn on the snooze. But it keeps going off! I realize it's my phone ringing, so I grab it.

INCOMING CALL – JASON

I look at the time and it's 12:32am.

"Hello?" I say, sitting up.

"Heeeeyyy pretty lady," Jason says drunkenly.

I sigh and say, "Jason, do you know what time it is?"

"Sexy tiiime!" he hollers.

"No, not sexy time," I say through a yawn.

"It could be if you come down and let me in," he laughs. *"Ha-ha, get it? Let me in, like in."*

"Real funny," I say, annoyed now. "Jason, I can't let you in, I was asleep. I have a really early morning and need sleep."

"Oh, come on, baby, I'll be really quick," he says as he hiccups.

"No, Jason, go home," I say.

"Fine, whatever!" he says and then hangs up on me.

Rolling over I close my eyes and try to go back to sleep. But all I keep thinking about is how if I go to sleep now, my alarm will just wake me up again in 20 minutes... then 15 minutes.

I throw my blanket off me and fling my legs out of bed angerly.

"Ugh, Jason!" I scream. I sit for a minute to calm myself. For a second, I contemplate calling him back and letting him in but that would only reward his selfish behavior. He'd do it again and again.

Take a shower, it'll help you wake up, and ease your frustration, I think to myself.

I get up and go into the bathroom and take a long, hot shower. It does ease the tension in my shoulders, and I can feel my anger with Jason waking me up almost an hour earlier than I needed to be, drain from me.

I get dressed quickly in blue jeans and one of my black button-up shirts that has my Rose Bud's logo on it, which is a red rose bud and Rose Bud's written in cursive underneath, also in red. I feel anxious so I don't do my hair like I usually do. I just throw it into a tight bun at the base of my neck and then I hurriedly put my makeup on. I grab my phone and go to the kitchen. I eat a bowl of yogurt and granola, then grab my bag, and toss my phone into it. I head down to the bakery's kitchen.

When I get to the kitchen, I turn the lights on, and plug in the smoothie maker machine. I grab the strawberries from the freezer and the spinach from the walk-in cooler and put them on the counter. I go back to the cooler and get strawberry yogurt and orange juice and put them by the strawberries and spinach. I walk out into the front and turn on the lights that are directly above our work area, leaving the seating area dark. I grab the bananas and go back into the kitchen.

I start by throwing a five-pound bag of frozen strawberries into the smoothie maker. I rinse a bag of spinach and throw it into the mixer. I open and cut up, four bananas. I dump a container of yogurt in, put on the lid, and turn on the machine. I stop it and add orange juice, put the lid back on, and mix. I do this until the consistency is to my liking. I repeat this until two of my 22-liter containers are filled to the 15-liter mark. I put the containers now holding my smoothie mix, in the back cooler.

After putting the containers in the cooler, I check the time and it's 1:47am. *Betty should be getting her soon, I think to myself.* I decide to make some of my frosting that I'll drizzle over the pastries. I was going to wait until Betty got here but I can whip it together pretty quick. Once I've finished making it, I put it in the cooler, next to the smoothies.

I grab more strawberries, raspberries, some pre-cut cantaloupe, honeydew melon, pineapple, and some grapes. I put the pre-cut cantaloupe, honeydew melon, and pineapple in large bowl. After washing the berries and grapes, I put the raspberries and grapes into the bowl as well. I cute the strawberries into halves and add them also. I gently mix up the fruit until it's looks evenly dispersed.

I grab a stack of my plastic fruit bowl to go containers and start scooping the fruity goodness into them. There's no rhyme or reason to how I do it, I just fill them up until the big bowl is empty. After closing all the containers, I put them all into the cooler.

Now that I'm done making everything, I run down to the basement to get boxes out of storage to use to load all the goodies. When my grandpa had the place renovated, he made sure the basement was redone so it was open and very well-lit. That way I wouldn't be scared to go down to get stuff. He knows how much I hate the dark.

I get back up to the kitchen and as I'm putting boxes back together and taping them securely, I hear the beep of the side door and hear Betty come inside.

"Abby, it's just me and Maggie," she hollers so I can hear her.

I holler back, "I'm in the kitchen."

She comes in and Maggie is right behind her, looking tired.

"Good morning," I say. "Maggie, you can go up and go back to sleep until you need to go to school."

"School's out for summer," Maggie says with a big grin,

"Oh! I thought you were doing homework last night," I say.

"No, that was just summer reading," she says.

"Good girl," I say. I see Betty smiling over at her. "Well, if you want to go up and go back to sleep or read or watch TV, whatever you want to do, you know where everything is."

"Thanks," Maggie says. She hugs her mom and then heads to the back door and heads up stairs.

"What do you need help with?" Betty asks.

"I've just got all the boxes put together so now we just need to box everything up and take it out to the van."

"Sounds good," she says as she grabs a couple boxes and goes over to an empty counter. Then she goes into the dry food storage, grabs containers of the baked goods, and brings them out.

"Thanks for doing all this," I say as I box stuff up.

"Of course," Betty says with a smile. We spend the next

few minutes boxing things into to-go boxes and then putting those into the bigger boxes.

"I'm going to go start the van, I'll be right back," I say. Betty just nods and keeps boxing things up.

I grab the van keys from the hook just to the right of the big delivery door and walk out to my catering van. I've only used it for catering weddings so far.

My van is black with red rose buds painted in an arc from the front of the cargo box to the back of it. Written in red, in the middle, is, 'Rose Bud's', with 'Bakery' written underneath that, also in red.

I unlock the van and jump inside and turn the ignition, it fires right up. I check the fuel gage, it's still on F. I always fill it up after each outing, so that I know I have enough fuel for the next day or event. I'm about to get out when my GPS system turns on, on the dash, and I realize something. Something very important! I jump out of the van, shutting the door, locking it with my keyless entry remote, and run to the bakery door.

I punch in my code and fling the door open.

"Betty!" I holler. She turns, startled. "I forgot to get the address to the studio I'm supposed to go to."

Her eyes go big, and her mouth falls open, "Wha—"

"I can't believe I forgot one of the most important things," I say, facepalming myself. "How could I be so stupid?"

"You had a lot going on yesterday and the fact they gave you less than 24 hours' notice..." Betty says, trailing off, trying to calm me.

I run over to my bag that I had tossed on to my desk

and grab my phone. I quickly open my contacts and hit Kallon's name.

It only rings twice before he answers.

"Hello?" Kallon says, groggily.

"Kallon, this is Abby, Abby Rose. I am so sorry to call you so early," I say in a rush.

"No, it's okay, what's up? Is everything alright?" he asks the sleep in his voice turning into concern.

"Yes and no," I stammer out. "We've got everything ready, but I just realized I don't have the address for the studio."

"Oh, that's my fault, I'm sorry. It's over on 22nd St, in Brooklyn. Dax should be there to help you. I'll call him real fast. I'll call you back—"

Before Kallon can hang-up, I ask, "Wait, what about Dax?"

"I'll call you back," he says and then the phone goes dead. I put my phone in my back pocket and wonder what the heck is going on with Dax supposedly being here. I had told him yesterday I'd drive myself because I'll have my van.

No more than two minutes go by when I hear a loud knock from the front of the bakery. I look at Betty and she looks at me. We walk out of the kitchen, into the front and see the silhouette of a huge man standing at the front door. I turn the light on that's closest to the front door and it immediately lightens Dax's face up through the door. My head tilts to the side and I walk to the door.

"What are you doing here?" I say, as I open the door. "I told you I was driving my van today."

"Yes, she just opened the door," Dax says into his

phone. "Yes, Sir."

"Kallon?" I ask, pointing to his phone. Dax nods. I put my hand out, asking for it.

"Umm, Sir, Miss Rose would like to talk to you," he says, again into his phone. He gets a smirk on his face. "A little bit, Sir."

He hands me his phone, and I wave him inside. After he steps inside, I pull the door shut and lock it. I turn and walk back towards the kitchen.

"What is Dax doing here?" I ask Kallon. "Who said I needed a car and driver?"

"He's there to help you get to the studio safely," Kallon says. *"He's driven me there more times than I can count, and he knows all the best short cuts."*

"I can drive myself," I say a little stubbornly, Betty looks at me questioningly.

"You had said driving in the city's traffic scares you. Stephanie didn't give you much time to mentally prepare for this, I thought Dax could help ease the stress of at least the driving part of today."

Taken aback by Kallon's thoughtfulness and how he seems to remember little details I've told him about myself, has me silent for a minute.

"Are you mad?" he asks. *"If you're really upset about it, I'll tell Dax to not worry about driving the van and you, but I will have him drive himself to the studio anyways, to help you unload and then load everything back up before 11, that's not negotiable."*

"No, that's okay. I'm just surprised is all. And if you're going to have him drive there anyways, it would be silly to take two vehicles. He can drive the van," I say, reluctantly. "But, what about him saying he's my driver now? That the Lexus is my car, and you have a new one and driver?"

"Sorry, Abby. I'm about to lose service, I'll talk to you later," Kallon says but I hear humor in his voice.

"Kallon, you were asleep when I called. You aren't driving and about to lose service."

"I…. eeet… mmm… ddrrr…" is all I hear from his end of the phone call and then he hangs up. I look at the phone, but it doesn't show me a 'dropped call' notification.

"Turd-head just hung-up on me," I say, handing the phone back to Dax, who just smiles down at me. I turn and walk back over to my boxes of baked goods and start loading them into the last of the boxes. I mumble to myself, "Pretending to lose service to avoid answering my questions."

I hear Betty and Dax chuckle. I just shake my head in their general direction. Betty knows how independent I am, so she should know how thrown I get when people do nice things for me unexpectedly. If Kallon thinks I'll drop it, I won't, we will have this conversation. I look at the clock and see it's 2:35am.

"We should start loading up the van," I say. "Let's put the smoothie containers in the refrigerator first, so we aren't tripping over the boxes trying to get back there."

Betty nods and heads to the cooler, she comes out with one of the smoothie containers, I go in and grab the other.

"How can I help?" Dax asks, looking around at all the boxes.

Might as well put him to work.

"If you want to grab the smoothie dispenser machines, and bring them out, that would be great," I say, pointing to the machines sitting on the counter to the left of the doorway leading out to the front of the bakery. I see the icemaker and add, "That ice machine needs to come too."

He nods and picks one up without showing signs of how much it weighs. I walk to the back door and I'm about to juggle the container against the wall and my arm so I can use one hand to open the door, but Dax reaches around me and opens it for us. I look back and he's holding the smoothie machine easily in one arm.

"Thank you," I say.

He just nods. I had already adjusted my container in my arms, so I go ahead and reach into my pocket and grab my keyless entry remote. I re-adjust the container back into my arms and walk out the door. I click the unlock button twice and Dax darts around Betty and I and opens the back door of the van for us.

"Thank you," Betty and I say together.

Again, he just nods. I step up and into the back and walk to the front of the cargo area where the smaller refrigerated area is located. It has just enough room to hold what I need refrigerated for any given event. The two containers of smoothie mix have plenty of room, but they also sit securely in a bin so that they don't tip over and spill while the van is moving. There's a nice spot to put my container of frosting and boxes of fruit bowls, as well.

Betty hands me her container of smoothie mix and I place it next to the one I just put down. Dax hands me the smoothie dispenser and I put it down next to the refrigerated area's door. We head back into the kitchen where Betty grabs the container of frosting and a box of fruit bowls. I then grab the other boxes of fruit bowls. Dax grabs a couple boxes of baked goodies and we start loading them into the van.

As I'm passing Betty on one of our trips in and out of the kitchen, I notice she's grabbed the tote that has my portable 3-tiered wire rack displays and 2-teir plastic pastry displays, in them. I have found that using these, makes set up and clean up a cinch. And a plus, the 2-tier displays are heated just enough to keep the pastries a nice warm temperature.

I grab the two commercial coffee brewers and as Betty comes back inside, she grabs the decaf and caffeinated coffee tubs full of freshly ground coffee. I point to a tote that has the coffee filters and teabags in it.

"Dax, if you don't mind grabbing that, that would be great," I say.

"Sure thing," he says. "Anything else I can take out now?"

"Umm," I look around. "If you can grab the cold brew coffee dispenser from in the dry storage room, that would be helpful too."

"I can do that," he says, heading into the storage room.

Betty and I take the brewers and coffee tubs out to the van and load them in. I put the brewers by the smoothie dispensers and coffee tub in a space meant just for a tub it's size, in the corner. I have Dax hand me the cold brewer and the tote with filters and teabags. I put the cold brewer by the other coffee brewers and put the tote with filters and teabags up on top of the coffee tub.

I throw in a couple cases of bottled water as I'm not

sure if I'm supposed to supply them or not. When I have to make a decision about bringing something or leaving it, I always think of my grandpa's wise words, "It's better to have it and not need it, than to need it and not have it."

However, I really should have taken time to get Stephanie's number from Kallon and called her for all of this so that I'm not bringing things I don't need but, it's too late now.

"I think that's it," I say, as we put the totes with serving utensils, napkins, plates, cutlery, cups, lids, and straws into the van.

Betty looks at her watch and then at me. She says, "Do you want me to go with you or stay here? It's barely after 3am, I can get things going for the bakery or come with you to help set up."

"Dax has been volunteered to help me set up," I look at him with raised eyebrows, he just grins. I shake my head and continue talking to Betty, "So why don't you go ahead and stay here. You can go up and take a nap if you need one. Most everything is ready to open this morning, just the coffee needs to be turned on and you can do that just before 5."

"A quick nap might be good," Betty says with a small smile. "Are you coming back after setting up or staying there?"

"I'll see how it goes," I answer. "I might stay there and nap in the van. If all goes well today and they want me to come back tomorrow, we'll have some baking to do this afternoon."

"Let me know as soon as they tell you and I'll get things started," she says.

"Thank you," I say. I give her a hug and grab my bag. "Ready, Jeeves?"

He shakes his head at my mock nickname for him, but he smiles despite himself, "Sure."

"Bye, Betty, thanks again. See you in a few," I say, heading to the back door.

"Bye, have fun," Betty says as she walks to the door to go upstairs.

CHAPTER 7

I walk around the van but before I can open my door, Dax is opening it, he has followed behind me.

"Even the work van?" I ask.

"Any and all doors," he says, smiling.

"Ridiculous," I say. "I appreciate it but when it comes to being at work, I can open my door."

Dax just looks at me and says, "Okay, I'll make you a deal. You can open your door to get out but getting in, I open it."

"I won't wait for you," I say.

"You won't have to," he says, shutting the door softly as I situate myself in the passenger seat.

"We'll see," I say to myself.

Dax gets in, buckles himself in, and pulls down the alley and onto the street. He starts driving towards what I assume is the direction of the studio. I know the general area but have never been there before.

"Will we get there in time?" I ask, looking at my watch, it's now 3:12am.

"Plenty of time," he says. "This time of night, or

morning, however you look at it, the traffic is pretty smooth."

I start patting my lap with my hands, a nervous habit I sometimes do if I don't have anything to do with my said hands.

"Nervous?" Dax asks.

"A little," I say. "I've never catered for a movie set before... for actors... famous people."

"You've catered weddings before, this isn't any different," Dax says.

"I guess that's kind of true, except for the people. And I usually have a few months of notice before the wedding day and the bride and groom pick out the foods they want," I say. "I don't mind the short notice. I just get nervous when I have to make quick plans and decisions."

"I'm sure your choices will be great. Just relax, take a nap if you want. I'll wake you up when we're close."

"I think I'm too nervous to sleep," I say, but I lay my head back and try to relax. The hard part was over, all the baking and decision making was done. Now, I just have to set everything up and keep my fingers crossed that they like my food. I turn my head and watch the lights from the cars as we pass them, and all the city lights zoom past as well.

If I don't think about how famous these people are and just think of them as just people, and treat them how I treat anyone, the stress does kind of ease up a bit.

I won't treat them any different than I do my customers at the bakery or at Rose's, or at the weddings I've catered, they are all people, I think to myself.

"Miss... Abby, we're getting close," Dax says, what feels like hours later. I open my eyes and realize I'd actually fallen asleep.

"Apparently I was more tired than nervous," I chuckle. "Thanks for letting me snooze for a minute."

Dax again, just nods. As I look at my watch, I see it's 3:48. We turn on to a street and up in front of us, I see a huge sign that indicates the studio is minutes ahead. My heart starts to race.

Calm down. They. Are. Just. People.... Breathe. I take a deep breath and try to calm myself. *I can do this. My food is delicious, and this will be an amazing opportunity for my bakery if all goes well.*

I watch as the sign gets bigger as we get closer. Dax stops at the gates, at a small security building.

"Can I help—" the security guard starts to ask but then she sees Dax "—Oh, Dax! It's you! I didn't recognize the van. What's up?"

"Hi, Stella. I'm driving for Miss Rose now and she's the new caterer for breakfast, for the 'Along Came You' crew," he says. He turns to me and says, "Miss Rose, this is Stella Brodden, she's usually here in the mornings. Stella, this is Abbigail Rose."

"It's nice to meet you," I say, with a nervous smile.

"It's nice to meet you also," Stella says, smiling. "They should be getting you a badge, so you don't have to stop and talk to me quite so long. You'll just show me your badge and be on your way."

"Oh, okay," I say.

"You guys have a good day," she says as she pushes a button and the gates open.

"Thanks Stella, see you later," Dax says as he pulls

through the gate.

"Thank you!" I holler out to her, hoping she heard me.

We drive around for just a couple more minutes before Dax turns beside a building with a big 'Studio 5' printed on the outer walls.

"Ready?" Dax says, as he pulls up to a side door, and parks.

"Yes," I say with more confidence than before. I'm now over my nerves and actually feel more confident.

"Atta girl," he says, smiling at me.

We open our doors at the same time, I grab my bag and sling it over my body so it's crossing me. I walk around to the back of the van where Dax has the door open already. Just as I'm about to grab a box, the side door opens, and Kallon walks out. Shocked, I just stand here, with one foot up on the back of the van and one on the ground.

"Good morning," he says, smiling at me. "You're catering van looks great!"

"Good morning... Thank you," I say, slowly. I put my foot back down on the ground. "I didn't think you'd be here yet."

"I told Stephanie I'd be here when you got here," Kallon says. "Did I not mention that to you?"

I look at Dax and then back at Kallon, and say, "There's a lot you haven't mentioned."

Kallon laughs and says, "We can talk about everything I've neglected to tell you, after we get everything set up. What can I help take in?"

I mock glare at him for a second and then a beautiful red head steps out from behind him, extends her hand, and says, "You must be Abbigail Rose! I'm Stephanie Steel. I am so grateful you were able to take us on, with such short notice. Kallon wouldn't stop raving about your breakfast pastries."

"Call me Abby, Ms. Steel. And I hope he hasn't hyped them up too much," I say, shaking her hand with mine as I smile. I look at Kallon a little nicer now.

"Not at all, they'll speak for themselves," Kallon states. He grabs a couple totes and moves towards Ms. Steel, who is now holding the door open.

"And you can call me Stephanie, or Steph, whichever you prefer but Ms. Steel is reserved for my mother," Stephanie says, laughing.

I grab the tote that has the display racks in it and Dax grabs a couple of boxes of baked goodies. We follow Kallon in through the door and then Stephanie hurries in front of us and leads us through a well-lit hallway. Along the walls I look at all the posters of past movies this studio has made and I'm in awe.

It doesn't take long before we're turning right, into a huge room where different sets for the movie are set up, but at the back, is a long table. Stephanie leads us that way.

"You can to set up here. And through the doors there —" she points to the right "—is a small kitchen. The other breakfast caterer used it for cleaning up afterwards. Did Kallon tell you what time we'd need you to have the breakfast stuff cleared out?" Stephanie asks.

"He did, he said before 11 o'clock. I usually like to have an hour of clean up time to make sure the area is how I found it before the next person comes in, so I'll start clearing stuff away at 10 o'clock, if that's okay with you?" I ask.

"That's perfect," she says. "I'll be over there talking to the film staff. If you need anything, holler. Actors will be here by 5 so everything needs to be ready by then. The film crew knows to wait until 5 also."

"Thank you, Stephanie," I say. She nods and then walks away from us.

"If you want to get things set up the way you want them, Dax and I will bring the rest of the stuff in from the van," Kallon says, putting his totes down next to me.

"That's okay, I can bring stuff in," I say. I add, in a teasing voice, "You don't need to help, what would your co-stars think?"

"I'd hope they'd think that they should pitch in and help as well," he says. "And don't you think it'll go faster if you start setting up now, while we bring in the rest of the stuff? It's really no problem at all."

"Don't you need to rehearse or something?" I ask.

"I'm not needed until around 5:30 and I have my lines memorized already," he says.

"Do you do this with all the caterers?" I ask.

"No, just the ones I'm friends with," he says with a smile and then winks at me.

Shaking my head, I finally say, "Okay, you aren't wrong. I could probably get everything set up quicker if I get started and let you guys help by bringing things in."

"Atta girl," Kallon says. "You'll learn to accept help sooner or later."

"I accept help," I say, shortly. "I'm just not used to it from people I just met."

"I think you mean men," Dax says. I look at him and he

just shrugs. "Am I wrong? The vibe I got from your boyfriend is that he doesn't help that much."

"He's busy," I say. "And I mean, people I just met."

Dax looks like he wants to say more but just shakes his head and walks back towards the hallway.

"He must like you," Kallon says chuckling. "He doesn't usually voice his opinions so freely."

"Does he with you?" I ask.

"Frequently," he laughs. "I can talk to him and tell him to keep it to himself, if it bothers you."

"It never bothers me when people speak their minds," I say. "Even if it's true and hurts to hear."

"Dax is a good judge of character, but he has been wrong a time or two," Kallon says. "He might not have a good read on Jason."

I shrug, not really wanting to get into this with Kallon now, or maybe not ever.

"I'll go out and help Dax bring stuff in," he says. He smiles kindly and walks away.

I grab my headphones and phone out of my bag and then I put my bag under the table, out of the way. I put my headphones in my ears and before putting my phone in my back pocket, I turn on music that helps block out thoughts. Thinking about Jason and comparing his behavior against Kallon and Dax isn't something I can do right now. It wouldn't be fair to Jason anyways. For all I know, Kallon and Dax's behavior may just be because we just met, and everyone is usually on their best behavior at first.

I grab the black tablecloth out of the box that has the utensils in it and lay it over the table. As I'm setting up all my tiered wire racks and pastry displays, Dax and Kallon bring the first few boxes of baked goods inside. I smile at them and start pulling the boxed goodies out and pull the pastries out one by one and put them in their display cases.

Kallon brings the coffee brewers in next and nods at me. I pull my headphones out of my ears, and he asks, "Where do you want these?"

"Let's put those at the end of the table down there on the right," I say. I'd been setting up the pastries on the left, hoping people would move from left to right to get things. "The cold brew dispenser can be set up to the right of them. Smoothie dispenser to the left."

"Sounds good," he says. He puts the brewers down and heads back out, without another word.

I put my headphones back in and my music starts back up. As I'm getting the baked goods set up, the guys keep bringing in box after box, tote after tote. It doesn't take long when I'm putting the last of the pastries in its display, when Dax walks in with a smoothie container and Kallon behind him with another, and the frosting container on top of it.

I take my headphones out and say, "Thanks, guys. That went a lot quicker and smoother than I thought it would. If you want to put the smoothie mix right there, I'll take the frosting and go warm it up so I can put it on the pastries that need it."

"Do you just dump this into the dispensers?" Kallon asks.

"Yeah, but—" I start to say but Kallon interrupts me.

"We can get these going, you just take care of the frosting, it's more important," he says, with a laugh. Shaking my head at his obsession with my blueberry scones, I smile as I grab the frosting.

"Fine. Each container will fit in one of the smoothie dispensers. Make sure they get plugged in and turned on, so the mix stays cold," I say.

"Easy enough," Kallon says.

I take the frosting and go into the kitchen. It's small but has what I need; a microwave and large pitchers in one of the cupboards that I can use to fill the icemaker and the coffee brewers up with water.

As the frosting is warming in the microwave, I check my watch, it's 4:27am. I have plenty of time to get the coffees made and ready, and the icemaker making ice.

I fill one pitcher and take it out with the frosting. Kallon and Dax are setting the cups and plates out when I get back out to the tables. They've already set the napkins and plasticware out, it looks good.

"Be careful, I might hire you," I say, laughing. "This looks great."

"I've eaten my fair share of catered meals," Kallon says.

I put the pitcher down by the coffee brewers and walk down to the pastries. I open the top plastic display and drizzle frosting over the scones and turnovers. I close these back up and open the bottom and drizzle it over the cinnamon rolls and berry rolls.

"How many of these do you need?" Kallon asks.

I look over and see him holding the pitcher of water.

"Enough to fill the coffee brewers and icemaker. The two hot coffee brewers have a lever for hot water for people that want tea," I say as I walk over to him, putting the empty frosting container in a box and push it under the table.

"We can help get them filled," Kallon says, handing me the water.

I show them how to fill the water reservoirs in the back of each of the hot brewers. I give the empty pitcher to Kallon and tell them which cupboard has the other pitchers. I put the filters and coffee in the hot coffee brewers and get the cold brew grounds put into the basket.

When I get into the kitchen, the guys have three of the six pitchers full.

"Go ahead and take these, we'll bring the others out to you. We can be your Gopher Men," Kallon says, smiling his heart stopping smile at me.

"Gopher Men?" I ask.

"Go get stuff for you," he says, laughing.

"I've never heard of that," I say, laughing as well. I grab two full pitchers and go back out to the table.

I need one more pitcher to fill the cold brew up. And just as I'm about to go back to the kitchen, the guys walk out with the other four pitchers.

"Thank you," I say as I trade them the four full ones for the two empty ones. "I just need five more."

They nod and each grab an empty pitcher and walk back to the kitchen. Once the cold brewer is full, I turn it on. I'm filling one of the hot coffee brewer's reservoirs when Stephanie walks up to me. I turn the brewer on once the reservoir is full.

"This all looks great and smells amazing. How's everything going? Finding everything you need?" she asks.

"It's going well. The kitchen is working well enough,

but it would be helpful for a way to have water be directly hooked up to the coffee brewers instead of packing water from the kitchen," I say. "But I know that's not feasible so, this will have to work."

"Nonsense, I'll have it fixed for you by tomorrow," Stephanie says as she pulls out her phone.

The guys come out with two more pitchers and grab the four empties. Dax looks like he's on a mission, while Kallon just smiles and nods a 'what's up' gesture to us.

"Mr. Keller has been helping you a lot," Stephanie says. "How long have you known him?"

"I actually met him Saturday," I say as I'm dumping some water into the icemaker. I finish dumping the rest of the water in this pitcher, into the last hot coffee brewer. "But Randy has been coming into my bakery for quite some time. I'm hoping to see him today."

"Mr. Keller must really love your coffee and pastries to be so adamant about hiring you," Stephanie says, smiling. "And I admit, if they taste as good as they smell, I see where he's coming from."

"Oh, thank you," I say, not really sure what else to say.

Luckily, the guys come back out with the last of the pitchers and I finish filling the decaf coffee brewer.

"So, what all do we have?" Stephanie asks, looking up and down the table.

I point towards the black handled Airpots and say, "Regular black coffee is in that one—" I point to the red handled Airpots, "—and in the red, that's decaf. I'm sure at this time of day, not a lot of people will drink it, but I wanted to offer it as an option for someone who can't have caffeine."

"Very thoughtful," Stephanie smiles.

"Each hot coffee brewer has a hot waterspout for tea," I say, touching the lever. I point to the baskets with sugar and single serve creamers, "There are single serve creamers and sugar here. As well as sugar free options for both."

"Already better than the last caterer," Stephanie says, beaming at me.

"This is cold brew regular coffee. Any of the creamers and sugars can be used in it," I say, smiling as well, pointing to the cold brewer. I put my hand on one of the smoothie dispensers and continue, "These are both strawberry, banana, and spinach smoothies, made with strawberry yogurt and orange juice."

"Now that is something we didn't have before," Stephanie says, looking giddy.

"And down here," I say as we walk back down the table to where the pastries are displayed. "I've made cinnamon scones and blueberry scones—"

Kallon interrupts and says, "Dibs on the blueberry scones, those are my favorite."

Stephanie and I laugh.

Continuing, I say, "There are cinnamon rolls and berry rolls. Raspberry turnovers and blueberry turnovers. Those six pastries get my homemade frosting drizzled over them. The blueberry and banana muffins are here with the fruit bowls beside them. I wasn't sure how many of those to prep, so they might run out. I didn't want to make too many and have too much fruit left over."

"I think it looks to be enough. If something runs out, they have other delicious options. But what are all these other identical pastries?" Stephanie asks, pointing to the other displayed goodies.

"Those are the sugar free, gluten free, fat free ones. I made the exact same things, just dietary friendly," I say.

"Wow, how thoughtful. The other caterer refused to do anything different," she says.

"That's too bad," I say.

"Other than needing constant access to water, is there anything else you need?" she asks.

"I can't think of anything, but I might by the time the morning is over," I answer.

"The kitchen isn't used by any other caterer, so feel free to leave things in there so you aren't having to pack things back and forth, things that are okay with leaving here," she states.

"Thank you, that'll help a lot."

"People should be arriving shortly," she says. "Thank you so much for this. Really, thank you."

"No problem," I say. "I'll be out in my van and will check on things throughout the morning. But, if you need me, call, or come get me."

"You can hang out in my dressing room," Kallon suggests. "I'll only be in one costume today, so I won't need it."

"Oh," I say, stunned. "That's okay. I don't want to be in the way."

"You won't be, I promise," Kallon insists. I see Stephanie look at Dax, who just shrugs.

"I—" I start to say but Kallon interrupts me, again.

"Just come look at it. It's a lot bigger than you think,"

he says.

"That's what she said," a voice says from behind me. I turn and see Chace Tanner standing not three feet way.

Chace Tanner is a famous actor who has been in the most recent romantic comedies, but he plays the tool who either tries to steal the leading lady or is dating her and the nice guy rescues her from him.

Chace is very handsome in the traditional movie star way. Blonde hair, blue eyes, and a fake tan that is starting to look unnatural.

"Whoa!" he says when he sees me. "Who's the little hottie?"

Chace looks from me to Kallon, who's gritting his teeth so hard, his jaw muscles are poking out of his jaw line.

Stephanie steps between us and says, "Mr. Tanner, this is Abbigail Rose. She's our new breakfast caterer. Miss Rose, this is Chace Tanner."

Mr. Tanner steps around Stephanie and offers me his hand.

"It's nice to meet you, Miss Rose. Not Mrs.?" he asks.

"No, I'm not married but I'm not single either," I say, taking his hand and shaking it. "And it's nice to meet you as well, Mr. Tanner."

"Call me Chace, all the pretty little things do," he says, looking me up and down. He pulls my hand up with his and then bends his head down and kisses it. I fight the urge to roll my eyes and scrunch up my nose in a show of disbelief at his arrogance. I pull my hand back, and again, fight an urge. But, this time, to wipe my hand off on my jeans.

"I'll show you to my dressing room," Kallon says

tightly.

"If you find yourself bored in there, my room is next door," Chace says with another wink.

I give him a half smile, half grimace, and turn to Kallon. And as a way to get away from Chace, I say, "Lead the way."

I see Kallon relax and he takes a step towards the hallway we'd come down from outside.

Once we get out to the hallway, Dax says, "I'll be outside if you need me."

"Wait!" I exclaim. Dax and Kallon both stop walking abruptly. "You don't want to come wait with me."

"I'm more comfortable outside," Dax states.

"I'll come outside with you then," I say, taking a step towards him.

"No, Miss Rose, you go to Mr. Keller's dressing room. It has a nice couch in there that you can take a nap on. You should get some rest. I'll be fine," he says and then turns quickly and walks down the hall.

"He enjoys his solitude, honest," Kallon says. "And I promise, this is not a trick. My dressing room is yours if you want it."

I look at him for a second and wave him on. We walk in silence for a minute.

"Sorry about Chace, he can be..." Kallon says, but trails off.

"Full of himself?" I suggest.

"Yes, to say the least. He'll confirm every bad thing you can think of about an actor or famous person. He uses anyone he can, to get what he wants. Please promise me you'll keep an arm's length away from him. He'd take full advantage of a sweet and beautiful girl like you."

Ignoring the fact that Kallon Keller just called me beautiful, I say, "How about I keep two arm's lengths away? He might think he's smooth and funny, but I won't fall for any of it."

"Even better," Kallon says, smiling.

We stop at a door and Kallon enters a code into the keypad. He opens the door, and we walk into what I can only describe as a large living room. There is a large sectional couch and a huge flat screen TV. A two-person table beside it. A sitting area with a mirror but the countertop is clear and doesn't look like it gets used much. There's a fridge in the corner of the room. To the left, is the bathroom, the door is open, showing off a shower and sink, the toilet must be behind the door. On the far wall is a long rolling rack with a ton of different outfits hanging on it.

"This is your dressing room?" I ask.

"Yeah," he says, as he shuts the door behind us. "The passcode to get in is, 8130. Randy, Dax, and Trevor, and I, and now you, are the only people that know it. You'll have privacy and a quiet place to rest."

"When will Randy be getting here?" I ask.

Kallon looks at his watch, "He should be here around 6am. I told him if he wanted to run by Rose Bud's, he could, but not to get me anything. This will be the first time I'll eat the catered breakfast. I'm sure my co-stars will be shocked."

"Will he drive himself since Dax is here?"

"No, Trevor is my driver now. After he dropped me off this morning, he left to go pickup Randy. Trevor will drive

Randy around when I have errands that need to be ran while I'm filming, just like Dax used to but now…"

I raise an eyebrow at him and he stops talking as he realizes he's brought up the subject about Dax driving me.

"I don't recall asking for a car and driver."

He takes a deep breath and says, "I know. I just thought it would be nice to have Dax and the Lex at your disposal since you go back and forth from Rose's to Rose Bud's so often. This way you don't have to wait for a taxi. And you did in fact say that the traffic terrifies you when you do have to drive."

"I can't afford to pay for Dax's services."

"You don't have to pay for his services. I have already paid for the rest of the year and all of the next."

"I'm sorry, what?"

"I pay two years in advance."

"But now you've paid for two drivers and two cars. I can never pay you back."

"I don't expect you to and I have always paid for both Dax and Trevor. Trevor is back up in case Dax is driving me and I need someone, or something picked up."

"Well…What will you do now? In those situations… No, I can't accept this."

"It's not for you to worry about. Trevor gets bored so this will be like I'm actually getting my monies worth," he laughs.

"I… I don't know," I start to protest again but then my phone buzzes in my back pocket. I look and see Kayla is calling. "Sorry, my best friend is calling."

"She's the one getting married, right? Kayla?" Kallon

asks.

"How did you remember that?" I ask, shocked.

"Good memory," he smiles and taps his left temple. "I'll give you some privacy. I'll head back to the set. I need to get a scone before they're all gone."

"I'll be back in there in a second," I say. And then add, "Thank you Kallon, for this opportunity. And for letting me use your room. And… for Dax and the car."

"You're welcome," he smiles a huge triumphant smile. "We're partners now, you'll get used to being spoiled."

My phone starts to buzz again.

"I don't know about that," I say as he walks out the door. I hit the answer button. "Hello?"

"Abby! Oh my gosh! My wedding is ruined!" Kayla says frantically.

CHAPTER 8

"What? What do you mean?" I ask.

"My wedding... is ruined!" Kayla pants out. I hear Peter in the background trying to calm her down.

"Makayla Lynn Smith, breathe!" I say sternly. I hear her take a sharp breath in. I never use her full name. "Now, blow it out. And take another deep breath in."

Kayla has always been one to go from 0 to panic mode 100, so I learned how to calm her down way back in elementary school when some boys weren't being nice to her. Our problems have changed through the years.

After I talk her through a couple of more calming breaths, I can hear her breathing start to relax.

"Better?" I ask.

"No... Yes... but no," she says quietly, and now I can hear her soft crying.

"What's wrong?" I ask.

"I just got off the phone with the florist," she takes another deep breath. *"All my Annabelle Hydrangeas were destroyed by bugs, and she won't be able to plant new ones in time for my wedding."*

She starts to get upset again.

"Okay, first, take another breath and blow it out," I say and wait as I hear her do it. "Good. Now, does Peter still want to marry you?"

"Yes, of course."

"Then your wedding isn't ruined," I say. I hear her laugh through another deep breath. "Keep breathing. I'm going to look something up. I'm putting you on speakerphone."

"Okay," I hear her say.

I click on the speakerphone and then open my search engine. I enter 'Annabelle Hydrangea look alike flowers' and 'Chinese Snowball' pops up. I save the picture and send it to Kayla in a text.

"Good news, I might have found a look alike. And in my opinion, it looks better," I say.

I hear the phone shuffle around and then I hear Peter a lot clearer.

"What did she find?" he asks.

"Look," Kayla says excitedly.

"That looks nice," Peter says, sounding like he has no idea what he's looking at but knows he had better like it.

"I'm going to text this to Shelly. I hope she has it," Kayla says, sounding hopeful. *"I like it too!"*

"Thank you for calming her down," Peter says.

"Yeah, thank you. I'm sorry I overreacted. I know I have a year but I want everything planned now. And thank you for thinking so quickly! I instantly thought the worst. I didn't even think to ask if there was anything similar, since I was so adamant on using the Annabelle's. I know the wedding is a year away, but I want everything to be perfect."

"Kayla, the only thing that makes it perfect is you and Peter. Everything else is just background noise," I gently say.

"*Absolutely,*" Peter agrees.

"*I know, you are totally right,*" Kayla says, sounding less stressed. "*Oh, Shelly texted back!*"

I cross my fingers and hold my breath.

"*She has it!*" Kayla shouts.

"Oh good!" I say, happy for my best friend.

"*Are you okay if I go back outside?*" Peter asks. "*I need to finish cleaning out the car before I head to work.*"

"*Yes, thank you,*" I hear Kayla say and then there's smooching sounds. "*Thank you, Abby!*"

"It's what I'm here for," I say and then remember something else. "Have you called a baker yet to talk about your cake?"

"*Yes, I did that last night,*" she says, sounding relieved.

"I wish you'd let me make it for you," I say. "I could save you so much money."

"*If today doesn't prove how much I need you leading up to, and definitely the day of, my weeding, I don't know what will. No, I'm going to be selfish and want your focus on me and not the cake. I know you'd do a better job than anyone we could hire but I know how much of a perfectionist you are, and I probably wouldn't see you until I was walking down the aisle,*" she laughs.

"You're allowed to be selfish, it's your wedding day," I laugh.

"*Yeah, but I can't be ridiculous, I need to lower my expectation of how perfect I want this day to be. But Peter deserves a beautiful wedding if he's going to be stuck with me for life,*" she giggles.

"Kayla, you two have been together since freshmen year of high school. He'd marry you in a courthouse just as long as he knows you are officially his life partner for... well life," I say. "He loves you. You love him. Remember that's all that matters."

"I love you! You always know what to say."

"Not always."

"Enough about me. How's work? I'm so sorry for calling you like this. You must be busy."

"Well... you won't believe what's happened!"

"What?!"

I take her off speaker and proceed to tell her about everything that's happened in the short three days since I left her on Saturday. Except for the restaurant part, obviously. Surprisingly, she's silent the entire time I retell my story.

"And I'm on the set right now, in Kallon Keller's dressing room!" I finish, out of breath. Kayla still isn't saying anything. "Kayla, are you still there?"

"You're kidding me, right?" she whispers.

"No?" I say as a question.

"You let me blabber on and whine about a stinking flower and you didn't stop me to tell me this? Heck, you didn't think to send me a quick text? Abbigail Rose! This is the most amazing thing!"

"The flower is just as important—" I start to say but she interrupts me.

"Ummm no, you said it yourself, it's just background noise. Meeting Kallon Keller and him referring you to cater the movie set he's currently working on, that is not background noise."

"The flowers are important to you. I don't want you to think they aren't. I only said they were background noise to get you to calm down."

"No, you were right. The only real thing that matters to me and Peter, is that our friends and family are there to help us celebrate," she says. *"But enough about wedding stuff for now. Tell me about Kallon. Is he as hot in person as he is in the movies?"*

I laugh. This is the first time Kayla has talked about anything for more than a minute other than her wedding. I honestly don't mind her talking about her big day. I truly am excited for her and Peter.

"He's better looking in person. But what's more than that, he's very kind. Like, genuinely nice and considerate of other people. His manners aren't a forced habit, they seem to be just how he is as a person. His driver, well I guess my driver, Dax and Kallon's assistant, Randy, are very polite and nice, as well. I really didn't expect that."

"I'm calling it now," Kayla says, laughing. *"You and Kallon are going to fall in love with each other."*

"Kayla!" I exclaim. "I'm with Jason."

"Listen, you know I love Jason. He was a great first boyfriend, especially in high school. But since college, he's kind of turned into..." she stalls.

"Into a what?"

"A corporate tool."

"Well, that's not fair," I say in Jason's defense. "You moved away. You only get to see him when you come home for a visit, and he's usually stressed from work."

"Can you honestly say he's still as attentive and loving as

he was before we graduated high school?"

"No, but neither am I. We've both grown up and changed. We aren't in that infatuated, always have to be together, stage anymore."

"Abby..." it sounds like she changes her thought. *"Let me ask you this, do you think Peter and I have grown up and changed?"*

"Of course."

"Do you think we've done that together or separately?"

"Together. You two are one in the same but also your own person."

"That's because we've made these changes together. We've grown together. We have also recognized our individual changes and have accepted them completely of each other. Can you say the same about you and Jason?"

I don't answer. I can't think of anything to say that could convince her, or me for that matter, that we have grown together. And if I honestly think about our relationship, we've been growing apart since our first year in college.

"Abby?" Kayla asks tentatively.

"Yeah," I say with a hitch in my voice.

"I didn't mean to upset you."

"I know," I say, sniffling. Apparently, Jason and I need to talk. "Look at you with your wise words."

"It's easier to see things from the outside looking in. You'd tell me if you noticed something off about Peter and me, wouldn't you?"

"Yes, I would but you don't have to worry about that, you've found your person."

I just need to figure out if Jason is still mine. I think to myself.

"Babe, Mom just called and wants you to call her back when you have a minute," I hear Peter say in the background.

"Okay," Kayla says away from the phone. And then to me, *"I better call her."*

"Okay. I wish I could be there to help with all this stuff."

"Thanks for being here for my manic phone calls and texts, that's all the pre-wedding prep I need from you."

"And your bridal and bachelorette parties!" I exclaim.

"Oh, yes, those two things as well," she laughs.

I hear a beep and look at my phone but there's nothing there.

"Do you have an incoming call?" I ask.

I hear a muffled scratch, like she pulled the phone across her cheek, and then a sigh.

"It's Vivienne," she says. *"She must really need to talk to me."*

"Okay, I'll let you go. Call me anytime if anything else happens or you just need to vent," I say. And then I remember, "Hey, ask your brother if his wife is coming to the bachelorette party. She's the only one left to RSVP."

"Oh, she probably won't come," she says in mock sadness.

"Why?" I ask, Kayla and Bree get along really well, so I'm a little surprised at this news. Mitch and Kayla are twins, they've always had the same qualities they looked for in friends.

"Because she's pregnant with baby number two!" Kayla

says excitedly.

"What?" I ask seriously surprised now. "Isn't James barely one?"

"Yeah, he turned one last month. They wanted them close in age, but Bree admits not this close," Kayla laughs. "Anyways, she's in the first trimester and is super nauseous all the time. Her work gave her extra maternity leave because she was getting sick in the office over everything. Smells are getting to her this go-around, which makes them think it's a girl."

"Well, that's exciting," I say. "That they think it's a girl, not that she's been so sick."

"Mom has been here for the last two weeks helping take care of James so that Mitch can keep working. Did I tell you he'll get paternity leave once baby is here? It was one of the perks that drew him to the company where Peter works."

Mitch and Peter are best friends, it's how Kayla and Peter met. Mitch brought him home from school and it was love at first sight for him and Kayla. At one point, Kayla tried to hook Mitch and me up, but we are too much like brother and sister. Mitch introduced me to Jason. They were on the same baseball team together in high school.

Beep-Beep

I look at my phone again, nothing.

"Vivienne calling again?" I ask.

After a quick second of silence, Kayla says, *"Yes. I better take this. I'll ask Bree about the party. Keep me updated about everything with you. Even if it's just a quick text."*

"I will."

"K, love you."

"Love you, too. Bye."

"Bye," she says and then she hangs up.

I look at the time before I put my phone away. It's 5:36am. I walk out of the room, making sure the door closes before I start walking down the hall. They made this building easy to navigate.

I've never done well inside big buildings. Especially ones with a lot of floors that are full of hallways, and they all look the same. I usually get lost. I really appreciate the people who drew and built this one.

I get to the set just as a large group of people are leaving the breakfast tables. I hear a lot of them mumbling satisfied compliments. There's only a tall, beautiful, dark-haired woman standing at the table when I get to it. As I walk up to her, she turns. It's Amelia Ray. I try to make my smile kind and not starstruck like I feel.

"Miss Ray," I say. "Good morning."

She glances down at my shirt and must notice my Rose Bud's emblem because she says, "Mmmhmmm, good morning you say? It would be if there weren't so many fattening things for breakfast. I guess I could just eat this little bowl of fruit."

"Oh, I'm sorry, I should have put out signs. These over here are all gluten free, sugar free, and fat free," I say, pointing to the dietary friendly foods.

"Really?" she asks skeptically.

"Yes," I say. Then I point to the other side of the table.

"These are all regular."

"Hmmmmph," she says a little snottily. She grabs a cinnamon and sugar scone and takes a tentative bite. I see utter delight cross her face before she gets control of her facial expressions. "Not bad. What about drinks?"

"Caffeinated and decaf hot coffee. Hot water for tea. And a cold brew caffeinated coffee. There are regular and sugar free creamers and sugar substitutes. Also, a smoothie option and bottled water."

"Your boss knows what he's doing," she sneers.

Before I can happily correct her, Kallon's voice comes from behind me, "Actually, Abby is the owner."

"Who is Abby?" Miss Ray asks, looking around.

"I am," I say, still politely. My patience are going to be tested today, I can feel it.

"Oh," is all she says.

"Pretty amazing, huh?" Kallon asks, smiling hugely at me.

"Sure," is all Miss Ray says with a half-smile, half-glare before she steps away and gets a coffee.

I try to smile at Kallon, but I can feel it looks fake, so I add a shrug. I turn to the table and start to arrange things so it's neater.

"Sorry about her—" Kallon starts say.

"You don't need to apologize," I say, interrupting whatever excuse he was going to use for her behavior.

"I forget how rude my co-workers are until there is someone new on set. I feel embarrassed when they act like that," he says, coming to stand next to me.

"Honestly, it's okay," I say, smiling up at him. "I'm used

to people acting a certain way towards me. Comes with the job, I guess."

"You should never get used to people being jerks and why are people rude to you because of your job?"

"People are usually cranky in the morning and that's when I see most people," I check the water in the coffee machines, they're still good. "I don't usually see customers at Rose's unless they ask to speak to the chef or management."

"Does that happen a lot?" Kallon asks, surprised.

"About once a week," I answer honestly.

"For what reasons?"

"Mainly to compliment on the food but every once in a great while someone will complain about service or something. It always turns out they've had a little too much to drink. I tell them I'll give them a complimentary dessert and it always seems to satisfy them."

"Ready on set!" a loud voice shouts. "Keller, let's go!"

"Shoot, I better go," Kallon says. "Please use my dressing room to rest. All of this looks great and will be here after you take a nap."

"I will," I say and yawn.

Kallon smiles and then walks over to the set they're filming on at the moment. It looks as if they're shooting on a dance floor. Kallon stands while a girl adds makeup to his face and then she moves away. He goes and stands next to a pretty, short, dark-haired woman. I don't think I've seen her in a movie before, but then again, she could have blonde hair but, in this movie, it's brunette. A bunch of other people, maybe extras, join Kallon and the woman on the dance floor, and act like they're about to dance.

A couple seconds later and the director shouts, "Action!"

I watch for a bit and marvel at how the actors transform into their characters. The music playing is country.

After I finish up straightening the plates and plasticware, I decide there's not much I can do, so I walk back to Kallon's room.

When I get to his dressing room door, I see it's open a little bit.

I know I shut it when I left, I think to myself.

I push the door open and ask as I step inside, "Hello?"

Putting some things down on the table by the couch, Randy turns with a start.

"Oh, Miss Rose, you startled me," he says.

"I'm sorry," I say, "I didn't know you'd be in here."

"I was just putting some new books in here for Mr. Keller. He likes to read when he's in between scenes or on a break and doesn't have time to go anywhere," he says as he stacks the last couple of books onto the pile.

He steps to me, sticking his hand out for me to shake, and says, "Hi, I'm Randy Johnsen. I don't think we've been properly introduced."

"No, we haven't," I say with a laugh, taking his hand. "I only know you're name because of your orders. Hi, I'm Abby Rose."

"It's nice to officially meet you," Randy says with a smile of his own.

"Nice to meet you also," I say. I let go of his hand and point to the stack of books. "So, what does Kallon like to read?"

"Oh, just about anything. Well, except horror. That is one genre he refuses to read," he smiles at me. "He likes to read about history, of both our country and other countries and the history of different things. There was a month where he had gotten into trains. Then another about different types of wines. He also likes fantasy fiction, suspenseful, sports, and romance."

"Romance?" I ask in disbelief.

"Oh yea, like I said he reads it all, except—"

"Horror," I finish for him and laugh. "I don't blame him. I don't read it either."

Randy goes over to the little counter by the fridge and pulls out some things from bags and puts them away. I see sitting next to some empty grocery bags, a to-go cup that looks familiar.

"How was Rose Bud's this morning?" I ask.

Randy looks over at me in surprise. I look over at the cup and nod my head at it, smiling.

"Oh," he says, laughing. "It was great as usual. Busy, but Miss Brown had it covered."

"I'll call her in a few and see how she's doing," I say and then yawn.

"I'm finished here, I'll leave you to the room," Randy says. "Mr. Keller said he was going to offer it to you. I'm sure he's pleased you took him up on it."

"I realized it makes more sense to get some rest than to babysit the table out there," I say.

"Stephanie does a good job at keeping an eye on things," he says, walking towards the door. "She'll take care of any messes and will let you know of anything you need to address. It's pretty low-key around here."

"That's good to know," I say and yawn again.

"There are blankets in that closet in the corner," Randy says, pointing towards the far-left corner. "Help yourself to whatever you might need."

"Thank you," I say sincerely.

Randy nods and leaves.

I walk over to the closet and find pillows and all sorts of uber soft throw blankets. I grab a pillow and blanket and head to the couch. I take my shoes off and lie down. After fishing my phone out of my back pocket, I snuggle down and get comfy.

I see that it's a little after 6am. I set a timer for 7, 8, 9, and 10 o'clock. I then open my text messages and send a quick text to Betty.

Me: All set up. Resting in Kallon's dressing room. :-D I'll tell you all about it when I get back. Text if you need me.

I then send Jason a text.

Me: Morning. How are you feeling?

I click my screen off and put my phone on my chest so when my alarm goes off, I'll be sure to hear it. I close my eyes and I'm asleep in what had to be seconds because the next thing I know, my alarm is going off.

I pick my phone up and look out of one cracked eyelid

and turn the alarm off and see it's 7am. I put the phone above my head on the armrest and roll onto my side. This couch is so comfy, and I feel so cozy under the blanket, I fall asleep just as quickly as the first time.

At some point I thought I heard my phone go off again, but I must have dreamt it because the sound only lasted a quick second.

BEEP—BEEPBEEP—BEEP**

I wake up feeling rested. It's amazing what a two-hour nap will do for you. I grab my phone and sit up quickly. My clock on it says it's 9. I look at my watch and it says the same.

I fling the blanket off me and hurriedly throw on my shoes. I walk quickly from the room and speed walk down the hall and into the set room.

I can tell the tables still look good, but everything is almost gone. I check the coffee brewers and see they've been filled.

"Crap," I say under my breath. Just then Stephanie walks over to me. "I'm so sorry, Stephanie. You shouldn't have had to fill these for me. It won't happen again."

"I didn't fill them," she says smiling.

"Then who?" I ask.

"Dax and Randy," she smiles.

"Who…" I trail off. I ask in a stern voice, just one word, well name actually, "Kallon?"

"He asked Randy to go get Dax and they filled them

up," Stephanie says, smiling still. I must look irritated because she adds, "Mr. Keller came back from a short break and checked on things. The coffee was getting a little low and he said you'd probably refill at that point. I asked if he wanted me to go get you and he said no, he'd have Randy and Dax take care of it."

A thought crosses my mind but only Kallon can confirm what I'm thinking. So, I muster up a smile and wipe down the machines with a napkin.

"That was nice of him," I say as kindly as I can.

Stephanie looks like she wants to say something but then she puts a finger to her ear where I see an earpiece.

"Oh, for heaven's sake. I'll be right there," she says. "I'm sorry, Abby. Drama in the costume design room."

"No worries," I say.

Stephanie smiles, squeezes my upper arm gently, and then turns and runs from the room.

I take the plastic case that had the regular scones in it off the table and put it in a box under the table. As I'm wiping the table off where the case was, I hear someone walk up behind me.

I turn and see Kallon with a smile on his face. I see behind him a group of the set workers rushing over to us.

"Break?" I ask shortly.

The smile on Kallon's face falls. His answer sounds like a question, "Yes?"

"Do you have a minute to talk to me in your dressing room?"

"I do," he says, confused.

Without looking at him, I turn and walk from the

room, not checking that he's following. I don't have to wait long before he's in step with me.

"Everyone is raving about your breakfast spread," he says. Probably to make small talk in the silence.

"That's nice," I say nonchalantly. I really wanted to jump for joy but before I can be too excited, I have a few questions for Kallon, first.

He looks at me in confusion but before he can say anything, we get to the door of his dressing room. I just step to the side, letting him do the honors of putting in his keycode. I figure that's the polite thing to do.

Kallon enters his code and then swings the door open. He doesn't go in first but motions for me to go ahead of him.

I walk in and sit on the couch. I pull my phone out and hold it in my hands. Kallon sits on the other side of the sectional. Far enough away, we aren't touching, but close enough he could probably touch my knee if he tried.

"What's wrong?" he asks after a minute of silence.

"You had Randy and Dax refill the coffee?"

"Yes," he answers matter-of-factly.

"Why?"

He's quiet for a minute. Then he answers, "You were sleeping."

"How do you know?"

He looks at his hands and then looks up with a sheepish grin. He says, "We had a 15-minute break. I came to check on you. You were asleep."

"That's all you did. Just checked on me?" he looks at his hands. "Did my alarm go off while you were in here?"

"Barely," he says.

"You turned it off, didn't you?" I ask in a little louder voice.

"Yes."

"I had it set for a reason. It was not for you to turn off," I say sternly.

"I'm sorry but you were sleeping, and you looked as if you were sleeping well."

"Apologies mean nothing if there is a 'but' in it," I say.

"I know. I truly am sorry. I knew you'd be upset but I told myself I would go check on things and if there was something out of my wheelhouse, I'd come wake you up myself. The coffees were the only things that needed refilled, and Dax and I watched you do the first ones, so I figured we could handle it."

"That's not your job. I was hired to do the catering. That includes refilling drinks when necessary, even if I'm sleeping. It's why I set my alarms."

"I'm sorry, truly. I was just trying to help," Kallon says. He doesn't sound offended, just sincere.

"I appreciate that but when, and if, I need your help, I'll ask for it."

"But will you though?" he asks with a smile. I can tell he's trying to lighten up my mood. It works a little bit.

"Probably not, unless it's something I really can't handle," I say, smiling even though I'm trying hard not to. I'm trying to stay serious.

"Why do I feel like the list of things you can't handle is slim to none?"

I shrug but then smile.

"Please, Kallon. This is my career. If they—" I wave to

gesture at the people out in the set room, "—see you and the guys doing stuff for me, they aren't going to believe it's my bakery or that I can't do it without help. My reputation will make or break me."

"Having me... the guys... help you, isn't going to ruin your reputation as a cook, baker, or business owner. Your food speaks volumes. But I understand and will obey your wishes. On one condition," he says, eyeing me.

"What's that?"

"You continue to rest in here," he says.

"Okay, but I have my own condition," I counter.

"What's that?" he says mimicking me and smirks.

"You don't turn off my alarm anymore."

"Deal," Kallon says, holding out his hand.

I take it and feel what is becoming a familiar spark of electricity shoot from our hands to my stomach. I look up at Kallon and for a quick second, I think I see a look of astonishment in his eyes.

I clear my throat and say, "Deal."

Kallon stands and when he does, I release his hand. I see him clench his hand into a fist.

Interesting.

"Are you staying in here for a bit?" he asks. His voice sounds a little shaky.

Interesting.

"No, I'm going to go back out and get what I can cleaned up. I want to head back to Rose Bud's as soon as I can," I answer.

"What time do you have to be to Rose's?"

"I get there around one to make sure everything is

good to go and to go over paperwork."

"Okay. If I don't see you again before you leave, I was planning on stopping in this evening after I'm done here, if that's okay with you. I was hoping to watch behind the scenes for a little bit. Just so I know how things work. You know, the kitchen hierarchy so to speak."

"That's fine. You don't ever have to ask or see if it's okay to come by. You can come anytime you want. You are part owner, after all."

"I appreciate that, but I don't want you to feel like I'm pushing myself on to you and the restaurant."

"You aren't," I say and then remember. "Has Randy signed a gag order?"

"He signed one that covers every business venture I undertake. That way he doesn't have to keep signing them," he laughs.

"Good idea," I laugh too.

I stand and follow him out of the room. We walk down the hall in comfortable silence, for a little ways.

"So, where is Randy now?" I ask.

"He ran some errands for me. He sure likes you."

"He seems like a nice guy."

"He is, I'm lucky to have him."

We slip back into silence and walk into the set room. I glance over to the set and see a ton of people mingling around. I see someone pat Stephanie on the shoulder and when she turns around, the girl points in our direction. Stephanie gets a big grin on her face and makes her way to us.

"Brace yourself, she's going to gush," Kallon says as he turns his back to Stephanie, so that only I can hear what he said.

"Abby, my girl!" Stephanie shrieks. "You are an angel here on Earth, sent to save the day! You've gone above and beyond anything we could have hoped for on such short notice. But also, it blows the other caterer out of the water. Well done! I'd like to officially offer you the catering job."

All I can do is just smile and let her hug me.

"Ummm thank you," is all I come up with after a second of awkward silent embracing. "This is an amazing opportunity for me and my bakery!"

"Everyone... and I mean, everyone, loves your breakfast. Not one complaint. Not even from you know who," Stephanie says the last part to Kallon.

"Really?" Kallon asks in surprise. "She always has something to complain about. Something is too hot or too cold. Too sweet or too bitter."

"Nope, not today," Stephanie says.

"Ooop, in-coming," Kallon says as he has just looked over towards the crowd of people and sees Miss Ray walking towards us. "Speak of the devil."

Miss Ray stops in front of me and looks me up and down, and says, "Not bad. Your, what did you call them? 'Dietary friendly' items were actually good and what you said they would be. I haven't felt this good after breakfast in a long time. And your coffee? It's the best I've had, and I've had a lot of different coffee from all over the world."

"Uh, thank you," I say, taken aback.

"Amanda!" Miss Ray shouts suddenly. I jump but the other two don't budge. She must do that often.

A little blonde girl, about my age, materializes beside

Miss Ray.

"Yes, Ma'am, I'm right here," she says politely and just loud enough to be heard.

"Get an application for my personal chef position and give it to..." Miss Ray looks at me.

"Her name is Abbigail Rose," Kallon starts to say, slightly irritated, before I can remind her of my name.

But before he can finish, I say, "I'm not looking for a job."

"Oh honey, nobody looks for this type of job, it's given to you," Miss Ray says in a tone I think she means to sound gracious but she just sound pompous.

"I'm sorry but I'm going to have to decline," I say before Amanda, who I guess is Miss Ray's assistant, can run off to get the application.

"You what?" Miss Ray asks, stunned.

"I decline your offer, Miss Ray," I say politely.

"I'm willing to pay you five figures a month. Plus bonuses for when I throw parties," she says. She's acting like she just gave me the best news I've ever heard.

"I'm sorry, Miss Ray. I run three businesses. My family's restaurant, my bakery and coffee shop, and catering."

"You could make twice, maybe even three times as much being my chef," she says.

"You have no idea what she makes," Kallon says.

"It's really not about the money. I love my career and what I do makes me happy. It truly brings me joy. So again, I'm sorry Miss Ray, but I decline your offer," I say as kindly as I can but also a little more sternly.

"Uhh," she says sounding confused. "Well, if you change your mind, you let me know."

I don't say anything. I just smile and turn towards the table and have to do a double take.

"Everything is gone," I say breathless.

Not one pastry or muffin is left on the table. I look down at the smoothie machines and they're empty also. I check the coffee in a hurry and find that they are empty as well.

"Well crap, I'm sorry," I say.

"Don't be, take it as a good sign," Stephanie says.

I look at my watch and it shows it's 9:56am.

"I'll get this cleaned up and then will you meet me in the kitchen to talk, Stephanie?"

"Absolutely!" she says.

"Ready on set, places please," the man who I think is the director, says.

"We'll talk later," Kallon says, smiling warmly at me. My heart stutters.

Get a grip! We are not catching feelings for him. Stop it!

I make myself think of Jason but then I think of my talk with Kayla. Luckily, Miss Ray distracts me from that depressing train of thought.

"Keep in touch," she says and then does the fake kisses to both sides of my face.

"Have a good day, Miss Ray," I say.

"Please, it's Amelia," she says with a wink.

I nod at her as she walks away. Kallon and Stephanie follow behind, talking to each other. I pull my headphones out of my pocket and put them in and listen to my music as I clean up. I can't help the smile that spreads across my face.

CHAPTER 9

Nothing to throw away or to eat later. Not even anything to drink. I just have to clean up. I say this was a massive success! I think to myself.

I take everything into the kitchen and hand wash it all. Instead of loading up the display cases, coffee brewers, and smoothie dispensers, I put them nicely arranged on the kitchen counter. I go back out to the table and take my remaining plates, cups, plasticware, and napkins, and put them in their tote and put that in the kitchen as well.

I take my tablecloth off and fold it up and put it in a box to take home to throw in the wash. I put the containers I brought everything in, into a different box to take home to use for tomorrow, because it sounds like I'll definitely be coming back.

A huge smile spreads across my face again. I'm putting the last of my stuff away and taking my headphones out of my ears, when Stephanie comes into the kitchen.

"Great first day," she exclaims.

"I'd say so," I laugh.

"Here is this," Stephanie says, pulling a small piece of

paper out of her pocket and a small black card. I take both and stare at them and then up at Stephanie, stunned at the little piece of paper.

"Wha—?" I stammer.

"It's the first week plus the bonus. The black card is to open any of the doors to get into the building. Stop in at the HR office before you leave, Dax knows where it is, and get your picture taken for your badge. You'll use that to get through the gates. This is all assuming you want to come back. Please tell me you want to come back?"

"I do, I definitely do," I say. "I just have a wedding I have to be at next year, but I will only miss the Friday and my assistant manager will be able to cover that day. That is, if the movie is still going."

"Good!" she exclaims again. She then adds, "No problem at all. Have your assistant manager come with you for a day to see how you set things up and our expectations. They'll need to get a security badge as well."

"Thank you," I say earnestly.

"Stephanie, the office said you needed us?" a man standing in the doorway says. There are two men standing behind him.

"Yes, thank you for coming so quickly," she says. "We need to have water access through this wall out to the table on the other side of them. We need it done by tonight."

The men look at each other and then the one in front says, "Will do. We'll get on it right now."

I look at my watch and it's 10:49am.

"I'll get out of your way then," I say as I scoop up all my stuff. Just as I'm stepping through the kitchen doorway, back into the set room, Dax shows up.

"How can I help?" he asks.

"How did you—" I trail off and look over at Kallon. He smiles and puts his phone back in his pocket.

I shake my head but smile at him and mouth a thank you. He nods.

"Let me take some of these," Dax says, looking at the boxes. He ends up taking them all. I grab the tablecloths because I don't want them getting forgotten about.

"Thank you, Stephanie," I say, turning towards her as she comes out into the hall with us. "I'll see you in the morning."

"No, thank you!" she says happily.

"Oh, is there anything I need to change?" I ask.

"No, nothing," she says. "Do exactly what you did for today, from here on out."

"Do you want me to make more of anything?"

"No, I think you made the perfect amount of everything."

"Okay, sounds good. See you tomorrow," I say to her with a smile. And then I remember another important fact I keep forgetting about it, "Oh, I forgot, I need your phone number."

"Yes! I need yours as well," she says. We pull out our phones and I rattle off my number for her. She hits call and I see a number pop up on my phone. I show it to her, and she says, "Yup, that's me!"

"Perfect, thanks," I say.

"Have a great day," Stephanie smiles back.

I follow Dax out into the bright sunlight, and we put

the boxes and stuff into the back of the van and then we get in.

"I guess I need your phone number too," I say, resigned.

"Don't sound so down, you'll learn to like being driven around."

"I don't mind that part," I say. Dax hands me his phone.

"Just put your number in and then call yourself, then you'll have my number," he says. Then he asks, "What part do you mind then?"

"I'm not use to people doing such big things for me."

"That's the thing about Mr. Keller, he sees something he can fix, and he fixes it. But he understands if he oversteps, you just have to tell him to back the hell off," Dax laughs. "In your case, you'd probably tell him that in a nice way."

I laugh a little and say, "He and I already had this talk today."

"Oh really?" Dax asks.

"When you and Randy refilled the coffee?"

"I knew you'd be upset about that," Dax says.

"You hardly know me. How could you have known I'd be upset about it?"

"You aren't as hard to read as you think you are."

"Meaning?"

"I watch people and have always prided myself on my judge of character. I can usually tell you about a person within a few hours of knowing them. You are good people. You love your friends and family. You treat your employees as friends... No, as family. You treat people extremely well, even if they don't return what you give. You are respectful. Kind. Hard working. You are independent, almost to a fault. You only allow people to help you if they work for you and that's because you feel like you have to pay someone to help you. So, when Kallon asked us to do that for you, small act as it was, I knew it would bother you. I know having me drive for you, bothers you, because you've never had anything given to you. You've always worked for it and you feel uncomfortable when you receive things that you feel you don't deserve. If anyone deserves good things in life, Miss Rose, it's you."

I stare at him in silence. This is the longest I've ever heard Dax talk. Granted, we just met the other day but my take on him was the strong and silent type. But he just sat here and described me.

"Did I miss anything?" he asks.

"Fiercely protective of said family and friends," I say. He nods. I add, "Funny. Smart. A blast to be around."

"Don't get too carried away," Dax says and then he winks at me. Having only known him for a couple days, I wouldn't have thought that gesture possible.

"I thought I could read people easily, not as easy as you can read people but easy enough. But then I met you," I laugh.

"Fort Knocks!" Dax says, flexing his chest muscles as he drives.

"Pretty much," I say, laughing. "You come off as a walled up, serious guy, but then there are moments where you're funny and somewhat relaxed."

"I do tend to be pretty serious. My line of work demands it."

"What did you do before driving for Kallon?"

"I was in the military and then secret service," he says. My mouth falls open. "But when my contract was up, I decided to retire that life, and do something less..."

"Dangerous?" I ask, still awestruck.

"I guess so," he says. "Being a bodyguard and driver still has its dangers but not nearly like it was for the government."

"Bodyguard?" I ask.

"Not in the way you're thinking," he says. "Well, not exactly. If Mr. Keller had an event, I just helped the more excited fans keep their distance."

"And Trevor? Is he like you?"

"Yes, we retired from the government together. Mr. Keller is our first civilian charge."

"And now you're stuck with me," I say sarcastically.

"I think I'll survive," he says, laughing a deep laugh.

We ride in silence for the rest of the ride home. I look at my phone and I have no new messages or calls. I send a text to Betty.

Me: Hey! Heading back to Rose Bud's. We got the job. They don't want us to change anything. See you in a bit.

Then I send another text to Jason.

Me: Hey, are you okay? I haven't heard from you. I have exciting news.

I lay my head back and enjoy the ride home in silence.

I guess having Dax drive me will have its perks. I'll be able to catch little cat naps between work. I didn't sleep while Dax drove us back to Rose Bud's, but I did daydream. Daydream and think.

I would never become Amelia's or anyone's personal chef. I've heard enough horror stories to turn me off of that career path. But I daydreamed about what it would be like to cook in a home and get paid for it, paid for it well. I wasn't lying when I told Amelia that I love what I do but I know I'm not going to be able to do all three of these things for ever. I'm young and can handle the crazy schedule and lack of sleep. But I know the day will come that I will have to make the decision on what goes first.

BEEPBEEP**

I look down and see I have a new text from Betty. Still nothing from Jason, though.

Betty: Hey! That's great news. I knew it would go well. I have some things already finished.

Me: You rock! Thank you! I don't have any plans tonight and depending on how busy Rose's is, I'll head out early to help finish up things.

Betty: No problem. The morning was pretty busy, but we've slowed down since around 9. How close are you?

I look around to figure out where we are, so that I know about how long it'll take to get back. It's taking us longer to get back than it had this morning.

Me: We're still about 20mins out. Traffic has been a little bad.
Betty: Okay. See you soon.

I stare out the window and think about how crazy the morning has already been. It feels like a whole day has already gone by but it's not even noon yet. Hopefully Rose's is busy enough, so that the rest of the day goes by quickly, too.

"Dax, if you don't mind stopping at the next gas station you see, I'd like to fill this up before we get back. I always have it full before I take it home."

"Yes, I can do that."

About 10 minutes later, we're pulling out of a gas station and on our way again.

We pull up to Rose Bud's at 11:56am. I jump out and hurry to the back of the van to start unloading things before I have to leave for Rose's.

"What are you in a hurry for?" Dax asks.

"I need to get to Rose's to start things there," I say, grabbing the tablecloth and a box of stuff. Thank goodness I had washed these before leaving the studio, that'll save some time tonight.

"I'll help get these boxes inside and then get the car pulled up," Dax says, grabbing the rest of the boxes.

"Thank you," I say sincerely. "Times like this is going to make having you around really handy."

Dax smiles at me and with full arms, he somehow shuts the back door of the van as we walk towards the door to the back of Rose Bud's. I punch my number into the keypad and the lock beeps. I open the door for us but before the door shuts, I put the box I'm carrying down, and take the key remote out of my pocket and lock the van.

"It's just us," I say to Betty.

She pokes her head through the door and says, "Hi!"

"Hi," I say.

"Hello," Dax says, nodding his head at her.

"I'm going to throw this in the wash and then run upstairs to change before heading to Rose's," I say. Betty walks up to Dax and takes a box out of his arms and puts it on a cleared off counter. "I washed everything. How's it going here?"

"Still good. The lunch rush hasn't hit but it's not quite time for it yet. I'll have Maggie come down and help me get things going for the studios breakfast once I lock up after lunch," she says, taking the last box from Dax and puts it by the others.

"Oh, that reminds me," I say. I pull the check out and show it to Betty. "Look at this!"

She walks over and takes the check. Her eyes go wide.

"Twenty-five thousand dollars?" she whispers. "They weren't kidding!"

"Yeah, apparently not," I laugh out.

"This is going to be so good for Rose Bud's," Betty says happily.

"Not just Rose Bud's, for you too. I'm giving you a raise," I say.

"What? No, don't do that," Betty says urgently. "I'm just doing my job."

"When I hired you, the job was part-time. You've surpassed that job description. You can now call yourself

Rose Bud's assistant manager. And I'll also figure out a way to pay Maggie. She's been helping out a lot as well. I'll talk to Craig this afternoon," I say. Craig is my accountant that does both Rose's and Rose Bud's financials.

"Really, Abby, you don't have to do that," Betty says, almost pleading.

"Betty, hard work, dedication, and willingness to go above and beyond what is asked of you, deserves to be acknowledged. That's all this is, acknowledging your hard work," I say.

"I'll go get the car," Dax says, sounding awkward standing in the middle of the kitchen listening to me and Betty debate on whether or not she deserves a raise.

"Thank you, Dax," I say.

Betty waves a goodbye as he excuses himself.

"Abby—"

"Betty, please," I interrupt her. "You've been working for me for over a year now. And you work here more than I do sometimes. And will be especially now with this catering job at the studio."

"I just don't want you to feel like you have to give me a raise because you feel like I might leave, because I won't. You already pay me more than any other bakery in town, and that's saying something, New York is a large city. I love working here and working for you. I love our location and our customers. I'm not going anywhere. Even with the heavier workload, which honestly isn't heavy, I'm not leaving because I love what we do here," Betty says, explaining her resistance to the raise.

"Although my fear of losing you is a factor, it's not why

I'm giving you a raise. You. Deserve. It," I say the last three words slowly, deliberately.

"I can't convince you not to give me one, can I?"

"No," I laugh.

"Alright, but don't pay Maggie," she counters.

"I'm paying her too. She needs to see that her work here means something," I say. "At 11 years old, if she sees hard work pays off, having her work later in life will be easy."

Betty thinks for a minute, "That's true. I've never thought I needed to worry about her work ethic, her grades are proof of that. Although, she loves school and reading, so that's not much of a struggle to get her to do any of that at any given time. It would be nice to show her the importance of working and sticking it out, especially when it comes to maybe doing something she doesn't necessarily want to do. Making a little money, and saving that money for something she really wants. Like the new e-reader she's had her eye on for the last month or so, could be a good experience for her."

"Exactly," I say, finally feeling like we've agreed on this whole thing. "I'll call Craig when I get to Rose's and have him set everything up for next week's paychecks."

"Thank you, Abby," Betty says with tears in her eyes. "For not only giving me an awesome environment to work in, but for giving my kiddo the chance to learn some good life lessons, and for being an amazing boss and friend."

"You make my life easier," I say. She walks over to me and hugs me. After a couple of seconds, I pull away and say, "Okay, I need to go change."

Betty steps away and tries to hide that she's wiping a tear away. I don't call attention to it, instead I turn and head for the door to the stairs. I hurry up them and walk into my apartment. I hear the tv playing and I walk in and see Maggie lounging on the couch, reading a book.

"Hey, kiddo," I say, smiling down at her.

"Hi Abby," she says. "How did it go?"

"Really good!" I say excitedly. "We got the job!"

"Yay!" Maggie says. "Did you get to meet any famous actors?"

"I met Amelia Ray," I say and wait for her reaction.

Maggie's eyes go wide and her jaw drops. She stammers out, "Shut up! Really?"

"I did," I say. "Maybe after a couple days of getting the routine down, I can take you with me now that you're on summer break. I'd like to take your mom as well."

"Oh, Abby, that would be the best thing ever!" Maggie says, putting her book down and clasping her hands together in front of her chest.

"Keep being good and I'll talk to you mom about it," I say, I look at my watch and see I really need to hurry now. "I need to go change really quick. I'll see you later."

"Bye, Abby," Maggie says as she snuggles back down into my couch and starts reading again.

I turn and walk quickly to my room. I change into my restaurant attire which is a black tank top , black slacks, my Chef jacket that I leave at Rose's. I and check myself in the mirror and see my eyes look bright and my cheeks look flushed. I look happy. I smile at myself and hurry from my room.

"Bye, Mags," I say as I head for the back door.

"Bye, Abby," she says, waving but not looking up from

her book.

I skip down the stairs and as I enter the kitchen, I grab my bag sitting on the table. I walk into the main part of Rose Bud's and see it's starting to fill up.

"Do you need me to help with anything before I go?" I ask Betty, as she's ringing someone up at the register.

"Nope, I've got this," she says, smiling over at me. "See you this evening."

"Thank you," I say, hugging her around the shoulders. To the customer I say, "Enjoy your lunch."

"I will, thank you," he says smiling at me.

As I walk through the sitting area, I say hello to our customers that I pass and nodding at the ones too far away to verbally greet. I look up and see Dax has pulled the car up right in front of the doors and is leaning against the front passenger door.

As I get to the door, he steps forward and opens it for me.

"Not every door?" I ask, shaking my head.

"Yes, every door," he quips, reaching around me to open the back passenger door.

Sighing, I get in and slide to the middle seat and buckle my seat belt. Dax hurries around the front of the car and slides into his seat. He buckles up before he starts the car.

"Straight to Rose's, correct?" he asks.

"Yes, please."

"You got it," Dax says as he pulls out into traffic with ease.

I hate to admit it but having Dax here really does make getting to places easier and quicker. Too many times I've had to wait for nearly twenty minutes for a taxi and during the holidays, it seemed like it was double that amount of time. I'm going to have to figure out a way to thank Kallon.

As Dax maneuvers us through the city, I lay my head back and take a nap, something I wouldn't have done in a taxi, not trusting the driver to tell me when we got to my destination. He'd no doubt let the meter keep running until I woke up, explaining that he wasn't my alarm clock, and it wasn't his job to wake me.

"Miss Rose," I hear Dax's voice say after what feels like the best nap I've ever had.

"Mmm," I say, waking up and stretching.

"We've arrived," he chuckles.

"Oh man!" I sit up quickly, startled at how long it feels like I had slept. Maybe I couldn't trust him to wake me. He's kind enough he might have just let me sleep because he guessed at how tired I was from the late night and early morning. "How long did I sleep for?"

"Just the twenty minutes it took to get here," Dax says as he gets out of the car and comes around to open my door.

"Just twenty minutes?" I ask as I get out.

"Yes ma'am."

"This car is such a smooth ride, combined with your driving... I was rocked into the best sleep I've gotten in months, and it was only twenty minutes," I laugh as I stand on the sidewalk.

"You're exhausting yourself," Dax says to brush off the compliment.

"I'm good, I had all weekend to rest while I was in Kansas," I say as I wave off his concern. Except, Dax gives me a knowing look like he highly doubts I rested. I've only known the guy for a couple of days, but he already knows me better than some people that have been in my life since I was a little girl. He looks at me with an eyebrow raised and a smirk on his face. Rolling my eyes, I say, "Fine, Kayla and I stayed up way too late talking and laughing and talking about her wedding plans and making a to do list for her for the next couple of months. But it felt like resting compared to working here at the restaurant and at the bakery."

Dax just laughs and nods, he says, "I'll be parked around the corner so when you're ready to head back to Rose Bud's, call me."

"Actually, there's a parking lot around back, you can park back there, if you'd like?" I suggest.

"Sounds good."

"Thank you, Dax," I say, smiling and touching his massive upper arm before turning and walking towards the front doors.

CHAPTER 10

As I enter my code into the keypad, I look at my watch and see that it's 1:14pm. *Not bad since I like to be here by 1 o'clock. Maybe I'll leave some clothes here to change into instead of running upstairs to my apartment to change. That might shave off the fifteen minutes of being late.* I'm only late because it's my standards for myself to be here by 1. My parents never expected me to be here any earlier than anyone else. I found that if I came in a couple of hours before everyone, I could get all my paperwork and pre-open stuff done in the quiet and solitude of the restaurant.

After the keypad beeps at me, I open the door and walk inside. I hurry to the back, to our office and hang up my bag on the coatrack behind the door. I go back out front and stop at the hostess desk and check to see that everything is clean and organized as usual. I pull out a drawer and put some new pens into the pen holder on top of the desk. We had custom pens made with our name and number on them so if customers accidently took them home, it is a reminder to them of our restaurant every time they use it. We've had quite a few people come in from borrowing the pen from a friend and their friends' raving review of Rose's.

I walk into the bar and check the tables. Again, everything is squeaky clean. I walk behind the bar, grab my inventory binder from a drawer under the register, and take inventory of the liquor, beer, and wine. I've done this so many times, it doesn't take me very long before I'm finished. I take my clipboard from under the register and clip my paper to it that I take notes on for which alcohol we're running low on. I'll go down into the basement to check our stock down there first before I have Bridget order more.

As I walk back to the front of the restaurant and make my way to the stairs leading up to the upper levels, I check the tables nearby. I know I don't need to check everything like this because my employees do their jobs above and beyond what we ask of them, but I would feel foolish if something was accidently forgotten and I needed to catch it before we open. Another reason I don't have to do it is because it's part of our servers opening duties to go around and check all the tables in their sections to make sure they're ready for opening. But again, I like to check to make sure or make notes about anything that needs changed that they might not notice.

Instead of taking an elevator up, I like to take the stairs to make sure they're nice and clean as well. I check the walls for any marks or dings that need fixed. I also check the carpet to make sure it's still in good shape. Our customers usually take an elevator but on the rare occasion they take the stairs, I like to make sure it looks immaculate as well.

I bypass the second floor and go up to the third. This floor is our event floor, and we haven't had an event for a couple weeks, but I like to check it just in case. Our next event is in two weeks, a couple is having their engagement party here. Luckily, it's still set up from the last wedding we had so we won't have to do much rearranging, just little things if the bride requests it. *I need to double check their menu and make sure Bridget has her copy of it so we can start ordering things.* I think to myself, making a mental note.

After my walk through, I go check the suite. It also hasn't been used since the wedding, and since myself and the head of the cleaning crew are the only ones who have a key, I'm not expecting it to be anything other than clean. I walk through and check the tables to make sure they're clean and the garbage's to make sure they're empty. I go to the guest bathroom and check the shower drains for hair and the sink to make sure it's sparkling clean. The living room looks perfect with the pillows on the couches arranged as they should be.

The one bedroom with the king size bed will be made the day before it'll be used so I'm not surprised to see it stripped down to the mattress cover. I check the extra-large jacuzzi tub's drain and check the large three shower-head shower for hair as well. I do a quick check of the toilet and it's just as clean as the guest bathrooms toilet. The sinks in here look spotless.

Now that I'm satisfied the third floor is still in top notch order, I walk back to the elevators and take Elevator 1 down to the second floor. Taking the elevator down allows me to make sure it's been cleaned top to bottom. When the door open, I step out and walk around the tables nearby and make sure they're clean. Making my way over to the wrap around bar area, I check the bar top and the tables in the vicinity. They all look great.

I go to the part of the second floor that we have our laundry room and the room off it that the cleaning crew keep their things stored. My mom was a genius when she had this section changed and turned into a centrally located laundry area. I check the washers and driers and find that they are empty. All the shelves are stacked full of clean linen.

As I make my way back to the elevators, I smile as I remember when I first came back from my time overseas, I had a clip board that I had to carry with me to check everything off to make sure I didn't miss anything. I've done this so many times now, I can do it from memory. I click the down button for Elevator 2 and wait patiently for it to come get me.

When the door dings open, I step in and check my watch. It's only taken me thirty minutes to do my walk through today. "I'm getting quicker," I say to myself with a smile.

When I get to the main floor, I go and check the customer restrooms and find them clean. I walk back out and walk down the hallway that leads to the kitchen. Before I start my checklist in here, I check the kitchen service elevators to make sure they're clean as well. It wouldn't be good to transfer food up to the next level with a dirty elevator. I'm happy to say that they are just as clean as everything else.

I do a quick run around in the kitchen and check the walk in cooler and dry storage to make sure everything is still stocked and in good standing. My employees make my manager job so easy because they do their jobs so well.

I go back to the kitchen elevators and take one down to the basement. The lights are automatic down here so when the elevator door opens and I step out, the lights turn on, one by one, starting with the closest one to me and out across the whole basement. I'm pretty sure Dad put these lights in when I started working here because, just like Grandpa, he knows how much I hate the dark.

Bridget's desk is down here even though we've offered for her to have one up in the actual office, but she refuses. She says she likes the quiet and she can double, and triple check our inventory any time she wants to make sure our stock is where we want it. She doesn't like the distraction of chaos the kitchen can cause. She likes to be able to sit at her desk, do her paper and computer work, and just focus.

I walk over to the shelves of hard liquor and check off the bottles. We still have plenty of backstock, but I make a note of the one we only have one case left in stock. Our wine selection is still pretty good, but our champagne stock is well below where I like to have it stocked at, so I make a note about that as well. I check our kegs of beer for our taps and those all look good, as do our cases of bottled beer.

I make my way back to the elevator and take the ride back up to the kitchen. I step out and walk to the office and look around realizing again how my parents won't ever sit behind those desks ever again. I go sit at my desk and remind myself that it's wonderful my parents are getting to retire and live the second half of their lives together doing the things they truly enjoy. One of which is visiting my brother and his family in Seattle. The other is traveling, which my parents have never really gotten to do because the restaurant took so much of their time and commitment.

To distract myself from the sadness of my parents not working with me anymore, I pull out this week's work schedule and make sure the servers are assigned the correct section for the week, as well as the bartenders. I check to make sure the busser's have their sections too. I do a quick check of our event calendar and see that we still just have the one wedding in two weeks, nothing was added to the calendar while I was gone.

I take the folder out of my desk organizer and open it to find the end of day reports for over the weekend while I was gone. It looks as if we had a really good weekend in both bars. I make a note for Bridget to order the liquor we're running low on and to order quite a few more cases of champagne.

"Abs, you in here?" I hear Royce holler from out in the kitchen.

"In the office," I holler back. Royce walks in a couple seconds later. I smile up at him and have a quick flash back to when I first met him at school.

He walked in looking more like a model than a student at culinary school. He was wearing clothes that cost more than my education and his black hair was cut short and stylish. He had smiled over at me and came over. He spoke in Italian and all I could do was stare. I had to clear my throat before I apologized for not understanding him, that I had only been in Italy for a week. He had laughed a dangerously sexy laugh and said he had asked if anyone was sitting in the empty chair next to mine. I had told him no and from that point on, we were inseparable. He taught me Italian and I helped strengthen his English, so that we were both fluent in the languages before our time was up at Italian Chef Academy.

I found that I was attracted to him but because I was with Jason, nothing ever happened. He had expressed a few months into our friendship that he wanted to date me, but I reminded him that I had a boyfriend back home. We put each other in the friend zone and thankfully, our friendship became stronger. Now, he's more like a brother to me than a friend. There was no one else I wanted to come work with me, when my parents told me to start looking for my Sous-chef. I instantly called Royce and asked if he'd be interested in coming to the States and work with me. He didn't hesitate, he packed up his life and moved to New York two weeks later.

"What are you doing?" he asks, coming in and taking a chair from the table in the middle of the room and putting it in front of my desk.

I hold up the papers in my hands and say, "Paperwork."

"You'll have more of that now that you're the boss lady," he says, winking at me.

"Don't remind me," I say with a sigh. "Between everything else, the paperwork is what's going to exhaust me."

"Everything else?" Royce asks as he leans forward and takes a candy out of my candy jar.

"Oh, I haven't told you," I say smiling ear to ear.

"What?" Royce looks up with his eyebrows raised.

"Rose Bud's got a catering job for a movie set," I say, biting my bottom lip to keep from giggling like an idiot.

"I'm sorry, what?"

"Yeah, Kallon's set manager called him up and said that the breakfast caterer wasn't working out and wanted to know where he always gets his breakfast from and if he could get her into contact with the owner. He asked her the details and told her he'd talk to me. He asked me after our meeting yesterday and I told him yes. This morning was our first morning and the set manager was thoroughly impressed and officially offered me the job," I say excitedly.

"Holy shit," Royce says. "Mr. Keller is just making all sorts of dreams come true, isn't he?"

I shake my head and says, "He's definitely not hurting anything."

"All the girls are tweeterpadded over him," Royce says, rolling his eyes.

"It's twitterpated and I can't really blame them," I say, averting my eyes away from Royce's.

"Not you too," he groans out. "We aren't going to get anything done around here if he's around."

"Oh stop, I'm not twitterpated. Was I a little shocked at first? Yes, anyone would be, but he's actually a really good guy. Genuinely, not just because he has a public persona to protect. If all famous people were like him, the world would be a better place. I'm not saying they're all bad, but you know we have some pretty snooty ones that come in here and demand things just because they're famous. Kallon knows this, which is why he has the gag order."

"I should get in the habit of calling him Mr. Webb, shouldn't I?" Royce says, sitting back in his chair.

"It probably wouldn't be the worst thing, it would help with any slips that might happen," I say, nodding at him. I look at my watch and see that it's 2:48pm. "We'd better get changed and start getting things prepped."

Royce nods and stands and without saying another word, leaves to go to the staff room to get his chef jacket put on. Royce and I are the only ones that wear chef jackets and black pants. My jacket is black with a red rose on my left chest pocket with Rose's stitched in red underneath it. Royce's jacket it white with the same stitching.

The other kitchen staff have white polo shirts with the same stitching and black pants. The servers have a choice of either a short-sleeve or long-sleeve, button-up shirt, but both are a nice rose red, with Rose's stitched in white over the left breast pocket. They're asked to wear black pants as well. My bartenders have the same choice in style as servers only their shirts are white with red stitching and they're asked to wear black pants too. The bussers and dishwashers have white t-shirts with Rose's stitched in black over their left chest area and are the only ones that can wear jeans.

Our hostesses wear dresses the same color rose red as the server's shirts, but they have a name tag that says Rose's on it instead of any stitching. The dresses are because Patty went through a phase of not liking to wear anything but dresses and getting her to wear the same uniform as the other hostesses was turning into a fight my parents didn't want to fight anymore. The other hostesses were wonderful and offered to wear dresses as well, to make Patty more comfortable. Mom found a great online store that had the dresses in the same color as the server's shirts, so she ordered a ton. We now have a stockpile of dresses, and shirts, in the laundry room for any of the staff that might need something new.

I walk over to the coatrack behind the door and pull my freshly laundered chef jacket off the hook and put it on. One of the things I did away with when I came back, was the chef hat. I got way to hot wearing the thing and decided it wasn't necessary. My dad had no problem with doing away with it either.

I walk out and see Bridget walking into the kitchen. She looks up and smiles at me.

"Hi Abby," she says.

"Hi Bridget," I reply with my own smile. "Did you happen to unlock the front door?"

"I did," Royce says from behind me. I turn and see him buttoning the last button on his jacket.

"Oh, thanks," I say. I turn to Bridget and say, "I did inventory in the bars already, but you might double check that I didn't miss something. I have just a couple notes on my list of things we need to order, it's sitting on my desk."

"Thanks, Ab," Bridget says, she blushes, nods at Royce and then to me and walks towards my office. I wait for her to go in and come back out and get on the elevator to go down to the basement before I turn to Royce.

"You didn't," I say in a whisper.

"Didn't what?" he says sheepishly.

"Bridget?" I ask with a raised voice. We don't have a rule about dating co-workers, but it was kind of an understanding that if you date someone you work with, you have to be able to act professionally while at work and not let the drama seep into the restaurant.

"Nothing's happened," he says but the smirk on his

face tells me otherwise.

"Yeah right," I say.

"We've kissed, okay," he says and now his face blushes too.

"You like her?" I ask in surprise. Bridget is beautiful but she's quieter and more laid back than Royce's usual girls. Royce's face gets a little redder, but he just shrugs without saying anything. I gasp and say, "You do! Like a lot."

"Shhhh," he hisses at me and pulls my arm towards the dry storage where we walk in as some of the other staff members come into the kitchen. "Yes, I do, okay."

"I haven't seen you like this since..." I try to think of the last time I saw him react to a girl like this, but I can't think of a time, at all. "I've never seen you like this."

"She's different than any girl I've ever dated. We're taking things slow and really getting to know each other. She's so smart and funny and beautiful," he says. He takes a breath and says, "And her kisses—"

"Okay, I get it," I say laughing before he can go into too much detail of what her kisses do to him. "Just don't get hurt and don't hurt her. She really is an amazing girl, but you are just as amazing."

"We won't get hurt, I can tell this is different," he states, dropping his eyes to the floor and then looks up at me.

"Just be careful, okay?"

"I will," he says. He nudges me with his hip before he grabs a couple of things off the shelf and walks back out to the kitchen.

Greeting the staff as they come in makes me smile. But I laugh at all the agreeing I have to do with the girls that, "Yes, it's amazing that 'Charles Webb' is now my partner and their other boss". Prep time goes by in a flash and by the time our first orders come in, time gets away from me.

CHAPTER 11

I'm focusing on a steak order when Pam, one of the hostesses on the main floor, comes on in my earpiece, *"Abby, we have a situation out here, can you come out please?"*

I take my gloves off and push on my microphone hooked to the top of my shirt and say, "Yeah, I'll be right there."

"I've got this," Royce says, coming to take over for me. He's got his own earpiece, so he heard what Pam said.

I check my watch as I walk through the door that leads to the bar, which is the quickest way to the hostess desk, and see that it's already 6:27pm. When I get to it, I see co-workers of Jason's standing in front of Pam, Patty, and Sherry. I look at Patty and see she's nibbling on her bottom lip, a sure sign she's upset.

"Thank you, Pam. Could you and Patty go check how the girls are doing upstairs?" I ask. It's a code we use when we feel like Patty needs a break. We found if we asked her outright to go for a break, she'd dig her heals in and refuse. Which would end up with her in tears because she was indeed needing a break and was overwhelmed.

"Sure thing," Pam says. "Come on, Patty, let's go see if they need more silverware."

"Okay," Patty says happily.

Before I turn to talk to Jason's co-workers, Shane and Deven and their wives, Lorrie and Mahleen, I take a deep breath and calm myself. These two are my very least favorite people that Jason works with and they just happen to be his closest friends as well.

"Hi guys, what can I help you with?" I ask politely as I turn towards them.

"As we were telling your help," Shane says in his snotty tone. *Breathe, Abby.* "We want a table and would like to meet Kallon."

I hide the shock on my face and do that by looking at him in a confused way. I force my tone to sound just as confused, "I'm sorry, Kallon who?"

"Don't play dumb," Deven says in a whisper. "Jason told us everything."

"Jason told you what about everything?" I ask in my fake confused voice that surprisingly sounds sincere.

"He told us that Kallon Keller bought out your parents and got you a sweet gig on his movie set," Shane says.

"I think Jason is confused," I say quickly.

"Oh, come on, he said he could only tell us and made us swear not to tell anyone else," Deven says laughing.

"Are you saying you don't have a catering job for his movie?" Lorrie asks me in a snide tone of voice. She turns to Mahleen and says, "I knew he was lying."

"He wasn't lying about that," I say. "Mr. Keller has been getting his coffee and breakfast from Rose Bud's for quite some time and his set manager asked him about it and without going into too much detail, I did get the job to cater breakfast for the set."

"So, he did buy out your parents?" Deven asks.

"Charles Webb bought out my parents," I say matter-of-factly.

"Who the fuck is Charles Webb?" Deven asks.

"He's a businessman, you can look him up on the internet. Jason must have gotten confused because this all happened around the same time," I say, now getting irritated. *I can't believe you, Jason.* "When did Jason tell you all of this?"

"Today at lunch," Deven says.

"Well, I'm sorry Mr. Keller isn't here," I say truthfully. "If you'd still like to have dinner, Sherry would be happy to find you a table. But sadly, you won't be meeting Kallon Keller tonight."

The wives look absolutely crestfallen, but the guys just shrug.

"We'll take a table," Shane says.

"Sherry, can you find them a table please?" I ask, as I turn to her with my eyes wide. Letting some frustration show only to her. She hides a smile as she clicks around on the computer screen.

"I've got a table for you, if you'd like to follow me," she politely says to them.

"Enjoy your evening," I say, as I plaster a smile back on my face. I nod at them before they start walking away. I keep my smile on my face as I walk back through the bar, smiling and waving at customers.

Once I get into the kitchen, I feel my face instantly

switch to a pissed off expression, which I'm sure makes me look like a raging bitch. When I look over at Royce, his eyes go wide.

I motion with my head that I'm going into my office and ask, "You got this for a little bit?"

"Yeah, you okay?" he asks.

"No, but I will be," I answer. I turn to Sarah and ask her, "Could you take over Sous-chef? This might take me a minute."

"Yeah," she says looking at me in concern.

I go into my office and shut the door, which is something I don't ever do. I sit down hard at my desk and put my face in my hands and whisper scream into them.

"JASON!" I scream into my hands again. I pick up my phone, go to contacts, and hit his name with little more force than necessary.

"Hey, baby," Jason answers but he sounds out of breath.

"What the hell are you doing?" I ask. I'm so pissed I can't form the correct way to ask the question.

"Ummm... I ahh... I... I just finished a workout, why?" he says defensively.

"No, I don't mean right now," I say through my teeth. "I mean, why did Deven and Shane just show up demanding to meet Kallon Keller?"

"Oh, shit, they did?" he asks laughing a little, somehow sounding relieved.

"Jason, you broke the gag order, and it took you less than a day," I say as I let the frustration soak into my words. "Do you know what this means?"

"What?" he asks, clueless.

"You have to pay the ten-thousand dollar fine," I say through clenched teeth again.

"What, no I don't. You can smooth it over with Kallon," he says this like it's a no brainer.

"The hell I will," I say. "I told you not to say anything to anyone. I told you to call him Charles, Charles Webb, or Mr. Webb."

"Oh, come on baby, don't be mad, please, I forgot," he says it like a whiney child.

"I am so mad at you right now, I can't talk to you anymore," I growl out.

"What do you want me to do?" he asks.

"Own up to your mistake and take responsibility for it," I shout.

"It's 10k, Abby," he groans out. *"I told those idiots not to say anything. Aren't you in breach of the contract too?"*

"NO, I, certainly, am not. I told your friends that you must have been confused because Charles Webb bought out my parents and Kallon Keller referred me to the set manager for the catering job."

"I can't lie to my friends," Jason says sounding like he's getting pissed at me.

"It's not a lie, Jason. Telling people that Charles Webb bought out my parents is not a lie. It's what we are legally supposed to tell people unless we... you... want to pay a hefty fine. Luckily your friends believed me, so they at least won't go around telling more people that Kallon is now co-owner of Rose's. I can't believe that my own boyfriend did this, did exactly what Kallon was afraid would happen. How could you!" I yell into my phone.

"I—" Jason starts to say but I hang-up on him. I can't listen to the excuse he's going to tell me right now. I am so mad.

Looking at my phone, I know the next phone call I need to make. I send a text first.

> **Me:** Hey, Kallon, could you call me when you have a free minute. Something's come up.

I put my phone down and cross my arms on my desk and put my forehead to my arms. I close my eyes and take deep breaths. There's a knock on my door just as my phone dings that I have a new text.

"Come in," I say, as I check my message.

> **Kallon:** Hey, I'm just about to head your way, can we talk when I get there?
> **Me:** Sure, that would probably be better.
> **Kallon:** See you soon. :-)

I smile at his little smiley face emoji but then shake my head. I'm too pissed at Jason. I look up and see Royce standing in my office. He's closed the door and has his arms crossed over his chest and he looks pissed.

"What's wrong?" I ask, standing up.

"I was going to ask you the same thing," he says. "Whose ass am I kicking?"

A laugh bubbles out of me and I sit back in my chair, and put my head back, "One guess."

"Jason?" Royce asks as he lets his arms drop. I just tap

my nose and point at him. "What did he do now? You looked like you were either going to murder someone or come in here and cry."

"I could definitely cry, but I won't. It's not so serious for someone to die but I'm sure Jason will want to," I say as I put my right arm over my face, the crook of my elbow over my eyes. I point out to the kitchen, "Is everything going okay out there? I don't think I can concentrate on cooking right now."

"Oh man, he must have really messed up but yeah, everything is under control. We're all caught up on orders. I wanted to come check on you," Royce says, coming and sitting down in front of me. "So, what did he do?"

"He broke the gag order," I mumble out.

"No shit?" Royce says in disbelief. "You made him sign one?"

"Are you that surprised that I did?" I ask instead of answering him. But then I answer in a defeated voice, "Of course I made him sign one. Out of everyone that we've told, I knew he was the only one I really needed to have sign because I thought losing his precious money would keep him from opening his mouth. I don't know what he was thinking... No wait, I do. He was using this little bit of information to one up his friends. Guh!! I'm so mad at him!"

"Have you talked to him already?"

"Yes, and he asked me to smooth it over with Kallon. Can you believe that?"

"Yeah, I can," Royce says. "You know how I feel about the guy. I only hide it when he's around for your benefit and so it doesn't start a fight with him. But I'm not surprised at all that he's asking you to fix his fuck up. I don't think I've heard of him take responsibility for anything. When he cancels your date on you last minute, it's because of work. When he's late, it's because of traffic. When he forgets something, it's someone or something else's fault. He's the definition of a narcissist."

"He didn't always used to be like this," I say sadly.

"What are you going to do?"

"I told him he has to take responsibility. Kallon is on his way here so I can tell him what happened," I say as I drop my arm from my face and look at Royce as I sit up.

"How do you think Jason is going to take that?"

"Not good. I'm sure it'll be my fault," I say.

"Don't let him get away with that, make him own up to his shit," Royce says. There's a knock at the door.

"Come in," I say.

Sarah pokes her head in and says, "We have a couple orders that just came in, but I can handle them if you guys need to talk more."

"I'll come out and help," Royce says, Sarah nods and leaves, shutting the door behind her. Royce stands up and says, "Don't worry about coming back out. We've got this. Just relax and remember that this is not your fault, and you did all you could to protect his dumb ass and he still chose to open his big mouth."

"But did I? I could ask Kallon to let this one-time slide," as soon as the words are out of my mouth, I hate myself for saying it. I feel myself wince.

"The look on your face right now says that you can't do that, and I know you really don't want to do that," Royce says, reaching for the door handle. "Asking Charles to let it go will only let Jason off the hook and if you do that, he'll do it again and again. And if word gets out that he let Jason off, other people will think they can too."

"I know, you're absolutely right. Saying it didn't even feel good," I say. Tears well up in my eyes and I say in a whisper, "I'm an awful girlfriend."

"No, you are not," Royce says, coming to me and pulling me up into a hug. "Jason is an ass of a boyfriend. And the fact that you feel bad for not enabling him to get away with shit, is another reason he's a narcissistic asshole. Abby, if he really cared about you, he wouldn't have asked you to smooth it over with Charles."

I nod because I truly believe what Royce is saying. But the girlfriend side of me, feels bad for not trying to get my boyfriend out of the trouble he's gotten himself into, once again.

"I'll pull myself together and come out there," I say, wiping my face.

"No, stay in here. Honestly Abby, we've got this covered," Royce says, as he squeezes gently and then looks down at me with a smile before he lets me go and walks over to the door again.

"Thank you," I say as I sit back down. He reaches for the door, and I say, "You can leave that open. Holler if you need me."

Royce nods and walks out the door, leaving it half open. I hear Royce's voice in my earpiece, *"Megan, could you bring Abby a glass of wine please?"*

I'm about to say no but then I change my mine. A glass of wine would really taste good right now. I grab my phone and send a text to Kallon.

> **Me:** I forgot to tell you, there's parking in the back. It's where have our event party attendees park and some employee parking, and we, owners and management, have our own parking spaces. There's a door to the right of the cargo door, use the code 7425 to get in. That'll be your code for the front door as well. Unless you want to come in through the front but there might be a mob scene from customers. Hahaha

I hope he uses the back door because if Shane and Deven see him walk in and come to the back, they'll get suspicious and think that maybe I was the one lying and not Jason. My phone beeps in my hand.

> **Kallon:** No mob scene for me, I'll use the back door. Thanks. And thanks for my own code. :-) I'm about 5 minutes out.

I put my phone down and before I can close my eyes, Megan walks in with a glass of wine.

"Thank you," I say.

"Just let me know when you need a refill," she says with a smile.

I take a big sip of my favorite Risata Moscato d'Asti wine. As hard as Royce has tried to get me to drink red wine, I just can't. I close my eyes and take another sip, letting the sweet nectar of the wine gods settle in my empty stomach. *I need to eat something before I drink more of this.* My eyes aren't closed for long when I hear my phone beep again. I pick it up and see a text from Jason. I sit up and open it.

Jason: I'm coming to talk to you since you hung-up on me like an immature child.

Me: I'm immature? Jason, I really don't think you coming here is a good idea.

Jason: Grow up, we can talk about this like adults.

Me: Are you kidding me?

I don't get a reply, so I toss my phone on my desk, feeling tears fill up my eyes again. I take a bigger gulp of my wine. I wipe away the tears that have fallen down my cheeks and I'm about to close my eyes when I hear the beep of my computer and our security camera screen pops up, showing Kallon walking up to the back door. He's wearing black slacks and a black long-sleeve button-up shirt but he has the sleeves rolled up to his elbows. A second later I hear the beep of the back door open and the chatter that I could hear in the kitchen ten seconds ago, cuts off. I sit up and try to dry my face and stop the tears that are about to spill over again.

"Evening everyone," I hear Kallon say as he walks into the kitchen.

"Hello, Mr. Webb," Sarah says back, and I hear Kallon chuckle.

"Abby's in the office," Royce's voice says.

"Thank you. Royce, right?" Kallon asks.

"Yes, sir, that's me," Royce's voice sounds astonished.

Kallon pokes his head in, his hair still looks wet from a shower, and you can see where he ran his fingers through it. He looks around the room before finding me sitting behind my desk. I still have teary eyes, so his smile instantly falls, and he shuts the door behind him.

"What's wrong, Abby?" he asks with so much concern, I feel like it could make me cry even harder.

I take a drink of wine again and take a deep breath. *Do not cry.* I take another calming breath and say, "Have a seat."

"This doesn't sound good," Kallon says, taking the seat that Royce had sat in earlier.

"It's not," I say and then laugh at Kallon's look of concern. "I mean it's not like the end of the world or anything, but it's not good."

"What's happened?" Kallon asks.

Not beating around the bush, I say, "Jason... my boyfriend, breached the gag order. He told a couple of his co-workers, who are his friends, and they showed up tonight asking... well no, they actually demanded to meet you."

"How did you handle that?" he asks, looking slightly amused.

"I told them Jason was confused. I told them Charles Webb was my new partner and Kallon Keller had gotten Rose Bud's the catering job," I say. "I told them Jason must have been confused on the details of the changes to both businesses because they happened so close together."

"You handled that very well," he says, encouragingly.

"That's not the problem" I say.

"Okay, so what is the problem?" he asks, confused.

"Jason told his friends," I say slowly.

"Yes, he did," he says. "Would you like me to talk to him to remind him of the gag order?"

"No, he knows full well the consequences of his actions. He works with contracts daily," I say. Kallon just nods and looks at me like he's waiting for me to ask him something. So, I hurriedly say, "I'm not going to ask you to let him slide on this. He needs to be held accountable just like you'd make anyone else. You would have made an exception for Maggie, Betty's daughter, but she's 11. Jason is 25, he knows better."

"Are you sure?" Kallon asks. "I know the order says ten-thousand dollars, but I could amend it just once to half that, see if it'll scare him enough to not do it again."

"I don't want any special treatment for me or him, just because we are partners. Say you did cut it in half, what if someone on staff finds out—" I wave my hand to gesture towards the kitchen "—or someone from a different business of yours somehow finds out and you made them pay the full amount. They could probably sue you for the other half, even though they were the ones who broke the contract. No, I won't put you in that position. Jason knew what he was signing. He knew what he was doing when he told his friends."

"Have you talked to him yet?" Kallon asks.

"Yes," I say as I take a sip of my wine again and I can feel my face getting warm from it.

"What did he have to say?"

For half a second, I want to tell him Jason admitted what he did and is taking responsibility for his actions, I want to tell him what I wish Jason would do, but I will not lie.

I let out a sigh and say, "He acted like it wasn't a big deal. I'm pretty sure he assumed I'd ask you to let him slide and not make him pay because he's my boyfriend."

"Do you typically cover for him when he messes up?"

"He hasn't messed up like this before, at least not this

big of a mess up. I'd make excuses for him if he canceled on me or if plans had to change and would forgive him quickly if he apologized. A lot of little things, I guess."

"Did you tell him you wouldn't ask me to let him off?"

"I did."

"What did he say to that?"

"I still don't think he believes me. He's actually on his way here to talk to me in person because I 'immaturely'—" I use air quotes "—hung up on him. He said we could talk about this like adults, like I'm the one acting like a child."

I go to take another sip of wine and find that my glass is empty. Before I push my microphone, I ask Kallon, "Do you want something to drink?"

Kallon looks at my empty glass and then up into my eyes. It looks like he's about to say no but then he changes the last second, "Sure, I'll have a 7and7 with ice."

I push my microphone and say, "Hey, Megan, could you bring me another glass and a 7and7 with ice, please."

"Sure thing, Abby," I hear Megan say immediately.

"So, where were we?" I ask. "Oh yeah, I'm as immature child."

Kallon's eyes tighten and his lips purse up.

I wonder what it would feel like to kiss his lips. The thought goes through my mind before I can stop it. I feel my face get a little warmer and I quickly look down at my hands, tearing my eyes away from his lips. *His soft, big lips...... STOP IT!*

Before I can say something to distract my errant thoughts, Kallon says, "Do you want me to be in here when he shows up?"

"Ummm, no, I think I should talk to him alone, but thank you," I say.

There's a knock on the door and my heart leaps into my throat thinking it's Jason. I have a bad feeling that if he comes while I'm talking to Kallon and I don't ask Kallon to let him off with a warning, Jason will fly off the handle.

"Come in," I say with a croaky voice.

Megan opens the door and walks in with a tray in her hand with our drinks on it but stops when she sees Kallon. She looks at me and then Kallon and then down at the drinks.

"Hello," Kallon says politely as he stands up.

Megan's eyes fly up to his and her cheeks turn red, "Hell… hello Mr. Webb."

She hands him his drink and then the wine to me. With her back towards Kallon, she mouths, 'Oh my gosh', and then rolls her eyes to the back of her head and then looks at me and mouths, 'Yum', before putting a smile back on her face and turning back around to Kallon. I let out a small giggle and smile.

"If you guys need anything else, just let me know," she says, nodding at Kallon and then smiling at me.

"Thanks, Megan," I say. I take a sip of my wine and look back at Kallon as he sits back down. "How do you handle all the women reacting to you like that?"

"Like what?"

"Oh, you just act oblivious," I say, laughing. Happy to change the subject off of Jason.

Kallon laughs and says, "I'm not acting."

"You really don't notice when girls get all flustered when they see you?"

"Was Megan?" he asks sincerely.

"Did you notice her cheeks were pink?"

"Yes."

"That wasn't from working in the bar. That was from walking in here and finding you sitting there looking like you do."

"And how is that?"

I put my wineglass to my lips and take yet another sip while I wave my hand in his direction, up and down, like I'm fanning him, "Like… that…"

Kallon smiles at me with a smile that makes me take in a raggedly deep breath. I clear my throat and take a sip. Somewhere in my mind a small voice is telling me to stop drinking and get something to eat.

"Abby, Jason is here," Pam's voice startles me in my ear.

I reach down and push the microphone, "Give me a couple of minutes and then send him back."

"You go it."

"Jason's here?" Kallon asks.

"Yeah," I say standing up. Kallon stands too. His eyes go from my face and travels down to my feet and then back up again.

"I'll step outside, I have a phone call to make," Kallon says with a smirk.

"Thank you," I say.

"No problem," he says as he goes to the door and walks out. He leaves the door open and I watch as he walks through the kitchen towards the back door.

When he leaves the room, I look down at myself and don't see anything that would make him smirk like he did. I shake it off and start pacing from one side of the room to the other.

"You can send him back," I say into my microphone.

"Yes, ma'am," I hear Pam say.

I don't have to wait long before Jason is walking into my office. I turn away from him, instantly angry, and walk to my desk.

"Shut the door," I say when I sit down. Jason huffs and shuts the door with a slam.

"I thought we were going to be mature about this," he mumbles. I see he's got a glass of amber liquor in his hand, probably whiskey, it's his go to right now. When he drinks whiskey, he turns into a raging asshole.

Great, just want this conversation needs.

"You're the one who slammed the door," I state.

"You told me to shut the door."

"I asked you to shut it, not slam it. Do you really want to have this discussion with the entire kitchen staff able to hear?"

"Oh, well... I guess not."

He sits in the chair that Kallon had just been sitting in and I can't stop myself from comparing them to each other. Jason is wearing his blue work suit, his tie has been loosened, and it looks as if he's been running his hands through his hair. He has light brown hair, clean shaven face, deep dimples in his cheeks, hazel eyes, and is fit in a lean type of way. I've always told people that Jason looks like a brother or cousin to Kevin Zegers.

Kallon on the other hand, has dark, almost black hair and has a matching scruffy beard. His eyes are blueish green, they were greener this morning, but they're more on the blue side now. He also has a brown spot in his left eye, not unlike the freckle in my left eye, but his is bigger. Kallon has a strong jaw and even through his beard, I can see his chin dimple.

"Why are you staring at me?" Jason asks and then takes a gulp of his drink.

"Just waiting for you to talk," I say and then clear my throat.

"What more is there to say?" he asks rudely.

"I don't know, maybe why on earth you'd blab when you knew you weren't supposed to?" I ask. "For starters."

"Babe it's really not that big of a deal," he says, taking another drink.

"But it is," I say. "You signed a legally binding contract, a gag order, and you broke it. You really don't see how big of a deal this is?"

"Oh, come on, you know he's not going to make me pay."

"And why is that?"

"Because of you."

"Me?"

"Yeah, you'll ask him to let me off and he'll do it because no one can say no to sweet little Abby."

"Okay, one, I'm not going to ask him. And two, what do you mean by no one can tell me no? You tell me no all the time when I ask you to go do things with me."

"You aren't going to ask him?" he asks, sitting up in his seat.

"No, I'm not. You knew exactly what you were signing, and you knew what you were doing when you told Shane and

Deven. They have two of the three biggest mouths at your office, not to mention their wives."

"Two of the three? Who's the third?"

I look at him pointedly, looking at him from his face down to his chest, and back up again.

He huffs and his face gets angry, "Screw you Abby. I do not have a big mouth. I can keep secrets."

"Oh yeah, like what?" I ask. When he doesn't answer I say, "Like when we thought I was pregnant last year and I asked you not to tell anyone? I had half your office messaging me telling me they were thinking of me. I had asked you not to tell anyone until we found out for sure. It ended up being a false alarm, but still, I had asked you to keep it a secret."

"I was scared and needed to talk to someone about it and I already apologized for that, why are you bringing it up again?"

"Because it's just one example of you telling people things I've asked you to keep secret."

"I do keep secrets."

"Name one that you haven't told anyone because I can't think of anything that I have told you that you haven't blabbed to someone."

"They aren't your secrets."

My mouth actually falls open and I'm stunned silent for a minute. I slowly close my mouth and shake my head. I can feel the tingle of my eyes, a sign I might start crying.

"So, you can keep secrets, just not ones that I ask you to keep?"

"I—" Jason starts to say. He can see my eyes starting to fill with tears. I take a deep breath and will myself to suck the tears back down.

"I'm not going to ask Kallon to not fine you," I say in a croaked voice.

"What!? All because I didn't keep the fucking secret?" Jason yells. It's so loud it makes me jump. "Or is this because I told you I can keep other people's secrets but not yours, not ours?"

"Not because you can't keep mine or our secrets, Jason, because you broke the contract. I'm not going to ask Kallon to go easy on you when I wouldn't ask him to do that for any of my employees. When I know he wouldn't do it for any of the other employees at his other businesses."

There's a knock at the door and Royce sticks his head in and looks from Jason to me.

"Everything okay?" Royce asks.

"We're fine," Jason snarls.

"I wasn't asking you," Royce snaps back. "Abby, are you okay?"

"Yes," I say, I wipe a tear away from my face. "I'm okay."

Royce looks at me like he doesn't believe me, but he nods and pulls the door shut.

"I'm not going to pay that pompous asshole ten-thousand dollars," Jason states.

"You'll go to court then," I say, sniffling again.

"You'll really let him take me to court? You're really going to make me pay him money that he doesn't even need?"

"Jason!" I yell and stand up with my hands flat on my desk. "How is this my fault!? I read the gag order TO you. You read it yourself. You signed it. You knew what it meant if you told anyone. YOU decided to open your mouth and tell your buddies about the buyer. You did. Not me. And him 'needing' the money isn't the point. The point is that the amount is supposed to make it so people don't say anything and keep his anonymity. YOU did this, not me."

"You've made your decision?" he snarls.

"What decision, Jason?" I say shocked at how he's still making this about me. "You made the decision for yourself when you decided to tell Deven and Shane."

"Yeah, well, I assumed you'd back me up. You know, your boyfriend."

"And I thought you'd finally be on my side and have my back for once. I thought you would understand the severity of keeping this information to yourself because you signed a damn legal document but not even that stopped you. It doesn't matter does it. It doesn't matter that I asked you. It doesn't matter that you signed the paper. If you have information or a juicy little tidbit to spread around work or maybe just to your friends, you're going to spread it, aren't you? To hell with who it affects?"

"How does this affect you? I'm the one that's going to have to pay a shit ton of money because you won't go to bat for me."

I laugh out a maddening laugh, "Oh my gosh, Jason! This is not my fault and you aren't going to make me feel like it is. This is affecting me because you are asking me to fix something that you did. Once again, fix something for you because you won't own up to it. And you paying a 'shit ton of money' has nothing to do with me not going to bat for you and EVERYTHING to do with you opening your mouth."

"I can't change your mind?" he asks as he takes the last large gulp of his drink.

"Nooo," I say, drawing the little word out in a duh kind of way.

"Well, I guess that's it then," he says standing up. "We're through."

And just like that, I feel like he's thrown a bucket of cold water on me. *Did that just happen?*

"You're breaking up with me because I won't fix your mess?" I ask in a whisper, sitting down in my chair slowly.

"I'm breaking up with you because you're a shit girlfriend. A girlfriend sticks up for her boyfriend. We've been together for... how many years now? 6? 7? I thought that meant something to you?"

Now I feel like he's slapped me. I can now feel the tears starting to fall.

"We've been together for 8 years you asshole, closer to 9. Strike that, we were together. You can see yourself out," I say, as I angrily wipe a tear away.

He shakes his head and goes to the door.

"I walk out this door and it's over," Jason says with his hand on the handle. "Over because of a stranger."

"No, it's over because you can't own up to your mistakes and take responsibility like a damn adult," I say. And then a thought hits me. "Remember, it's not a one and done."

"What does that mean?" he glares at me.

"It means you don't just get fined once," I say. "If more people come in and ask about Kallon, and they're associated with you, you will get fined for each one of them."

Jason's face goes pale. He splutters out, "That's… that's ridiculous."

"Keep your mouth shut then," I say. "That's my parting gift to you."

"Abby," Royce's voice comes from the other side of the door.

Jason flings the door open and gets into… well not Royce's face because Royce is a good six inches taller, but Jason still gets into his space none the less.

"I told you we were fucking fine, dude," Jason snarls.

"I'm not your dude and I suggest you step back," Royce says in barely contained anger.

Before Jason can say anything, Kallon steps up behind Royce and puts a hand on his shoulder.

"Good evening, gentlemen," Kallon says. Royce turns his head and looks at him over his shoulder. Royce relaxes and steps out of the way. Jason takes a step back inside.

Kallon steps in the office and he doesn't wait for Jason to say anything, he just grabs a chair and pulls it around and puts it next to me. He sits and rests his elbows on his knees.

"I'll be out here," Royce says. Before he shuts the door, he says, "Holler if you need anything."

I look at Jason and then at Kallon, waiting for Jason to say something but it looks as if the wind has been knocked out of him.

"Kallon, you remember, Jason," I finally say in a small voice because I'm trying not to cry.

"I do," Kallon says, not taking his eyes off Jason. "So, what's going on in here?"

"I was just… I came to talk to Abby about—" Jason

starts to say. He clears his throat and says, "I accidently let slip that you bought out Stephen and Viki."

"Mmm," Kallon says, not letting Jason know he already knew. I glare at Jason because he uses the word 'accident' when I know he did it on purpose. "And how did that information accidently come out?"

"Well, it... My friends... my good friends... were asking how things were going for Abby and her parents looking for a new co-owner and instead of using your alias, I said your real name," Jason stammers out.

"Oh," Kallon says. He looks over at me just as I'm wiping a tear away. "Did you or did you not sign the gag order?"

Jason looks at me with a look that's asking for help, but I just stare at him. He glares at me and then looks back at Kallon, "I signed it."

"Were you of sound mind when you signed it?" Kallon asks.

"Yes?" Jason answers as a question.

"Were you coerced into signing it?" Kallon asks in his calm voice.

"No, absolutely not," Jason answers like he's offended.

"So, Abby did not force you to sign the gag order?" Kallon asks a little more sternly.

"No, she asked me to," Jason says.

"And you read it?" Kallon asks.

"Yes," Jason says resigned, finally seeing where Kallon is going with this line of questioning.

"Well, there's not much I can do," Kallon says.

"What do you mean? You're the only one that can do

anything," Jason says, almost pleading.

"You see, Jason, I stand by my morals and ethical principles. If I don't have my integrity, I don't have much of anything. If I were to let just one person off for breaching the contract, I'd have to let everyone off. And in that case, I wouldn't need the gag order at all. My businesses would be ruined and I'd be bankrupt within a year," Kallon says.

"I promise I won't tell anyone," Jason says, definitely begging now.

"You've already broken the promise you made when you signed the gag order. I'm sorry, I just can't trust you," Kallon says with finality.

Jason looks at Kallon and then at me.

"Abby?" he pleads.

I just shake my head, I have nothing to say to him, and then look down at my glass of wine sitting on my desk.

"Thanks," Jason says. I look up and he's glaring at me. "Thanks for nothing."

He walks to the door and throws it open and walks out.

Kallon instantly turns to me, puts his hand on my back, and asks, "Are you okay?"

"He broke up with me," I whisper out.

CHAPTER 12

"What do you mean he broke up with you?" Kallon asks.

"He said, and I quote 'I'm breaking up with you because you're a shit girlfriend. A girlfriend sticks up for her boyfriend. We've been together for... how many years now? 6? 7? I thought that meant something to you?' Can you believe he couldn't even remember how long we've been together?" I ask, wiping a tear away. I grab my wine and take a drink.

"He said that to you?" Kallon asks, he sounds sick to his stomach. "Because you wouldn't ask me to let him off with a warning?"

"Yup," I say, popping the 'p'.

"Call him back in here and I can tell him I'll give him one last chance, but I'll have him sign a gag order that would require him to pay double the amount, maybe that will scare him into not saying anything," Kallon says, rubbing my back.

"No, I'm not going to let him off. He was blaming me for his mistake," I take another drink of wine but then decide to down it all. My cheeks feel warm and my tears feel cool as they roll down my face. "I'm not going to allow him to do that anymore. He needs to step up and be a man. A man like you with integrity and who own's up to his fuck ups."

"Abby, have you eaten anything today?" Kallon asks, wiping a tear from my cheek.

"Mmm, I honestly can't remember," I say, I pick up my glass and try to take a drink, momentarily forgetting it's empty. I push my microphone and says, "Megan dear, would you mind bringing the bottle for me. And Mr. Webb would like another drink as well."

"*Absolutely, Abby,*" Megan says into my ear. I smile up at Kallon. He smiles for a second and then he stands and goes to the doorway.

"Royce," Kallon says and waves for my Sous-chef to come here. Kallon steps back in as Royce comes to the door and when he sees me crying, he walks quickly to me and moves the chair Kallon was sitting in and bends down in front of me.

"What happened?" Royce asks.

"Jason dumped me," I say with a shrug.

"Because you wouldn't let him off?" Royce asks but his tone says he already knows the answer.

I tap my nose twice and then point to him but he's so close that I tap his nose too.

"How much wine have you had?" Royce asks, looking at my glass.

"Not enough," I say and then laugh.

"I don't think she's eaten anything today," Kallon says. He walks over and sits down in front of my desk.

"I'll go make you something to eat, how does that

sound?" Royce says, rubbing my back.

There's a knock at the open door and Megan steps inside.

"Here's that bottle—" she starts to say but then sees me and stops talking. She walks the bottle in quietly and hands Kallon his drink.

"Thank you, Megan," Kallon says politely.

"Yes, thank you Megan," I say and smile at her. I reach for the bottle and pour a healthy amount into my glass. She smiles at me and nods at the guys before she leaves the room.

"Maybe you should hold off until you get some food?" Royce says.

"Maybe I should drink my dinner tonight?" I answer with my own question.

"How about I go make you your favorite and you visit with Mr. Webb, does that sound like a good plan?" Royce counters.

"I don't think hashbrowns and eggs over easy will go well with this wine," I say, looking at the wine in my glass.

"Okay, I'll make your second favorite," Royce says with a laugh.

"Oooh, fettuccini alfredo?" I ask excitedly.

"Yes," Royce says, laughing a little harder.

"Will you make some for my new business partner?" I ask. I look at Kallon and say, "Do you want to have dinner with me? Are you allowed to eat pasta?"

"I don't know what you mean by 'allowed' but yes, I'll have dinner with you," Kallon says, laughing. He looks at Royce and says, "I'll have the same. Thanks, Royce."

I grab my glass and take a pull. I put my glass down

and put my head back on the back of my chair. I close my eyes but before they close all the way, I see Royce nod for Kallon to go over to the door with him. I think they try to whisper but I can hear them as if they're still standing next to me.

"I've never seen her like this before, not even when she and Jason took a break last year," Royce says.

"I think it has to do with what he said to her," Kallon says. He sounds pissed. I open my eyes a little to look at his face. *Yup, he pissed.* I don't feel bad for eavesdropping. They are standing in my office and talking about me, after all.

"What did he say?" Royce asks, sounding like he's about to be upset. Kallon repeats what I told him Jason had said. Royce says in astonishment, "What?"

"That's what Abby said," Kallon says.

"That little weavel," Royce growls.

"Weasel," Kallon corrects.

"Yes, that," Royce says. "Now it makes sense why she's like this. Their breakup last time was mutual. There was no name calling or blame thrown around. I honestly didn't think he'd stick to it, blaming her for his mistake. He really is a narcissistic asshole."

"Here, here," I say, raising my glass to cheers to that last statement, forgetting that I was supposed to not be listening.

"I'll go make you guys some dinner," Royce says.

I look over and see Kallon nod at Royce and then he shuts the door as soon as Royce is gone. He looks at me and smiles as he walks back over to the desk. He sits, picks up his glass, and takes a sip.

"So," Kallon says, putting his glass on the table but

wrapping his big hands around it, interlocking his fingers.

"So," I repeat. "Nice to see that your new business partner can't handle a breakup or her liquor... Fun, isn't it?"

"You're human, we all handle breakups bad," Kallon says. "And I actually like that you can't handle your liquor."

"Why, so you can take advantage of me later?" I giggle and then put my hand over my mouth.

Kallon looks shocked and then he laughs too. He says, "No, that's not what I meant. I meant that you're a light weight. My other business partners out drink me ten to one."

"You're a light weight too?"

"When it comes to the guys I drink with yes, but compared to you, I'm a well-seasoned alcoholic," he laughs.

"How many drinks until you're buzzed?" I ask.

"I'm on my second 7and7 and I'm starting to feel it. So, I'd say, three of these and I'll be buzzed. Four and I'll be leaning more towards drunk, but these taste pretty strong," he says, lifting up his glass and looking at the liquid inside.

"Our drinks are why people like to come here. We make our drinks strong, but it costs them. I don't usually drink and I honestly can't think of the last time I got drunk. With my schedule... I can't afford to be hungover," with that thought, I push the bottle away from me. "Don't let me have any more to drink tonight."

"I promise," he says, smiling at me as he pulls the bottle further away from me.

"I haven't been drunk in a long time, hopefully Royce's food will help sober me up," I say, laughing.

"I'm sure it will. An empty stomach and any type of alcohol is the perfect combination for it to go straight to your blood stream."

Before I can respond, my phone starts to ring on my desk. I pick it up and see that it's Jason calling.

"It's Jason," I say in surprise.

"Do you want me to step out?" Kallon asks, getting ready to stand up.

"No, no, it's okay," I say. I hit the green answer button and in a monotone voice, I say, "Hello."

"Abby," Jason says.

"Yup," I say.

"Will you please tell me why you won't ask Kallon to drop this?" Jason says.

"Because all you care about is yourself, Jason," I say. Now that I'm a little tipsy, all my bottled-up emotions from the last little while start to bubble to the surface. "Because the only time you call or text me lately is to see if you can swing by for a quicky. Because when I told you I had some exciting news about Rose Bud's and I told you about it, all you could ask was how much they were going to pay. There were no congratulations or anything. When I went to spend the weekend with Kayla, you were always too busy when I called, and you never replied to my texts. You blame me for everything. When we have plans to go on a date, you cancel. When I call for a spur of the moment date, after you've told me you're just hanging out at home, you're suddenly busy, that something else came up or you remembered you had a project from work you needed to finish. Jason, I'm just now realizing that you've been pulling away from me for a while now. If you wanted to breakup with me, you should have done it a long time ago."

"I didn't want to until now and it's not just me that's been pulling away. What about you? Every time I call to see if we can hook up, you're always too busy," Jason says.

"Hook up? We were in a relationship, Jason. We don't hook up anymore. And I've only been busy-busy for the last couple of days. I got home from Kayla's, and I haven't stopped. I went from the airport— which you didn't even bother to come there to pick me up by the way— straight to the meeting here at Rose's. I got home and went straight to bed because I was up for nearly 24 hours because of my layovers, and you still never replied to my text that I was home. I got up early yesterday morning and opened my bakery. I had another meeting yesterday morning with the restaurant staff and then dinner at my parents. Which you know I have every Monday, you used to go with me regularly, but you stopped coming with me about six months ago. Remember, you suddenly started having meetings at work those night? I got home from family dinner and found that Betty and Maggie had worked their butts off and had everything prepped for this morning, my first morning catering breakfast for the movie set. I was able to go to bed last night around 8:30 because of them prepping everything for me. I've been up since you called me last night around 12:30, asking for a quicky. You called me after I had already told you I had to be up earlier than usual, to get things done for the movie set. I have always been there for you, Jason, always."

"When you were stressed out waiting to hear if you got hired at Financial Structures, I was there for you. When you were debating about switching departments after being there for a year, who was there to talk you through all the pros and cons? I was. When you thought you'd made a bad investment for your biggest client, who was there to listen and do research for you to make sure it was the best investment for them? Me. And each time your parents cancel coming home for a holiday or your birthday, who's there to make it special for you?... Me... These last few days, I've needed you there for me. But you can't be here for me, can you?" I ask.

"*First of all, I didn't even know you went to Kayla and Peter's,*" Jason says, and I gasp.

"Are you kidding me?" I yell into the phone. "I called you the night Peter called me to say he was purposing and wanted US there. I told you I was going to fly out over the weekend and that I'd be back Sunday. I invited you to come with me. I told you that Peter would enjoy some guy time with his high school best friend. You responded with a, 'That sounds good babe, tell Peter hey for me.' I tried calling you while I was there, but you said you were busy and would call me back, but you never did. I would text throughout the day and like I said before, you never replied."

"*Yeah, well... you're never around when I need you,*" he replies.

"Meaning I wasn't around to give you a blow job or a quick fuck?" I ask, seething. I see Kallon look at me quickly and then back down at his glass, I see him smirking a little. I ignore the burn in my cheeks from embarrassment. "That was only twice, Jason. And I had good reason to send you away. This right here is what I'm talking about. You couldn't see that I needed to get some rest, all you knew was what

YOU needed in the moment, and that was all that mattered to you."

"So, we're done?" he asks.

"You made that perfectly clear before you left here," I say.

CLICK

I look at my phone and see that Jason hung up on me.

"Guh!" I growl out and put my phone down on my desk a little harder than I mean to. I pick up my glass of wine and take another sip, a smaller one this time. I look up at Kallon and say, "Sorry."

"I think you handled that very well," Kallon says. He smirks again and says, "You made very good points and kept your cool."

"I still feel like crap though," I say, spinning my glass around in my hands.

"That's to be expected, you just broke up. Even if you're realizing it's for the best, it still sucks," Kallon says.

"Don't take this the wrong way but, how would you know what it feels like to get dumped?" I ask, laughing a little at the absurdity of the thought of Kallon Keller getting dumped.

"I've been dumped," he says, sounding taken aback.

I stop smiling and look at him with no expression on my face. I stammer out, "You have?"

"Of course, I have," he laughs. "If someone tells you they've never been dumped they're either lying to you or they've always dumped their significant other before they could do it, you know, beat them to the punch so to speak."

"What crazy girl broke up with you?" I ask, seriously concerned with the mental state of a woman that would dump Kallon Keller. The little bit that I've been around him has shown me that he's what most women look for in a man.

"Well for one, my first girlfriend in high school," he says.

"Why did she breakup with you?" I ask.

"Because I told her I was going to Juilliard instead of going to play college football. She thought I had a better chance at becoming an NFL football player than an actor," he says, laughing.

"I bet she's kicking herself now for that," I say laughing.

"It's good to hear you laughing," Kallon says.

"Thank you for sitting with me. I'm sure you've got better places to be tonight," I say.

"Nope, I had planned to come here and hopefully get a chance to visit with you some more," he smiles at me. "I'm sorry you and Jason broke up, but from what I could see and what I've heard, you deserve better."

I just shrug, and say, "After emptying my bottled-up feelings during our call, I do feel better about us breaking up, it really is the right thing. I just hate that he's blaming me for everything."

There's a knock at the door and Kallon gets up and goes and opens it. Royce is standing with two plates of delicious looking food.

"Dinner time," he says. He walks in and places a plate in front of me and one where Kallon was sitting.

"Thank you, Royce," I say.

"You sound like you're feeling better," he says, smiling down at me.

"I am," I say. "Jason called and I let him know what I've been feeling lately, and I had Kallon promise to not let me have any more wine after this last glass."

"That's probably wise," Royce says, laughing. "I'm sorry Jason is an ass."

"It's okay. I'm realizing this for the best," I say.

"Well, enjoy," he says as he leaves the room.

Kallon shuts the door and walks back over to the desk.

"This does look good," he says, picking up his fork and scooping up some noodles and chicken. He takes a bite and says, "Mmmm… this is so good!"

I smile at him and then reach under my desk where I have a little minifridge and pull out two bottles of water. I hand one to Kallon and open mine up. Before I take a bite of my food, I down about half my water bottle.

"Thanks," he says around a mouth full fettuccini alfredo.

I take a bite and my taste buds explode with delight. Royce has out done himself again. We sit in silence and eat for a little while. I finish off my water and grab another one. I look and see that Kallon still has half a bottle.

"So what movie are you working on right now?" I ask, breaking the amiable silence, realizing I haven't asked this question yet.

"It's a movie adaptation of a book, 'Along Came You'. I play the lead role, Dalton Young," he says after he takes the last drink of his 7and7.

"I love that book!" I say excitedly. "I didn't know they were going to make it into a movie."

"I enjoyed reading it as well, which is why I agreed to play the male lead."

"That's right, Randy mentioned earlier when I was in your changing room, that you enjoy reading. He was putting new books in your room."

"I do enjoy it very much. Just like acting, books allow me to immerse myself into someone else's life. I can go on adventures without leaving home, which is nice if I've been gone for a long period of time filming."

"I completely agree," I say. I look at him and tilt my head side to side and then blurt out, "You'll make a good Dalton."

He laughs and says, "You think so?"

My cheeks go red, so to distract myself from looking at him, I pick my wine glass up and mumble out, "Mmmhmm."

"Well, I'm glad I have your approval."

I laugh and just as I'm about to tell him he doesn't need my approval, my phone dings.

"This better not be Jason," I whisper as I pick up my phone. I look and see it's a text from Betty.

Betty: Hey, just wanted to let you know we have everything prepped and ready for tomorrow. Get some rest tonight and I'll see you around 3. :-)

Me: Betty, you are a godsend. It's been a hell of an evening. Just a heads up, Jason broke up with me. It's a long story, I'll fill you in more in the morning.

Betty: Are you okay?

Me: Yeah. It's taken me a minute, but I've realized it's probably for the best, maybe. I don't know. We can talk more in the morning. Thank you so much for your hard work, you seriously have no idea how much I appreciate you.

> **Betty:** Get some rest. Night, Abs.
> **Me:** Night Betty.

"It's Betty, she's a saint. She and Maggie have everything prepped already for tomorrow morning. I guess I can get to sleep at a decent hour again tonight," I say. "I can't believe it's almost 8."

"It's definitely been a long day," Kallon says. He looks up at me and says, "I can't believe you've been up since 12:30am. How are you still functioning?"

"Coffee and sheer will," I say, laughing. I grab my wine and take a sip. I know I said I wouldn't have more but I can't let what I already poured, go to waste.

Kallon just smiles and goes back to eating the rest of his dinner. We sit in silence, enjoying this amazing food that Royce cooked for us.

CHAPTER 13

"Are you finished, or would you like something else? Desert?" I ask Kallon after we've finished our dinner in silence. I go to stand with my empty plate, but I sway a little.

Kallon jumps up and puts a big hand on my shoulder, "You okay?"

"Yeah, I think I just stood too quickly," I laugh. I reach my hand out and nod towards his empty plate.

He hands me his plate and as I go to take a step, I feel dizzy and sway again.

"Maybe we should get desert to go and eat it in the car, I'll take you home," Kallon says as he steadies me and takes the plates from my hands.

"I don't feel drunk in the silly kind of way I usually feel, but I do feel very dizzy," I say, I put my hand on my desk to keep myself from leaning more into Kallon.

"I'll take these, and I'll be right back, don't move," he says and then he smiles.

I shake my head and instantly regret it, if I thought I was dizzy before, it's nothing to this feeling right now. I close my eyes tight and breathe in through my nose and out my mouth.

"Are you okay?" Royce's voice says from the doorway.

I open one eye and say, "I'll be fine. A little too much wine, too fast, on an empty stomach. I'm hoping the food will help soak it up here in a few minutes."

"It might be too late for that," Royce says, laughing. "Kallon says he's going to take you home?"

"Are you okay with me leaving? I've totally messed up and won't be any good to anyone here," I say sadly.

Royce walks over to me and pulls me into his big arms, "You're allowed to feel this way, Abby. Don't beat yourself up over it. We've got this covered, it's our slowest night of the week. Go home and rest."

"Thank you, Royce," I say. As he steps away from me, I click my microphone and say, "Hey guys, I'm going home, Royce is in charge. Patty, could you come to the office for a minute?"

Royce squeezes my shoulder and then walks back out to the kitchen. I grab my phone off my desk and send a quick text to my mom.

> **Me:** I'm heading home early, you'll have to come pick up Patty, I'm sorry. Jason broke up with me, a few minutes ago and I may have indulged in a little too much wine, too quickly. I'll call you when I get home to explain.

I put my phone in my back pocket and as I'm taking my chef jacket off, Kallon walks back into the room. He freezes for a minute, looking at me up and down, and then quickly raises his eyes to meet mine.

He clears his throat, smiles, and says, "Trevor will

drive us to your place. And if Patty is okay with it, Dax will drive her home to save your parents from having to come get her."

"Oh, that's okay, I already sent my mom a message that she'd need to come get her," I say, awestruck that he's so thoughtful. I hang my chef jacket on the coat rack and grab my bag off the hook it's hanging from.

"There are two drivers already here, but I don't want to tell you what to do, although, it's really no problem. Dax has grown fond of you and is the one that offered to take Patty home, since she's met him before. He thought it would help take some worry off your shoulders," Kallon says.

I'm about to reply but my phone dings in my pocket. I grab it and see a response from my mom.

> **Mom:** Oh sweets, I'm so sorry. Don't worry about Patty, Dad will come get her shortly.

I look up at Kallon and then down at my phone and then back up at him. I ask, "Are you sure?"

"Absolutely," he says with a smile.

Shaking my head a little, I send Mom another text.

> **Me:** Change of plans. Dax is going to bring her home.
> **Mom:** How will you get home?
> **Me:** Kallon's other driver, Trevor. I'll explain when I call you later. Just don't send Dad.

After a quick thought about Patty, I hurry and send another text.

Me: Actually, let me ask Patty if she's okay with this before we decide on anything.

Mom: She couldn't stop talking about Dax last night, I'm sure she'll be fine with it. But yes, ask her and then let me know.

As I'm putting my phone back in my pocket, Patty walks into the office.

"Are you okay?" she asks, she's chewing her bottom lip again. "Jason was really mad when he left."

"Yes, I'm okay, Sis," I say, wrapping my arm around her shoulder when she comes and gives me a hug. I will myself not to sway, luckily it's not noticeable to Patty. "I have a question for you."

"What is it?" she says, looking up at me.

"How would you feel about Dax driving you home tonight?" I ask, squeezing her shoulder gently.

"The big scary looking guy that came into our house last night?" Patty asks flatly.

Oh no, she's afraid of him. I say, "Well, yes, but don't be afraid, he's a really nice guy, Patty. He just looks scary because he's so big. He has to be big to protect people like Kallon."

Patty looks from me to Kallon and asks, "Why do you need protected?"

Kallon laughs and is about to say something, but I jump in quickly and say, "Patty, it's not about why he needs protection. Just know that Dax is a really good, nice guy, and you don't need to be afraid. Are you okay with him driving you home? If not, Dad can come and get you."

"I'm not afraid of him, I know he's nice, I can tell,"

Patty says. And that is one thing about her, she just always knows when someone is genuinely a good person. "He can drive me home."

I squeeze her shoulder again, and say, "You are the bravest person I know."

"I know," she says bluntly.

Kallon and I laugh a little and I pull out my phone to let my mom know.

Me: You were right, she has no problem with Dax. I'll ask him to come in and get her at 9. Love you Mom, I'll call you once I'm home.

"Okay, Patty, Dax will come in and get you at 9, okay. Do you want me to let Sherry and Pam know?" I ask.

"No, I will," she says, pulling away from me but then comes back quickly and gives me a big hug. "I love you, Abby."

I hug her back and say, "I love you too, Patty."

She lets go and walks away but before she leaves, she stops at Kallon and gives him a big hug.

"I love you too, Kallon," she says to him, putting her head to his sternum.

He smiles at me and then down at her, wrapping his big arms around her too. He replies with, "I love you too, Patty. You are a very sweet, beautiful person."

"I know," she says as she pulls away.

"Patty..." I say with a chuckle. She has all the self-confidence in the world but sometimes needs to be reminded to use her manners.

"Sorry, thank you, Kallon," she says as she waves and walks out of the room.

"I adore her," Kallon says, still looking out the door, probably watching her walk through the kitchen.

"She's my favorite," I laugh. I go to take a step and the office tilts. Big hands are on my shoulders steadying me again. Ignoring the zing shooting from where his hands are touching me, I look up and see Kallon looking at me with concern. I say one word, "Dizzy."

"Let's get you home. I don't think being sleep deprived is helping you any," he says, wrapping an arm around my back, and putting his hand on my right shoulder, holding it gently but with strength too.

"Triple… no quadruple mixture," I say with a giggle, now feeling the giddiness in my head that I feel when I'm getting drunk. *No, no, no, don't let it get to you.* I take a deep breath, trying to clear my head, it doesn't help though.

Kallon chuckles as he urges us forward slowly, "What do you mean?"

I laugh and say while I hold up my right hand, one finger for each point, "One, no food all day. Two, wine. Three, emotional turmoil. And four, lack of sleep."

"Well, let's get you home so you can get to bed, that'll cure most of those," he says.

"Most…" I agree, knowing he means sleep won't help with my emotional turmoil. "But not all."

"Time will help," Kallon says with a small squeeze to my shoulder.

I can feel my emotions starting to boil up. Even if I know that Jason and I need this break, because our relationship hasn't been good since… *No, don't think about it. Wait until we're home.*

"Thank you for being here," I say to change my train of thought.

"Like I said, I wouldn't want to be anywhere else."

"No plans with Miss Shell tonight?" I ask, realizing too late that he should be out with her.

"Not during the week. She has modeling gigs in L.A. and will be back Friday evening. I told her I'd be here tonight, getting to know my new business partner better, and seeing behind the scenes of the restaurant."

"I can't imagine how busy your guys' lives are," I say, in awe.

"Yes you can," Kallon chuckles. We get to the doorway and I pull away from him slightly. I don't want to walk through the kitchen with him holding me like this. He looks down at me with a questioning look.

"Sorry, I can walk from here," I say. I step away and then instantly feel like I'm falling. I reach out and grab the linen closet door that's to the right of the office door.

"Please let me help you," Kallon whispers from beside me.

"I can't have rumors starting that there's something between us," I whisper back. I then slap my hand over my mouth and my face feels warm.

"Would they think that? Even if I'm helping you walk out the door?" Kallon asks. He doesn't wait for a response before he says, "Royce, will you come here?"

I look over and see Royce look up and then finishes doing something on the stove before taking his gloves off and heading our way.

"They are great employees, but they're still humans,

there's still gossip that gets spread. Yes, I think they'd read more into you with your arm around me than it just being a helpful hand out the door."

"Is it okay that I called Royce over?" he asks. "It looks as if you two are close."

"He's one of my closest friends, so yes, it's fine," I say as Royce gets to us.

"What's up?" Royce asks.

"Could you help Abby to the back? Trevor is parked out there," Kallon says quietly. He then raises his voice and says, "She's not feeling well. I think the lack of sleep from the last couple of days are catching up with her."

I elbow him in the side and look up at him angerly, "I'm fine."

Royce chuckles and puts his arm around my shoulders and pulls me towards the back door. I reluctantly go with him, letting him hold me up and keep me walking in a straight line.

Once we get outside, Kallon steps up and Royce releases me so that Kallon can put his arm around me.

"I'm fine," I say as I step away and then slide down the six steps, on my ass. "Oooph."

"She's stubborn," Royce says with a chuckle. He then adds, "Good luck."

I start laughing at the picture in my head of me falling down the stairs, but I look up over my shoulder and say to Royce, "Screw you, I am not."

"Okay, Abby," he says laughing and walking back into the kitchen, letting the door swing shut. I hear the automatic lock click into place.

I'm still laughing when Kallon walks down the steps and crouches down beside me. I hear a car door open and when I look over, I see a man that looks similar to Dax walking over to us.

"Please let me help you," Kallon says as he tries not to laugh.

"I'm mad at you," I say, still laughing.

"Are you?" he asks, putting a handout to wave off who I think is Trevor. Kallon then turns his attention back on me and puts a hand under my right upper arm, close to my armpit, and his left hand on my back and helps me up.

"Yes," I say, standing up.

"Why?"

"Because I feel fine. My employees don't need to think I'm getting sick because I can't handle my schedule," I say annoyed.

"It's okay for them to see that you're human, Abby. Even if you can handle it all, it's okay if you can't."

I look up at him and huff out a sigh. He's right, there's absolutely no reason I should feel embarrassed that he made up an excuse for me to need Royce's help outside. It was a better alternative than them thinking I was snuggling up to Kallon, my new partner, and their new co-boss.

"You're right, I'm sorry."

"It's okay," he says laughing. "But are you alright? You did just slide down six steps on your ass."

I laugh and can feel my face turning red. Thank goodness it's nighttime, and even with the well-lit parking area, it's still dark enough he can't see my embarrassment.

"I'll be okay," I say as I rub my tailbone which smarts

just a little bit. I start walking and my steps aren't in a straight line. "I don't know what's wrong. I don't even feel that drunk. I mean, I do but not like I have felt in the past. I don't understand why I can't just walk."

Kallon reaches out with his hands and puts them on my shoulders, steering me towards the car.

"Abby Rose, this is Trevor Anderson. Trevor, this is Miss Abby Rose," Kallon says as we get closer to the dang near carbon copy of Dax.

"It's nice to meet you Miss Rose," Trevor says as he opens the rear right passenger door.

"It's nice to you meet you also," I say as I start to sit on the seat. "Thank you."

Trevor just nods and gently shuts the door after I've gotten my legs inside the car. I hear Kallon says something, but the car must be a little soundproof because it just sounds like a muffled mess of sound. When I look out the window, I see Trevor nod once at Kallon, a gesture of understanding at whatever Kallon had been saying. Kallon walks back behind the car, over to the passenger door, Trevor following close behind him, where he opens the door and shuts it once Kallon has slid inside.

I stare at Kallon as he adjusts his pants and jacket. As he's putting his seatbelt on, he looks over at me. I look away quickly, embarrassed at getting caught gawking. Kallon pulls out his phone as I slip my bag off and put it down between my feet and then reach behind my right shoulder, looking for the seatbelt.

"I'm letting Dax know to go in to get Patty in a few minutes," Kallon says, looking down at his phone.

"Thank you," I say.

Trevor has gotten into the car and starts to pull out of the parking lot, taking a hard right, which makes me fall to the left. Trying to keep myself from falling over, I fling my left hand out to stop myself. My hand lands on Kallon's thigh, his upper thigh, like any higher and I would have been holding on to his...

"Eeek," I let out a squeal of embarrassment and lift my hand up. But just as I do, Trevor turns right on to the one-way street out of the alley entrance to our back parking lot, causing me to fall right into Kallon's lap.

Face flaming, I use my left hand again to find leverage to push myself off Kallon. My hand finds the seat and as I look down to see where my hand is between Kallon's legs, my eyes fly up to Kallon's face. His lips are pulled into his mouth, into a tight line, he looks like he's trying not to laugh. Both of his hands are up in the air, like he doesn't know what to do with them. With my right hand still holding on to my seatbelt, I pull it until there's no more give, and I pull myself away from Kallon.

"I'm so sorry," I say in a voice just a touch louder than a whisper. I close my eyes and put my head back against the head rest, mortified.

"No harm, no foul," Kallon says, chuckling.

Shaking my head, I pull on my seatbelt, trying to get it to come out so I can buckle myself in securely so that awkward situation doesn't happen again. But my seatbelt seems to be stuck.

"Here let me help you with that," Kallon says. He turns and reaches over me with his left hand. I look up and his face… his lips… are a mere inch away from mine.

I hold my breath and stare at his lips for a long second and then up to his eyes. Kallon is frozen in place, looking at my lips for more time than is necessary. My tongue, having a mind of its own, pokes out between my lips a little and licks my bottom lip before I pull my bottom lip into my mouth, biting down on it. If I hadn't been staring at Kallon's eyes, I wouldn't have seen his eyebrows raise a little higher, and then his eyes are slowly moving from my lips up to my eyes. We stare into each other's eyes for what feels like minutes but, it's really just a couple seconds.

Don't kiss me… No, kiss me… NO, don't kiss me! My brain is warring with itself. I let out my shaky breath and pull my head back ever so slightly, but not taking my eyes off Kallon. *I don't want to kiss you. Jason just broke up with me. Aaaand you're my business partner for goodness sake! But look at your lips, they're so… perfect…* I look back down at Kallon's lips, his bottom lip bigger than his top one. They make the perfect lip heart shape.

Kallon shakes the seatbelt and then pulls it slowly out and as he leans back into his seat. He pulls the belt across me and buckles it in for me.

With a shaky voice, I say, "Thank you. And sorry about… that… I've definitely had way too much to drink."

"It seems so have I, my apologies as well," Kallon says with a little deeper voice than what I've heard from him. I glance over just as he swallows hard, his Adam's apple dips down low and back up slowly.

I look out my window and try not to laugh at the absurdity that this night has turned into. But I can't hold it in, a little snort escapes, which makes me put a hand over my mouth and I start to laugh hysterically now.

"What's so funny?" Kallon asks, laughing with me.

"Just… tonight," I say between breaths. I start laughing so hard I can't talk for a minute. It's one of those laughs that no sound comes out except for when I try to take a breath in but it's a sound between a snort and a wheeze. I start fanning my face with my hand and tears start to roll down my cheeks.

I look over at Kallon and he's laughing but his eyes are wide. I take a couple more minutes to calm myself down, taking in deep breaths and then blowing them back out.

"Are you okay?" Kallon asks.

I'm about to answer him but a different thought hits me, "Aww we forgot to get dessert."

Kallon laughs and says, "We can stop somewhere, if you'd like."

"Noo," I say sadly. "It's probably better for me to get home. The sooner, the better."

"If you're sure," Kallon says.

"Yes, I need sleep more than I need ice cream," I laugh.

"Is ice cream your preferred dessert?"

"Mmm," I think for a minute. "Yes, either ice cream alone or a scoop of vanilla with a warm chocolate chip cookie or brownie. Or a banana split."

"Man, I haven't had a banana split in a long time," Kallon says with longing in his tone. "What's your favorite ice cream alone?"

"Probably Oreo or a salted caramel. What about you?"

"I don't think I have a favorite. I'll be completely happy with any ice cream that's put in front of me. But your cookie or brownie with vanilla combination sounds really good too."

"Oh, come on, you have to have a favorite," I laugh. "Say your favorite ice cream parlor can only have one flavor from here on out, what flavor do you hope they keep?"

Kallon thinks for a minute and then smiles. He says, "I guess that'd be Strawberry."

My mouth falls open, "Strawberry? Really?"

"Yes, why is that so surprising?" he laughs and then angles his body so he's facing me more.

I turn so I'm facing him as well and say, "I don't know. I guess I figured you for a... maybe a Rocky Road type of guy."

"I do like Rocky Road but if I had to pick just one ice cream to have at my favorite parlor, it would be Strawberry."

"Interesting," I say smiling. "So, what's your favorite dessert?"

"Your chocolate chip cookie brownie thing at Rose's," he says.

"No way... Really?"

"Yes, really," he laughs. "Apple pie used to be it but after I had that combination the first time I ate at Rose's, my favorite changed. It's the perfect balance of cookie and brownie."

"I made it because I couldn't decide between the two one time when I was having a rough night. So, I decided to make half a batch of each and combine them. It turned out better than I could have imagined. I took it to my parents' house the next day and had them try it. They immediately told me to put it on the dessert menu at Rose's. It's one of our top sellers."

"I don't doubt it."

"Sir, we're about 10 minutes from Miss Rose's building, where would you like me to pull up to it?" Trevor asks from the front seat.

Kallon looks at me and I say, "Just out front will be fine. Thank you, Trevor."

I lean the left side of my head against the head rest and close my eyes, suddenly exhausted.

"Are you alright?" Kallon asks.

"Mmm, yeah I think so," I say, and then yawn. "I just think the excitement from today has caught up to me."

I keep my eyes closed and listen to the hum of the tires on the road. I must have fallen asleep because my leg is being gently shaken by a large, strong hand.

"Abby, we're here," Kallon says.

I open my eyes and turn my head. We're parked out front of Rose Bud's.

"Oh," I sit up and turn to face forward. "Thank you."

Trevor gets out and walks around to the sidewalk and to my door. He opens it, holding out his hand for me. I take my seat belt off, grab my bag from between my feet, and scoot out of the car. I take his hand and let him help me out. I turn to lean into the car to tell Kallon thank you and goodnight, but I see him sliding out of the car behind me. I take a step back just as Trevor is letting go of my hand. I close my eyes to blink but find it hard to open them again and then I feel myself falling backwards towards the ground.

Big arms are around my back, catching me before I can fall completely. I feel another set of hands on me, one holding tightly to my hand, and the other onto my forearm.

"Oh, Miss Rose, I'm so sorry," Trevor says.

I open my eyes and see Kallon to my left, his arm around my back. I look up at Trevor who's holding my right hand and arm, and say, "It's not your fault. I've had a touch too much wine on what was an empty stomach and I'm running on about four hours of sleep in the last 48 hours. I think I've hit my limit."

"I'll get you up to your room," Kallon says, standing up and putting me back on my feet.

"I'd say I can make it myself, but we know that'd be a lie," I say sheepishly.

"It's really no problem," Kallon says to me. He picks up my bag and puts the strap over his left shoulder. He then puts his right arm around my shoulders, wrapping his hand around my right shoulder and squeezes gently. He offers his left hand to me and I place my left hand in it. It's warm and big and my hand disappears into it.

"I'll be back in a couple of minutes, Trevor," Kallon says.

"Yes sir," Trevor says. "Good night, Miss Rose."

"Good night, Trevor," I say as I watch him walk around the car to the driver's side.

"Let's get you to bed," Kallon says. I look up at him with mock surprise on my face and wide eyes. He looks down at me when I haven't moved a step and he laughs a quite laugh, "Not like that, Abby."

I start laughing and say, "I know. It was just funny how you said it. I had to give you a little crap."

"You're funny," he says, laughing.

"Am I?"

"Very," he says honestly.

"Jason never said I was. I always had to explain things to him when I'd try to be funny or a joke that I thought was hilarious," I say a little sadly as we start walking up the sidewalk and turning around the corner of the building to head down to my door.

"Maybe his humor is different from ours," Kallon says kindly.

"Ours?" I ask, looking up at him.

"Yes, I think you and I might have the same type of humor."

"Well, that's good," I say as we get to my door. I punch in my code, the door unlocks, and Kallon lets go of my shoulder to let me go inside. He doesn't let go of my hand though.

We go up the stairs in silence, my right hand on the railing, and my left hand still in Kallon's. I can feel his right hand lightly on my back. When we get to my front door, the keypad swims in front of me and looks to have too many numbers for me to focus on.

Kallon offers me my bag, so I dig for my keys. I find them and try to concentrate to get the key in the hole. I can feel when the key catches the opening but by the time I push the key forward, I've apparently moved the key just enough in either direction that I can't get it to go in.

"Can I help you?" Kallon asks. He brings his right hand out in front of us and asks for the keys.

"If you think you can get it in, go right ahead," I say. I start laughing and cover my mouth with one hand as I hand him my keys. I mumble out, "That sounded bad."

He laughs as he slides it in the first try and turns it.

"How did you do that so easily? I thought you said you had too much to drink too?" I ask.

"Not enough to affect my eye coordination," he laughs.

"Hmmph," is all I can say as I open my door and step inside. I turn on the light to the living room and turn to Kallon as he pulls the key out of the lock and hands them to me. He then hands me my bag and I throw my keys inside and then place my bag on the long skinny table by my door.

"Do you want me to help you to bed or do you want to lay down on the couch for a while?" Kallon asks.

Willing myself not to make an inappropriate comment about the bed, the thought of him being in my bedroom has my face heating up. *Abby, stop it!*

"Couch would be great. Thank you," I say as I motion to my sectional. "I need to call my mom before I pass out for the night. If I go to bed now, I have a feeling I'll fall asleep as soon as my head hits the pillow."

"Okay," Kallon says, helping me over to the couch. I sit down and lean back. I put my head back on the big pillow and close my eyes. Kallon asks, "Can I get you some water?"

"I'll be okay," I stammer out.

I hear him chuckle and then he walks away. I open one eye and see him heading towards the kitchen. He turns on the light and sees my case of water on the counter. He goes to my fridge and opens it, looking for a cold water, maybe. He closes the fridge door and walks back to the water on the counter and grabs one. As he walks back to me, he opens it.

He squats down in front of me and says, "Sorry, I couldn't find any cold water."

"I prefer room temperature," I say as I look up at him. He's got a look on his face that finds my preference interesting.

He hands me my water and says, "Drink all of this before you fall asleep. It'd be a good idea for you to take some Tylenol or something before you fall asleep as well. Ward off any headache you might get in the morning."

"Thank you," I say, leaning forward and taking it from him. I take a big swing before I put it on the end table.

"Are you sure you'll be okay by yourself tonight?" he asks with concern on his face.

"Yes. I'll call my mom and then go right to sleep," I say, touched again by his thoughtfulness. "Thank you, though."

"You're welcome, Abby," Kallon says. He pats my leg before he stands up and then says, "Please call me if you need anything."

"Thank you," I say again.

"Make sure you lock this before you go to sleep," he says. He goes to open the door and finds that it's locked.

"My grandpa made sure that my doors automatically lock," I say with a smile at his impressed look. "I have to unlock it from in here for it to be truly unlocked. You just turn the lock to the left to get out and it'll relock again when you shut the door."

"I like that," he says, looking at the door and then at me. "Have a good night."

"You too," I say with a big smile.

As soon as Kallon leaves, I kick off my shoes, and I reach into my back pocket and pull my phone out. It's 9:23pm. I click on the icon of the phone and then tap on

'Mom'. The phone doesn't ring more than twice before she picks up.

"Oh honey, is everything alright?" she says in a hurry.

"Yes, Mom, everything's fine," I say and then pause. I add, "Or it will be."

"What happened?" she asks.

"Jason broke the gag order and wanted me to ask Kallon to ignore it. I wouldn't, so he broke up with me."

"Oh honey, I'm sorry. But this will blow over and he'll apologize. He'll see that he was in the wrong."

"And if he does, do you think I should take him back?"

"Don't you love him?"

I take a minute to think about it and when I answer, I have a hitch to my voice, "I'm not sure Mom. I thought I did. But the way he was talking to me and acting, it doesn't show me that he loves me."

"Sounds like a break is needed. For you both to think about what you want."

"Yeah," I say as a tear rolls down my cheek. I wipe it away and ask, "Has Patty gotten home yet?"

"She got home just a couple minutes ago but went right to bed. Dax walked her to the door. He's a very sweet man."

"Yes, he is," I say as I smile into the phone.

"You get some rest. If you need anything, you let me know, alright?"

"I will Mom, thanks."

"Good night, sweetheart."

"Night, Mom."

She hangs up before I do so I exit out of the phone app and go to my messages. I open Kayla's and send her a message.

>   **Me:** Hey, you awake? :-(

I don't have to wait long before I see the three little dots pop up.

>   **Kayla:** Yes. What's with the sad face? What happened?
>   **Me:** Jason broke up with me.
>   **Kayla:** What?! Why?!
>   **Me:** He breached a contract and assumed I'd smooth it over for him. I wouldn't, so he called me a shit gf for not having his back.
>   **Kayla:** He's really turned into such an asshat. But how could you smooth over a contract?
>   **Me:** It's a long story and a ton of details. I'll explain to you next time I see you.
>   **Kayla:** I'm sorry, Abs. Are you ok?
>   **Kayla:** Hang on, I'll call you. Give me a second to go to another room, Peter is watching a movie.
>   **Me:** It's OK, we can just text I'm tired and a little drunk. If I talk out loud, I might bawl. So, no... I guess I'm not OK... Mom thinks he'll apologize and realize that he was in the wrong.

I see the three dots appear and then disappear a couple of times, like Kayla can't decide on what to say.

>   **Me:** Just say what you want to say, Kay.
>   **Kayla:** Let me ask you this. Do you still love him?
>   **Me:** Mom asked me the same thing. I don't know if it matters if I still love him or not, he hasn't shown me that he loves me.
>   **Kayla:** I think it matters.
>   **Me:** I honestly don't know. Ever since last year, with the pregnancy scare and how he went around and told everyone at his work. I don't feel like I've been able to trust him. I didn't even tell you until after we found out I wasn't.

Kayla: If he does apologize for being a total tool, will you take him back?

Me: I don't know.

Kayla: You guys have a long history together but Abs, that's not the most important thing to have in a relationship. If there's no more chemistry... connection... love, it might be better to let it go.

Me: I know...

Kayla: You going to be ok?

Me: I will be, but I have some thinking to do.

Kayla: I'm always here for you, Abs.

Me: I know, thank you. I'm going to go to sleep. I'll talk to you later.

Kayla: OK, night.

Me: Night.

Before I put my phone down on the table, I double check that my alarms are still set. I also turn my notifications off so if anyone, especially Jason, tries to call me, it won't wake me up. I need some uninterrupted sleep, even if it's just a couple of hours. After setting my phone down, I pull the blanket that I have folded on the back of the couch, over me and lay down.

Today definitely didn't end as good as it started. It started off amazing with my first day on the movie set being a success. Work at Rose's started off smooth. And then the crap flood gates opened when Deven and Shane came in. Although, if I'm completely honest with myself, I'm glad they came in, or I wouldn't have known that Jason opened his mouth. Who knows how many people he would have told before we found out. Damage control would have been well out of reach. At least with those bone head friends of Jason's and their superficial wives, I feel like I covered it pretty well.

I roll myself over and face the cushions and pull the

blanket up to my chin. Some sleep will help clarify my thoughts.

CHAPTER 14

BEEPBEEP**BEEP**

BEEPBEEP**BEEP**

I roll over and fumble around to find my phone. My fingers finally hit something on my screen to stop the beeping from going off. I roll to my side, away from the cushions, and snuggle down into my couch and the blanket.

I was having a delicious dream about someone eating ice cream off my...

I sit up quickly and then regret it. A throbbing pain fills my head.

I forgot to take Tylenol like Kallon suggested. I hurry and glance around my living room. No one is here but me. I wipe a hand across my face and take a deep breath in and my mind goes back to my dream.

"We are not going to start having dreams about him," I say to myself sternly. "Absolutely not!"

BEEPBEEP**BEEP**

My phone startles me, the annoying alarm clock sound making my headache pound even harder. I reach over and grab it. When I pull it to my face, I see that it's 1:06am and that my battery is dangerously low. I put my phone on my lap and stretch my arms above my head and then stretch my neck, first to the left and then to the right. As I fling the blanket off me, the phone goes flying off my lap onto the floor. When I bend down to pick it up, the throbbing increases to the point I let out a painful groan.

"Okay first, Midol and water. Second, plug my phone in while I get ready for the day," I say to myself.

I walk sluggishly into my kitchen and not bothering to turn on the light, grab two bottles of water. I down one before I head to my bathroom. Walking even slower, I try to stretch my back and neck as I go. Sleeping on the couch might not have been the best idea.

I get to my room and turn my light on, immediately dimming it so it doesn't make my headache turn into a migraine. I put my phone on my charger on my nightstand. I go into my bathroom, not bothering to turn on the overhead light, but turn the light on in my shower. It's less offensive to a pounding headache. I open my medicine drawer and pull out my bottle of Midol.

In school, a classmate introduced me to Midol as a hangover cure when we had stayed up too late trying different drinks, she was trying to improve for her Mixology certification. Midol has the perfect combination to help with hangover symptoms, but for me it mainly helps with headaches and any nausea I may feel.

I pop two in, down half my water, and then walk over to my shower and turn it on. I turn it to just a little hotter than I normally like it, hoping it'll help get the kink out of my neck. I strip out of my clothes and toss them into my laundry basket. As I step into the hot stream of water, I go over everything I need to do today.

It's no different from yesterday. Get the smoothies made and fruit bowls filled. Make the frosting for the baked goods. Then pack everything up. I'm hoping everything goes as smoothly today as it did yesterday. I need to talk to Royce and see how last night ended up going. I didn't have any missed calls or texts from anyone, so I'm hoping that's a good sign. And most importantly, I need to apologize to Kallon for my behavior last night. From what I can remember, I was acting inappropriately.

I have a flash back about how close we were to kissing. Or, when I thought about kissing him. He was just so close. I shake my head to get the mental image out of my mind.

"No," I say sternly to myself as I wipe water out of my face. "I'm not going to think about that. I'm going to keep Kallon in the business partner box where he belongs. I'm with… was with Jason. We just broke up yesterday. Kallon is with Tina. We. Are. Business. Partners."

I finish my shower and get out. I wrap a towel around my head, and then wrap one around myself. I wipe my big mirror off and look at myself in the mirror. I don't look as tired as I feel, so that's a good sign. I grab my half drank water and finish it off as I walk into my room.

I go to my closet and pull out another black Rose Bud's shirt, a black camisole tank top, and a dark pair of jeans. As

I walk over to my bed, I grab a pair of undies and socks from my dresser. I hurry and change into my clothes. I go into the bathroom, finally turning the overhead light on, now that the Midol has worked its magic, and run a brush through my hair. I do a side braid, starting up by my right temple and bringing it down and around the back of my head until I stop right behind my left ear. I finish it with a tight messy bun. This is my go-to hairdo because it keeps the hair out of my face and most importantly out of the food I'm cooking.

I put on some eyeliner and mascara. I decide to keep my small hoop earrings in and after putting deodorant on, I turn the light off and walk over to my nightstand to grab my phone. I see that it's 1:36 and feel a little panic that I'm behind schedule from yesterday.

"Breathe Abby, we've got plenty of time," I say, taking a deep breath in and letting it out slowly.

Even with that itty bitty pep talk, I still hurry and put my phone into my back pocket and run into my closet and grab a black pair of pants for Rose's. I grab my empty messenger bag and through the pants into them. I can get back to Rose Bud's, unload, and then head to Rose's and get that shift going. The good thing about it being the second day on set is that I don't have to load up the cases and extra stuff today, just the food.

I hurry out of my room and turn the light off as I go. I get out into the living room and grab my bag off the table by the door. I set it and my messenger bag down on the couch while I throw on my shoes. After getting them on and grabbing my bags, I turn the lights off in the living room and head to the kitchen. I grab another water bottle and then head to the door that leads down to Rose Bud's.

When I get to the kitchen, I see that the kitchen light is on.

"That's weird," I say to myself as I put my bags down on my desk, next to the clean tablecloths that I'll be taking with me. "Betty is usually good about turning things off before she leaves."

Just as I finish talking to myself the doors leading out to the front, swing open and I jump and yelp in surprise.

"Oh, sorry, Abby," Betty says in surprise to my startlement.

"It's okay, Betty," I say with my hand over my chest. "I didn't know you were here already."

"I decided to come in early to help," she says with a shrug.

"You've already helped out so much," I say sincerely.

"With how your evening went, I just wanted to make today easier for you."

"Well, thank you," I say as I look around. "Is Maggie here?"

"She's out front, asleep on one of the super comfy chairs," Betty laughs.

"Go wake her and tell her to go up to my place. You should have sent her up when you guys first got here."

"I didn't want to wake you or startle you even more than what I just did. She's okay. When we finish getting everything finished, I'll take her up."

"When did you get here anyways?"

"Just after 1," she says, not looking at me. "I heard the water pump turn on not to long after I started getting things going, so I figured you were up and getting ready. I should have sent you a message to let you know we were here, sorry."

"Don't apologize, I really appreciate you coming in this early."

Betty gives me a warm and happy smile and then we get to work. She already has the smoothies finished. We work quickly and quietly getting the fruit bowls thrown together. As we're boxing up the baked goods, Betty breaks the silence.

"So, do you want to talk about you and Jason?" she asks tentatively.

"Long story short, he broke the gag order, and demanded I ask Kallon to let him off. I told him I wouldn't. I told him that he needed to start taking responsibility for his actions. I think he's forgotten that when he does something wrong, there's consequences. And that's mainly my fault because I've been making excuses for him for so long now."

"No Abby, it's not your fault. It's natural to want to help the person you love and who you're in a relationship with, but it's not okay that he made you feel like it was your fault for his mistake," Betty says as she puts her hand on my shoulder. "Please believe me."

"My head is telling me that you're right, it really isn't my fault. He knew the consequences if he broke the contract but... my heart is telling me I should have gotten Kallon to waive the fine, just this once because Kallon would have," I say as I put a finished box on the other table. I come back to our worktable and start loading another box up but then stop and take a deep breath, and say in defeat, "Then my head yells at my heart that it's time for Jason to grow up and take responsibility for his actions. I know my head is correct but loving Jason for so long, has made it hard to listen to it sometimes."

"Maybe some time away from him will help your heart and head reconnect to be on the same page," Betty says with a shrug.

I nod my head without saying anything.

KNOCKKNOCK**KNOCK**

We hear knocking coming from the front, which makes us look at each other. I look at the clock on the wall and see it's 2:32am.

"Maybe it's Dax again," Betty asks as her cheeks turn pink.

"What's with the blush, Ms. Brown?" I ask her as my eyebrows raise up and I try to hide a smile.

"I'm not blushing," she says, turning away from me, the pink in her cheeks reddening.

"Mmm, I think you are," I say. "Do you like Dax?"

"Don't you?" she asks turning around with a small smile.

"Sure, he's a nice guy from what I've come to know of him. Not bad to look at either, wouldn't you say?" I waggle my eyebrows at her.

"Oh, I would definitely say that," she laughs.

KNOCKKNOCK**KNOCK**

The knocking is louder now.

"I better go see who that is before they wake Maggie

up," I say as I hurry through the doors. I flick the light on to light up the front of the bakery and see Dax standing by the door. He waves at me when he sees me walking towards him. I look around and find Maggie fast asleep on my biggest oversized chair. She has a book in her hands.

If I ever have kids, I hope they love reading as much as she does, I think to myself as I reach the front door. I unlock it and step aside to let Dax in.

"Good morning, Miss Abby," he says, nodding his head at me.

"Morning, Dax," I say smiling. I laugh and say in resignation, "There's no way to get you to stop feeling like you have to drive me everywhere, is there?"

"It's not a 'feel like' situation, Miss Abby. I really enjoy driving for you. And plus, my services are paid for, remember?" he asks with a chuckle. "And I wanted to be here to help load things up again. I know you left quite a bit of the big stuff at the studio, but I'd hate to see you hurt yourself by trying to load everything by yourself."

"I'm not doing it by myself, Betty is here also," I say as we make our way through the customer sitting area.

"Is she?" Dax says with some excitement in his tone. I glance over at him and see he's smiling.

"She is," I smile back at him. "She's finishing up boxing the last of the baked goods."

Dax glances over and sees Maggie sleeping. His smile gets bigger and his eyes get softer.

"That's a good kid there," he whispers, knowing now that Maggie is in the room sleeping.

"She's a very good kid."

We walk through the doors into the kitchen and see that Betty has everything packed up and is now wiping down the counters.

"Everything is finished, we just have to load it up now," she says, looking up at me and then glancing at Dax. Her cheeks pink up again, and she says, "Morning, Dax."

"Good morning, Mrs. Brown," Dax says as he smiles hugely at her.

"No Mrs., just Ms. but you can call me Betty," she says as she runs her fingers over her ear, like she's pushing her hair behind it. It's a nervous tick she has, she never has hair to push behind her ear unless it's down and it's never down when she's a work.

"Alright, Betty," Dax says, and I can hear the caress in his voice as he says her name.

"I'm going to go start the van," I say as I turn away so that they don't see my smile and that I'm trying not to giggle at them. *I'm going to have to do some investigating here.*

I grab the keys off the hook by the back door. I open the back door and walk out to the van. I unlock it quickly and jump in and turn on the ignition. I jump out and after shutting the door, I lock it back up. When I get back into the kitchen, I see that Dax and Betty have gotten everything pulled out of the cooler and everything is ready to be loaded.

"Shall we start loading?" Dax asks.

"Yes please," I say, not bothering to argue about him not having to help. I'm just going to have to learn how to accept it and not fight it.

I grab the containers of smoothies and Betty starts to load Dax up with boxes of baked goods. I walk over to the back door, put the smoothie container in my right arm down so I can open the door, but Dax steps forward and pushes it open with his foot and then leans his back against it to keep it open.

"Thanks," I say, smiling up at him.

Dax just nods.

It doesn't take long before we have everything loaded and ready to head to the studio.

"Betty, please go up and rest. You and Maggie have gotten into a weird sleep schedule because of me, and I hate that you're running yourself ragged," I say as I see Betty yawning by the doors leading out into the front of the bakery.

"I'm not running myself ragged, I'm getting plenty of sleep. Don't worry about me, I'm more worried about you," she says, eyeing me sternly. "But I'll take Maggie up so she's a little more comfortable and I'll try to rest as well, seeing as everything is ready again for this morning."

"You guys make a great team," Dax says, looking between Betty and me.

"She makes my life so much easier," I say, giving Betty a hug.

"No, you are who makes my life easier," she hugs me back tighter.

"Let me know how opening goes, I'm sure it'll go smoothly," I say as I pull away from her.

"I will. And you let me know how everything goes on set," she says with a wave.

"Thanks for everything. See you later," I say to Betty as I grab my messenger bag, and the table clothes. I leave my bag with my Rose's clothes in it for later. I turn to Dax and say,

"Ready Jeeves?"

Dax shakes his head and walks towards me. He turns and nods to Betty and says, "See you later, Betty."

"Bye Dax," she gives him a small wave. "See you, Abby."

She turns quickly and walks out of the doors and into the front. When Dax turns back around towards me, he's got a goofy smile on his face.

"What?" he asks a little startled.

"Nothing," I say, smiling up at him. I reach for the door, but he reaches around me and opens it. "Thank you."

"Welcome," he says in his deep voice. "But what was that smile about?"

"I was just smiling."

As soon as he shuts the back door, I wait to hear the locks slide back into place before I start walking again. I reach into my pocket and unlock the van. I hand the keyless entry remote over to Dax and he just smiles.

"That was hard for you, wasn't it?" he asks with humor thick in his voice.

"Yes, but I've decided I'm just going to accept this," I point to him and the van. He follows me around to the passenger side and opens the door. I say a little drier than I intend to, "Thanks."

"You'll get used to this as well," he says with a wink and a throaty laugh.

Shaking my head and laughing a little, I jump into the van and start to buckle myself in. Dax walks around the front and hops in too. He buckles his seatbelt before he puts the van in drive and we're on our way to the studio.

Checking my watch, I see that it's 3:03am. I look

around at the traffic and see it's fairly light for a Wednesday morning. We should get to the studio with plenty of time to set things up.

I turn to Dax and say, "So, Dax. Tell me more about yourself."

"What more is there to know, Miss Abby?"

"Are you married?"

"No."

"Have you ever been married?"

"No."

"Any kids?"

"No. If I had kids, I would be married," he says shortly.

"Well, there are co-parents, you know," I say tentatively. *Am I being too nosy?* "Are my questions bothering you?"

"Not at all," he says, glancing at me. "I'm just a man that believes that if he has kids, he does his best to make his marriage work."

"Even if it's toxic?" I ask.

He thinks for a minute and says, "No, I guess not. If the relationship between the parents to stay married is harmful to the kids and all avenues to fix whatever is causing the issue or issues, have been exhausted and there are still problems? Then co-parenting would be the healthiest option."

"So, no kids and you've never been married. Are you seeing anyone?"

I see Dax's jaw muscles flex as he clenches his teeth. He lets out a breath and says, "No."

"Why not? You are a good-looking man and very nice. Well-mannered and you are very chivalrous. Any woman would be lucky to have you," I realize that maybe I'm now getting too personal. "I'm sorry, Dax. You don't have to answer that. It's really none of my business."

"As your driver, it's important that you get to know me. So, I don't mind answering these questions," he says smiling over at me. He laughs and says, "It's just been a long time since I've been asked any of this."

"Does Kallon not ask you anything personal?"

"Oh, he asks all the time, but my personal life never changes."

"Why is that?"

"Women don't tend to understand the demand my job has on my personal life. I don't have a lot of free time."

My face falls a little as that realization hits me.

"I guess you really don't," I say, sadly.

"Miss Abby, I love my job. Please don't look like that, like it's your fault I don't have someone special in my life. I choose this. I also believe that when the right woman comes into my life, she'll understand my job and realize that all my free time will be spent with her. However limited it might be and she'll be okay with it."

"Maybe someone that works at a job that demands a lot of her time as well, so she truly understands where you're coming from?" I ask, side eyeing him.

Dax's eyes squint and his brows furrow a little. He side-eyes me and says slowly with caution, "Yes, possibly."

"Would you ever consider dating someone with a kid?" I ask and I can't help the smile that spreads across my face.

Dax's features relax and he gets the biggest smile of

his own and he says, "Yes, I would."

"Good to know, good to know," I say, laughing a little. I'm about to say something else but I'm interrupted by my phone buzzing in my bag. I dig through it and find my phone.

New Text – Kallon

"It's Kallon," I say to Dax. I turn away from him, so he doesn't see me smiling like an idiot, and open the text.

Kallon: Good morning, Abby. Just wanted to say good luck on your second day. :-)
Me: Good morning to you too, Kallon, and thank you. :-) But aren't you up a little early?
Kallon: Maybe but only by 45 minutes.
Me: You're missing out on 45 minutes of precious sleep.
Kallon: I couldn't sleep any more. I kept waking up wondering if you were ok. How are you feeling?

My smile gets bigger. *Stop it... Stop it. He's only curios because he had to drag my drunk ass home last night.*

Me: I'm good. Midol took care of any after affects the wine had.

I bite my bottom lip and type out another quick text.

Me: Thanks again for last night. I'm sorry you had to see me like that. And I'm sorry you had to bring me home.
Kallon: I'm happy to hear that you don't have a headache or anything after the wine. But I was more curious about how you're doing with your breakup with Jason?
Me: I honestly haven't even thought about it. Whatever that means.
Kallon: I'm sure you have closer friends that you'd probably prefer to

talk to but know that I'm here for you too.

    Me: Thank you, I appreciate that.

    Kallon: Well, I need to go shower and get ready. I'll see you in about an hour.

    Me: See you.

I have to bite my bottom lip harder to keep from smiling as my mind strays to the thought of Kallon taking a shower. I physically shake my head and shut my eyes. I instantly start debating with myself in my head like there are two people inside there. *Nope. Don't go there. But… it's so easy to think about. How many times have we fantasized about- NO! He's our business partner now, we can't think of him like that anymore.*

With a little pout now on my face, I open my eyes and put my phone away. It's a good thing no one can hear my thoughts, they'd think I was crazy with the way I talk to myself. I lean my head back and make myself think about Jason, NOT Kallon. I'm only thinking of Kallon so that I don't have to think about Jason and how much it hurts that we've broken up. But does it hurt? My heart aches a little but it's not the brokenness I've read about in books or seen in movies.

I honestly haven't been around anyone who's personally gone through a breakup and had been totally devastated by it. Kayla has never gone through a breakup. She's marrying the one and only person she's ever dated. Betty went through her heartbreak years ago, long before we ever met. So, I never got to see firsthand how she handled it. We've talked about it, and she said it was hard, but it was the right thing for her and Maggie.

I feel like I should be a little bit more heart broken

over the fact that my relationship with my one and only boyfriend is over. But I just feel… numb. I guess that's what I feel. Numb and empty. And mad, mad that he's not taking ownership in his mistake, yet again.

When we broke up last year, after he'd told everyone in his office about how he was worried I was pregnant, after I had told him not to tell anyone until I'd gotten a home test and taken it. I was sure I was pregnant. I was five days late. When the test came back negative, I was still certain I was and that the test was wrong. I again, told Jason not to say anything to anyone, until I had managed to get in to see my doctor and have a blood test done to be sure. Only when that came back negative did I feel reassured that I wasn't. When I left the doctor's office and turned my phone back on, and all the notifications were coming in from his coworkers, that's when I found out he'd blabbed.

After I got home and waited for him to show up, I thought about why I was so relieved that I wasn't pregnant with a baby from the man I was in love with. I thought I wanted to have a family with Jason. I thought I wanted to marry him. I chalked it up to my ideal of being married first and then having a baby. I told myself I was relieved because the steps I wanted to take, hadn't been skipped. But I was so furious with Jason for telling his coworkers and he couldn't understand why I was so upset, he decided we needed a break. So, we took a break.

He was the one that called me up and said he was missing me and apologized for what he had done. He promised he'd do a better job at keeping my secrets from now on. I took his word for it. Looking back on the last year or so, I can see how we didn't really go back to how things were before the pregnancy scare. I didn't have any real secrets to tell him until recently and what did he do? Even after signing a damn gag order? He opened his mouth and told people.

I toss my phone into my bag and with a little more force than I mean to, I toss it to the floor. I stick my left foot under my right leg and cross my arms over my chest, fuming.

"Everything okay?" Dax asks.

"Yes," I say a little too hotly. "I mean, no. I don't know."

"Do you want to talk about it?"

"I guess it's only fair since I was asking you about your personal life," I say. "Jason broke up with me last night."

"Patty mentioned that last night."

"Did she?" I ask. "How did she know?"

"She said she figured it out because Jason left in a bad mood and—" Dax pauses and tightens his grip on the steering wheel.

"And what?"

"Patty said he'd called you a bad name."

"What?" I ask, shocked. "He said something to Patty? What did he say?"

Dax takes a deep calming breath and says, "She said he told her, 'Your sister is such a bitch.' Only Patty said, 'the b-word'."

I laugh a little because Patty has never cussed a day in her life. But then I'm fuming again.

"Right, I'm the bitch," I say, shaking my head. "I'm the bitch because I wouldn't fix his big mouth mistake."

"Miss Abby," Dax says seriously. "I'm sorry, but if I ever see him again, I don't know if I'll be able to hold my tongue.

No matter what happened, he should never call you names, especially to your family members."

"Oh, I agree," I say. "He broke the gag order and I wouldn't ask Kallon to waive the fine."

"Mr. Keller would have, if you'd have asked," Dax says, looking at me.

"Yes, Kallon said that, but I'm tired of fixing things for Jason. For enabling him to do stupid things and not have to deal with the consequences. He's 25, he needs to start acting like an adult and not a teenager anymore. Between me and his parents, I don't think he's ever been held accountable for anything in his life. I helped him out of the sticky situation by figuring out how to make what he did work. Or I'd help him figure out a plan B so that his mess up wasn't noticed or that he had a way to fix it before authorities or his boss found out. Most of the time, he'd go to his parents first but if they couldn't help him by literally paying for it, then he'd come to me."

"I'm sorry you're going through this," Dax says sincerely.

"I love him, but he needs to grow up. Maybe this will be his wakeup call," I say with a shrug.

I close my eyes and lean my head back against the seat again, I can feel my headache trying to come back. *I'll take some more Midol when we get to the studio. And no more wine on a work night.*

I let the van rock me to sleep. Sleeping in a vehicle always makes the time seem to speed by. The next thing I know, Dax is gently shaking my shoulder.

"Miss Abby, we're about to pull up to security," he says

as he slowly rolls up to the booth just like yesterday. He pulls his badge out of his wallet to show it to the security guard. "We never did stop to get your picture taken for your badge. We should make time to do that today before we leave."

"Oh shoot, yeah I definitely need to do that today," I say, palming my forehead. I reach down for my bag and pull it up onto my lap. I grab my phone out of it and enter a reminder, so I don't forget. I also see that it's 3:48am.

"Morning Stella," Dax says. I look up and see he's parked next to the security building.

"Morning Dax. Hi Abby," she says nodding at me.

"We didn't get a chance to get her badge yesterday," Dax says, nodding sideways at me. "We'll make sure to get it today though."

"No worries," she says waving us on. "It just makes it quicker for you guys to go on through."

"Thanks, Stella," Dax says.

"Yes, thanks Stella," I say, leaning towards the dash so I can see her better.

Dax pulls away and drives us around the buildings. It will take me a couple of more times coming here before I know my way around. All the buildings look the same. They just have big numbers on them to tell them apart. I remember our building is Studio 5.

Dax drives around what I figure is the front and he pulls next to the building like we had yesterday.

"Ready for day two?" he asks as he puts the van in park and pulls the keys out of the ignition.

"Ready or not, here we come," I say jokingly as we get out.

CHAPTER 15

The first thing I notice is that the construction workers had done amazing work at getting water ready for me. There is a hot and a cold outlet with restaurant quality water lines already hooked up to them. They even built in holders into the wall for the end of the hoses that I'll connect to the coffee brewers, so that they aren't hanging down on the ground. That was an unexpected, thoughtful, surprise.

Dax makes quick work of unloading the van while I get the tables set up. I have my headphones on, listening to my pump-up playlist. I've just put the last of the pastries into their display cases when Dax puts the last coffee brewer on to the table from the kitchen.

I pull my left headphone out and say, "That's it, right?"

"Yes, this is the last of it," he says. He reaches into his pocket and pulls out my van keys. "Would you like these back?"

"No, you can hang on to them. I won't be going anywhere."

"Would you like some help setting the rest of this up?" Dax asks, looking at the table that's pretty much all done.

"No, that's okay, I'm almost done. I just need to plug the coffee in and get them going. I've got the smoothie machines already filled and going. It's—" I look at my watch "—4:32 and everything else is set up. Having the display cases already here and not needing to bring them, saved a lot of time. Thank you so much for your help, Dax."

"No problem at all, Miss Abby," Dax says with a nod.

I'm just finishing hooking up the water hoses and turning them on, when I feel someone come up and stand right behind me. Big hands cover my eyes and I freeze.

"Guess who?" a male voice says trying to sound deeper than normal.

"Umm, I have no idea," I say honestly. It could be Kallon, but this would be weird of him to do, unless he's being playful.

"It's me," the male voice says as he turns me to face him. It's Chace Tanner.

"Oh, Mr. Tanner," I stammer out. I feel my face heating up because I'm standing so close to him.

"It's Chace, please," he says, winking at me.

"Ok, Chace," I say trying to smile but I feel so awkward standing this close, my face muscles aren't cooperating. I hurriedly stammer out, "Good morning."

"You really didn't know it was me?" he asks.

"No?" I say as a question.

"What kind of fan doesn't know the voice of her favorite actor?" he asks arrogantly.

"The kind where she's not really a fan," I hear coming from behind Chace. I recognize Kallon's voice immediately.

As Chace turns to look at Kallon, he relaxes his hands

enough that I step back, and put some space between us. The uneasy feeling I had in my gut instantly goes away as soon as the physical connection he had on me is broken. I breathe in a shaky breath but hurry and blow it out as I see Kallon walk around Chace.

"I think she's more of a fan of mine than yours, Keller," Chace snaps back. He turns back towards me and a look of surprise crosses his face when he sees that I'm no longer in his hands. He quickly lowers his hands that are still hanging in the open space between us.

"Well, she's my friend," Kallon says. "You'll save yourself a lot of issues if you keep your hands off of her."

"Ha! Your friend, sure," Chace says. "Does Tina know about your new friend?"

"Kallon and I are friends and only friends," I say in a rush. I leave out that we're business partners because I can tell that Chace would be one of those types of people to exploit his friends and co-workers. "There is no reason for Tina to be upset about us being friends."

"You keep telling yourself that, sweetheart," Chace says leaning in and winking at me.

"Chace!" Kallon bellows. "Stop being a dick."

"Boys, boys," Stephanie says as she walks up to us. "No need to stake a claim, Abby is already taken, remember?"

Chace says in a cocky tone, "That can change."

And Kallon says, "I'm not staking a claim."

I don't say anything, it's probably better for Chace to think I'm still taken. Even if he's arrogant enough to think he could have any sway in my personal affairs. The more he talks, the less I like him.

I look at my watch and it's 4:48am, finding an excuse to leave this delightful show that's embarrassing me, I say, "I'm going to go into the kitchen and make sure all my extra stuff is ready to be put out once things need refilled. The coffee will be ready in 10 minutes, the hot water for tea should be filled in 5. Thanks again for the water access, Stephanie."

I turn and walk away quickly, before she or the guys can say anything. When I walk past Dax, he raises his eyebrows, and then pats my shoulder as I go by. I don't acknowledge his gesture and go into the kitchen. I'm putting the leftover icing in the fridge when I feel a presence behind me. I turn and see Kallon leaning against the door frame.

"I'm sorry about that," he says. "I hope you don't think I was staking a claim or anything like that. I saw how uncomfortable you were with Chace touching you, so I thought I'd come over and help you. He can't comprehend that a woman wouldn't feel anything but grateful to have his attention on them, he wasn't reading your facial expressions at all."

"Was it that obvious?" I ask.

"To anyone who cares about other people's feelings? Yes," Kallon says. "Chace doesn't care about anything unless it's what he wants. Please be careful around him and let me know if he bothers you."

"I'll be okay, thank you though," I say as I shut the fridge door.

"Actors to the set in 5," we hear bellowed through what I can only assume is a megaphone.

"Are we good?" Kallon asks.

"Absolutely," I say, giving him a reassuring smile.

"Okay, good," he smiles back at me. "I better get out there. Use my room to rest."

"Thank you," I say.

I spend the next hour checking on the food and refilling everything that needs filled. Having access to water directly to the coffee makes keeping them filled a breeze. I just have to change out the coffee grounds and filters and it's ready for a new brew.

They started filming around 6am so the food and drinks don't need filled as much as before. I decide to take Kallon up on his offer and go to his room. I set my alarm for 7am, 8am, and 9am. I'd use the last hour to make sure everything was set out to be eaten so at 10 o'clock I could start cleaning up again.

I grab a pillow and blanket and get set up on the couch. It doesn't take long before I fall asleep. I wake up when my alarm goes off and hurry out to check on my set up. I have to fill everything up but luckily nothing is completely empty. I check the coffee and see the regular needs refilled already but the decaf is still a little more than halfway full. I take the lid off the regular coffee brewer and dump the grounds and filter in the trash. I go into the kitchen and grab a new filter and my coffee grounds. Once I'm finished, I walk back to Kallon's dressing room.

I must be exhausted because I'm asleep as soon as my head hits the pillow. I wake up to a familiar smell and when I open my eyes, I see Randy putting a coffee cup and pastry bag on the coffee table in front of the couch. I sit a little, which makes Randy jump.

"I'm so sorry for waking you, I meant to be quiet," Randy says with a sheepish look on his face.

"I didn't hear you, I smelt that," I say, smiling while I point to the goodies on the table. "It's from my shop, isn't it?"

"Yes," Randy smiles in response. "Mr. Keller said he noticed you hadn't eaten anything while you've been here. Dax said you hadn't had anything on the way over, so Mr. Keller asked me to pick you up something while I was at Rose Bud's. I asked Miss Betty what she recommended because Mr. Keller said you mentioned your order changes. Miss Betty said you'd probably need something with an extra shot, so she made you a Caramel macchiato, double espresso. She said it's your usual when you need a little extra pick me up. She also sent a cinnamon roll."

"Thank you," I say, sitting up all the way and grabbing the coffee. I take a sip and about moan. It's delicious and exactly what I need. *I'll have to talk to Kallon about him still sending Randy for an order.* I look up and ask, "Please tell me you got something for Dax and Trevor?"

"Miss Betty insisted on sending something for them, she knew you wouldn't want them left out," he smiles at me as he answers.

"She knows me too well," I laugh. "Well, thank you again."

"My pleasure," Randy nods at me and then turns to leave. He shuts the door behind him and I'm left in the room alone again.

I pick up my coffee and take a couple good, long drinks from it before I pick up the cinnamon roll and, while using the wrapper, I take a big bite. I hadn't realized how hungry I was but in four more big bites, it's all gone. I use the napkin that Randy had put down beside it and wipe my face. I pick up my coffee again and take a couple more drinks and grab my phone.

I see it's 7:48am so I decide to go check on my tables. I turn my 8am alarm off so it's not going off while on set and their recording. I would be horrified if it went off and they had to stop filming because my phone interrupted them.

When I get to my tables, I see that everything is again about halfway gone. I pull the rest of the pastries and fruit bowls out of the kitchen and refill all the containers for the last time. I'm guessing they're about ready for a break so hopefully they'll come finish everything, so I don't have leftovers again. This go around, I have to fill both coffee brewers. It doesn't take more than a couple of minutes before I've finished with both and I'm walking back to Kallon's room.

Not feeling as tired as I had earlier, whether it has to do with the double espresso that I all but inhaled or if the cat naps I just took really helped, or maybe the combination of the two, whatever it was, I'm actually feeling pretty good. I fold the blanket up that I was using and put it and the pillow away. I sit and grab my phone. I send Betty a quick text.

Me: You are a life saver. Thank you so much for the coffee and cinnamon roll. I needed it.

I don't have to wait long before I see the three little dots signifying that Betty is replying.

Betty: Don't thank me, I just made 'em. Sounds like Kallon has been keeping an eye on you.

I shake my head as I type out my response, a small smile spreads across my lips.

Me: Yeah, it was really thoughtful of him to do that. And thanks, also, for sending something for Dax and Trevor.
Betty: I did what I thought you would do. :-)
Me: How are things going there?
Betty: Pretty good. It's slowed down. The Trio left not too long ago. How's everything going there?
Me: Good, so far. I'm hoping things go just as good as yesterday and cleanup won't take long.
Betty: That's good. Have you met anymore actors?

I'm about to tell her about Chace Tanner and Amelia Ray, but I hear someone entering the code in the door and I watch as it opens and Kallon walks in. I quickly add a reply to Betty.

Me: I'll tell you about them when I get back.

"Hi," Kallon says as he walks into his dressing room.

"Hi," I say back. Feeling awkward for some reason, I start to stand but Kallon waves at me to sit back down. He walks over to an armchair and sits down.

"How's your second morning going?" he asks.

"So far, so good, I think," I answer with a shrug. I pick up my coffee and finish the last of it. I hold up the cup and tip it towards him. "This has helped a ton. Thank you."

"It's the least I can do," he says as he takes a sip from his own cup.

"How's the movie?" I ask.

"Pretty good," he says with a small laugh and his face turns a little bit pink. "We're filming the trampoline scene."

I don't have to think too hard to remember what scene in the book he's talking about.

"Oh... oh my," I say, feeling my own face warming up. "How's that going?"

"Interesting," he says. "We aren't actually... doing... it... which probably makes it a little bit more difficult to portray that particular scene. I don't have a lot of experience on trampolines in the normal sense, so it's taking a couple takes to get it just right. We're taking a break now so that we can come back not feeling so... awkward, I guess is the word I'm looking for."

"Who's the actress playing Lainey?" I ask. When I read, 'Along Came You', I didn't necessarily have an actress in mind, but I could definitely visualize what the character looked like from the authors writing. I hope they chose someone who will look like her, like they did Kallon for Dalton.

"Amy Shakons," Kallon says.

"Oh, she's perfect!" I exclaim. "I've always thought that she and Emma Watson could be sisters. Are they related?"

"No, but they do look similar enough to be sisters," Kallon says with a smile.

"Is it difficult to act out those scenes?" I ask before I know what I'm saying. My face instantly goes red. "I'm sorry, you don't have to answer that."

Kallon laughs and puts his cup down. He leans back in his chair and kind of stretches his back out while leaning his head back. He situates himself back into his chair and says, "We are professionals but sometimes, if the writing is really good and we're really into a scene, it can become... uncomfortable. No one ever takes offense. It's kind of hard —no pun intended—" he laughs "—not to react to someone if we're both into the roles we're playing. In my experiences, nothing has ever happened... too severely, and breaks are taken if things do start to get too intense. But like I said, it's all done in a very professional, civilized way. That way no one gets embarrassed and lines don't get crossed."

"I could never be an actor. You guys do such a good job. You make it all seem so believable on screen, that I've heard of fans becoming so obsessed with an onscreen couple that when they find out they aren't actually together in real life, they almost grieve the loss of the couple they thought were meant to be together. I bet that can be an intense and crazy experience, I don't know how you do it," I say. I stop myself from asking if he was on a break because the scene was causing him to get carried away or if it was just difficult to maneuver on a trampoline. I remember thinking when I read the book, that having sex on a trampoline would take quite a bit of rhythm and finesse.

"Keeping a firm grip on reality helps," Kallon laughs.

"I'm sure it does," I laugh with him.

KNOCKKNOCK**KNOCK**

Kallon and I both look at the door after we hear the soft

knocking and then he stands and walks over to it. He opens it and I hear Dax's voice.

"If Miss Rose is awake and would like me to, I can take her to get her picture taken for her ID badge," Dax whispers.

As Kallon steps back and lets Dax into the dressing room, he says, "She's awake."

I stand before Dax is all the way into the room. He looks like he's about to say something, guessing it's what he had told Kallon, I cut him off and say, "Yes, please, Dax. That would be great. Maybe by the time we're done, it'll be time to clean up."

Dax nods at me and steps out of the room. I pick up my coffee cup off the table and toss it in the garbage can next to the door.

"Thanks again, for the coffee and cinnamon roll," I say to Kallon as I pass him at the door.

He touches my shoulder as I walk by and says, "No problem at all."

"See you later," I say as I walk out into the hall where Dax is standing. I laugh a little and add, "Enjoy your break."

Kallon tilts his head down, eyes closed, and a quiet laugh comes out, "Thanks and see you in a few."

As I follow alongside Dax down the hall, I hear the door shut softly behind us. I glance back and see that Kallon didn't step out with us. *He must really need a break.* I laugh quietly to myself. Or so I thought.

"What's so funny?" Dax asks.

"Nothing," I say but I giggle again. To change the subject so I don't have to explain why I think it's funny Kallon needs a break, I ask Dax, "So what have you been up to?"

"Reading," he says.

Intrigued, I ask, "What have you been reading?"

"The book that this new movie is based off of," he says, looking down at me as if he's expecting me to laugh at him.

"I didn't peg you for a romance book kind of guy," I say. I don't laugh but I do smile up at him.

"I read all kinds of books. If Mr. Keller's acting in a movie that's based off of one, I like to read it, so I know what the movie is about."

"I do that if I see a new movie coming out and find out there's a book. Sometimes I don't find out until after I watch the movie but either way, I usually end up watching and reading both."

"Which do you prefer?" Dax asks as we turn down a different hallway that I haven't been down yet.

"I don't have a preference. I take each as a separate form of entertainment. The movie version is just based off the book and I go into it not expecting it to be done exactly as the book was written. Some of the thing's authors write about are easier to imagine but difficult to portray onscreen. I can see why screen writers have to change things. Also, some books would take way longer than a normal one and a half to two-hour movie if they did it exactly as the author wrote it. Some things must be cut, while some things are added to get the gist of what was written in the book across to the audience. I can see how some people get upset if they expect the movie to be done precisely like the book but that's because they go into it wanting it to be the book coming alive on screen."

"I don't think I've ever heard anyone explain it like you

just did. Everyone I know that has a deep love of books, have strong feelings about the way a book has been conveyed into a movie. I'll have to remind them that it's just a movie based off the book, not the book coming to life, like you said," Dax says with a big smile.

"So, you're reading 'Along Came You', where are you in the story?" I ask.

"She just got to Montana," he says.

"Oh, the fun has just begun," I say laughing. "What other books have you read? What's your favorite genre?"

"I don't really have a favorite genre. I'll read anything. Mr. Keller lets me borrow any of his books he's finished reading. He'll recommend one occasionally, if it's one he especially liked. What about you?"

"I'll read just about anything, except horror. I don't do horror. I don't even watch horror movies. My imagination takes hold, and it takes something already scary and makes it terrifying. No thanks, I like my sleep."

Dax laughs and says, "I'm not a big horror fan either. I'm not one who enjoys blood and gore. I got enough of that while in the Military."

"I can see how you'd want to steer clear of that genre," I say, patting his big arm.

We come to double doors that say HR and Dax opens the door for me. I walk in with him right behind me. A grandmotherly type of woman is sitting behind a big L shaped desk with a large computer to the left of her. She looks up from a book she's reading and smiles at us.

"Good morning," she says.

"Good morning, Mrs. Clearing. This is Abbigail Rose,

she's the new breakfast caterer for the set of 'Along Came You'. She needs to get her picture taken for her ID badge. Miss Rose, this is Deloris Clearing, head of Human Resources," Dax says nodding towards Mrs. Clearing.

"Good morning, Mrs. Clearing," I say, reaching my hand out for her to shake.

"Good morning, Miss Rose, I was wondering when I'd be seeing you," she shakes me hand and smiles sweetly at me. She stands and walks around the desk and while she motions towards a door to my right, she says, "Follow me and I'll get your picture taken."

"I'll wait out here," Dax says, taking a seat in one of the three chairs lining the wall.

Mrs. Clearing opens the door and waves me inside the room. As soon as I step inside, a light turns on automatically. It's a small room with a blue sheet hung up on the wall and a tripod with a fancy looking camera on top of it.

"If you'll just stand on the big X on the floor, that would be wonderful," Mrs. Clearing says. I walk over and stand on it, turning to face her behind the camera. "Now, look at the camera and smile. I'll take a couple just in case you blink."

"Okay," I state. I smile and hold still, trying not to blink.

"Relax a little honey, you look like you're grimacing a little," she says kindly.

"Oh, sorry," I say. I try to think of something that'll bring a true smile to my face. I think of my family.

"That's better," she says. As I'm thinking of my parents, my thoughts turn to Jason. I feel my smile slip a little, so I refocus. My thoughts transfer to Kallon and how kind he's been through everything the last couple of days. Mrs. Clearing cheers and says, "That's it! Hold that thought!"

The flash goes off a couple of times before she steps away. She fiddles with something on the camera and then pushes the button. She motions her hand towards the door, so I walk over to it. I open it and she walks out ahead of me.

"All set?" Dax asks.

"Yes," Mrs. Clearing says. "I'm certain one of those last pictures will do the trick. When do you leave?"

"I'll be cleaned up and packed by 10:30," I say.

"Perfect, I'll have your ID badge to you before then. Have a great rest of your morning," she says as she sits back down at her desk but instead of picking her book back up, she turns to her computer. I see that my pictures are on her screen. The camera must have Wi-Fi capabilities for them to be instantly transferred to her computer. *Cool!*

The walk back is a quite one. It's nice that I don't feel the need to fill the silence with small talk. Dax has a comforting essence about him. And I know he's not a huge fan of small talk either.

"Would you like to go back to Mr. Keller's dressing room or back to the set?" Dax asks, finally breaking the amiable silence.

I look at my watch and see that it's almost 9 o'clock.

"Back to the set would be great," I say. "Thanks for taking me to HR. I would have gotten lost along the way. I'm not great with directions in doors."

"My pleasure," he says with a nod.

Dax leads us down another hallway that I'm pretty

sure we didn't come down, but it leads us to the set but on the other side of where I've come in from. I can already see that most of the food is already gone. I hurry over and start packing the empty display cases into the kitchen. All that is left are a handful of scones and a couple fruit bowls. The smoothies are tapped out also.

I move the scones onto a plate and set them aside. With Dax's help, yet again, we have everything brought into the kitchen so I can wash it all. I put my earbuds in before I start washing things. I'm washing everything by hand, not wanting to wait for the dishwasher to finish its cycle to put it all away, so I have the drying rack already full. I'm about to pause my washing so I can dry some things to make room for the rest of the dishes, but then Dax is here with a towel, grabbing a display case tray and starts to dry it.

"You don't have to do that," I say as I pull an earbud out from my ear.

"I don't mind," he says as he grabs the clear case and dries it off.

"Well, thank you," I say hip bumping him. Although, my hip is well below his.

"You're welcome," he says with a chuckle and continues to dry things.

I take my other earbud out and put them both in my pocket. I only listen to my music if I'm alone, I don't want to be rude to the person I'm working with. Betty and I will turn on the radio if we want to listen to music while we're baking.

With Dax's help, clean up happens quickly. He wipes the tables down as I fold up the last tablecloth. I look at my watch and see it's 9:45am. I'm placing the tablecloths on top of things in the tote I'll be taking back with us when Kallon walks up to us.

"Looks like another successful morning," he says with a huge grin. It does something funny to my stomach.

STOP IT! There is nothing funny going on with your stomach. I internally chastise myself.

To Kallon, I say, "Yeah, it looks like everyone enjoyed everything again. I might change up the scones tomorrow. Maybe do a chocolate chip one with a chocolate drizzle and a poppyseed with a lemon glaze. I don't want people to get bored too quickly."

"I don't think anyone could possibly get bored of your food, even if you served the same thing for the duration of the movie. But I do admit, those new scones sound amazing," he says as his smile gets bigger.

I smile back at him. I appreciate him thinking no one could get bored but after a couple days of eating the same thing, someone is bound to get tired of it. If I make sure to switch things up, even if it's just changing the scones out every other day, that will help keep it mixed up. If people start requesting something specific or if I notice something isn't getting eaten as much as the previous, I'll make adjustments.

"Do you think I need to stay any later or since everything is clean and put away, I can go?" I ask Kallon.

"You can go. If Stephanie has anything she needs to talk to you about, she'll call you," Kallon answers.

"Okay, I'd really like to get back and take a quick nap before going to Rose's," I reply.

"Miss Rose?" I hear my name being called. I turn

around and see Mrs. Clearing walking towards me. "I have your ID badge ready for you."

"Thank you, Mrs. Clearing," I say as she hands it to me. I turn it over and look at the picture. I'm shocked at what I see. She nods to us all, turns around, and walks back the way she came.

"That's the best ID badge I've ever seen," Kallon says, sounding a little shocked himself. I look up at him and he says, "I'm serious. That's a really good picture of you."

My face heats at his complement so I look back down at my picture. It really is a good picture of me. I don't think I've ever had a picture of myself turn out this good. My smile doesn't look forced. The smile reaches all the way up to my eyes. It's one of the most genuine smiles I've ever seen on my face, at least one that's been captured by a camera.

"Kallon, they need you on set," a man says as he walks up to us.

"Thanks Braydon," Kallon says. Braydon smiles and winks at me before he turns around and walks back towards the set. Kallon looks after Braydon for a second, shakes his head and then turns to me. He gently takes my left upper arm in his right hand, causing that same feeling to bubble in my stomach. I ignore it to listen to what he's saying to me. "I'd like to come to Rose's tonight and look over some things with you, if that's alright?"

"Kallon, you don't have to ask to come to the restaurant. You have your code to unlock the doors. If you come before we open, it works on both the front and back door. If you don't want to be seen coming in the front once we have opened, you can come in through the back like you did last night."

"I know, I just," he pauses for a second. "I just don't want you to feel like I'm imposing or over stepping."

"We've been over this," I say as I reach out with my right hand and touch his hand that's still holding my arm. I smile at him and continue, but in a lowered voice so only Dax can hear us, "You are co-owner. You have just as much right to be there as I do. You won't be over stepping."

Kallon doesn't say anything for a minute, he just stares into my eyes. He nods at me and finally says, "Okay. I'll see you later then."

I put my hand that is touching his hand, quickly into my pocket. He squeezes my arm gently before pulling his hand away. I instantly miss the heat of his touch.

Co-owner. You said it yourself. Co-owner. Business partners. Pull. Yourself. Together.

"See you," I say. He nods at Dax and then walks quickly over to the set. They had just called his name again through the megaphone.

"Ready?" Dax asks me. I look at him and see that he's holding the tote of stuff that I wanted to take back to Rose Bud's.

"Yes, thank you," I say. I reach for the tote, but he pulls it away.

"I've got this," he says nodding for me to start walking. I give him a mock glare before I lead us out of the building.

I open the back of the van and wait for him to put the tote in before I shut the door. I head to my designated door and go to get in, but Dax reaches in and grabs the handle before I can.

I don't try to argue with him because I know what he'll say, I just smile up at him and say, "Thank you."

He nods his head and then shuts the door gently after I've situated myself into the seat. I've got my seatbelt on before he gets to his door. He hops in and buckles himself in before he pulls us away from the building. I try to keep my eyes open on the way back home, but I can't keep them open for very long. Before I know it, Dax is gently shaking me awake.

"Miss Abby, we're back," he says quietly.

"Just Abby," I groan out. "I let you open the door for me without complaining, please just call me Abby."

I hear him chuckle as he opens his door and gets out. He doesn't respond to my request. I grab my bag that was on the floorboard and open my door. I look at my watch before I get out, it's 10:55am. I walk to the back of the van and realize something.

"Shoot, I need to fill this up with gas," I say, hitting the van hard enough to make a noise but not so hard that it's obnoxious.

"I already did that," Dax says as he pulls the tote out of the back.

"What?" I ask, stopping in my tracks.

He answers as he nudges the back doors of the van shut with his shoulder and then gives a little shrug, "You were out cold and I didn't want to wake you. I stopped at the same gas station as yesterday."

"How much was it? I have cash inside," I say, as I walk over to the back door to my bakery and punch in the code.

"Don't worry about it."

"You either tell me so I can pay you back or you get free coffee and baked goods until further notice," I say, holding the door open for him.

Dax glares at me as he walks inside but he doesn't offer up a price of how much it cost for the gas. I know how much it cost to fill up yesterday but if he doesn't tell me, I'm keeping to my word of free stuff.

I walk in and see that Betty has the dishes all finished. I walk to the doors leading out front and poke my head through.

"We're back," I say. I see her at the register, she's counting the till. She just nods in response, not wanting to lose track of where she's at in her counting.

I turn and walk back into the kitchen and help Dax unload the things in the tote. I grab the tablecloths and toss them into the washer. I turn to start putting the other stuff away, but Dax is already doing it. It's amazing how fast he's picked up on where stuff goes.

"How was it?" Betty asks as she walks through the doors, she's zipping up the bank bag as she comes in.

"Great," I say. "Everything was devoured again."

"That's amazing," she says with a grin.

"I think I want to switch up the scones. How do you think a chocolate chip with a chocolate drizzle and a poppyseed with a lemon glaze would work?" I ask her.

"Oh, those sound good! We haven't made those in a while," she says excitedly.

"That's what I was thinking," I smile back at her. I yawn and shake my head.

"You go take a nap, I've got this," she says as she comes

towards me and pushes me towards the door to my stairs.

"No, I'll be fine. I'll help you," I say but I yawn again.

"Abby, I've got this. Maggie is finishing out front and can help me," she says, pushing me from behind.

"I'll help too," Dax says, surprising us both so that we turn our heads and stare at him. "If you'd like the help."

"I... I... Yeah, that'd... be great," Betty stammers out. She starts pushing me again and says, "See, I've got all the help I need. Go lie down for an hour or so. You need rest or you're going to make yourself sick."

"I just feel like I'm leaving all the hard work for you to do," I say as I reach the door.

"Please don't feel like that. We've talked about this. I need to earn my raise that you've given me," she says as she walks back towards the work area.

"You more than earn it," I say just as another yawn comes out. I laugh and say, "Fine, I'll go lie down. I'm hoping once this first week is over, my body will adjust to my new schedule so I'm not so tired."

"And if it doesn't, I'm here," she says as she starts pulling out the flour and sugar.

"Thank you," I say. "To both of you."

Dax and Betty just nod and wave me away. I see Dax walk over to the sink and start to wash his hands before I shut the door behind me and head up to my apartment. As I walk up the stairs, I yawn once again and realize just how much I need this quick nap.

CHAPTER 16

BEEPBEEP**BEEP**

BEEPBEEP**BEEP**

I roll over in bed and look at my phone. My alarm is going off, it's 8am. I yawn and stretch, thankful it's finally Sunday. To say that the rest of the week went by in a blur would be an understatement. My nap Wednesday lasted an hour before I got up and went downstairs to help with some prep work. I got to Rose's around 1. Work there went great, we were pretty busy right at opening, but at 9pm when it slowed down a little, Royce kicked me out and told me to go home and go to bed. It took some convincing, but I finally gave in and went home and fell right to sleep. Thursday and Friday went about the same. Saturday, my first day off from the catering business allowed me to sleep in a couple more hours but I was still down in the bakery at 4am.

My new routine had become me waking up at 1am, prepping the smoothies and fruit bowls. Betty and Dax would show up around 2:30 and help package up the baked goods that Betty and Maggie prepped the day before and then they'd help me load the van. I'd work the movie set in the mornings and get home around 11. Betty wouldn't let me help with anything at Rose Bud's, she had actually marched me upstairs Thursday to make sure I laid down. So, from about 11 or a little after until noon, I'd nap. I really started to wonder if I could make 2 o'clock work getting to Rose's since Bridget was doing such a great job at inventory. I needed to relinquish some duties to her, I know I don't need to double check her bottle counts.

Stephanie told me that I was bringing enough food to last the five hours and if it was gone before 9:30, 10 o'clock, then I could start cleaning up and not to worry about leaving early. She said it was a sign that everyone was loving the food. They also really enjoyed when I switched up the scones. The new chocolate chip and poppy seed were a hit. They all liked that I started to alternate the days I brought them and the cinnamon sugar and blueberry. As well as making them the healthy way.

So, I'd get home around 11 and take an hour nap. I'd wake up and change for Rose's, and then I'd work there from about 1pm until about 9pm. Royce reassured me that he and the crew could handle the rest of the night and they didn't disappoint. I'd come in, in the afternoons, and the place would look amazing.

Betty made me promise that I'd sleep in this morning. She was worried I'd make myself sick if I didn't get in some decent sleep. I only had to worry about Rose Bud's today and tomorrow because Rose's is closed. Today is another day off from the movie set. Betty was trying to get me to take the whole day off but finally agreed on 9 o'clock being the earliest she'd 'allow' me to step foot into my bakery. I'm so lucky to have her.

I stretch and roll out of bed. Sleeping for close to twelve hours straight feels good. I hadn't realized how much I needed to sleep in longer stretches than the four or five hours I had been getting. But feeling how good I feel right now, it was definitely needed.

I walk to the bathroom and take my watch off. I turn on the water in my shower, I step in once I'd stripped out of my pajamas, and take a leisurely shower, something I haven't been able to do all week. It was usually a quick, 'wash the hair and all the stinky parts, and shave really quick' type of shower. This morning, I'm letting the warm water work its magic to loosen my tight shoulder and neck muscles. The only down fall to sleeping for so long, sleeping like a log, was that I now have a slight kink in my neck.

Without the rush of my mornings, I have a minute to think as well. Which allows me to think about Jason. I close my eyes as I rinse my conditioned hair and feel the sadness I had been pushing down since our breakup, it's almost been a week already. With how busy I've been, I haven't allowed myself to think about him or how it makes me feel, and now that I have a minute to think, all the feelings are hitting hard.

My relaxing shower now ruined, I step out after I've rinsed everything off and wrap myself in a big fluffy towel and wrap my hair into my hair towel. I make my way out to my room, sit on my bed, and let myself cry some more.

RING-RINGRING-RING**

RING-RINGRING-RING**

Hiccupping I reach for my phone and see that it's Kallon calling. Taking in some deep breaths to calm myself, I swipe right to answer.

"Hel-lo," I say. I pull the phone away and clear my throat. I put the phone back to my ear and try again. "Hello?"

"*Abby?*" Kallon asks.

"Yeah, it's me," I say. I put my hand over my mouth, I can feel another sob about to pour out of me.

"*What's the matter?*" I hear Kallon ask. I hear him say something away from the phone, but I can't understand what he said.

"Nothing," I croak out.

"*Abby,*" he pleads. "*I can tell you've been crying, or you still are, what's the matter?*"

"It's nothing," I sniff out. "I've just had a minute to think about Jason and me. I've been so busy that I haven't had time to think and now that I have, I'm just sad. I'll be okay."

It's quiet on Kallon's side for a minute and then he says, "*I'm sorry you're hurting, Abby. How can I help?*"

"I just need to sit with it for a minute. I wasn't meaning to ignore it... my feelings, I mean, but I guess I was and that's never good. But I'll be okey," I say, wiping my nose with one of the tissues out of the box next to my bed.

"*Are you sure I can't do anything?*" he asks.

"No, but thank you though," I stammer out before I start crying again. "Hey... I'm going to... get off here."

"*Abby...*" I can hear the concern in Kallon's voice.

"Really, Kallon... I'll... be fine," I say. "Bye."

I don't wait for him to say anything or get to why he was calling, I just click the end button and put my phone down on my bed. I lay back and fling my arms over my face and let myself feel for a minute.

◆ ◆ ◆

After what feels like hours, and my last tear is drying on my cheek, I sit up and walk back into my bathroom. I look in the mirror and sigh.

"So much for my shower," I say to myself. My eyes are puffy and red, along with the rest of my face.

I look at the clock on the shelf to the right of my mirror and see that it's 9:30. My cryfest lasted only 45 minutes. I turn on the cold water and grab a washcloth. I get it soaking wet and hold it to my face, focusing on my eyes. After a couple of minutes, I pull it away and look back at myself. I'm not as red but I'm still puffy.

"This will have to do," I say as I put the washcloth down and pull my now semi-dry hair out of my towel. I reach over and grab my watch, putting it on quickly.

I pump a dime size amount of conditioner into my hand out of the travel size pump I keep next to the sink and add a little conditioner to my hair before I brush it out. My salon lady told me once that it's good for hair to add a little to the ends after a shower, it helps keep them hydrated. I've been doing it ever since and she and I have noticed a huge difference. I don't have nearly the number of split ends anymore.

Grabbing my brush, I run it through my hair, it glides through easily. I do a quick side braid and end with a messy bun just behind my left ear. I put some moisturizer on my face and put on some mascara and eyeliner. It's amazing what just those two products can do to my eyes. I don't look as puffy, but I can definitely tell I've been crying. Hopefully Betty won't notice or maybe the puffiness will have gone down by the time I get downstairs.

I hang up my hair towel and walk back into my room. I pull out a pair of white underwear, a white bra, and socks out of my underwear drawer and a pair of blue jeans out of another drawer. Walking to my bed, I take my towel off, placing it on my bed and put on my undies, bra, and socks. Once I've finished with that, I walk to my closet and pull out a Rose Bud's t-shirt. I pull it over my head and then put on my jeans.

Once I'm dressed, I put my phone in my back pocket, and then walk out of my room and make my way to my living room. I sit on the couch where I'd sat last night and took my shoes off. I put them back on and then go into the kitchen. My bag is sitting on the counter where I left it and decide to leave it there. I'm not going anywhere today so there's no need to bring it down to the bakery.

I head to the back door and take the stairs slowly. I'm giving my face some time to simmer down on the puffiness before Betty sees me. If she makes me talk to her about why I've been crying, it'll make me cry all over again. I usually need a good couple of hours after a good cryfest before I can talk about what happened or the tears will spill over again.

I get down to the kitchen and see that Betty has once

again already cleaned up. I walk out into the front part of the bakery and see Betty talking to a young couple at one of the tables by the front windows. I go over and make myself a coffee. I look around the seating area and see an older man sitting by himself reading a paper. There are four, maybe mid to late twenty-year-old girls, sitting at different tables, but all are reading books. One college looking guy has his laptop out, with books and papers spread across one of our bigger tables. I smile and finish my coffee.

When I envisioned my bakery, this is what I had hoped for. For a place people could come to for some peace and quiet. To hangout for a morning date, read a paper and enjoy a good cup of coffee, or to check out new books and eat some yummy baked goods while doing it. I had also hoped some college students would find me and use me as a study sanctuary. The library is a great place to go but it's always nice to have another quiet place you know you can go to, to get some last-minute studying in before final exams. Or more time to look over a paper meant to be turned in, in just a couple of days. At least, I'd always wished I could find a place other than the school library or my bedroom to study in.

I take a sip of my coffee, causing my eyes to close. *It's so good!* I take another sip just as the front door opens and I hear the tinkling of the bell ring. I turn and open my eyes and freeze. Kallon and Dax are standing just inside the door. I see Betty turn to greet the newcomers, but she also freezes. We both hadn't planned on seeing them today.

Kallon slides his sunglasses off his face and a soft smile spreads across his lips as he starts to walk towards me. Betty walks up beside Dax and says something to him, but he just shrugs, head nods towards Kallon, and mumbles something to Betty. I see her smile and laugh a little, and then she shakes her head before walking up to the counter.

"Morning, Abby," Betty says with a sweet smile as she gets closer.

"Morning," I say, eyeing her. She's acting like she knows somethings off. I glance over at the side of the display case that's so shiny it can almost be mistaken for a mirror. My eyes don't look very puffy anymore and all the redness is gone.

"Morning," Kallon says.

"Morning," Dax says also.

"Morning," Betty and I say at the same time.

"Can I get something for you guys?" Betty asks, walking over to stand beside me.

"We're good," Kallon says.

"So, what can we do for you?" I ask with confusion in my tone.

"Well," Kallon starts to say. He looks at Betty and smiles and then back at me. "See, Tina and I were going to go to a baseball game today but she's still in L.A. So, I have an extra ticket and I was wondering if you'd like to come with me?"

"Like, Major League baseball?" I ask, shock taking place of confusion.

"Yes, the Mets," Kallon answers with a small laugh. "They're playing the Cardinals at 1:40 today."

"What about Dax?" I ask. Then I turn to Dax and ask him directly, "Don't you want to go?"

"I already have a ticket," Dax replies quickly.

I eye him for a minute before I look at Betty and her

eyes look a little too wide with surprise.

"I can't. It's my first day where I'm not needed anywhere but here," I say.

"You deserve a day off. Off from everything," Betty says, grabbing my upper arm and turning me towards her. She reaches up with her other hand and grabs my other arm. "Abby, please. When was the last time you took an actual day off? Not the weekend you took to go to Kayla's, but an actual day off?"

"I... I... It was..." I say, trying to think.

"Exactly, you haven't taken a day just for you. Granted, it's a baseball game but you'll still have fun," Betty says with a laugh and wink at Kallon.

"You don't like baseball?" Kallon asks. "We can do something else."

"I like baseball," I say. "I just have never been to a game before."

"It'll be fun, you'll love it," Betty says as she turns me and half pushes me towards Kallon.

"Wait," I say, leaning back into her. "You said it doesn't start until 1:40, I can work for a couple of hours, can't I?"

"No," Betty says as Kallon replies with his own response.

"Well, actually..." he pauses while I glare at Betty. When I look at him, he continues with, "I was planning on getting there around noon to talk to the owner and some of his business associates."

"Oh," I say. "What about you, Betty? You haven't had a day off in a long time either."

"I get afternoons off, I'm fine," she says matter-of-factly.

"That's not having a day off," I say.

She answers with a shrug.

Shaking my head at her, I look at my watch and see it's just after 10am. I look up at Kallon and ask, "How long does it take to get to the ball field?"

"I always plan on 45 minutes," Kallon says. He turns to Dax and asks, "Does that sound about right?"

"With the extra traffic that'll be in the area for the game and the construction going on, it'll take at least 45 minutes. I'd probably say an hour," Dax replies. He shrugs at me when I shoot him a glare.

"So, we should leave around 11?" I ask.

"Does that mean you'll go?" Kallon asks excitedly.

I look at Betty and say, "Are you sure, Betty? I've been gone so much. I feel guilty leaving you here again. Especially when I don't have to be anywhere else. And I slept in this morning."

"Absolutely!" Betty says equally as excited as Kallon. "Like I said, you deserve an actual day off. I've got this."

I look at her skeptically for a second, not that I think she is lying about being able to handle the bakery or that she really doesn't want me to go, but because I just can't wrap my head around taking the day off.

I turn to Kallon and say, "Okay, fine. Yes, I'll go."

"Yes!" he exclaims as he gives me a high-five. I can't help but smile as I high-five him back. "Okay, go change. Or don't. You can wear you Rose Bud's shirt."

"No, I'll change," I say. "I don't have anything baseball though."

"That's okay," Kallon says. He waves at himself and says, "I'm just wearing this."

I look him up and down and admire the way he looks. He's wearing blue jeans that fit him nicely and a heathered gray t-shirt that stretches over his pecks and almost looks too small for his biceps. I look back up at him and see he's grinning ear to ear.

"Fine," I sigh. "I'll run up and try to find something."

I grab a scone and then my coffee. I stop in the kitchen and write down in my notebook what I took. Betty and Maggie write their stuff down too. It's so I can keep track of where product is going. I told Betty it was one of the perks of working here, free food and drinks as long as you're working. But now, I think I'll tell Betty she and Maggie get free food for life. I owe her so much.

I hurry up to my room and fumble around in my closet. I pull down a white t-shirt. It's supposed to be really warm today, the white will hopefully keep me cool. I go to my dresser and pull out a pair of jean shorts. I trade out my work shoes for sandals that I haven't worn since I bought them.

Looking at my feet in my sandals, I realize I haven't painted my toes in a really long time. I grab my box of nail polish and pull out the fast-drying colors and choose a hot pink. I hurriedly paint my toes, hoping it truly is fast drying. *How embarrassing would it be to have fresh paint on my sandals?* I ask myself. I test it one more time before I stand up, to make sure it's dry. I look at myself in the mirror and check my makeup.

"It's not a date, what does it matter?" I ask myself. I answer with, "It matters because you're going out in public with Kallon Keller. Just as friends, but still, you shouldn't look like a wreck."

I add a little more eyeliner and mascara, just enough to touch up what I did before going downstairs. I grab my little hoop earrings and put them on.

"This isn't a date," I say to myself out loud again. "Just as friends, no, business partners spending the day together."

I instantly think of Jason and think of how he'd feel if he ran into Kallon and me out together. Even though I know it's not a date, Jason would instantly think it was one. I shake my head. I should not be worrying about how he'd respond to me being at a baseball game with another man. I should only feel angry with Jason and the way he acted. For blaming me for his mistake but we were together for so long. And I miss him. Taking the time to think on our relationship, I can really see how much we had started to drift apart.

I can't even remember the last time Jason called or texted just to see how I was doing. We haven't been out on a date in months. I know part of it is my fault for working at both the restaurant and bakery, but I always made time to take him lunch on Monday's. That is until he had told me that the office was going to start providing lunch for staff so I wouldn't need to stop by anymore. I had asked if I could still stop by to see him, and he said it would just be a waste of my time because it would be a working lunch and he wouldn't have time to visit.

I was hurt at first, but then decided to focus on what I could control. I started focusing on the restaurant and bakery's menus. Seeing what could be tweaked or done away with because it wasn't a popular item. There wasn't much to change at Rose's but there were a few ideas I had added to Rose Bud's.

As I'm walking out of my bedroom, I hear a knock at the back door. I walk through the kitchen and open the door to see Maggie, holding a package.

"This just came for you. Mom asked me to bring it up," she says with a smile.

"Thank you," I say as I take the package she's holding out for me. I open it and see a black leather folder. I pull it out and see the boudoir photos I had done two months ago. I had decided to get them done as a surprise for Jason for our upcoming anniversary that's supposed to be next month.

I shut the folder and put it on my kitchen counter. I grab my bag and nod to Maggie to head back down the stairs. I start breaking down the box my folder came in to toss it in the recycling downstairs.

As we're walking down the stairs, Maggie asks, "So, you're going to a baseball game with Mr. Keller?"

"Yes, as friends," I reply.

"I'm glad he's taking you."

"Why is that?" I ask. She's quiet and seems to not want to answer. So, I nudge her and ask again, "Why do you say that?"

She shrugs one shoulder, stops, looks up at me with a little sadness in her eyes, and says, "You haven't had any fun lately. You're either running from the restaurant to here to sleep for a couple hours, just to run to the movie set, and then back to here and back to Rose's. The last time you took time off, the only time I can remember you ever taking time off, was to go be with your friend when she got engaged. You just seem like you've been putting in a lot of time for other people and not putting in anytime for yourself. Mom told me Jason broke up with you, I just have to say he's an asshole for doing that."

"Maggie!" I say but can't help the small laugh the escapes. "You shouldn't talk like that."

"It's the truth though," she says with a double shoulder shrug. She starts to walk down the stairs.

"Maybe but your mom will wash your mouth out with soap if she hears you cussing," I say tugging on her ponytail since she's a couple steps ahead of me.

She looks over her shoulder with big eyes and says, "Please don't tell her."

I laugh and don't respond as we reach the bottom of the stairs. She opens the door and steps though into the kitchen. I can hear shouting from out front.

"What in the world?" I ask, looking at Maggie and then the door leading to the front. Maggie looks just as confused as I do and shrugs. I point to the chair by my desk and say, "Stay here."

I hurry through the doors and see Jason standing in front of Dax, who's standing just slightly in front of Kallon. Betty is standing behind the register with her hands on the counter, she looks like she's about to start yelling herself.

"I want to see..." Jason is screaming in Dax's face but stops when he sees me. He exclaims, "Abby!"

"What is going on?" I ask. I walk out from behind the counter, around Dax, and Kallon, and walk by Jason. I wave at the customers now looking up from their work or leisurely reading. I say to them, "I'm sorry for the disturbance folks."

I turn and glare at Jason and point towards the back. He gives Dax and Kallon a triumphant smile and literally pushes past them. Fuming, I say to Dax and Kallon, "I'm so sorry. I'll take care of this and then we can go."

"Miss Rose, should you be alone with him?" Dax asks.

"I'll be fine," I say, I pat his arm as I walk past him.

"We'll be right here if you need us," Kallon says to me but he's staring at Jason's back as he storms into the kitchen.

"Thank you but it'll be alright," I say to him, touching his arm as well, I get zapped by static electricity. I turn to Betty as I rub my hands together and say, "Offer the customers a free scone or another coffee, please."

She nods and grabs a pad of paper to write down what they would like. I hurry into the back and see Maggie shooting daggers with her eyes at Jason.

"Hey, Mags, will you go help your mom?" I ask her.

"Sure," she says. She doesn't stop glaring at Jason until she walks through the doors.

"Even the kid hates me?" Jason asks with a small chuckle. I just stare at him as I cross my arms across my chest. He lets out a breath and his shoulders sag in what looks like defeat, "I'm sorry. I know I fucked up."

I just raise my eyebrows at him, but I don't say anything. It's quiet, almost to the point of feeling awkward.

"Please, babe, I said I was sorry," he groans out.

"And—" I start to say. I can feel my anger rising. I take a deep breath to calm down and then continue "—and you've said you were sorry multiple times before now. How do I know you actually mean it this time? Saying sorry doesn't mean anything unless you change your behavior."

"I am... I will," he says, walking towards me.

I put my hand up to stop him from getting any closer and shake my head, luckily he stops.

"Please, babe," he begs.

"Please what?" I ask.

"Let's try again," he pleads.

"I don't know, Jason," I say. I can feel my defenses starting to fall. "I'll have to think about it."

"We've been together for so long, we can't let this little fight end it all for us," he says.

"You said some really hurtful things. I just can't forget that," I say.

"You know how I get when I drink whiskey," he says with a half-smile.

"Are you serious?" I ask. "You're blaming the alcohol?"

"I wouldn't have said it if I hadn't been drinking," he says with a shrug.

I shake my head. "You're still not taking responsibility for anything. Blaming the alcohol for how you ended things, for what you said to me... That's not showing me you're willing to change."

"I've apologized," he says. "That's more than what you've done."

"What do you mean by that?" I ask.

"You haven't apologized," he states matter-of-factly.

"What do I have to apologize for?" I ask, shocked.

"For not having my back," he says it like I should already know.

I throw my hands in the air and then cover my face. I say through my hands, "You need to go."

"What? Why?" he asks. I hear him walking towards me and I have enough time to pull my hands from my face before he grabs on to my wrists and holds them tightly.

"Jason, let go of me," I say sternly, trying to pull free from his grip.

"Tell me why I have to leave?" he asks. He looks at me, really looks at me. He looks down at what I'm wearing, down to my sandals, and then back up at my face and asks, "Are you going somewhere?"

"I am," I say. I pull on my hands again and say, "Let go."

He looks back at the doors leading to the front and then back down at me, "You're going somewhere with him?"

"Yes," I say, a little louder than a whisper. I clear my throat. I have nothing to be ashamed about. I say with a stronger voice, "His girlfriend couldn't make the baseball game he's going to, so he asked if I wanted to go."

"So, you'll take a day off for him but not me?" he asks, throwing my hands down and away from us. My shoulders protest at the angle they rotate as he throws them.

"When was the last time you ASKED me to do anything?" I ask.

Jason glares at me and says, "You are MY girlfriend."

He takes a quick step to me and kisses me roughly on the mouth. I push him away and he stumbles back. But he recovers quickly and goes to stalk back to me.

"Jason, stop!" I holler at him, my hands thrust out towards him. He stops immediately but the doors from the front fly open and Dax is standing there, looking so mad he might rip the doors off their hinges. Kallon is trying to push beside him, but Dax is holding him back, barely.

"Abby?" Dax says my name as a question but he's staring at Jason.

"I'm fine," I say as I wipe my mouth off, since I didn't reciprocate the kiss and open my mouth, Jason was left tonguing my lips and face. Dax takes a step inside which allows Kallon the chance to step in. He comes to my side but puts himself in front of me. "Jason was just leaving."

"I meant what I said," Jason says, seething as he stars back at Dax. "You're my girlfriend."

Not waiting for my reply, Jason storms out of the kitchen.

"What was that about?" Betty says from the doorway behind Dax.

"Jason being Jason," I state.

"Are you okay?" Kallon asks, turning to face me. He bends down so our eyes are level with each other.

"Yes," I say. "Honest. He didn't hurt me."

"We heard you yell at him to stop," Betty says with her hand over her heart.

"He kissed me and when I pushed him away, he acted like he was going to try again," I say. Seeing the look on Kallon's face, I add quickly, "He stopped when I told him to."

"Do you still want to go to the baseball game?" Kallon asks. "We could do something else if you aren't up for being around people."

I laugh and say, "I'm fine, really. The baseball game sounds great and plus, I'm not going to be the reason you miss your meeting with the owner."

"I can reschedule the meeting," he states.

"No, we'll go," I say, patting his arm. Again, the static

electricity zaps me. I pull my hand away and say, "I'm good, I promise."

Kallon looks at me for a second with squinty eyes but then smiles and says, "Okay. Let's go then."

Kallon motions for me to go first, he follows behind. Out of the corner of my eye, I see Dax motion for Betty to go ahead of him. I turn and see her step to the side and stand behind the register.

"Have fun!" Betty says as she waves.

"Thank you, Betty," I say. She just waves me on and then goes over to Maggie who is standing over by the coffee maker. I wave to them both and turn to walk out the door.

Dax hustles around us and reaches for the door and opens it. I look around and as I'm sliding into the back seat, I ask, "Where's Trevor?"

"I was hoping you'd say yes to going to the game with me, so I sent him off to drive Randy around to get some errands done for me," Kallon says as he slides in beside me.

"And Tina's still in L.A.?" I ask.

"Yes, she said her modeling gig ran over their projected time but..." he pauses and looks out the window.

"But...?" I ask. He looks at me with what looks like sadness in his eyes. "Oh, never mind. You don't have to finish your sentence."

"I don't think she's coming back," he says.

"What? Why do you say that?"

"She's put off coming back for a while now. I could understand the photo shoot taking a week longer, but it's been a month," he says. "When we talked yesterday, we FaceTimed... She was at the beach with some of her friends."

"Oh," I say. "She'd be crazy not to come back for you."

"It was only a matter of time," Kallon says with defeat. "I'm not the typical actor. I don't like parties. Well, that's not true. I do like a good party but not the crazy and wild kind. I like having a few friends over for a BBQ. Swimming in the pool, playing games, just hanging out. Tina knew all this, but I have a feeling she thought she could change or persuade me to turn into who she wanted me to be. I won't. I'd rather be in the company of a handful of great friends, than to be surrounded by a bunch of fake people."

"I can understand that. I'm the same way," I say.

"Yeah?" Kallon asks. He smiles an encouraging smile and says, "I feel a story behind that statement."

I laugh and say, "I have more stories than a noncelebrity should have. Jason stopped inviting me to his work parties because I 'didn't act the way the other girlfriends did.' I started to be stand offish. I would sit in a corner, sipping my one drink, counting the minutes before we could go home. Half the time, it was well after 3am. I saw things there that I was not impressed with, not just the excessive drinking but drug taking as well. The last party I went to with him, was at his friend, Deven's house. I needed a break from the loud music and the drunk people. I went to find a bathroom. I walked into what I thought was a bathroom, but it turned out to be a bedroom. There was an orgy going on, more legs and other body parts than I could count. I walked out, embarrassed, and ran to the bathroom. The door was open so I didn't think anyone was in there but there was a guy in there snorting something off the counter. He smiled at me and asked if I wanted a hit. I didn't know what he meant, but at the same time, I knew what he meant. I turned around and left. I found Jason and told him I wanted to go home but he was too busy taking shots. He 'needed to stay to build rapport with his coworkers.' This was after he'd worked for the company for over a year. I figured the rapport was already built with the number of parties we had gone to, and he went to more without me. I went outside and called a taxi. They picked me up 20 minutes later. Jason didn't come out once to see if I was alright. He didn't call me until two days later, wondering how I got home. He couldn't remember me asking to go or that I left."

"Wow," Kallon says. "That sounds very similar to parties I've been dragged to."

"I'm more like you," I say with a small laugh. "I'd rather sit around a patio, smelling the burgers on the BBQ, playing games, or just visiting. Jumping in the pool to cool off just to go back to sitting around hanging out. When you have your close, good friends, you can relax, and the fun just happens naturally. When you're trying to impress people, that's just stressful and then things can be taken too far."

"You are good people," Kallon says, wrapping his arm around me and giving me a quick hug. That zap of electricity zaps us and he pulls away quickly. He says, "Sorry, I don't know why we keep getting zapped."

I hear Dax clear his throat quietly from upfront and I look at the rearview mirror. He has a smirk on his face but doesn't say anything, he just winks at me. I look from him to Kallon, but Kallon just shoots Dax a look that says, 'be quiet'. I look out the window to hopefully get out of this now awkward situation.

"So, can I ask you something?" Kallon says with a sheepish tone.

"Sure," I say.

"It's none of my business so if you don't want to answer, you don't have to," he says quickly.

"What's your question?" I ask with a laugh.

"Are you going to get back together with Jason?"

I want to say, 'you're right, that's none of your business' but he was just open with me about him and Tina, I can be open with him as well. I can see Kallon being a good friend.

"I... don't know," I say. "I'm not happy with how he was acting or what he said to me. He apologized but I don't believe he meant it. He'd have to really show me that he was changing for me to give him another chance."

"So, you would take him back?" Kallon asks.

"We have history," I say quietly.

"Sometimes having history isn't enough," Kallon says. "I'm only saying this as your friend and because in the short time that I've known you and him, he hasn't shown me anything that proves he cares about you. You as a person. You as his girlfriend. Or you as his future wife."

"Oh, I am not his future wife," I say quickly. "We haven't revisited that since... last year."

"When you guys took a break?" Kallon asks.

"Yeah," I say. I decide to tell him the whole story. "I had told you we'd broken up only once in the 8 years we've been together. It was over him telling a secret to his coworkers. I thought I was pregnant. He told me he only told them because he was worried and stressed out. It ended up that I wasn't pregnant but my trust in him was shaken. We talked about where we wanted our relationship to go, we both decided a break was needed."

"I'm sorry he broke your trust," Kallon says. He seems like he's going to say more, but I can see he changes his mind and says, "Do you not want to marry him?"

I shrug, "I'm not sure what I want anymore. I know that I'm too busy with the restaurant, bakery, and catering job, that I don't have much time to think of anything else. My best-friend's wedding is in a year and if the movie is still going, I'll have to bring Betty to the set, so that she can take over that while I'm gone. Which means we'll have to close Rose Bud's while I'm gone, at least over the weekend. It's not a big deal, closing for a wedding, especially my best-friend's wedding, is important. I'll keep the bakery closed that Sunday also and give her a full day off. Lord knows she needs one. I might even consider closing on Sunday's and Monday's until the catering job is finished. I feel like I'm—" I stop talking and look over at Kallon, my face going red. "—I'm sorry. I'm rambling."

Kallon smiles a kind smile and says, "Don't apologize for talking out your thoughts. That's what I'm here for. Do you think your customer's will understand if you close Sunday's and Monday's?"

"My Trio and their wives might be the only ones that are flustered by it, but they are like grandparents to me, so they'll understand why I'm doing it. And maybe if I promise them some to go orders special for them on those days, they won't mind as much."

"You really care about your customer's, don't you?"

Kallon asks.

"Absolutely! If I didn't, my business would fail."

"Sir, we're pulling up," Dax says.

I look around and see that we've arrived at the baseball stadium.

"Wow, that didn't take long," I say. I look at my watch and see it's actually been an hour since we left my bakery.

Dax drives slowly and then drives around to the back where a security booth is maned by a big security guard. Dax pulls up and rolls his window down.

"Mr. Kallon Keller and Miss Abbigail Rose are here to see Mr. Cowen," Dax says.

The security guard pulls out a clipboard and looks at it. He nods to Dax, and says, "Follow the lane, the next guard will point you to your parking spot."

He pushes a button, and the poles stopping us from going forward, sink into the ground. Dax gives a quick nod and then we're driving forward.

We drive straight and then the lane dips down like it's going under the stadium. We come around a corner and a security guard is ahead of us, about 100 feet, shinning a flashlight at us and then a spot in front of him. Dax maneuvers the car into the parking spot. He jumps out and opens Kallon's door. I reach into my bag and pull out all the cash I have in my wallet and my driver's license, and my sunglasses, and then put my bag on the floor. The security guard steps forward and opens my door.

"Thank you," I say as I step out. He just nods and then walks away and goes towards Kallon. I put my money and ID into my front pocket and put my phone in one of my back pockets. I slide my sunglasses on my head.

"If you'll follow me, I'll get you to the elevator. Mr. Cowen will be waiting for you once it stops," the guard says.

"Thank you," Kallon says.

The guard starts walking, Kallon follows. I step up next to him and walk with him. The underground parking garage is kind of creepy. The little lights don't give a ton of light to see from. The flashlight the guard has shines brighter than that lights do.

"You okay?" Kallon asks.

"I don't like the dark," I say, glancing around quickly.

Kallon takes my hand and says, "You're safe. Between the three of us guys, nothing will get to you."

I squeeze his hand, my terror taking over. I try to take a calming breath when I say, "I... I know."

Dax steps up beside me and his body heat radiates towards me. Being sandwiched between these two men, I feel a little bit better.

A bang behind us has me squealing and jumping ahead of us, I almost land on the security guards back.

"What was that?" I shout.

"Don't worry," the security guard says, I can tell he's trying not to laugh. "The other guards are just setting out parking cones for more guests and the ball players."

I let Kallon pull me back to walk between him and Dax. Luckily, the elevator is in sight, and it's bathed in light. I pick up my pace and Kallon chuckles beside me. I bypass the guard and practically run to the elevator.

"She doesn't trust you?" the guard says.

"She doesn't trust the dark," Kallon says, which is true.

For the short amount of time that I've known Kallon, I do trust him more than some people I've known my whole life. But I don't trust the dark even more.

The guard steps up and passes his badge over a pad and the elevator door opens immediately. He reaches in, passes his badge over another pad, and then pushes the button for the 6th floor.

The guard motions for us to step inside and once we're all in, he says, "Have a great day and Go Mets."

As the door closes, I let out a deep breath, letting it calm me down.

CHAPTER 17

As we stand in the elevator, Dax is standing in front of us, in his protective stance. Kallon puts his hand on my back and gently rubs up and down for a second. The motion sends tingly feelings straight to my stomach.

"I'm sorry about the darkness, I should have planned for that," Kallon says nonchalantly.

"I'm surprised you remember me saying anything about being afraid of the dark," I say, trying to not let him see how much his touch is doing to me. *He's your business partner Abbigail! Pull it together!*

"You told me about it when you were telling me how your grandparents renovated your basement in your building. I also noticed you have extra lights behind your bakery, where your van is parked. You didn't have to tell me you were afraid of the dark, I could just tell."

"I didn't think anyone had noticed I'd added those flood lights," I say. If anyone did, they never said anything. "I try not to tell people how much it bothers me. Jason... he thought it was funny and took every opportunity to scare me."

"I don't think it's funny to use someone's phobia against them. It can cause unnecessary trauma and make the phobia even worse," Kallon says as puts his arm around my shoulders and pulls me into a gentle hug.

Without time to say anything else, the elevator stops, and the door opens. A man in a fancy looking suit is standing in front of us, beaming. Dax moves off to the side so that Kallon and I are in full view. Kallon doesn't move his arm completely off of me but slides it back to my upper back. He urges me to step out of the elevator and he steps along with me. Dax coming up to my other side. The doors to the elevator shut behind us.

"Mr. Keller," the man in front of us says. He puts his hand out in front of him, towards Kallon and says, "It's nice to finally meet you!"

"It's nice to meet you too, Mr. Cowen," Kallon says, shaking his hand. He lets Mr. Cowen's hand go and turns to me and says, "Let me introduce you to my good friend, Abbigail Rose. Abby, this is Mr. Cowen, the owner of the Mets."

Mr. Cowen extends his hand to me with a smile and says, "It's nice to meet you as well, Miss Rose, I've heard a lot about you."

"Oh, thank you, it's nice to meet you too," I say as I reach my hand out to him. *Kallon talked to him about me?* I think to myself as Mr. Cowen kisses the top of my hand softly and lets my hand go. I pull it back and resist the urge to wipe it off on my leg. It's not that I feel like he's being a creep, I've just never liked having my hands kissed before.

"And this is Dax Wilson," Kallon adds. "My head of

security."

"Mr. Wilson, a pleasure," Mr. Cowen says as he shakes Dax's hand. He turns to Kallon and says, "I do have to say that his services won't be needed as my security is top notch here."

"I appreciate that, but he'll still be around," Kallon says. I notice he looks at me quickly and then back at Mr. Cowen.

"No problem at all. I'll get him a security pass from one of my guys, so they know he's to come and go as needed and to do what he feels necessary," Mr. Cowen says.

Do they think something is going to happen? I ask myself. *We're just at a baseball game. Could something seriously wrong happen here?* I don't get a chance to ask my internal questions before Mr. Cowen turns and motions us into his huge box office.

"We have a lunch spread set up, please help yourself," Mr. Cowen says. He steps next to Kallon and adds, "My associates are all here, you can see them at the other end of the room. If you'd like to get a plate of food and a drink and meet us down there, we can start our meeting."

"I can wait for food and a drink, I'll be down there in a second," Kallon says.

Mr. Cowen nods at him, slightly bows his head at me, and then turns and walks away. Kallon turns to me and says, "Help yourself to the food. Are you going to be okay for a few? The meeting shouldn't last very long."

"Go ahead, I'll be fine," I say. I pat Dax on the arm and add, "I've got big brother here to keep me company."

Dax chuckles, which makes Kallon smile hugely.

"Okay, I'll be back in a few," Kallon says, he reaches his

hand up and squeezes my upper arm gently and then walks after Mr. Cowen.

"Alright, big brother Dax," I say teasingly. "Let's go check out the food situation. I'm starving."

"Big brother Dax?" Dax asks.

"If you don't like that, I could call you babysitter Dax, is that better?" I tease.

"What does that mean?" he asks completely confused.

"Don't play dumb, I know Kallon wants you to keep an eye on me. So, you're either a big brother or a babysitter, which is it?"

"I don't know what you're talking about," Dax says unconvincingly.

"Mmmmmhmmm… I'm going to go with big brother. Even though babysitter is more accurate because you are getting paid to watch me. But I know you aren't ridiculous enough to try to put me in time out if I do something I shouldn't. You would tell Kallon though, and that's definitely big brother territory."

Dax just shakes his head and laughs, "You're funny when you're nervous."

I look at him shocked. I was nervous but how did he know. I start to ask him, "How—"

He interrupts and says, "You tend to ramble and your eyes haven't stopped scanning the room since Kallon stepped away. I assure you, you're safe."

"I'm not scared of anything. I just feel out of place up here," I say. We'd gotten to the food table which is pushed up against the wall of windows that look down on the baseball field.

I look over the food and see all the types of food really rich people serve. Food they think other rich people would enjoy. There's the really fancy stuff like caviar, pate de foie gras, and raw oysters on the half shell. There's a very colorful veggie platter, some of the veggies I can't imagine being good eaten uncooked, in fact I know they aren't good uncooked because I've tried them. There's a meat and cheese platter, all the expensive type though. A big platter of shrimp cocktail. A plate of truffles, another plate of fish, cod and smoked salmon. Little fruit platters scattered around the table. And then a platter of sardines with crackers and green olives.

I look up at Dax and see his face is mirroring mine. It's a very disappointed look.

"See anything you like?" I ask him.

He looks down at me and then at the table of food, "Not really. You?"

"No, I was hoping for a good ol' fashion hotdog," I say sadly.

Dax looks around the room and then grabs my elbow. He turns me slightly and starts to pull me towards the opposite side of the room of where Kallon and the other men are talking.

"Where are we going?" I ask Dax, slightly surprised.

"To get a hotdog," Dax says matter-of-factly.

We come to two doors where a security guard is standing. He puts his hand out and stops us.

"I'm Dax Wilson," he says as he pulls out his wallet. I notice he has some kind of badge like a policeman would have, along with his ID.

"I've got Dax Wilson here—" he says after he pushes an

earpiece, he's quiet for a second, listening "—Copy that. Wait here," he says to us.

He opens the door on the left and steps inside, the door shutting quickly behind him. We don't have to wait long before the door is opening and he steps back out. I glance behind him and see it's a security office. There are three other guards in there sitting in front of a wall of screens.

"Turn these back in when you leave for the day," he says. He hands Dax a pass on a lanyard, just like he has around his own neck. And then he has something small in his hand. "The earpiece will allow you to hear everything we say and it allows you to reach out to us. Just hold the little button to talk and then let go when you're finished. They work like Walkie-Talkies. The pass has the ability to open any door you need to get through but be advised each door that isn't for the common person will have a security officer by it, so you'll need to explain why you're needing to go through, even with having the pass around your neck. Will you be enjoying the game up here or do you have seats?"

"We have seats," Dax says. He then looks down at me and says, "Unless Miss Rose would prefer to watch up here."

"No! Our seats will be great," I say quickly.

"May I see your tickets then?" the guard asks.

Dax pulls out his phone and swipes through a couple of things and then he shows it to the guard.

"Oh okay, those are easily enough to find. They're right behind our dugout. If you're wanting to head down there now, you can go out this door and take the stairs all the way down, it'll stop at the lower level. You just step out, turn left. If you'd like to hit the bathroom or concessions before going to your seats, hang a right as soon as you are down from the stairs and out of the door," the guard swipes his pass by the pad to the right of the door and opens it for us to head down the stairs.

"Thank you," I say. Dax just nods.

"Enjoy your day and go Mets," the guard says. I'm starting to wonder if they're supposed to say 'Go Mets' every time they're done talking to someone.

Dax steps over to the door but motions for me to go first. I smile and nod one more time at the security guard before I step past him. We start walking down the stairs when we hear the door shut behind us.

"Will Kallon mind that we're leaving?" I ask.

"He told me to make sure you're comfortable and having a good time. If he knew how uneasy you were, he'd be upset if I made you stay up there. Plus, they didn't have any hotdogs and you're starving," he says with a smile.

I bump him with my shoulder but don't say anything else. We continue the walk down in silence. When we finally get to the bottom, Dax tries to open the door, but it's locked. He swipes the pass across a similar pad as the one from upstairs and we hear a click of a lock. Dax opens the door and we walk out. He puts the pass around his neck and then puts the earpiece in his ear.

"Do you want to go find our seats first and then get food or would you rather go get food first?" Dax asks.

I look around and see that a lot of people have already shown up. I glance out into the little bit of the concession area that I can see and see that it's already packed.

"Let's go find our seats."

"Lead the way," Dax says, waving me to the left.

I put my sunglass on and start walking down the steps, taking in all the seats and people. We have to wait a couple minutes while a large family— about 20 people wearing matching shirts that say something about Switzer's Family Reunion— find their seats. It doesn't take us long before we've gotten to the Mets' dugout.

"What seats are ours?" I ask him.

"Section 114, row 1," he says, after he pulls out his phone and checks. I follow the little numbers painted on the steps all the way to the bottom, directly behind the dugout. Dax points to some seats and says, "These are ours, pick which ever one you want to sit in."

I pick one and sit, Dax folds himself into one beside me and looks around. I look around as well and see the seats far behind us are filling up. Dax pulls out his phone and taps away on it. After a minute, he puts it away into his front pants pocket. I look out on the field and see both teams are warming up. I tilt to the side and pull my phone out of my pocket and look to see it's 12:32pm. The game should start in a little more than an hour.

"Would you like me to go get you something to eat?" Dax asks, looking around.

"Why don't we wait and see if the hotdog guys start making their rounds? If they don't in a few minutes, we can go get something. From what I could see, the lines looked really long for concessions," I answer.

"I don't mind waiting in line. You could stay here and enjoy yourself."

"I'll be okay for a few more minutes, promise."

We sit silently looking around, taking in the sights and sounds as the excited crowd starts to fill the stadium. I see several dads with their kids, happily pointing and getting situated in their seats. I see couples getting to their seats and putting on their baseball team fanwear. I'm watching a group of guys about my age painting their bare chest with paint to spell 'Go Mets', when I hear a familiar voice behind us.

"That seat taken?"

We turn and look and see Kallon coming down the steps. He's wearing sunglasses now and a Mets baseball cap. From a distance he wouldn't be recognizable but from this close, you can totally tell it's him.

I smile up at him and say, "Well I was saving it for someone, but I guess you can sit here instead."

"Gee, thanks," he says in mock disappointment.

Dax stands up and lets Kallon sit in his seat. He moves and walks up the steps away from us.

"Where's he going?" I ask, watching him leave.

"He likes to check things out," Kallon says. "He'll be back."

"Oh," I say, turning back around. "Hey, how'd you know we were done here?"

"Dax texted me that you guys found the seats. Weren't a fan of up there?" he gestures with his right thumb back behind us.

"Mmmm, no, I'm sorry. I felt out of place," I answer honestly.

"Don't apologize for that. I'm glad you guys left and came out here. After we were done talking business, they just wanted to keep talking about random stuff. When I got Dax's text, it was the best opportunity for me to leave," he says with a laugh.

I tap the bill of his hat with my finger and ask, "What's with the disguise?"

"Makes being able to watch the game a little easier. Luckily, Mr. Cowen had a couple extra lying around. Here, I got one for you too."

He holds up a hat he has in his hand. I hadn't noticed it at first. Well, honestly, I hadn't looked away from his face to notice anything else. It's black with a blue 'N' and 'Y' that are outlined in orange.

"May I?" he asks, motioning to put it on my head.

"Sure."

He turns in his seat and gently puts it on my head. He softly pushes the little hairs around my ears behind them and then resituates my hat.

He taps the bill of my hate and says, "Perfect."

I smile and then shape the bill so it's more rounded. I laugh and say, "Now it is."

"A girl who knows how to wear a hat? I like it," he says with a laugh.

I laugh and nudge him with my shoulder when my stomach growls. Thankfully it's gotten loud enough in here that Kallon didn't hear it. I'm about to say something to him about us going to go get something to eat when I hear from behind us, a guy yelling, "Hotdogs! Get your hotdogs!"

"Ohhh," I say, looking behind us.

Kallon looks at me and then back to where I'm looking. He then jumps up and raises his hand at the guy and hollers, "Over here!"

I watch as the hotdog guy comes down the steps and smiles at us when he gets to our row. I see he has a nametag that says, 'Walter'.

"How many?" he asks.

Kallon looks at me and I raise my index finger. Even though I know I could eat two, I want to save room for a stadium beer. Kallon eyes me and then turns to the hotdog guy.

"We'll take eight," Kallon says.

"You go it," Walter says with a large grin. "That'll be fifty-six dollars."

I internally grimace at the price but then hurriedly reach into my pocket to give some cash to Kallon, but he completely ignores me. He pulls his wallet out and hands the guy some cash.

"Keep the change," Kallon says as Walter hands him the hotdogs and some condiment packets.

"Thanks, man," Walter says happily.

"Hey, do you know if there will be drinks coming out soon?" Kallon asks. *I love this man!* I think to myself and then amend quickly. *As a friend! Love him as a friend.*

"They're starting to make their rounds. What are you looking for? Beer or soda?" Walter asks.

Kallon looks at me and raises an eyebrow. I lean around him and say to Walter with a smile, "Both but maybe a beer first."

"My kind of girl," Walter says with a wink. Kallon coughs one short, deep cough, which makes the smile on Walter's face disappear. He clears his throat nervously and says, "I'll send him your way."

"Thank you," I say. Walter nods and walks away. Kallon hands me two hotdogs. I say in protest but as kindly as possible, "Thank you so much, but ummm, I just wanted one."

"Well, if you don't finish the second one, I'll eat it. You know like a good big brother would," Dax says with a bark of a laugh from behind us.

Kallon and I turn and see him coming down the steps. He walks behind us and with one easy step, steps over the seats and then sits beside me.

"Big brother?" Kallon asks curiously.

Dax leans forward and says, "It's a long story but it's better than the alternative."

"Which is?" Kallon asks, now really intrigued.

"Babysitter," I say matter-of-factly.

Kallon laughs and says as he lifts his sunglasses to rest on his hat, "Do I want to know?"

"I'm sure if you think about it for a second, you'll figure it out," I say teasingly.

"No hints?" he asks.

"I don't think you'll need any," I laugh.

"Hmmm," Kallon says. He pretends to be thinking hard but reaches across me and hands Dax three hotdogs and some condiments.

"Thanks," Dax says.

"Condiments?" Kallon asks me.

"Yes please. Mustard, ketchup, and relish please," I reply.

"No onions?" Kallon asks, holding up a little packet of prepackaged onions.

"Oh, I didn't know they came in these little packets too. Are they any good?" I ask.

"Surprisingly, yes," Kallon says.

"Sure, I'll take one," I say. I turn to Dax and watch what he puts on his hotdog. I don't know if he's serious about eating part of my hotdog if I can't finish it, so I don't want to put everything on it if he doesn't like it all. But my worries are put to ease as I watch as he puts everything on his hotdogs.

I unwrap one of my hotdogs and open the little condiment packets and starts dumping the content onto my dog. I save half the onion packet to use on the second hotdog if I decide I'm hungry enough to eat it.

"Cheers," I say as I pick up my hotdog and tip it in Kallon and then Dax's direction. They laugh and do the same. I open my mouth and take a big bite. My mother would be horrified by the lack of manners I'm displaying right now but I'm too hungry to care. I can't help mumbling, with my mouthful and using my hand to cover it so I'm not being completely rude, "Mmmm... mmmy gerd. This is so good."

I glance over at Kallon and see he's frozen with his hotdog an inch away from his mouth, which is hanging open. He's got a weird look in his eyes as he looks at my hand over my mouth. I turn my head, so I'm looking straight at him and that jolts him out of his stare because he clears his throat and finishes putting the hotdog in his mouth and takes a bite.

I hurry and finish chewing and swallow. I say, "Sorry about that, that was rude of me."

Kallon's face turns a little red for some reason, he swallows his food, and says, "You are totally fine—" he clears his throat "—I didn't think you were rude at all."

I'm about to ask him what that look was for when I hear the beer gal calling out from behind us.

"Cold beer! Get your cold beer here!"

I look behind us and see the gal halfway down our section.

"Will you hold these for me?" Kallon asks as he puts his glasses back on, holding out his hotdogs towards me.

"Sure," I say, taking them quickly.

Kallon then stands and waves the girl over. She looks him up and down and smiles. I laugh internally. Even with his sunglasses and hat disguise he's still very, very good looking.

"How many, handsome?" she asks. Her name badge says, 'Lucy'.

Kallon looks down at me and asks, "Abby?"

"Just one for now, thanks," I say. The girl's smile faulters a second when he said my name, but I smile back at her kindly. Hopefully conveying it's okay for her to smile at Kallon, I have no claim on him.

"We'll take two," Kallon says.

"That'll be thirty-one dollars," Lucy says as she grabs one of the two beers. I try to get cash out of my pocket without dumping our hotdogs off my lap, but Kallon is already handing her some from his wallet again.

"Keep the change," he says to her as he hands me the first beer.

"Thank you," she says just as happily as Walter the hotdog guy.

She hands him the second beer and then turns and

starts back up the steps. Calling out to see if anyone else is in need of a beer. Kallon turns and sits down, taking a sip of his beer.

"What about Dax?" I ask belatedly.

"I don't drink," Dax says.

"At all?" I ask.

"No," he says. "I've never really liked it. The taste or the way it makes me feel."

"Well now I feel bad," I say.

"Don't be silly. Enjoy the beer. I'll get a drink when the soda guy comes around," he says with a laugh.

"Okay," I say, still feeling guilty for drinking when he doesn't.

"I can take those back, if you'd like?" Kallon says, drawing my attention away from Dax. Kallon's pointing to his hotdogs in my lap.

"Oh yeah, here," I say, scooping them up and handing them to him. "Did you not eat after your meeting?"

"No, I don't really like any of the food they had. Did you guys try anything?" he asks.

"No, we wanted a hotdog," I say laughing.

"What do you think of them?" he asks as he takes a bite. I watch as some ketchup and mustard smears on the middle of his top lip. I subconsciously lick my lip when Kallon's tongue pokes out to lick it off.

I shake myself and answer him, "They're delicious."

He laughs and takes a sip of his beer. I pick mine up from my cupholder and take a sip also. It's good but it's definitely not worth the fifteen dollars. I take another sip anyways.

"What do you think of the beer?" Kallon asks.

"It's good," I say and take a big gulp, but I can't avoid the grimace that crosses my face.

"Not as good as your wine, though?" Kallon asks, teasing me.

"The only thing better, and I mean a little better, than the wine I like is a vodka cranberry," I laugh. "But I only drink those when I don't have to work the next day."

"So hardly ever?" Dax comments from beside me.

"Yup," I laugh and nudge him. I take another big pull of beer and then put it down. I can feel it going straight to my blood stream already. *Grr, I'm such a light weight!* I take a bite of my hotdog and chew it fast. Taking another bite quickly, hoping it'll help with the affects the beer is already having on me. I laugh and shake my head.

"What's so funny?" Kallon asks. He's taking a drink of his beer now. He's got a little foam on his upper lip this time. I'm silently memorized as I watch him lick it off and then he wipes his mouth with his hand. Luckily, I ignored the urge to lick my lip this time.

"Nothing," I say, looking down at my hotdog and taking another bite.

"No, tell me, please. I want to know what you find funny," Kallon says, elbowing me gently.

"I was just laughing at how the beer has already started to take effect on me," I shake my head and look down at my cup. "I still have three-quarters to go and I'm already feeling it."

"Well, what did you have to eat today?" Kallon asks.

"A scone and my coffee," I say.

"That's hardly anything," Kallon says, easing my embarrassment. He then asks, "What did you have for dinner last night?"

Crap, what did I have last night?

"Ummm... some garlic toast?" I say uncertain.

"If you don't eat something decent and get some decent sleep, you're going to make yourself sick," Dax says.

"Okay, big brother," I say nudging him with my shoulder again. "I'll do better."

Before they can comment, we hear, "Ice-cold drinks! Get your ice-cold drinks!" being called from behind us again.

Kallon again stands up and waves his hand. I touch his leg and say, "I'll hold your wieners again if you want me too."

My face goes red as I hear Dax bark out a laugh and Kallon turns around quickly and looks down at me.

"You'll hold my what?" Kallon asks with a smirk on his face.

"Your hotdogs... I meant your hotdogs," I say, putting my hands on my cheeks. "I didn't mean your—" my eyes go to his crotch, and I look quickly back up to his face "—I meant your hotdogs."

"Mmmmhmm, oookay," Kallon says, teasing me again. He hands me his two remaining hotdogs and then turns back to the guy with the drinks. I can hear Kallon laughing.

Dax laughs again and I elbow him.

"Shhhh, I didn't mean it like that," I say, my face reddening even more.

"What can I get for you folks?" the drink guy asks. I look over and see his name is Ben.

"Three waters and... Dax do you want a Dr. Pepper?"

Kallon asks, looking over his shoulder at Dax.

"Yeah, that'd be good, thanks," Dax says.

"Abby, do you want anything other than a water?" Kallon asks, looking at me now.

"A Sprite, please," I say in a small voice.

"Three waters, a Dr. Pepper, and two Sprites," Kallon says as he turns and looks at Ben squarely.

"That'll be forty-three fifty," Ben says as he hands Kallon the three waters first. Kallon smiles and winks at me as he hands me the waters. I glare at him and shake my head. *I'm never going to live this down.* After Kallon hands Ben the money for the drinks, and tells him to keep the change, Ben hands Kallon the sodas.

"Enjoy the game," Ben says as he turns and walks away.

I hand Dax a water and then hand him his Dr. Pepper after Kallon has passed it to me. Kallon then hands me a Sprite and I give him a water and his hotdogs. I put my drinks down by my feet, telling myself I need to maybe start drinking the water sooner rather than later.

We sit in silence and eat our hotdogs and sip our drinks. I've eaten about half of my second hotdog when I nudge Dax and ask him if he wants the rest.

"Sure," he says. I hand it over and finally pick up my beer and take a sip. I'd been nursing it and my water at the same time for the last little while.

"So, you've never been to a major league game before?" Kallon asks, breaking the silence. I look over and see he's finished eating all his hotdogs and his beer is gone too.

"No, we don't have a favorite team but if a game happened to be on while we were at my parents, we'd watch it, but we don't go out of our way to watch a game. Same goes for basketball or football," I say with a shrug. "However, my grandpa, my mom's dad, loves the Dodgers. Anytime he's here visiting and there was a game on, we watch. I remember sitting with him in the summers when I'd go visit them and watch the game with him. But other than him, no one else is interested in pro-sports."

"Jason isn't a fan?" Kallon asks tentatively like he's not sure if he should bring Jason up or not.

"He's a big enough fan of the game to make bets, but not a big enough fan to have a favorite team. Well, I guess he'd probably says he's a Yankees fan, but I don't think he watches their games religiously."

"Where was the last place he took you out on a date?" Kallon asks.

"The last time we went out on a date was kind of a fluke thing. I hadn't heard from Jason all day. He hadn't replied to any of my text or called me back. So, when he called to see if I wanted to go out to dinner with him and his work friends, I was surprised, but he also honestly sounded surprised when I said yes. He assumed I had to work, but he somehow forgot that Rose's was closed on Monday's. He had hurriedly told me he'd pick me up at 7 o'clock and then hung up on me. I had felt like it was a weird interaction but shook it off as him needing to reconfirm with the guys that I would be coming," I say. I think for a minute and say, "That was over a month and half ago."

"You guys haven't been out on a date in that long?" Kallon asks sounding honestly surprised.

"We had some planned, but he'd cancel for one reason

or another. He'd reschedule for another time and then end up canceling the night before or the day of," I say. I can hear how sad my tone of voice sounds. I shrug and pick up my beer and take another drink. "What about you and Tina?"

"When we're in the same city, we go to dinner at least twice a week, sometimes more. She usually has some party she wants me to go to with her, but I typically don't stay long. Just long enough to say hi to her friends and the person hosting and have a drink and make small talk. I'm usually on my way home two to three hours later," Kallon says, looking down at his water.

"You really don't enjoy big parties?" I ask earnestly.

"I really don't," Kallon says.

"What is it about them you don't like?" I ask. "If you don't mind me asking."

"I don't mind in the slightest," he says with a smile. "I don't like them because the majority of the time, people just want to know how much money I made on my last movie. How much I'm making on my current one. Or how much I'll ask for during negotiations for the next one. They ask about all the houses I own, how many planes I own, cars too. I don't think I've had one conversation that didn't center around the people I know or have met now because of my popularity, or the amount of money I have, or what materialistic things I now own. I've also gotten tired of my date or girlfriend's friends hitting on me. I've never felt comfortable having that type of attention on me while I've been on a date or in a relationship. Whether the relationship is brand-new or if we'd been together for weeks, maybe even months."

"You have to know how handsome you are, though

right?" I ask.

"You think I'm handsome?" Kallon asks. His face turning a little pink.

I look at him with a duh face and say, "I'm serious. Are you uncomfortable with that type of attention because you really don't think you're handsome enough to attract that type of attention? Or is it something else?"

"I'm confident enough to know I'm a good-looking guy. I don't like that my looks are what most of the attention is from. It's not from what's in here and here—" he points at his head and then his heart "—it's just from this and this—" he points at his face and then waves down his body "—None of my past dates or girlfriends wanted to talk about any of the books I'd read. Or about the places I'd traveled for work to find out if I was able to enjoy it or not. Only a handful even know my schooling history. Even less know that I have businesses, actually, I don't think I've told any of them."

"Why's that?" I ask.

"I guess it's the same reason I have the alias. I'm embarrassed to say that the girls I tend to date are very materialistic and don't mind being offered or even mind asking for free things. They get free things offered so often, they start to expect it. I can't even imagine what they'd say if they found out about the hotels I own and other businesses. And forget about them signing the gag order, they'd be offended I'd even ask. So, I don't tell them."

"I'm sorry. It seems like it would be hard to be completely yourself around someone who you should be able to be yourself around, without telling them all about your life," I say, touching my left hand on to his right forearm.

He looks down at my hand and then places his left hand over mine, "It's hard but I'm sure the right girl for me is closer that I'm aware."

I laugh and give him a smile and say, "I'm sure you're right. And my list of words for you, keeps on growing."

"I keep meaning to ask you about that list," Kallon says, turning towards me a little. When he turns, his arms slide so my hand is on top of his hand, so I pull it back into my lap. He glances down and then moves his hand into his lap as well. He smiles up at me and say, "Can I hear what words are on it now?"

"I'll give you a couple but not all of them, it's a private list," I laugh.

"Oh really?" he says and turns towards me even more. "Now I really want to know."

I laugh again and say, "Well, for starters, kind and considerate are at the top of the list. Giving, intelligent, and talented are up there too. Thoughtful and in the week that I've known you, you've proven to be trustworthy and reliable. And the last one I'll give you for now is... compassionate."

"Wow," Kallon says, sounding sincerely shocked. "Those are some nice words. You really think those things of me?"

"I do. Should I be double checking my list?" I ask teasingly.

"I don't think so but that's just me," he says with a laugh. "I try to think of myself in the most positive light, but I sometimes wonder if I don't see myself as clearly as I should. Because I can't say the same about the majority of the people I attract."

"You attract those people because you make people want to be better. You attract them because the alternative isn't nearly as good and they want to be near something wonderful, something better than themselves. Because those people know deep down that they are miserable, and they don't like the way they act or treat others. And then, I'm sure there are some that know how much people like you, so they use that to get in with people. Those are some of the worst types of people because they don't care about what people think of them, so they don't care how they come across to others. They fake what they need to fake until they have their claws in a person," I say with a shrug.

"She's not wrong," Dax says. "She's the first person I've met that's explained it how I know it to be."

Kallon's quiet for a minute, looking down into his hands that are still in his lap. When he finally looks up at me, his smile is so heartwarming, it makes me smile back just the same.

"Thank you, Abby," he says sincerely. "I'm going to keep trying to live up to your list of words."

"I don't think you have to try. I think it's just who you are," I say honestly. "Unless you are the best damn actor I've ever met and you're pulling the wool over my eyes."

That makes Kallon and Dax both burst out laughing. I start laughing to and when we finally catch our breath, the baseball game starts!

CHAPTER 18

The game has been entertaining to watch so far. The guys have made it exciting and interesting. Sitting behind the dugout has been a lot of fun. I never realized how big baseball players were until they were mere feet away from me. It's now the 7th inning and Kallon and Dax are standing up.

"What's going on?" I ask.

"It's the 7th inning stretch," Kallon says.

"The what?" I ask.

"Just stand, you'll see," Kallon says encouragingly with a big smile.

So, I stand and wait. I don't have to wait long when all of a sudden, a song from my childhood comes over the speakers.

"Oh my gosh, I totally forgot they do this," I say. I start swaying with the song. And when the words start, I'm stunned at how the whole stadium is singing along.

"Take me out to the ball game. Take me out with the crowd.
Buy me some peanuts and Cracker Jack.

I don't care if I never get back.
Let me root, root, root for the home team.
If they don't win, it's a shame.
For it's one, two, three strikes you're out, at the old ball game!"

By the end of the song, the stadium feels alive. I'm cheering and whistling with everyone else around us. I look over at Dax and see he's even smiling broadly and laughing. I glance over at Kallon and he's whistling and cheering too!

"That's amazing," I say with a huge smile on my face as we sit down. Just as Kallon is taking a seat, someone from beside him taps his shoulder.

"Sir, here's those things you asked to be delivered right now," the guy says. I lean around and see he's a younger kid and he's holding three boxes of Cracker Jacks and three small bags of peanuts. He looks at me and smiles as he hands them to Kallon.

"Thank you," Kallon says. He takes them and gives the guy some cash.

"You already paid for them, sir," the kid says.

"That's for you," Kallon says. The kid stands for a minute and then beams at Kallon.

"Thank you, sir," the kid replies. Kallon smiles back at him and then turns and sits down beside me. The young kid takes off up the steps.

"Here," Kallon says as he hands me a bag of peanuts and a Cracker Jack. I hand them down to Dax, who laughs and leans over me to say thank you to Kallon. Kallon then hands me another thing of both snacks.

"Thank you!" I say excitedly. "I can't remember the last

time I had Cracker Jack!"

I open the box and dump some into my hand. I pop it in my mouth and squeal like a little girl. I smile and pour some more into my hand. I stomp my feet excitedly and smile over at Kallon.

"Thank you, thank you," I say. I lean over to him and give him a hug and he hugs me back by putting his arm around me.

"Uh, Mr. Keller," Dax says in an urgent voice. I hear a faint chant starting.

"*Kiss! Kiss! Kiss! Kiss!*" the crowd starts to chant together.

Kallon looks over at Dax and Dax points up to the mega screen. I look up too and see the camera is on us. I burst out laughing at seeing myself with Kallon's arm around me on the huge screen. Then the kissy face frame with the crowds chant makes everything clear.

My eyes go big and I look at Kallon. He's still looking at the screen. I look back up just as he's look at me. The people behind us start chanting.

"Kiss! Kiss! Kiss!" they say.

The guy right behind Kallon leans forward and grips his shoulder and I hear him say, "Dude, kiss the beautiful girl or I will!"

I look startled at Kallon but then I start laughing. He tips his head in a 'I'm willing if you are' type of way so I just shrug and nod.

Over the chanting crowd, I say, "Rated G!"

Kallon nods and leans towards me, and I lean towards him. Our lips touch and it's as if my heart is attached right behind my lips. It starts to race and then that electrical zap zings through me. My ears start to buzz and I can hear my heartbeat pounding with the buzzing sound. I open my eyes and see Kallon's eyes open in shock as well. For a second, I melt into him, my eyes closing again.

Kallon's hands go to my face and he pulls me to him a little more. Our lips part just enough that I can feel his bottom lip in my mouth, my tongue instinctively reaches out to touch it. The tip of my tongue quickly rubs against his lip and I can feel he's doing the same to my upper lip. Another zap of electricity runs through me.

Suddenly the sound of the crowd going wild with whoops and hollers of joy and encouragement, breaks through the buzzing and my heartbeat throbbing in my ears. I smile and slowly pull away. I open my eyes and see Kallon looks how I feel, slightly stunned but smiling. He turns away from me and waves out towards the field, I'm sure being filmed on the big screen. I turn my head into him and hide my face. He laughs and when I look, the camera is still on us. I shake my head and pick up my Cracker Jack and put some in my mouth. I lift it and tip it out to the field. The crowd starts cheering wildly. I can't help but think it's a good thing we're still wearing our hats and glasses.

The camera finally spans away from us and finds some other people to torment. I'm laughing and putting more Cracker Jack into my mouth as I reach down and grab my Sprite and open it. I take a swig, my cheeks still feeling warm. I look over at Kallon and see him staring at me.

I swallow my pop and ask, "What?"

Kallon clears his throat, shakes his head, and says,

"Nothing."

He grabs his Sprite as well and opens it, drinking about half of it. I smile up at him and as he pulls the drink away, he smiles back.

"What?" Kallon asks me in the same tone I asked him.

"Nothing," I return in the tone he used. He narrows an eye at me while puckering his lips just a little.

I have to face the field, or I know I'll stare at his lips for too long. Our, small, semi-innocent kiss still tingles on my lips and my heart is still slightly racing. I take another sip of my Sprite, willing the tingle to go away.

I can't have these feelings. We can never kiss again. As the thought crosses my mind, my smile disappears. We watch the 7th inning and as the 8th inning begins, Dax stands.

"Is there something else going on this inning?" I ask as I stand with him.

"No, I'm going to go pull the car around out front," Dax says with a laugh as he steps in front of me to pass.

I glance over at Kallon and see he's standing now too, letting Dax walk in front of him to get to the stairs. I look at him a little closer and see his face doesn't look as relaxed as it was before we kissed.

Great. It totally changed something. No, it only changes things if we let it.

We finish watching the game and both Kallon and I stand at the same time. I glance up at him and he smiles down at me.

"Ready to go home?" he asks.

I nod my head and stand. I glance at my watch and see it's almost 4:30pm. I grab my phone from my pocket and see I have a text from Jason from an hour ago.

Jason: Abby, baby, I'm sorry. I really am. Please, can we talk? Just us. Please.

Sighing, I text him back as Kallon and I wait our turn to start the long process of climbing the stairs to exit the stadium.

Me: Yes, we can talk but Jason, there's going to have to be some changes. Honest to goodness changes.

I don't have to wait long to see the three little dots appear.

Jason: Text me when you get home. I'll come over... if that's ok.
Me: Ok.

I put my phone away and cross my arms. Sighing as I feel my mood instantly changing. Kallon turns, at the sound.

"Is everything okay?" he asks. He takes his sunglasses off to look at me better.

"Yeah, everything's fine," I say in a tone that says otherwise.

"Listen, about the kiss—" Kallon says with concern in his voice but before he can continue, I interrupt him.

"No, no, no, my sigh doesn't have anything to do with that," I say. I take my phone out and shake it a little. "Jason texted me, he wants to talk when I get home."

Kallon looks at me skeptically, but he doesn't say anything.

"What?" I ask.

He seems to decide on something and asks, "Do you think it's safe to meet with him?"

"Jason wouldn't hurt me, if that's what you're thinking," I say.

Kallon puts his sunglasses back on and looks over his shoulder to see that it's our turn to join the que on the steps.

"Are you sure?" Kallon asks, turning sideways so he can talk to me and watch the people in front of him.

"Yes," I say. But then I think about how aggressive he'd gotten at the shop this morning. I shake my head and say, "Yes, he wouldn't hurt me."

"Okay," Kallon says. He seems to take my word for it and turns as the line in front of us starts moving at a faster pace.

I take the time it takes to walk up the steps to think about Kallon's question and Jason's actions this morning.

Before this morning, I would have had no doubt in my answer but now... I just don't know how Jason might react if our talk doesn't go the way he wants. The thought of him physically hurting me makes me cringe on the inside. *No, he wouldn't do that. Would he?*

I'm still thinking of my own question as we walk out of the stadium and make our way to the front where some cars are parked. Kallon sensing my distraction, gently grabs my elbow to lead me in the right direction. The zap of electricity and sudden change of direction startles me.

"Oooh," I say, stumbling as I wasn't prepared for the shock and I wasn't watching where I was going, just following the crowd.

"Sorry about that," Kallon says as he catches me before I completely fall to the ground.

"It's not your fault, I was in deep thought and wasn't paying attention."

Kallon nods his head in understanding and smiles at me kindly. He points up ahead of us and I see Dax standing by the car. As we get closer, he opens the back passenger door and I get in. I grab my bag from the floor and then slide over to the other side and buckle myself quickly.

I stare out the window as we pull away from the stadium and keep thinking of Jason. And how much he's changed in the last year or so.

"Is everything okay?" Kallon asks, touching my arm with feather soft pressure. The zap returning. *I wish it would stop.*

"Yes," I say, shaking my head and looking around to see how much of the city has already passed by, which tells me quite a bit of time has gone by as well. "Sorry, just thinking."

"Can I ask about what?" Kallon asks.

"Jason," I say quietly.

Kallon's face falls a little and says, "Oh. If you're worried about the talk you're going to have, I can be there as moral support."

I laugh a little and say, "Thank you but I don't think you being there will be helpful."

"Why not?"

"Jason seems pretty jealous about our friendship. He was upset when he found out I took the day off to come to the game with you. I've explained that we're friends and business partners, but I think he's threatened by me having another man in my life. Even if it's in a total platonic way."

Kallon looks to the front of the car for a couple of seconds and then looks back. He wiggles his pointer finger between him and me and asks, "Is this platonic?"

No! I don't want to have this conversation... Grow up, Abby! We can be mature about this. Just tell him yes. Point out he has a girlfriend, and we have... well, Jason, whatever it is we have with him.

I take a steading breath and say, "Yes, it's platonic. You have Tina and I'm trying to figure out what's going on with Jason. Plus, we're new business partners."

"Did you not feel anything during that kiss?" Kallon asks, turning to face me full on.

"It doesn't matter if I did or didn't, Kallon, it was an innocent peck during crowd entertainment at a baseball game. Like I said, you have Tina, your girlfriend," I state again, enunciating 'girlfriend'. I want to ask him if he felt anything, but I know if he says he did, my will to keep us in the business partner and friend zone will crumble to the ground.

But before Kallon can respond, Dax clears his throat from the front seat and says, "We're back at the bakery."

As Dax gets out and walks around to Kallon's door, Kallon looks at me for a quick second but then turns as his door is being opened and gets out. I let out a sigh and scootch over to the door. I sling my bag over my shoulder as I stand up next to Kallon.

"Are you sure you're okay?" Kallon asks.

I put my hand on his arm and smile up at him as sweetly as I can and say, "Yes, I'm sure. Really. Thank you so much for today. It was a lot of fun and just what I needed. I'll see you tomorrow."

Without thinking, out of pure habit, I reach up, wrap my arms around Kallon's neck and give him a hug. He hugs me back tightly and I feel his face on the space between my shoulder and neck. I feel my eyes start to shut in contentment but pull myself out of wherever my mind was going. I pat him on the back, quickly lowering myself back down and step away.

"Have a good evening," Kallon says. He smiles at me and then gets back into the car.

"See you in the morning," Dax says as he nods at me.

"Bye," I say.

I watch as Dax walks around the other side of the car and gets in. I can't see Kallon through the darkened window, but I wave anyways. I stand there and watch as they drive away.

I look at my bakery and see that the closed sign is on and instead of going in, I reach for my phone and send Betty a quick text.

> **Me:** Hey, going to the park for 20mins, Jason wants to come over and talk, but I'll tell him to come over later so I can help prep stuff for tomorrow.

I walk down to the closest crosswalk and join the throng of people waiting to cross over the busy street. I feel my phone vibrate in my hand. I look at it and see that Betty has replied.

Betty: Don't worry about it, Sweets. Maggie and I are just about done. Do you need back up for Jason? I don't like the way he acted this morning.

Me: No, I'll be alright.

Betty: Are you sure? I can head up and make dinner in your place, so that I'm doing something but there in case if he gets... carried away again.

Me: I appreciate it, but I'll be alright. If you finish before I get back, just head home. You two have been working so much lately, enjoy the evening.

I don't wait for a reply, I just put my phone in my bag and wait to cross the street. I have a special tree at the park that I like to go to if I need space to think. My condo is great for quiet but sometimes, I need to get out to let myself process my thoughts.

I follow the crowd across the street and then take the familiar sidewalk through the park and soon I'm at the tree. I sit with my back against it and lean my head back, closing my eyes.

Do I want to get back together with Jason? My heart says yes but my mind says no. My mind is saying he needs to do some work on himself and figure out how to take ownership in his mistakes and to stop blaming me for everything. My heart is saying that we can be together and help him grow and mature. We don't have to be separated, broken up, for him to learn these things. We can help him.

I open my eyes and look around the park. There are families all around, having Sunday picnics and playing with their kids. There's a group of people having a game of football and a lot of people on the trails, walking, running, and riding bikes. I listen to the sound of kids laughing, birds chirping, and dogs barking. I'm in a part of the park where you can barely hear city noises, which is exactly why I like coming here.

I have to think for a minute about the last time I was here. It's been way too long, about two months. I typically come on Sunday's and Monday's once we've closed Rose Bud's for the day. I'll bring a book to read and just sit for an hour or so, depending on how engrossed I get in the book. I let out a quiet laugh as the memory of the time I read until it was getting dark crosses my mind. I had totally lost track of time. The park can turn into a scary place once the sun goes down, I don't usually hang around long enough to see just how scary. That day, I'd practically ran home.

Today though, I know I can't stay long. I pull my phone out of my bag and set an alarm for ten more minutes and decide it will be plenty of time to rest my mind. Then I'll have to head back to either help Betty or call Jason to come over to talk.

CHAPTER 19

Before my alarm goes off, I feel my phone vibrate. I open my eyes and hold my phone up to see I have a text from Betty.

Betty: Hey Sweets, we finished up. We're heading home. Call me if you need anything. See you in the morning.
Me: Thank you so much, Betty. I know I probably sound like a broken record, but I don't think I'll ever be able to truly express how much I appreciate you and Maggie.
Betty: Don't you worry about that, I know you do. Good luck when you talk with Jason. Get some rest tonight.
Me: Thanks.

I open my text history with Jason and send him a quick text.

Me: Hey, I'll be home in 10. Come over soon if you want to talk. I really need to get some sleep tonight before the catering job starts back up tomorrow.

I'm surprised again to see the three dots appear so

quickly. In the past... I don't even know how long... Jason has never replied so quickly as he has today.

> **Jason:** Sounds good babe. I'll head that way now.

I stand and start making my way back home. As I walk, I turn my alarm off and then put my phone back in my bag. I don't have to wait at the cross walk this time. Just as I'm getting to it, the light changes. The crowd and I make our way across the street and then I make my way to my bakery.

I decide to go in through the bakery and make myself a coffee. I'd really like to have some wine, but it won't help my point with Jason that alcohol hasn't helped our relationship. I decide to make Jason his coffee as well.

After making our coffees, I head to the back and see that Betty and Maggie have everything ready for me for in the morning. I just have to do my morning prep and load things up. As I walk by my desk, I make a note that I need to talk to Stephanie tomorrow about bringing Betty and Maggie in to take over for when I'm gone for the wedding. In fact, I might as well just send her a text now.

> **Me:** Hey Stephanie, I was wondering if my assistant manager, Betty Brown, and her daughter, Maggie, can come in with me, to see how things are set up and where everything goes. Will that be okay? Would there be a day that would work best to bring them in?

I put my phone in my pocket and head up to my apartment. I plop my bag on my kitchen counter and grab a bag of plain popcorn from my snack cupboard and go to my living room. I sit down, put my phone on the table, and drink my coffee and eat my popcorn while I wait for Jason to come.

My phone buzzes on the table.

Stephanie: Hey! Yes, Betty and Maggie can come anytime. Whatever day works for you guys. Just let me know and I'll let security know you'll be bringing in two extras. We can talk more about details tomorrow.

Me: Thanks Stephanie. See you in the morning.

Just as I'm putting my phone back on the table, I hear my intercom buzz. I get up and walk to my door and push the button.

"Hello?" I ask into it.

"Hey, babe, it's me," Jason's voice says from the other end.

I push the button to unlock the bottom door and then wait at the top door until I hear him knock. I open it and see him standing there, smiling broadly, and holding red roses. He looks really nice, too.

I smile up at him and say, "Come on in."

He steps inside and kisses me gently on the cheek.

"Thanks," he says. "Oh, I brought your favorite flowers."

I don't let me smile faulter and I don't remind him that roses aren't my favorite. It's the thought that counts, right?

"Thanks, Jason," I say. As he takes his jacket off and hangs it up, I walk into the kitchen, and pull a vase out of a bottom cupboard. I have to wipe it off because of the dust that's on it. I put some water in it and then put the roses inside. I put the vase on my coffee table when I get back into my living room.

I pat the couch and says, "Come sit. I made you a coffee."

Jason smiles and walks over and sits down. He picks up his coffee and takes a sip.

"Perfect, as always," he says. He takes another drink before he puts it down. He pulls his phone out of his pocket and puts it on the table next to my phone.

We stare at each other for a minute, in silence. Just as it's getting awkward, we both start to say something at the same time.

"So," I start to say.

"I—" Jason says.

We both stop and then laugh.

"You go first," I say with a smile.

"Thanks," he says. "I've been going over in my head all day today to figure out what to say. I practiced a speech, but it just ended up sounding insincere. So, I threw it out. What I really want to say is… I just want to apologize again for this morning. I acted like an idiot. I seem to be acting like that a lot lately. And for that I'm sorry as well. I know I've said that so many times lately that those two words don't really have a lot of meaning anymore. But I'm willing to do what I need to, to show you I'm changing. I want to be that person I used to be. The person you loved and didn't hurt you with everything that comes out of my mouth."

"Okay," I say. "What do you have in mind?"

Jason takes a deep breath and then says, "I know I need to do better at staying in touch. I drifted away and I'm sorry about that. I'll do better about texting and calling. I've also realized I've become a bit of a drunk. I drink as soon as I'm finished with work and well into the night, if not early mornings. It started with a way to take off the edge at the end of the day, after a stressful day that is. Then it became something to do with the guys. We'd stop at the... bar down the road from the office and have a couple. Then a couple turned into a few and then it turned into an all-night thing. Now, it's more of a habit than something I enjoy. So, I won't be drinking anymore. I'll figure out a different way to destress after a hard day, but I know drinking isn't the best way."

"How will Deven and Shane feel about that?"

"It doesn't matter how they feel. If they have a problem with it, I won't hang out with them. I know it's what I need to do to prove to you I'm willing to change for you."

"Jason, it won't work if you're doing it for me and not yourself. If it's not what you truly want, you'll only be able to withhold from drinking for a couple of days before your will caves and you're back at the bar with them."

"No, babe, this is what I want too. I want you and I thought about what you said this morning. I can't blame alcohol for all my mistakes. I made them, I need to own up to them," he says as he leans to the side and pulls something out of his pocket. It's a folded-up piece of paper. He hands it to me and says, "Here."

I take it and unfold it. I see it's a check for ten-thousand dollars. I look up at him and say, "Really?"

"I messed up. I told Deven and Shane and I have to pay for it, literally. I won't make that mistake again," he says. "Can you give that to Mr. Webb?"

I smiled at his use of Kallon's alias.

"Thank you, Jason," I say.

"So does this mean we're back together?" he asks.

"Well, I do have to tell you something," I say. While I sat here and listened to Jason, I decided I was going to give him another chance. But that meant I needed to come clean to him.

"What's that?" Jason asks, turning to face me.

"Today at the baseball game, Kallon and I got put on the kiss cam. We kissed, it was a little peck, it was a silly thing."

Jason's hands go into fists and I see the vein in his neck starting to pop out. He closes his eyes and takes a deep breath.

"Did it mean anything to you?" he asks a little louder than a whisper.

"No, he's my friend and business partner," I say. *HA!* My brain shouts but I ignore it.

"Then why do you feel the need to tell me if it didn't mean anything to you," Jason says, sounding like he's getting angrier.

"Because I would never hide something like that. Even as innocent as it was, I'd never hide it," I say. "Think about it. What if you go home and see it on the tv or the guys tell you they saw it when they watched the game. If I didn't tell you, you'd think I was keeping it from you, and you'd think it was because it meant something."

Jason lets out a deep breath and says, "You're right. I'm sorry. I just... you know I don't like him."

"You don't even know him," I say in Kallon's defense.

"I don't want you around him," he states.

I let a short laugh escape and say, "Jason, no. Kallon and I are business partners and friends. Nothing has happened and nothing is going to happen. I'm not even kidding when I say the kiss was barely even a kiss. We only did it so the crowd and cameraman would leave us alone. He has girlfriend, a freaking model for crying out loud. You have no reason to be jealous of him. At all."

"Then why is your face turning red?" he asks. "It's your tell, you know, when you're lying."

"I'm not lying and my face is turning red because you're starting to upset me. You're making me feel like I've done something wrong when I haven't."

After a minute of Jason staring out the window, he turns to me and says, "I guess I'm just jealous that he gets to spend so much time with you."

"We can spend time together. We just have to make the time. We both do. I know I haven't been the best at giving my time to you and I'm sorry about that. I've got my routine down now for the bakery, restaurant, and catering gig. I'll do better at being here for you."

"So does that mean we're back together?" he says with a big smile.

I can't help but smile back at him and I say, "Yes, it does. But Jason, you have to do the things you said you'd do."

Jason scoots closer to me on the couch and puts his hand on my knee. He smiles down at me and says, "I will."

His hand squeezes my knee and when I look down at it, I watch him slide it up to my thigh. I look up at him and see desire flaring in his eyes. He leans in but instead of attacking my mouth, he waits for me to meet him.

I lick my bottom lip and lean in to kiss him. His lips meet mine and I hear a soft moan escape his lips.

"I've missed you," he murmurs around my lips.

"Mmm... me too," I say.

Jason shifts on the couch and puts his other hand to the back of my head and pulls me closer to him. His hand remaining on my thigh, shifts so is thumb is on the inside and his other fingers are splayed on the outside of my leg.

Our kissing deepens. He leans back and pulls me so I'm straddling his lap.

"Baby," he says in a whisper against my lips. He presses his hand against my back, pressing my chest into his, and he kisses me passionately.

I can't think of the last time we've kissed like this and the last time we had sex was... too long ago. I can feel my heart racing in my veins. Jason pulls his mouth from mine and kisses across my cheek, to my ear. He pulls my earlobe into his mouth and gives it a little suck.

A moan escapes me and my head rolls to the side, giving him better access to my neck. He takes the hint and kisses down my neck, to my collarbone. In one movement, he pulls my t-shirt off and throws it to the floor.

"God, babe, you're beautiful," he says before he kisses down my chest. He kisses my cleavage, running his left pointer finger down inside the bra cup of my right breast. He then pulls the cup down and pulls my nipple into his mouth. His other hand is on my back, unclasping my bra.

"Jason," I say breathlessly.

"Mmm, baby, I love when you say my name," he says.

He gets my bra off and my breast are pebbling from the combination of the cool air of my condo and how turned on I'm becoming. Jason's hand cups my right breast, pulling the nipple into his mouth as his right-hand cups my left breast, kneading it gently. His thumb and forefinger pinch my nipple and roll it around a little.

"Oh, yes," I say. I rock my hips and I feel how turned-on Jason is by his hardon pressing into the inside of my thigh.

"I need you," Jason says.

"Yes," I say.

Jason stands in one motion and I wrap my legs around his waist. He carries me to my bedroom. I kiss down his neck and pull his shirt off as we go. I kiss down to his collarbone and then across his chest to the other side and make my way up to his neck.

"Baby, you're driving me crazy. I'm about to cum in my pants just from that, easy," he says with a chuckle.

I giggle and continue kissing his neck. Soon my back is against my comforter. I open my eyes and see Jason stepping back. I toss his shirt to the floor as he unbuttons his pants and in one swoop, his pants and underwear are off. His erection standing at attention.

I've never been with anyone but Jason so I've never seen another man's erection so I can't say for sure if he's average, above average, or small. I stop staring at him and shimmy out of my pants and undies.

Need flares in Jason's eyes. He reaches down to his pants on the floor and pulls out a condom. He slides it on and then he's on top of me. He kisses me deeply before going to my breasts again. His legs slide between mine, pushing them apart, I can feel him at my entrance.

"Not yet," I say. I reach down and start rubbing myself.

A growl comes from Jason, and he says, "I'll do that."

With his mouth on my right breast, Jason reaches down with his hand and takes over for me. He starts to rub where my fingers were, but then his fingers move to the side a little. I try to move my hips so that his fingers are back to my spot, where I need him, but he then slides a finger inside me, and I freeze.

"Awww baby, you're so tight," he says into my breast. His starts to thrust his finger in and out slowly. He then adds a second finger before I'm ready for it and I cry out. "Yeah baby, cum for me."

I'm startled at the thought that he thinks that outcry was of pleasure and not pain.

"Hang on Jason," I say as he speeds up his pace. I reach down and start to rub myself again. Hoping that the combination of his fingers inside me and me hitting my spot, will help ease some of the tension.

"I don't know if I can wait much longer, baby," Jason says. I feel him rubbing his erection against my leg.

"Just… a couple… more… seconds," I beg. I'm almost there, almost ready.

"I need you now," he says in a rush. His fingers disappear and then in one thrust, Jason is inside me. My breath catches as he moans out, "Oh god, yes!"

As he starts to thrust into me, I slowly breathe out. Willing myself to relax so it doesn't hurt as much. I try to get back to where I was a minute ago, I could tell I was close. I rub my spot with my right hand and take my right nipple into my left hand and pinch it gently. Jason opens his eyes and sees me. With his head, he knocks my hand away and starts sucking on my nipple.

"Yes," I say. "But... but... Jason, stop for a second."

Jason stops sucking on my nipple and leans back but he keeps thrusting and grunting.

"No, I meant, hold still for just a second, please," I say. I need a second to get there and to do that, I need him to stop moving for just a second.

Jason grunts out but stops moving. He goes back to sucking on my nipple. I rub myself a little harder and faster, begging myself to get there. I need this. I can feel how much I need an orgasm.

"Baby," Jason pleads. He can feel me just starting to tighten around him. "Baby I can't."

He doesn't wait for me. He puts his head to my right shoulder, and he starts thrusting again but faster this time. In no time, he's stiffening, and I can feel him jerk inside me.

"Uuughnaaaah," he groans out into my neck. He thrust one more time, but weaker this time, before he collapses on top of me, breathing hard. I try to keep rubbing myself, I'm so close, but with his body on top of me, it makes it hard to move my hand.

Feeling defeated that it's not going to happen, I pull my hand out from between us and put it on his back.

"Baby, that was amazing," Jason says into my shoulder. He kisses my neck, leans up and pulls out of me, and then rolls on to his back.

Even though I didn't get my orgasm, I'm still out of breath when I say, "Mmm... yeah."

Jason rolls to his side and kisses my shoulder. He laughs and says, "Make-up sex is always the best sex, don't you think?"

I smile at him and nod. *Sure, for you.* I think. I've never been able to get Jason to listen to what I need or want in the bedroom, which is probably why I've never had an orgasm with him.

I get up, grab a large pajama shirt from my dresser, and walk to my bathroom. When I come out, Jason is dressed.

I stop just inside my room, feeling discouraged, and ask, "Leaving already?"

"Well, it's almost 6, don't you need to get to bed soon? You've gotta be up early for the movie set, right?" he asks as he tucks in his shirt. He reaches onto the floor and picks up a tissue. He must have used it to take the condom off.

He walks into my bathroom as I answer him, "Yeah I have to be up early."

When he walks back out, he stops and kisses me on the cheek, "Then I'll talk to you tomorrow. Get some sleep, love ya."

"Yeah, okay," I say, feeling confused as he walks out of my room. I follow him and walk behind him as he walks to get his phone off the table. He checks it and he chuckles at something on his screen. I pick up my phone and hold it in my hand. He walks to get his jacket and puts it on. We stop at the door and he kisses me deeply.

"Thanks for giving me another chance babe," he kisses me quickly, slaps my ass— which I hate— and with another chuckle, he opens the door and walks down the stairs. He doesn't turn around. He just opens the bottom door and walks out. I hear the lock click into place and then I shut my top door. The door locks and I walk into the kitchen to get some water.

"What the hell?" I ask out loud. "Did Jason just use us getting back together as a way to get a quickie?"

Before I let myself think about the answer to that question, I let it go. If I think about it too much, it'll irritate me. I shake my head and drink my water. I look in the freezer for something to eat and decide on a chicken stir fry meal. It takes 5 minutes for it to cook, so I walk back to my room and put on a pair of underwear and shorts.

By the time I come back out, the microwave is off, and my food is the perfect temperature. I sit at the bar and eat in the silence of my apartment, and I try not to think about what just happened. Maybe I'll talk to Jason about it the next time he's over. Maybe he doesn't understand that it would be nice if I could get some attention and join him on the orgasm train. Hopefully it won't hurt his feelings to find out I've never had one with him.

After I'm done eating, I throw my garbage away and wash my fork and put it away. As I'm heading to my room, I feel my phone vibrate in my pocket. I pull it out and see Kallon is calling.

"Hey," I say as I answer. I walk into my room and lie down on my bed.

"*Hi, Abby. I hope I'm not interrupting your talk with Jason, I just wanted to see if everything was going okay,*" Kallon says. I take a minute too long to answer because Kallon says, "*Abby? Is everything okay?*"

"Yeah, yeah, everything's fine," I rush out so he can

stop his worrying. *Everything is fine, right?* Ignoring my question to myself, I say to Kallon, "Jason and I talked and we're giving us another go. He took responsibility of his mistakes and even wrote a check out to you. He says he's done drinking and is willing to get back to the guy I fell in love with all those years ago."

It's quiet on Kallon's side for minute and then he says, *"I'm happy for you, Abby, if this is what you want."*

"It is," I say to him but think to myself, *I think.*

"Good," Kallon says. I can hear the smile on his face. He genuinely sounds happy. *"What do you guys have planned for this evening?"*

"Nothing," I admit. "Jason already went home. I'm going to bed here shortly so I can get up early to start the week off right."

"Okay, well if you need anything, let me know. I'll see you tomorrow," Kallon says.

"Yeah, see you tomorrow."

We hang up. I put my phone on my bedside table and go into my bathroom. After brushing my teeth, I turn off all the lights, and go to my bed. Turning the lamp on, I grab my phone and plug it in, and then double check that my alarms are set.

I snuggle down into my blankets and fall to sleep quickly.

CHAPTER 20

The week goes by in a blur and before I know it, it's Friday. After talking to Stephanie and Betty on Monday, we decided that Friday would be the best day to have the girls come along. It would give us enough time to let the regulars know we would be closed for the day, but we'd be open first thing Saturday morning.

My alarm goes off but I'm already awake. I'd been woken up at 1am from Jason. He'd called to see if he could come over, he'd worked late at the office. He'd been good all week, texting and calling to see how I was doing. He replied to my texts fairly quickly and I don't think there was a phone call in the evenings that he didn't answer.

We haven't seen each other since Sunday night though, so I was tempted to tell him yes he could come over, but I decided against it. I told him we had to be responsible adults, but I didn't tell him that I knew why he wanted to come over and 1am sex wouldn't do well for me and my sleep.

He hasn't quite grasped that I don't get a ton of sleep. He grumbled a little about not coming over, but he said he understood and apologized for waking me up. He said he'd try to remember my sleep schedule from now on.

I roll out of bed and take a quick shower. After getting dressed in my blue jeans and Rose Bud's polo, I throw my hair into a low bun and add on a little eye make-up. I put on my socks and shoes and head out to the living room after grabbing my phone off the nightstand.

I walk to the kitchen and grab my bag off the counter and make my way downstairs. I stop at the cupboards by my desk and pull out a Rose Bud's polo for Maggie. It's the smallest shirt I have but I'm hoping it'll fit her well enough. If it doesn't, I'll order her a couple of her own. She's been helping here long enough that I decided last night that it was time for her to have her own shirt. I set the shirt on my bag by the back door and then get to work doing all my prep work.

By the time I have everything done and ready, I hear the beep of the side door and look up at the monitor to see Betty and Maggie walking in.

"Good morning," I holler from the kitchen.

"Good morning," Betty says as she walks in.

"Morning," Maggie says excitedly.

I walk to the shirt on my bag and bring it over to her.

"So, Mags, you've been a part of the Rose Bud's family since the first day your mom started working for me but how about we make it official?" I ask, holding out the shirt.

"Really?" Maggie asks in surprise.

"You help your mom and me out so much around here, I think it's time you have your own shirt. Plus going to the movie set today, you'll look extra professional," I wink at her.

"Thank you, Abby!" she squeals and throws her arms around my neck.

"You're welcome," I say as I hug her back.

"Look Mom, it's just like yours and Abby's," Maggie says as she holds up her shirt.

Betty takes her jacket off and I see she's wearing her polo instead of her usual Rose Bud's t-shirt.

"It sure is," Betty says patting Maggie's head. "Now, when you wear that shirt, it's like a uniform. When you're wearing it, you show respect to Abby by behaving in a way that will show Rose Bud's in a positive light."

"Yes, ma'am," Maggie says as she walks into the dry food storage room and emerges a couple seconds later with the polo on and her t-shirt in her hand. She says excitedly, "It fits!"

"It sure does," I say, laughing at how excited she is about her own business polo.

I hear a knock out front and go open the door for who I'm assuming is Dax at the door. When I turn on the light, I see him standing there.

"Abby, do you want a coffee?" I hear Betty ask from behind me.

"Yes please, mocha today please, double shot," I say over my shoulder as I unlock the door. I open the door and say while I move to the side to let him in, "Good morning, Dax."

"Good morning, Abby," Dax says with a smile. I pull the door shut and lock it as he steps beside me and says back towards the counter, "Morning Ms. Betty, Miss Maggie."

"Dax, if you don't start dropping the Ms. nonsense, I'm going to stop making you your coffees," Betty says sternly. "Please, call me Betty."

"Yes, ma'am, I'll try harder," he says. Betty turns slowly with her eyebrows raised. Dax laughs and amends, "Sorry, yes, Betty, I'll try harder."

"That's better," she laughs. "Now, would you like a coffee?"

"Yes, please," he says as we make our way to the counter.

"Can I have one this morning?" Maggie asks.

Betty looks at her and then at me. Maggie looks pleadingly at her mom and then at me.

"It's up to you, Betty, but I'd do half a shot. It's way early enough that I don't think the caffeine will affect her this evening, but we don't need her a jittery mess while on set," I say jokingly as I gently tousle Maggie's hair.

"Hey, I've had caffeine before," Maggie says defensively.

"When?" Betty asks as she turns to hand me and Dax our coffees.

"I've snuck drinks of your coffee," she says timidly, like she's going to get into trouble.

Betty laughs and says, "Taking sips and having your own coffee is completely different, honey."

"Please, Mom," Maggie begs. "Kids my age are drinking energy drinks. One coffee with half a shot of espresso isn't going to hurt me."

"Kids are really drinking those things?" Dax asks, surprised.

"Yeah, they're gross though," Maggie says.

"Alright," Betty concedes. "You can have one this morning and we'll see how it goes. But don't expect to have one every morning."

"Thanks, Mom!" Maggie says happily.

"What do you want?" Betty says laughing.

"Whatever you usually have," Maggie says bouncing on her toes.

"Are you sure you want to add to your already bouncy self?" I ask, teasing her again.

"I'm just excited," she laughs.

"Come on kid, let's start loading some boxes while your mom finishes your drink," Dax says. He turns to me and asks, "Are your keys where they usually are?"

"Yeah, on the hook by the back door," I say.

I wait with Betty while she finishes up the drinks. As we walk back to the kitchen, I turn off the lights to the front and then we start helping Maggie and Dax load the van. As soon as we have everything loaded a realization hits me.

"Shoot, there's not enough room for all of us to ride in the van," I say.

"That's okay, I had already planned on driving," Betty says.

"Are you sure?" I ask.

"Yes, no problem at all," she says with a smile. "Are we ready?"

I look at my watch and see we're on track for time, so I nod.

"I'll wait to see you guys pull out on to the road and then I'll follow you. But just in case, will you send me the address and I'll have Maggie put it into my GPS in case a traffic light or traffic separates us?" Betty asks as she puts her jacket back on. She grabs her purse from the coat rack and puts it over her shoulder.

"Yeah, I'll do that right now," I say. I pull out my phone and send the address to Betty.

"Ready?" I ask.

"Yes," Maggie answers first, excitedly.

"Okay, see you guys out front," I say. I watch as Betty and Maggie head out to the front to use the side door.

I follow Dax out to the van and we get it. Dax is an amazing driver and makes sure Betty is behind us before we take off. He's so considerate of making sure she stays behind us that every time we come to an intersection with a light, he doesn't go through unless he knows there's time for Betty to make it through as well.

Traffic is its normal early morning speed, so we get to the studio lot with plenty of time. Dax and I talked Wednesday and decided we needed to leave a little early to make sure we got through security. I'm glad he did because I hadn't even thought about needing to bring a separate car. We had checked with Stella yesterday as we were leaving to make sure Betty and Maggie were on the list to get in. She confirmed that they were.

Stella is at the gate this morning and greets us. We explain Betty in her Honda Accord behind us. She nods and waves us in. We pull ahead and wait for Stella to check Betty's ID and to give Betty and Maggie guests passes and a parking pass.

When we see Betty start to pull forward, Dax starts to lead the way to the studio. Once we get to the side door, I see it open, and Kallon is standing there with a big smile on his face. Stephanie is standing to the side but behind him.

Kallon comes down the steps and opens my door for me. I look up to see Stephanie looking at him in a strange way. When she sees me looking at her, she smiles again.

"Good morning," Kallon says.

"Good morning," I say back to him. I look at Stephanie again and say, "Morning, Stephanie."

"Morning, Abby," she says as she walks down the steps. Dax comes around the van just as Betty and Maggie walk up to us, they'd parked behind us.

"Morning," Betty says to Kallon. Then she turns to Stephanie, "Good morning."

Kallon smiles and nods at her and then beams at Maggie. He says to her, "Good morning, kiddo."

Maggie doesn't say anything, she's staring at the door behind Stephanie, and she's suddenly extremely quiet.

"You okay?" I ask her as I walk over to her.

She just nods.

"I think her nerves have caught up to her excitement," Betty says, rubbing Maggie's back gently.

I put my arm around her back and say, "It's easier if you think of them all as just people. Because they are. They get paid a lot of money to entertain people, but they are just people, like you and me. Treat them the way you treat everyone else, and you'll be just fine."

"I... I don't think I can..." Maggie stammers out. "What do I say to them?"

"Hello, hi, how are you," I say with a gentle laugh of encouragement. "Talk to them the way you talk to our customers at Rose Bud's."

"You don't have to say anything," Stephanie says

kindly to Maggie. "If you feel uncomfortable talking to anyone, just give them a nod and smile and then leave to go somewhere else."

"Hi, I'm Betty Brown," Betty says, extending her hand to Stephanie.

"I'm so sorry, I forget that I haven't officially met you. Abby has talked so much about you, I feel like we met before today. I'm Stephanie Steel, welcome to the set," she says as she shakes Betty's hand.

"Thank you and thank you for the opportunity to help Abby out," Betty says with a smile. She turns to Maggie and says, "This is my daughter Maggie. Maggie, this is Ms. Steel."

"It's nice to meet you too, Maggie. You can call me Stephanie, both of you," Stephanie says with a warm smile.

"Nice to meet you," Maggie says timidly.

I go to the back of the van and open it up. I turn and see Dax standing there with open arms. I laugh and start handing him things. Then Kallon is there and out of nowhere, Trevor is standing behind him.

"Where did you come from?" I ask with a startled laugh.

"I was at Mr. Keller's car, Dax sent me a text that you guys were here. Load me up," he says with open arms.

Maggie hurries over and starts grabbing things as well, soon the guys are back.

"Why don't you take a load in and start showing Betty and Maggie how you like things set up? The guys and I can bring the rest of these things in," Kallon says.

"Kallon, when are you going to listen to me when I tell you this—" I wave my hand at the back of the van and towards the building "—isn't your job? You should be inside getting ready for your scenes."

"When are you going to listen when I tell you, my job is to help my friends," he says as he steps up to me. We glare at each other for a second and then he smiles at me. "Plus, I'm not due on set until 7, so I have some time to kill."

I shake my head, but smile, and say, "You're ridiculous."

"Take what's in your hands inside and start setting up, we've got this," he says as he steps aside for me to go to the building.

"Fine," I say. Shaking my head still and walk to the door that Stephanie is holding open.

She takes one of the boxes from the top of the pile I have and walks with me.

"I've said it before and I'm going to say it again, Kallon is different around you," she says with a smile.

"Is he normally not so nice and helpful?" I ask. I can't believe he could be anything but those things.

"Oh no, he's one of my favorite people because of how nice and helpful he is but with you… I don't know, his smile seems more genuine. He's happy and you can just see he truly enjoys being in your presence, like he can be his real self around you."

"He's not usually happy?" I ask, ignoring the rest of what she had said.

"He's happy but guarded. I know the way some of the other actors behave irritates him, but he doesn't say anything unless they get out of hand. The female lead, this is her first big film. Some of the other actors were giving her

a hard time and he stuck up for her. He doesn't let people...
whether their actors, set workers or production crew, bully
other people. He doesn't work for directors or producers
who have a reputation of being cruel or... let's just say not
nice people. He tries to surround himself with good people
but sometimes, he gets stuck with some that just aren't. It
can cause him to become gloomy. He only comes out of his
dressing room to do his scenes and then he's back in his room
because he doesn't want to argue and fight with costars when
they start acting a certain way," Stephanie says as we get to
the tables. She sets the box down and turns to me. "It's just
nice to see him relaxed and happy."

I smile at her and nod because I don't know what to
say. I walk into the small kitchen and start grabbing the
things in here that I need and put them on the counter.
When I come back out, Betty and Maggie are standing beside
Stephanie. I grab the tablecloths out of the box and Betty
helps me put them out.

I spend the next twenty minutes explaining to both
Betty and Maggie, who's so intent on what I'm saying, she
doesn't know some of the actors have arrived on set. But
I explain to them how I set things up. After we've got
everything out and the coffee is filled and brewing, I take
them into the small kitchen.

"When it's time to clean up, I wash everything and let
it dry while I pack up the things I'll take home. Once I have
the tables cleared off, I come back in and put everything
away. We're the only ones that use the kitchen, but I like
to have it clear in case the other caterers need the space," I
explain.

"How often do you check the food and drinks?" Betty asks as we walk back out to the table.

"Every hour. At 10, I start clearing things away unless things get devoured before then, then I clear it away as the displays become empty. We need to be cleared out by 11 but any time after 10, Stephanie says is okay. Smoothies are hit or miss on if they go fast or one of the last things to go but I've never had anything leftover," I say with a smile.

"That's because your food is the best we've ever had," Stephanie says with a smile of her own. Dax, Trevor, and Kallon are standing off to the side and they give nods of agreement.

"Well, well, well," a man's voice says from behind me. "Not only do we have our beautiful Abby today, but she's brought in two more beauties. How lucky are we?"

I turn to see Chace standing five feet behind me, Betty, and Maggie. I turn to introduce him to the girls, but I see Kallon walking over to us in a defensive manner. Dax and Trevor are right behind him.

Trying to ignore the guys' behavior, I smile at Betty and Maggie and say, "Mr. Tanner, this is Betty and Maggie Brown. They're going to be taking over for me in a few months for a Friday and Monday. Betty, Maggie, this is Chace Tanner."

"It's nice to meet you, Mr. Tanner, I'm Betty," Betty says, nodding at him.

He smiles at her and says, "Please, call me Chace, all the pretty ones do. Except, this one," he puts his arm around my shoulders. Out of the corner of my eye, I see Kallon stiffen. Chace chuckles and says, "She still refuses to call me anything but Mr. Tanner, even though I keep telling her to call me Chace."

He taps my nose and I shake my head and step out of his arms.

"And like I've told you, Mr. Tanner, I like to keep things professional," I say with a smile.

"Except with Kallon," he says with an eyebrow raised.

"I met him outside of the movie set, before I got the job to cater. He's a friend," I say with another smile. I can tell that offending Chace is something I don't want to do, so I try to make light of this conversation.

"We can be friends too," he says, putting his arm back around my shoulders, pulling me in tightly. The feeling is a little too intimate for my liking and I'm about to say something when Kallon steps forward.

"She's got enough friends, Tanner. Take your hands off her and quite hugging people to you who don't want to be hugged," Kallon says as he steps up and offers me his hand. I take it and look at him gratefully. He pulls me from Chace's embrace and pulls me to stand beside him. I turn and see Chace glaring at Kallon and then his eyes go to where my hand is still in Kallon's. I drop it quickly.

"I'm sorry if I made you uncomfortable," Chace says with a bow of his head. "That wasn't my intentions."

"It's okay," I say. I feel Kallon stiffen beside me so I add, "But I'm not really a hugger, so handshakes would be okay from now on."

"Handshakes?" Chace asks with a laugh that doesn't sound in the least bit humorous. "Sure."

Movement to the side of us catches our attention and I

see Maggie moving to stand closer to Betty.

"So, your Maggie, Betty's sister?" Chace says, smiling kindly to Maggie.

Maggie shakes her head but doesn't say anything.

"She's my daughter," Betty says with a smile as she puts her hand around Maggie's shoulders.

"You're a mom?" Chace asks in surprise.

"Yes?" she says as a question.

"And not married?" he asks, looking at her left hand. His eyes dance with something that looks like excitement.

"No, not married," Betty says but her smile faulters a little.

"Not married and a MIL—" Chace doesn't finish what he's saying, as Kallon tenses beside me and I can tell he's about to say something but Stephanie steps forward and interrupts him.

"Betty would you and Maggie like a tour?" she asks. She shoots a glare at Chace but then turns to smile back at the girls. Betty had looked down at Maggie, so she didn't see the look Stephanie gave him.

"That'd be great, if we're all set here?" Betty asks looking at me.

"Yeah, we're good," I say.

"You can take them to my dressing room when you're finished," Kallon says. "I'll have Dax meet you there."

Stephanie nods and motions for Betty and Maggie to follow her. Maggie grabs on to Betty's hand and they start walking. Dax looks at me and then at Kallon, we both nod at him and he turns and follows the girls. Kallon and Trevor turn and glare at Chace. I turn my attention to him too and I can feel my face mirroring the same glare.

"What?" Chace asks in genuine astonishment.

"You seriously have to ask what?" Kallon asks.

"Did I do something wrong?" Chace asks, looking at us all.

My face goes blank and my head tilts to the side, "You truly don't see anything wrong with what you just said to my friend? How you're behaving?"

Chace shrugs and looks at us like he doesn't know what we're talking about.

"You don't tell someone you just meet that you think they're a MILF and comment, twice, on them being unmarried," Kallon says. I see Trevor grip his fists into tight balls at his side. His shoulder muscles are straining under his shirt.

"Don't single moms like hearing things like that?" Chace asks earnestly as he looks at me.

"I don't think so. At least ones who value other things other than sleeping around. My friend, Betty, is not one of those moms," I say.

"So, it's rude to say things like that?" Chace says. He sounds a little slow to the conversation which makes me think he's never had to worry about what he has said to people. Which also makes me think he's always been around people that gives him what he wants so he's never had to think before he's talked before.

"Very rude," I say.

"Noted," he says. He walks over to the table and starts filling a plate with food and then gets a cup of coffee. He doesn't say another word to us before he walks away.

I turn to Kallon with my eyes wide in a 'What the hell' type of way.

"He's—" Kallon starts to say but I put my hand up.

"You do not need to explain or apologize for him. It seems he's had people do that for him his whole life to the point he doesn't even know how to have a normal conversation with people without filtering what he's thinking before he speaks it. His behavior does not reflect on yours. I promise," I say, touching Kallon's arm. At my touch, he relaxes.

"Do you want to walk with me to my dressing room?" Kallon asks.

"Sure," I say. I look one more time at the table before we start walking.

"I'll be outside if you need me, Sir," Trevor says with a nod. He excuses himself and leaves the set.

"So, how's your week going?" Kallon asks as we start walking.

"Good. I'm glad it's Friday though. We have that big wedding we're prepping for, for tomorrow night at the restaurant. Thank goodness for having a staff at both places who are competent," I say with a laugh. "I don't think I could do any of this without them."

"And you are the reason they stay," he says as he nudges me with his arm. I laugh but don't say anything. We walk in silence for a minute. Kallon clears his throat and says, "So how are things going with Jason?"

"Good," I say.

"That's good," he says with a smile.

"How are things with Tina?" I ask.

His smile disappears and he says, "We broke up. She finally confessed that she wouldn't be coming back to New York and was hoping that I'd move to L.A. after the movie was over. I told her I wouldn't be moving to L.A., ever. I have businesses in L.A. that I would be checking on and if a movie is being filmed there, I'd be there but I wouldn't move there. She didn't like that. So, we decided it was best that we end things."

"I'm sorry," I say, I touch his arm and squeeze gently. I ineffectively ignore the zig in my arm. I move my hand from his arm and put it in my pocket.

"It's okay," he says. "Somethings aren't meant to be and it's better to acknowledge it sooner rather than later."

I feel a twinge in my chest, but I brush it aside and nod in agreement.

"So, who's next on the list?" I ask, joking with him.

"Ha!" he barks out a short laugh. "No one. I'm taking a break from dating."

"Hmmm, I don't think that'll last long," I say with a laugh.

He laughs and nudges me again, "What? Why do you say that?"

"Because, as soon as the eligible women find out your single, they'll come ah-flockin'," I say with another laugh.

"Just because they come 'ah-flockin'—" he uses air quotes "—doesn't mean I'll want them."

"So, you're telling me that if some beautiful girl walks up to you and says, she wants you, you're going to tell her no?" I ask, looking at him doubtfully.

"Yes, I'll tell her no."

"Bull," I say with a loud laugh.

"I guess it would depend on the girl," he says, looking down at me with a look in his eyes that has me looking away.

I clear my throat and ask in a teasing tone, "Amelia Ray?"

"Hell no," he says with absolute conviction in his voice.

"Why not? She's nice enough," I say.

He looks at me doubtfully and says with a chuckle, "You don't know her very well."

We reach his room, he enters his code, and then opens the door for me. Betty, Maggie, and Dax aren't here yet, so Kallon leaves his door open a little and walks over to the fridge.

"Would you like something to drink?" he asks as he pulls out a water bottle and holds it up.

"No, thank you, I had a coffee on the way over," I say.

I sit on the couch and pull a book off the table. I hold it up to him and ask, "Have you read this one?"

"Finished it last week," he says.

"Did you like it?"

"I did, it was full of adventure and—" his voice trails off and his face turns a little pink.

"And what?" I ask, I open the book and fan the pages.

"Romance," he says quietly.

I laugh and look down at the book, "May I borrow it? I haven't read a good book in a while."

"Sure," he says. "Chapter twelve is a good one."

I look up at him and he smiles, but his face has gotten a little redder. I look back down and feel my face warming as well at his implication of what the chapter holds in store.

He reaches forward and grabs a book and opens it. I take my shoes off and get comfortable on the couch and open the book.

"Abby?" I hear my name being called and a big warm hand touches my arm. I look up from the book to see Kallon's hand on me. Betty, Maggie, Dax, and Kallon are looking at me, they all have an amused look on their face.

"Oh, sorry," I say, I look at the page I'm on and close the book. I put it on my lap and move on the couch to make room for someone else to sit.

"Good book?" Betty asks.

"Yes," I say excitedly.

"You seemed really into it," Maggie says. "Can I read it after you?"

"No," Kallon and I say at the same time. We both look at each other and laugh.

"Why not?" she asks.

"It's an adult book," I say.

"What chapter are you on?" Kallon asks with his eyebrows raised.

"Five, but I can see where the story is leading," I say with a laugh.

"I read adult books," Maggie says and then she slaps a hand over her mouth.

"Maggie Lynn Brown!" Betty says shocked.

"I skip the love scenes, promise I do," Maggie adds quickly.

"And how do you do that?" Betty asks with her hands on her hips.

"I ask the librarian to put Post-it notes over the parts I

shouldn't read," she says sheepishly.

"The librarians allow you to check out adult books?" Dax asks, flabbergasted.

"Well, it's not their job to monitor and limit us on what we read. If we read at a higher level than our age, we can check-out whatever we want. It's up to the parents to set limits on their kids' library card," Maggie says. She sounds so grown up. She then looks at Betty and adds, "Mom, I promise, I don't read anything I shouldn't. I don't read horror or anything with a ton of violence. And when the book starts to express that the couples are about to... you know—" she looks over at Dax and Kallon and I can tell she's a little uncomfortable talking about this in front of them. If it was just me and her mom, she would have said exactly what she thought, but she continues "—I stop reading until I can have the librarian cover it for me. We've talked about... it... so I'm not stupid. I know what's going on, but I don't want to read about it. I'm not ready for any of that."

I smile at her, proud of her in a way that I can only describe as motherly. I look at Betty and see her facial expression matches how I feel.

Betty smiles at Maggie and says, "We'll talk about this at home but just so you know, you aren't in trouble."

Maggie sighs in relief and sits down, "Thank you."

"How was your tour?" I ask, trying to change the subject. Maggie shoots me an appreciative smile and then beams at me.

"It was great," Betty says. "We stopped at HR and they got us ID badges to wear while we're here. With not knowing if you'd need us to help again, Stephanie decided to just go ahead and get us ID's. She also said she'd put us on the list of cleared people permanently, so that way we could come with you anytime we wanted and you wouldn't have to clear it with her."

"That was nice of her," I say with a smile.

"Guess who we met?" Maggie says practically bouncing off the seat.

"Who?" I ask.

"Amelia Ray!" she says excitedly.

I see Kallon tense across from me and he asks, "Oh, how did that go?"

"Amazingly!" Maggie beams at him. "She was so nice. She even signed a napkin for me! Look!"

She pulls out a folded napkin from her pocket and shows it to us.

"That is… nice," Kallon says, surprised.

"And Mr. Tanner apologized for his behavior," Dax says, looking at Kallon and then at me.

"He did?" I ask.

"Yeah, he did," Betty answers. Her face turns red, and she adds, "He gave me those flowers too. I told him it wasn't necessary, but he insisted."

"He said he has a lot to learn when it came to talking to pretty momma's," Maggie adds with a laugh.

"That was nice of him," I say to them both. I look over to where Betty pointed to and saw a huge bouquet of flowers sitting on the table beside the door. I turn back and smile and add, "I'm glad he apologized."

I look at my watch and see it's been an hour already. I jump up and say, "Holy crap, I need to go check the table!"

"We did that on our way back here," Betty says. "We filled what was about half gone and checked the coffee, they were all still about three-quarters of the way full. It's good for another hour."

"Thank you for that, I need to set my timer to go off. I got distracted," I say, holding up the book.

"I was thinking," Betty starts to say and comes to sit beside me. "What if, Maggie and I take over today while you're here. That way we have a run through before we do it ourselves."

"What will I do?" I ask.

"Read that book of yours," Betty says nodding at the book sitting on my lap.

"I couldn't," I say, putting the book on the table.

Betty reaches over and grabs it and puts it back on my lap. She says, "Yes you can. This will be the perfect opportunity for me, and for Maggie, to get practice in before we're here alone. If we need help, we'll call you."

"I don't know," I say. I don't like feeling as if I'm pushing my responsibilities off onto someone else.

Seeming to have read my mind, Kallon says, "Your responsibilities aren't just doing everything by yourself. I can understand where your resistance is coming from but delegate today. Betty's right, today would be a good time for her to do it herself, with Maggie helping of course, while you're here."

I mock glare at him. He already knows me so well. I sigh and say, "Fine."

"Yay!" Betty says, clapping her hands.

I laugh and shake my head.

"See, letting people help isn't so bad. Letting go of some of that control is good for your health, too," Kallon says, reaching over and squeezing my knee. The zing that shoots to my stomach almost makes me gasp. I smile instead and lean back.

"I let go of control," I say.

"You're getting better at it," Betty says, positively.

"I'm trying," I laugh.

Betty stands and says, "I'm going to go out there and keep an eye on things. Maybe meet some more people. The crew seems really nice."

"Can I come too?" Maggie asks, standing up excitedly.

"Yes, you can come help me," Betty says with a grin.

I see Kallon pull his phone out of his pocket and types away on it.

"Please let me know if there's any problems," I plead to Betty as she walks to the door.

"I will," she says. She smiles and walks out of the room.

Dax goes to walk towards the door, but Kallon says, "I've got Trevor meeting them at the tables."

"Are they in danger?" I ask. I think about all the times that I've been here and I realize that Dax was always close by. "Am I in danger being here?"

"Oh, no, you ladies are perfectly safe. I just like having the guys be close to you girls in case you need help with something," Kallon says nonchalantly. I can tell he's hiding something.

"Kallon?" I say his name sternly and he looks at me. I don't say anything else but raise my eyebrows at him.

"Okay, there might be some guys who... they might

have a reputation of taking what they want. Not in the extent of it being illegal per se, but definitely not in the most gentlemanly way."

"I don't like the sound of that," I say, getting nervous.

Kallon slides over on the couch he's sitting on, so he's closer to me, and puts his hand on my knee.

"Abby... you and the Brown girls are safe, I promise. I only have Dax and Trevor around to make it clear you guys are off limits to that behavior. They can come talk to you but the moment they start behaving in any way that makes you uncomfortable... Dax and Trevor have permission to act," Kallon says.

"Who is it?" I ask.

"I'm not at liberty to say, unfortunately. It was put in our contracts that we can't out anyone but if they act out, or if something happens, you'll know, and they'll be dealt with. Again, they haven't hurt anyone and no crimes have been committed. They just toe the line of morally grey," Kallon says.

"Is Chace Tanner one of them?" I ask.

"No, oddly enough. He's just a self-centered, egotistical ass, who honestly doesn't know how to talk to people in a normal way. When he's corrected, he actually learns from it. The other guys, they take the slap on the wrist and carry on with themselves," Kallon says as his voice drops down into a low growl. "I don't think they'll learn until they step over that line and find themselves in handcuffs. I hope that day neve comes, not for their sake, but for the person that lands on the other end of their behavior."

I shiver at that statement. An alarm on Kallon's phone

goes off and he looks down at it.

"Time to head to the set?" I ask him.

"Yeah," he says. "You'll be okay here?"

"You tell me?" I ask in a half joking way.

"You'll be okay here," Kallon states it this time instead of asking it like a question. He smiles and adds, "Dax will be just outside the door, or he can hang out in here, if you'd prefer."

"Whatever you want to do," I say to Dax.

He nods and says, "I'll be outside, Miss Rose."

Kallon stands and leaves his dressing room with Dax. I lean back on the couch and think about what Kallon just told me. There are some guys here that take what they want but do it in a way that isn't illegal? How does that work? Maybe they sweet talk girls into doing things because of who the guy is? I can see that being true.

I shake my head, clearing the thoughts out. If we were in real danger, Kallon would have told me. If we were in real danger, those men wouldn't be here. Right? I hope the answer is that they wouldn't be. I shake my head again and open the book on my lap back up and start reading.

CHAPTER 21

I had set my alarm to go off at 10 o'clock and when it goes off, I'm surprised at how fast the time flew. I check the page I'm on and set the book down. I stand and stretch. I haven't moved since I started reading the second time. Kallon wasn't joking, chapter twelve was a good one. I'm only a couple chapters past but man, that chapter left me wanting more.

I pick the book back up and walk to the door. Dax is standing just outside and when he hears the door open, he looks down at me.

"Hi," I say. "Why didn't you come in and sit?"

"I sit in the car all day, standing out here is nice," he says matter-of-factly.

"Okay," I say. "I'm going to go check-in with Betty and start getting things cleared away."

Dax just nods and then falls into step next to me.

We walk in silence as we go. I can't help my mind wandering back to that chapter. I had thought of Jason, during that scene. About how it would have been like for him to have done the things to me that the male character had done to the female character. I wasn't one for sex in public places but a secret place with a pond, after having a nice picnic, that sounds like something that could be fun.

As we walk into the set room, I look up and see Kallon on set with no shirt on and a towel wrapped around his waist. Without warning, my mental image of Jason doing the things to me turns into Kallon doing them. I bite my lip and turn quickly. I walk fast over to the table, put the book down on it and then walk into the kitchen. Luckily, Betty hadn't noticed me and I'm free to splash water on my face. I grab a bottle of water and take a drink.

STOP THINKING OF HIM LIKE THAT! I scream at myself in my head. But just that thought has me rethinking how the male character— Kallon —had kissed his way down the female character's— me — stomach until he was down at her— *STOP IT! No, no, no! Jason, think of Jason!* I shake my head and force myself to stop thinking of the book completely.

I look around and see that Betty has everything washed and now drying. I take a steadying breath and walk back out to the table, keeping my eyes away from the set. I look around and see that everything is packed up and the only thing left is the tablecloths.

I reach for the one my book is sitting on. I pick the book up and grab the cloth and then put my water and book down on the bare table. I turn my back to the set and start to fold up the cloth. I look over and see Betty talking to Stephanie, they seem be in the middle of a cheerful conversation. I see Maggie standing by Trevor while he points out people on the set. I fight the urge to turn and succeed. I place the first tablecloth in the tote to take home and as I'm reaching for the second, a strong hand squeezes my shoulder.

Please don't be Kallon. I think to myself as I turn around. But it's him.

"Hi," he says with a big smile. He's still only in a towel. My eyes, acting on their own, travel from his face down to his neck, to his massively muscular chest that has just the right amount of hair on it to make him look deliciously masculine. My eyes travel to his washboard abs, down to the V that leads to his—

My eyes fly back up to his face, I see that his Adam's apple dips down, as if he gulped, like he's nervous about me checking him out. There's absolutely no way he didn't notice me doing that. I reach for my water on the table and open it up and take a quick drink.

"Hi," I say after I swallow the water and force my eyes to lock with his. I clear my throat and ask with a stronger voice, "What's with the towel?"

"Shower scene," he says with a lopsided smile.

"Oh," I say. Then my mind goes to 'Along Came You' where the characters have sex in the shower. My face heats to an embarrassing shade of red, and I say, "Oooh."

"I wanted to catch you before you left, sorry about this," he says, waving at his body. I mentally congratulate myself for not looking. "How did you like the book?"

I had just taken another drink and inhaled at his question, causing the water to go down the wrong pipe. I start to cough uncontrollably which makes Kallon pat my back.

"That good, huh?" he chuckles. "You must have gotten to or past chapter twelve."

I shake my head and cough again and hold up a finger for him to wait a minute. After my coughing fit is over, I take another drink.

"Better?" Kallon asks.

"Yes, thank you," I say, laughing.

"So, the book? You liked it that much?" he laughs.

"No... well yes, it's good but—"

"You haven't gotten to the good part yet?"

"Well yes, I have but it's all good parts," I say laughing. And then my face flames red hot, my mind just went back to him staring as the lead male character. I take another drink.

"What chapter are you on now?"

"Fifteen."

"I might have fibbed, chapter seventeen is even better than twelve," he says with a wink.

"What?" I ask in surprise. Not waiting for him to reply, I shake my head and laugh, then say, "You're awful."

"Keller on set!" a loud voice shouts over a speaker.

"Sorry, I have to run," he says. "I'll talk to you later."

"Yeah, go, go," I say waving at him as he walks away. Even with a towel on, his ass looks good. *STOP IT!* I shake my head and insert a visual of Jason's ass instead of Kallon's.

I finish folding up the last tablecloth and toss it in the tote. I walk into the kitchen and put away all the things staying here. As I'm putting the last display case away, Betty walks in.

"Stephanie is awesome," she says with a laugh.

"She really is," I say in agreement.

"Trevor and I will load the van up," Dax says as he pokes his head into the kitchen.

"Thank you, we're finished in here," I say, as we walk out.

I grab the book, put it in my bag, and sling my bag over my head to cross my body. We find Maggie helping the guys load things into their arms. They're able to carry just about everything so Betty and I load ourselves up and follow them out.

"Maggie, will you get the door for us?" Betty asks as we all come to the door to outside.

Maggie runs forward and opens it for us, holding it so it doesn't shut on anyone. We get to the van and Dax puts the totes he's holding down and gets the keys out of his pocket. After he unlocks and opens the doors, we put everything into the back.

"Following us back to the bakery?" I ask Betty.

"I thought I'd swing by and get us all lunch at the pizza place just down the road from there," she says.

"Ooh that sounds good, I haven't had pizza from there in a hot minute," I say, my mouth watering at just the thought.

"I'll call ahead so it'll be ready for me to pick up when we get back," she says. She looks at Dax and says, "Pepperoni alright with you, big man?"

Dax laughs and says, "Yes, just fine. Thank you, Ms.... Thank you, Betty."

The smile she gives him is the brightest I've ever seen. I smile over at her and wave goodbye as I walk to the passenger side of the van. Dax opens the door and waits for me to get in before he shuts the door.

When he gets in, I reach over and hand him my credit card. It's become a compromise for me to nap on the way home. I convinced Dax to use my card to pay for gas though. It took some stern talking to him last week, but he finally said that if I'd sleep, he'd use my card.

◆ ◆ ◆

"Miss Rose, we're back," Dax's voice says as he gently touches my shoulder.

I sit up and see we're parked back behind the shop again. I stretch and get out. It hasn't stopped surprising me how fast and hard I sleep on the ride home.

"Thank you, Jeeves," I say.

Dax chuckles as he comes around to the back. We grab an arm load each and head for the door. I punch in the code and open the door for us. We step into the kitchen and I turn on the lights. We put our stuff down, I put my bag on my desk, and as I turn to go back out, Dax stops me.

"I'll get the stuff out, you put it away," he says with a raised eyebrow, daring me to argue with him. But oddly enough, I don't feel like arguing.

"Okay," I say and yawn.

"Maybe you should go take a nap?" he says with concern in his eyes.

"I'm fine. I just need to wake up from the nap I just had," I say with a little laugh.

Dax shakes his head and heads out to get more stuff

from the van. I start putting stuff away as he brings it all in. After he's done, I hear the honk of the van, and when he comes back in, he hangs the keys up onto the hook.

I hear the beep of the side door and look at the monitor to see Betty and Maggie walking in with pizza boxes and a cup carrier full of soda pop.

"Lunch is here," I say, suddenly starving. My coffee I had this morning no longer filling my belly. I need to do better about eating something in the mornings.

"Lead the way," Dax says, sweeping his arm in front himself.

I walk out to the front and grab some plates as I go.

"Hi!" I say excitedly. And then the smell of the pizza hits me. I groan and say, "Oh that smells delicious!"

"Doesn't it?" Maggie says, enthusiastically. "Mom made me wait until we got here."

"Mean mom!" I say teasingly to Betty.

We all grab a seat at a four-seat table and I pass around the plates. Betty opens the top box and we all inhale deeply.

"Wow, that does smell good," Dax says.

We all reach in and grab a slice and then eat in silence for a moment. The only sound in the room is quite chewing and an occasional sip from a straw drawing soda pop out of the cup.

After we've all had a second slice, I look at my watch and see that its almost noon. I stand and stretch again.

"Thanks for lunch, Betty," I say as I start to walk to the back. "I need to go change and head to the restaurant."

"Do you need help with anything?" Betty asks.

"No, I have everything put away. Go ahead and head

home for the day if you'd like. We can prep stuff in the morning," I say.

I see Betty and Dax share a look but I'm already disappearing into the kitchen before I have a chance to ask what it was about. I rinse my plate off and put it in the dishwasher. I hustle up the stairs and make it to my room quickly. I change into work pants and then a black tank top, knowing I have my chef jacket at the office at Rose's.

I check my hair and make-up and see that it's still all put together. I stop at the kitchen counter and see my black folder of boudoir pictures and remember I still needed to do something with them. I'm no longer wanting to give them to Jason, not yet anyways. Our relationship is still rocky, and I don't want to give them to him unless I know for certain they won't end up in someone else's hands or worse, online. I take it to the living room and put it on the coffee table, so I won't forget about them again.

I head back down the stairs to the shop and grab my bag. I take my phone out and check it. I see I have a missed call from Jason, so I call him back.

"*Hey babe,*" he says when he answers.

"Hey, Jason, sorry I missed your call. I got back from the set not too long ago but then had a quick lunch. But now I'm heading to Rose's, what's up?" I ask.

"*Do you want to come to my place for dinner tonight?*" he asks. I skid to a stop. He never offers to have me over, let alone cook for me.

"Sure," I say. "What's the occasion?"

"*No occasion. Can't I invite you over just because?*"

"I mean, yeah you can but you haven't in a very long

time. I'm just surprised is all," I say honestly.

"*I know, and I'm trying to make up for that,*" he says a little sternly.

"Okay, okay, yeah I'll come over," I say.

"*When do you think you'll get to my place?*" he asks.

"Depending on what all we have left to prep for tomorrow, I might be able to leave at 8."

"*Okay, that'll work,*" he says. "*See you tonight, babe.*"

He hangs up before I can say bye. I put my phone back in my bag and walk to the front of the bakery. When I get out to where everyone is sitting, I see that they've started on the second pizza. Or I should say, Dax has started on the second pizza.

He sees me and stands quickly, wipes his lips with a napkin, and just as he's about to grab his plate, Betty grabs it for him.

"I'll take care of that for you," she says smiling at him. I look at Maggie and see that she's reading a book.

"Thank you," Dax says. "And thanks again for lunch. It was really good."

"Do you want to take the rest of it?" Betty asks.

"No, that's okay," Dax says, waving her off as she tries to hand him the box. He turns to me and asks, "Ready?"

"Yeah," I say. "Thanks Betty! Bye, Mags!"

Maggie raises her hand and waves a hand at me but doesn't look up from her book. Betty smiles and rolls her eyes at her daughter before she looks at me and waves goodbye. We walk out and Dax opens the door for me. I buckle up and pull my phone back out.

I'd made a list last night of all the things we had left

to do for the wedding tomorrow. We have some appetizers to finish prepping and I had the cake to make but I'm going to do that tonight when I get home from Jason's. The bride wanted a plane white, two-tier cake for her and the groom, and then cupcakes for the guests. I had made the cupcakes last night. I just have the bridal cake to make now. The main course will be made tomorrow, but I need to triple check that we have all the fish and steak that they've requested. The pasta salads will be made tonight, as will the rolls. The green salad will be tossed together tomorrow but I need to make sure Tim and Lee, two of our station chefs, have all the veggies chopped and ready.

I see that we need to use our white seat covers and table clothes, the bride will be bringing people in to decorate. I look and see that they'll be arriving at 6 in the morning to start decorating. Bridget has volunteered to come let them in and be onsite if they have any questions for her.

I lean my head back and close my eyes. The stress that tomorrow will bring starts to creep its way into my mind and body. *This is why we don't do weddings on Saturdays.* I tell myself. Saturdays are one of our busiest days and now we have a two-hundred wedding party with the ceremony at 6, appetizers at 8, and dinner at 9. Tomorrow is going to be a long day.

I open my eyes and watch the city and traffic go by. It'll be over in 48 hours, then I can breathe and relax. My bag falls from my lap and the book inside falls out. I reach down for it and open it up to the page I remember reading last. I pick up where I left off and let the pages carry me the rest of the way to the restaurant.

"Abby... Abby!" Dax says a little louder. I look up and see him laughing at me. "That book really pulls you in, doesn't it?"

My face turns a little red, embarrassed that I can't seem to NOT get sucked into the story, but I say, "Yes, it's a good one."

"Well, we're here," Dax says, pointing in front of us. I see that he's parked in the back again. I had told him we could start parking back here, since I have a parking spot that I hardly ever use.

"Thank you," I say. "Hey, come in and sit in the office. No sense in you waiting out here all by yourself. You can sit at one of my parents' desks, Kallon hasn't claimed one yet."

"Okay, thank you," Dax says. I'm surprised that he takes me up on the offer but happy that he does.

We walk to the back door, and I enter my code and go inside. I lead him to the office and turn on the lights.

"Sit anywhere you like," I say as I put my bag and the book on my desk. I reach into my bag and grab my phone and put it in my pocket.

"Thanks," he says with a smile.

"If you need a computer to use, use which ever one you're sitting at," I offer up as well.

"Oh, that's not necessary," he says waving me off.

I start to walk out but then I say, "I have to go do my rounds, do you want to come with me? I can't remember if I've given you an official tour or not."

"Yeah, that'd be great," he says again with a smile.

I wait for him at the door and then we walk to the front where I start my rounds every time. When we get to the third floor, and I'm showing him where the wedding will be, I remember about my plans tonight.

"Dax, I'm supposed to go to Jason's tonight, will that be okay?" I ask.

"Abby, I drive where you tell me to. I have no opinion on if it's okay or not," he says with a smile that doesn't meet his eyes.

"Well, I never want to assume that you don't have plans," I say.

"I won't and never will have plans," he says sternly.

"That's not right, you should have some time off for yourself," I say as I stop and turn towards him.

"Time off is not for me," he says. "I like to stay busy or at least know that I'm on call 24/7."

"What if you find a woman that you want to settle down with?" I ask, thinking of a golden-haired woman that we left not too long ago.

Dax doesn't say anything as he just looks down at me. I wait patiently for him to say something. He finally exhales and says, "Then she'd have to understand my line of work."

I roll my eyes and say, "Okay big guy."

I laugh as his eyes go wide at the nickname Betty had used earlier today and then he glares at me. I laugh again and start walking. We finish the tour and I finish my rounds and we're back down in the office. I'm quietly going over paperwork, as Dax does something on his phone.

As usual, Royce is the first in the door. He greets us and talks to Dax for a few minutes about his military history and then he's off getting ready to start work. Soon, the sound of everyone else is filling the kitchen and the staff room.

I get up from my desk and put my chef jacket on. I walk out and greet everyone. Everyone gets to their stations and starts prepping for dinner and the wedding tomorrow. I walk out and find Patty at the hostess desk.

"Hi Patty," I say as I walk up to her.

"Hi Abby," she says walking over and giving me a big hug.

"How was your day?" I ask.

"Good," she states. "Dad will be picking me up at 8 tonight."

"Okay, that sounds good," I say. "If you need me, you know where to find me."

"Okay," she says and turns back around to finish organizing the menus again.

I say hi to Sherry and Pam. I walk into the bar area and say hi to Cammy, Joel, and Brent as they start to get their stuff ready. Stacy, Megan, and Jay are walking around their sections, getting their chairs put down, and checking their tables.

I walk into the kitchen and it's a flurry of happy talk and kitchen utensils. I go to the office and find that Dax isn't in here anymore. I turn to walk back out to the kitchen and see Dax walking back in from the back door. I'd given him his own code to get in, in case he was outside and needed to get in quickly.

I smile over at him and he holds up a book. I tilt my head, knowing that my book is in my bag in my office.

"What's that?" I ask as he walks up to me.

"How I spend my time waiting," he laughs.

"I like it," I say. I look and see it's a book on the history of Greece. I laugh and say, "Enjoy."

I go into the kitchen and begin my work. Letting the time slip away from me.

CHAPTER 22

The evening went by so fast that when my phone started vibrating in my pocket, I couldn't have told you the time. I pull it out and see that it's my 7:45 alarm going off. I look around the kitchen and see everyone either cleaning their station from the food they just made or cleaning up from prepping foods for tomorrow.

I walk around for a minute and get an idea on how everyone is doing. It seems like we're ahead of schedule. Most of the prep work for the wedding food is done. Tim is finishing up the veggies for the salad and then all that was left was the cake I was doing later.

"Royce," I call out. When he turns, I point to the office. He nods and asks Sarah to finish plating the food he was working on. We walk into the office, and I sit at my desk, rubbing my neck.

"What's up, Ab?"

"How do you feel tonight's going?" I ask.

"Pretty great, all things considering," Royce answers.

"I feel the same, but I wanted a second opinion," I say sounding edgy.

"What's wrong?" he asks.

"I just feel like everything is going too smoothly. The dinner rush was insane, but we handled it amazingly. We're all but done with the prep work for the wedding. I just keep feeling like I'm forgetting something," I say, rubbing my face with my hand now.

"You made your list, yes?" Royce asks.

"Yes, of course," I say.

"It has everything the bride and groom wanted, yes?" he asks again.

"Yes, of course," I say again.

"You've checked your list?"

"Yes, multiple times. Everything is here. The food, the beer, wine, alcohol. I'll bring the cake and cupcakes over tomorrow. We have the dinnerware she picked out already upstairs and ready to be placed."

"Then relax," Royce says with a smile. "You have it all under control."

"I just feel like the other shoe is going to fall, you know what I mean," I say sounding stressed out. "Rose Bud's is doing great and the catering gig is too. Rose's has been steadily busy all week. I just have a feeling something bad is going to happen."

"You're just stressed. Go home, we've got this covered," Royce says. "You've got that cake to make, remember?"

"Yeah, but I have dinner at Jason's first," I say with a sigh. I don't know why I'm so apprehensive to go over to have dinner. I really do think it's sweet that he invited me.

"You do?" Royce asks, sounding shocked. When I told

him I was going to give Jason another chance, he didn't seem surprised. He said he knew I would, but he also told me to be careful, that giving someone too many chances led to people repeating bad behavior or their behavior getting worse.

"Yeah, he called earlier and asked if I wanted to have dinner at his place tonight," I say with a smile.

"Well, I'll be an ape's uncle," he says.

I laugh and says, "It's a monkey's uncle."

"Monkey's uncle, yes, yes," he says waving off his mistake. "You should go. We have this."

"Are you sure?" I ask.

"Yes, we've been telling you, you do too much. Even if you came in as manager for a couple hours, we'd have this covered," he says as he pulls me up from my chair and gives me a hug.

"I know but—"

"I know what you're going to say, but maybe you need to reevaluate your responsibilities," he says with a gently shake to my shoulders. "Remember, you are co-owner and manager of this restaurant now. You don't have to be head chef if you don't want to be."

"Are you trying to steal my job?" I ask, pretending to be horrified.

"No, no, Abby, I would never do that," Royce starts to say in earnest. I start laughing and he says, "Oh you little… that wasn't funny."

I laugh hard and say, "It was a little funny."

Royce starts to laugh too and I hear Dax laughing as well. I look over at him and see him give me a thumbs up.

"I'm serious though, Abby. Think about what you're

willing to let go of to free up a little bit more of your time. You should be enjoying this time in your life, not working yourself to death," Royce says more serious.

"I agree with him on that," Dax says. I look over at him again, but shoot him a glare this time. He lifts his hands in a show of defeat and then goes back to his book.

"I will," I say. Royce looks at me skeptically so I say in a tone to match his, "I will."

"Okay," he says with a smile. "Now go and have dinner with Jason. We'll see you tomorrow."

"Thank you, my friend," I say. Then I lean up and give him a quick kiss on the cheek.

"Of course, il mio adorabile amica," he says as he kisses me on the cheek.

I turn from him and step to the coat rack and take my jacket off. I reach over and grab my bag and look at Dax as Royce walks out of the office.

"I'm going to go say goodbye to Patty and then I'll be ready to head out," I say to him with a smile.

"Sounds good," he says.

I walk out of the office and through the kitchen to the doors that lead to the bar. I walk through the bar, saying hello to the customers and letting the employees know I'll be heading out and Royce is in charge. I get to the hostess area and see Patty talking to our dad.

"Hey Dad," I say as I walk up.

"Hey, Buds," he says as he gives me a hug. "You heading out?"

"Yeah, we've got everything caught up back there and Royce and Sarah can handle the rest of the night. Plus, Jason invited me over for dinner," I say. He's got a surprised look on his face too, so I say, "Yeah, I was just as surprised when he invited me over."

"Well, that's good sweety, you deserve to have some fun in your life," he says as he kisses the top of my head. He turns to Patty and says, "You ready to go home, honey?"

"Yes," Patty says. She comes around and gives me a hug. "Bye, Abby."

"Bye Patty, see you tomorrow," I say. She waves and walks towards the doors.

"Bye, Buds," Dad says as he gives me another quick hug and then he hurries from the restaurant to catch up with Patty.

"Bye girls, Royce is in charge," I say to the other hostesses. They all wave and go back to looking at the computer screen.

I walk back to the kitchen and see Dax standing at the back door. As I get closer, he opens the door for me and I walk out with him on my heels. The night has gotten a little chillier than the previous nights.

"It feels like spring's trying to hang on," I say as we get closer to the car. Dax pulls out the key fob and starts the car before we get to it.

"It sure does," Dax says as he opens the car door for me and I jump in quickly. I lean forward and turn the heat on and the air up as Dax runs around and gets in. I sit back and buckle up.

"Where does Jason live?" Dax asks.

"35 Hudson Yards," I say.

"Really?" Dax asks surprised.

"Yeah, why?"

"It's only about 20 minutes from Mr. Keller's place," he says.

"Oh," I say. "I guess I never asked him where he lived."

We ride along in silence. I pull out my phone and send a text to Jason that we're about 15 minutes away. I put my phone in my lap and lean my head back. I think about what Royce had told me. That maybe it's time for me to take a step back from cooking. Just for now, while I've got the catering gig going.

It would free up some of my time. I could leave the restaurant a little earlier at night and get home. Maybe have some evenings to spend with Jason. I did tell him I'd start making free time with him a priority. Maybe stepping back and just being owner, manager of Rose's is what I need to do, just for now?

My phone buzzes in my hand and I see Jason is calling me.

"Hello," I answer, forcing myself to sound more chipper than I feel. I still have that ominous feeling inside.

"Hey babe, you said you're about 15 minutes out?" Jason says sounding out of breath.

"Yeah, maybe closer to 10 now. Traffic is moving along and we've hit a lot of green lights," I say. "You sound out of breath, is everything okay?"

"Oh yeah, everything's fine. I was just… running around picking up the place," he says with a chuckle.

"Okay," I say. "You know you don't have to do that for me."

"So, I'll see you in about 10 minutes?"

"Yeah," I say.

"*Okay, see you then,*" he clicks off without letting me say goodbye, again. I'll have to tell him how much it bothers me that he does that.

I put the phone in my bag and my hand touches the book. I pull it out and my face heats up again. I push it back into my bag and close my eyes. *DO NOT start thinking of Kallon like that.*

I have to figure out how to make myself not think of Kallon in that sort of way. It's hard not to when he looks and acts the way he does. Especially when he walks around the set half naked.

I'm with Jason, I shouldn't be thinking of another man while I'm in a relationship. And I definitely shouldn't be thinking of my business partner. I let a groan of frustration out and sit up, opening my eyes.

"Is everything okay?" Dax asks from up front.

"Yeah, just tired I think," I say.

"I'm at your beck and call. You just say the word and I'll take you home," Dax says. He pulls up to a building and I look to see we're already at Jason's apartment building. I check my phone and see that the ten minutes flew by in what felt like two.

"Thank you, Dax."

He gets out and comes around to open my door.

"It's my pleasure, Miss Abby," he says. I let the 'Miss' part slide, I know he says it out of utmost respect.

"I'll call you when I'm about ready to leave. I'm guessing two hours tops."

"Whenever you're ready."

I nod at him and make my way to the doors. I'm waiting for the elevator and when the doors open, a tall, thin, and very beautiful red head gets out.

I about bump into her on accident, and I say, "Ooop, sorry."

"No worries," she says. She hurries past me and out the door. I get in and push the number for Jason's floor.

When the doors open, I walk down the hall. He's lived here for a couple years now. You'd think I'd be more familiar with this place, but I can count on one hand how many times I've been here. That thought alone, makes me feel sad. A woman should know her boyfriend's apartment building better than I do. A girlfriend should be invited over to her boyfriend's building more times than just a handful.

By the time I get to his door, my mood is piss poor, at best. I knock and wait. I hear running and then the door opens, and Jason is standing there smiling but looking shaken up.

"What's the matter?" I ask.

Jason shakes his head, and the scared look disappears, and he says, "Nothing, babe. Time just got away from me and your knocking startled me. I took a quick shower."

"Okay, if you're sure," I say tentatively. I look at him closely and see his hair is damp and he's in shorts and a t-shirt.

"Of course," he shakes his head again and then smiles at me. He pulls me to him and says, "Hi."

I smile back and say, "Hi."

He pulls me into his arms and kisses me deeply. He shuts the door and then leans against it, pulling me against him. His kissing becomes almost frantic, his hands wandering my body like he's looking for something.

I pull away and ask, "Jason?"

He had started kissing my neck but pulls away and say, "Yeah, babe?"

"What's wrong?"

"Nothing, I'm just really excited to see you," he says. "Sunday feels like a long time ago."

And then he's kissing me again. His hands trail down my back and when they get to my ass, he squeezes and then lifts me up. His hands go to my thighs and he wraps my legs around his waist.

I guess sex before dinner works. I think to myself as my stomach growls quietly. He stops kissing me and offers me his neck. I take the hint and start kissing him. Instead of going to his room, we go to the couch. He puts my back down against the cushions and then he's on top of me.

He instantly starts dry humping me, pulling the top of my tank top down so he can get to my breasts. He pulls a nipple out of its bra cup and sucks it into his mouth, while his other hand is unbuttoning my pants. He pulls my pants and undies off in one pull, not even taking his mouth off my nipple.

His fingers find my entrance but before he can go any further, I reach down and grab his hand.

"What?" he asks in a husky voice. "I want to make you feel good."

I pull his hand to the spot I want him to rub and he starts to rub. I show him how much pressure to use and he follows my lead. He growls into my ear and says, "It's hot when you show me what you want."

I smile into his neck and kiss him. *Of course, he'd want to know, he wouldn't get upset. He loves me and wants me to feel as good as he does.*

I run my hands up his chest and then to his back. I get to the hem of his shirt and pull it up. He stops kissing me so I can pull his shirt over his head. After I toss his shirt to the floor, he bypasses my lips and pulls my nipple into his mouth. I then go to my tank top and pull it up, he again stops his nuzzling long enough for my tank top to pass between him and my breasts. I reach behind me and unclasp my bra and I pull it away.

"There they are," Jason all but growls the words out. He moves his lips over to my other nipple and starts to roll his tongue around it.

"Jason," I breathe out. He took it as a sign to increase his speed with his fingers but in doing so, he position moved. He isn't on the spot anymore.

My hand goes down to move him back, but he grunts out, "I've got this, can you take my shorts off?"

I wanted to tell him he doesn't, 'got this', but before I can, his lips are on mine and my mouth is full of his tongue. I go to his shorts and try to push them down as much as I can. When I left my leg up to use my feet to pull them down, it causes me to open up to him and his fingers find their way inside me.

"God damn, you're so tight," he says. He presses his body into me as he uses the hand he was using to hold himself up off me, to take his shorts the rest of the way off. He wasn't wearing underwear. I can feel his head at my entrance.

"Not yet, please," I say.

"Okay baby, we can play a little longer," he says with a laugh. "But I'm telling you, I'm primmed and ready to go, so we can't play for long."

When his arm is back by my side, holding himself up a little, I reach down and start rubbing myself. With his fingers inside, and me rubbing, I'm hoping I can reach an orgasm before he decides it's go time.

Jason leans back and gets off me, but his fingers stay inside. As he watches me rub myself, his fingers pick up speed.

"Damn, babe, this is hot. Why have you never done this for me before?" he asks.

I want to tell him that 'this', isn't for him, it's for me but I just smile and then close my eyes. He reaches up with his free hand and starts playing with my breasts.

"Yes, Jason, please," I say. "Don't stop doing that."

"Shit, babe," he says in a voice full of desire and need.

I look down and see his erection is indeed ready and willing to join the party. I reach down with my free hand and start to rub him. I look up at him and his eyes roll to the back of his head.

"Fuuuuuck me," Jason says. His eyes pop open and he stairs down at our hands at my center.

"I'm close, Jas," I say, breathing hard.

With that, Jason hollers, "Fucking hell, babe! I can't wait any longer, this is fucking hotter than shit. I gotta get inside you."

He reaches to the table behind the couch and grabs a

condom and puts it on, thankfully he didn't take his fingers out. I start rubbing harder, faster, trying to get there before he takes his fingers out.

So fast, in almost one motion, his fingers are out of me but then they're replaced by his erection. He lets out a sigh that's almost a growl of relief.

"You feel so fucking good," he says. He leans over me and starts to thrust in and out. He pulls almost all the way out and then slams in.

My breath catches and comes out in a whoosh. He does it again and my breath does it again.

"You like that baby?" he asks. He pulls all the way out and then slams into me.

"Ugh, a little too rough on that one," I say.

"Sorry," he says and kisses me deeply. He keeps himself inside of me but picks up the pace.

I start rubbing harder, willing myself to beat him to the finish line, just this once. I can feel the tightness starting in my stomach and then it makes its way lower. Just a little more... but the slapping sound that our bodies are making is starting to distract me.

I pull my mouth away from Jason's and say, "Can you stop for just a second, I'm so close, please?"

"You want me to stop?" Jason asks, thrusting in harder. My breath comes out in a whoosh. "Nah, you like it like this."

He pulls back and comes back in, not as hard as the time that hurt me but close to it.

"Jason, please, I... I... I want to orgasm too," I say, my face heating at my words.

"You will baby... cum with me," he says. He sucks on

my nipple and stills for just a second. I think he's going to give me the minute I needs so I start to rub my spot again. After a couple seconds, I can feel myself getting closer. But then Jason pulls on my nipple, almost painfully and then starts thrusting faster and harder.

"Please," I breathe out. "Please... just... a... second longer."

""UUUGHNAAAAH!" Jason bellows out. He jack hammers for a second and then he slumps into me, breathing harder than I've ever heard him breathe before.

My orgasm that was right there dissipates in a wisp of sadness. And now I'm pissed. I push Jason off me and stand up. I storm to the bathroom and shut the door.

"Do not cry," I whisper to myself as I stare into my eyes in the mirror. I hate that my tears are so closely associated with my anger. Sure, I'll cry when I'm hurt or sad, but that takes a lot. Now, when it comes to be being mad, it comes way to easily. And right now, I'm pissed as hell. I sit on the toilet and let nature do its thing.

After I wash my hands, I splash some water on my face and try to calm down. *Why should I calm down? I was trying to tell Jason what I needed and he didn't listen.* I throw open the door and Jason's standing there.

"Are you okay?" he asks. "I didn't hurt you, did I?"

"No, and no you didn't," I say as I push past him. I track down my clothes and put on my underwear.

Before I can put on anymore clothes though, Jason wraps his arms around my waist and asks, "You're not okay?"

"No, I'm not," I say. I push his hands off me and grab my bra and put it on. I can't look at him right now. I don't want him to see the tears that are forming in my eyes.

"What's wrong?" he asks.

I stand and turn slowly towards him. I throw my hands in the air and the first tear falls, "What's wrong Jason is... I was telling you what I needed, so that I could orgasm with you and you didn't listen to me... again."

I look to the floor and find my pants. I rip them up my legs, flinching as the zipper scratches my leg. I find my tank top and pull it over my head.

"Wait, what?" Jason says. "You didn't or—"

"No, I didn't!" I interrupt him.

"I thought you did," he says sounding sad. He grabs his shorts off the floor.

"What gave you that idea?"

He takes a second to think and then his head hangs down. I look and see he's still naked, his erection gone just like my forgotten orgasm.

"I got so lost in the feeling, of you getting tighter, I thought you were close enough that I could finish and have you follow right behind me," he says, running a hand through his hair and then puts his shorts on.

"That's not really how it works, a girl has to be right there too before a guy falls over the edge or she loses it," I say, sitting down.

"Shit babe, I'm sorry, we can go for round two after dinner and I promise it'll be all about you," he says, sitting next to me.

I look at him and a small smile crosses my face. I'm hit with a wave of exhaustion and hunger. I don't say anything about round two, but I do say, "Dinner sounds good, what are we having?"

"Whatever you want to make babe, I made sure I stocked the fridge and cupboards, so you'd have options."

I'm shocked silent. No thought in my head. My body freezes. I'm just staring at Jason with my eyes wide, my eyebrows have to be lost in my hairline now, and my mouth is hanging open dumbfounded.

"Babe?" Jason says. He rubs my arm and says with concern, "Abby?"

My breath comes out in one quick whoosh. I feel a sob about to break through me, not one of anger but sadness this time. I close my mouth and let my body sag. I put my hands to my face and shake my head.

"I'm cooking?" I ask through my hands.

"Well, yeah, you're the cook," he says in a humorous tone that also sounds like he's saying 'duh'.

"You invited me over for dinner," I say, pulling my hands away. And as I do, I tell myself not to cry.

"Yeah, for you to cook for us, like you always do," Jason says. He sounds confused now.

"When have I ever cooked over here? And when is the last time I cooked for you at my place? We always get takeout," I say, standing up. I walk into the kitchen, to see if he's messing with me. But no, there's nothing ready. There's not even any takeout on the counters. I turn and put my hands up and out to the side. "Seriously?"

"You thought I was going to cook for us? You know I can't cook," Jason says rudely.

"At the very least, you could have gotten us takeout," I say. I walk past him and go to my shoes that he'd somehow gotten off me quicker than I thought possible. I sit and start to put them on.

"Why are you going to get takeout when I have a kitchen full of food? Just make something here," he says as he pulls on his shirt.

His words feel like a slap. I slam my foot into my shoe, not worrying to tie them. I storm to the door, but he jumps in front of me.

"Just make something here," he says.

"I'm not making anything here and I'm not going out to get food," I say in a snarly tone. "I'm. Going. Home."

"What, no, stay," Jason says. He puts his hands on my shoulders, but I shake him off.

"I am so upset with you right now that I can't even begin to want to stay here. Move," I demand. I look at him and raise my eyebrows, expectantly.

"I don't know what I did wrong," Jason says angerly.

"Then take some time to think about it," I say as I get to the door. I pick up my bag and storm out, slamming the door behind me. I dig in my bag for my phone and call Dax."

"Hello, Miss Abby," he says cheerfully.

"I'm ready to go home," I snarl out.

Dax takes one breath and says, *"I'm out front, where you left me fifteen minutes ago."*

A manic laugh erupts from me, and I say, "It's only been fifteen minutes?"

"Yes," Dax says uncertainly.

"Of course it has," I say laughing without humor. "I'll be right down. Bye."

"Bye," Dax says.

I don't bother hanging up the phone and throw it into my bag as I wait for the damn elevator to get to me. I look back down the hall to see if Jason is following me but of course he's not.

The elevator finally dings and the doors open. I get in and hit the button with the star and the L on it. As I make my way down, I try to calm myself down.

He never said he was going to cook. Yeah, but he invited us over. If he wasn't planning on cooking, he should have gotten something delivered or picked something up. You don't just assume the person you invite over is going to cook just because that's what they do for a living.

Talking to myself was going to land me in a mental institution if I continued to have these conversations with myself. As the doors ding open, Dax is standing in front of them waiting for me.

"Did he hurt you?" he asks. He looks madder than I feel.

"No, he didn't," I say.

"You sounded upset when you called," he says. I start walking through the lobby towards the doors to go outside.

"I was, I am," I say.

"What happened?" he asks.

"I don't want to talk about it. I'm hungry, I'm tired, and I want to go home," I say.

We get to the car and Dax hurries to open the door. I slide in and put my seatbelt on. I cross my arms around myself and hold myself tight. *I will not fall apart in the car with Dax here.*

Dax gets in and he looks like he wants to say more but he just puts the car in drive and pulls away from the curb. We aren't moving but more than a couple seconds when I feel my phone buzzing in my bag. Anger flaring, I pull my phone out. I'll let Jason have another piece of my mind, but then I see it's Kallon calling.

"Did you tell Kallon something happened?" I ask Dax.

"No, I haven't talked to Mr. Keller since the movie set," he states.

"Why's he calling me then?" I ask.

"Answer and find out," Dax says kindly. I know he can tell I'm on the verge of losing it.

"Hello?" I ask as I answer the phone. I try to change my voice, so I don't sound so upset.

It's quiet for a second and then Kallon says, *"What's the matter?"*

"Who says anything's the matter?" I ask back.

"I can tell by the tone in your voice. What's wrong?"

I shake my head and say, "Nothing."

"Something."

I laugh and say, "Just... nothing. I'm hungry, tired, and want to go home."

"Didn't you have dinner plans with Jason tonight? Have you not left for his place yet?"

"Yes, and yes," is all I say.

"Yes, you had plans and yes you've left?"

"Yes."

"It didn't go well."

"Yes," I say sadly. I feel a tear go down my cheek.

I hear Kallon pull the phone from his face and he says something in a muffled voice, but then he's back and says to me, *"Are you okay?"*

"Yes," I sniffle.

"No, you're not. Did you guys break up again?"

"No… I don't think so. Somethings happened and it pissed me off. He didn't know what he did wrong, so I told him to take some time to think about what I could be upset about."

It's quiet on his end and then he says, *"Do you want to talk about it?"*

"Not particularly," I say.

"You know you can talk to me about anything, right?" he says in such a kind and sweet voice that my hold on my tears, breaks.

I pull the phone away, close my eyes, and let a sob out.

"Miss Abby?" Dax says with so much concern that another sob rocks through me. He reaches back and grabs the phone from my hand and pulls it to his ear. "Sir, it's me."

I don't know what Kallon says but Dax says, "Umm, it's pretty bad."

Kallon says something else, and Dax says, "Yes, sir. About twenty minutes out."

He must have hung up the phone because he doesn't say anything else. I put my head against the door and let myself cry.

I cry because these two men who I just met a couple of weeks ago, seem to care more about me than my boyfriend of 9 years. Or what should have been 9 years. Another sob rips through me. *What am I doing with Jason?*

CHAPTER 23

When the car finally stops moving, I've almost cried myself to sleep. Before Dax can get out of the car, my door is opening, and a big body is reaching over me. Hands unbuckle my seatbelt and then strong arms are lifting me out of the car.

"I've got her, Dax, just get the door," Kallon's voice says from behind me. I take a deep breath, smelling his intoxicating cologne. It smells so good. I remember smelling it the night we had dinner at Rose's and I drank too much wine. The night that Jason and I broke up. Another sob comes and more tears roll down my cheeks. "It's okay, Abby, I've got you."

He starts walking, carrying me, and then we come to a stop.

Dax says, "Abby, what's the code to get through your door?"

"568... 363," I whisper out between hiccups.

Kallon carries me up the stairs like I weigh nothing and then we stop again.

"And the one for the top door?" Dax asks gently.

"5683... 968," I say. My hiccups subsiding a little bit more.

Dax opens the door and Kallon carries me in. He walks over to the couch and sets me down. I open my eyes and see Trevor had been with us and he walks to the kitchen with bags of food. Another wave of sadness rolls through me and I curl into myself.

"Thanks guys," Kallon says. Someone walks over and he says, "Oh, yeah, thanks, she'll need something to drink in a minute."

"We'll be outside if you need us," Dax's voice says, full of concern.

"Thank... you... both," I manage to get out.

"No problem, Miss Rose," Trevor says. Dax must have already left. I start crying again.

"Shhh," Kallon says, rubbing my leg. He's sat down beside me. "Abby, please, talk to me."

I shake my head and cry some more. Kallon stands up and then he's lifting me and then wrapping his arms around me, holding me tightly. We sit with just the sound of me crying for a while, long enough for me to finally stop crying. I take a deep breath and sit up, away from Kallon's arms.

"You okay?" he asks.

I nod and wipe my face with my hands. Kallon reaches into his suit jacket pocket and pulls out a brand-new handkerchief.

"Men actually carry those around still?" I ask with a small laugh.

"I do," Kallon says.

"Of course you do," I say with another laugh. I wipe my

face and hold it in my hands. The silky softness feels cool and nice in my fingers.

"Wanna talk about it now?" he asks.

"Not really," I say.

"If you don't give me something, the thoughts that are going through my mind right now are going to cause me to make Dax drive me over to Jason's place and beat him to a pulp. Did he hurt you?"

"Not in a physical way," I say. But my mind says, *Well, the sex wasn't the gentlest, but he doesn't need to know that.*

"In what way?" Kallon asks in such a sincere way, that I look up and see concern all over his face and his eyes look as if he's as upset at I am.

"It's really embarrassing to talk to you about this but seeing as you're the only one here for me to talk to and my best girlfriend lives too far away to go to her house and Betty has Maggie, I guess you'll have to suffer through this with me," I say wiping my face again.

"Like I said on the phone, you can talk to me about anything."

"You might change your mind about that after tonight."

"I doubt that. There's nothing you can tell me that will scare me away."

Like a Band-Aid, Abs. "I've never orgasmed while having sex with Jason and since the only person I've ever been with is Jason, I've never had an orgasm during sex."

Kallon's quiet for a minute but I don't dare look at him. He takes a breath in and says, "Ooookay. Not where I thought this was going but okay. Have you told him what you like?

What you don't like?"

"I've tried but… he either doesn't listen, doesn't care, or gets too carried away and by the time I'm… close, he's done. I tried to finally explain it to him tonight because I actually got upset enough that he noticed. He told me after dinner we could use round two just for me."

"Round two?"

"Yeah, I barely made it through the door before he was on me."

"Make up sex will do that," he chuckles. "So, round two didn't go any better?"

"Round two didn't happen."

"How come?"

"Because we didn't have dinner and I was pissed, I left."

"Why didn't you have dinner?"

"Because he assumed I was going to cook," I can feel myself getting upset again. I take a steading breath and play with the handkerchief in my hands.

"He what?"

"He assumed I was going to cook dinner."

"After he invited you over?"

"Yup. Oh, but he graciously stocked the fridge and cupboards for me," I say snarkily. "Now, I could see how he'd think that was a generous thing to do if I ever cooked at his place. Honestly, the only time I've cooked for us, is on special occasions. Like our anniversary or his birthday. If we had plans for a dinner date, we ate out or got something to go or delivered."

"He didn't get anything ready for dinner? He expected

you to do it after being at work all day?"

"Yes."

"Okay, I can see why you were so pissed," Kallon says with a little laugh. He then says softly, "But why all the tears?"

"I wasn't crying because of Jason, well not really. I was crying because... I realized that you and Dax, and Trevor for that matter, have shown me more consideration and thoughtfulness in the few weeks that we've known each other, than my boyfriend of nine years ever has, and it just hit really hard."

"I can see how that could affect you."

"I don't know what to do anymore," I say sounding completely defeated.

"I do," Kallon says. He gets up and walks into the kitchen. He turns and says, "Do you eat in the living room?"

"I eat anywhere," I say with a laugh.

He laughs too and brings in a bag of food.

"What's this?" I ask.

"Chinese," he says. "We happened to be driving by this place when Dax got ahold of your phone. I had Trevor stop and I got food."

"I haven't had Chinese food in so long," I say, sitting up and reaching for the bag. I look at him and say, "Thank you."

"You're welcome," he says. "But I get to eat some too. I was in a business meeting that ran late, and I haven't had dinner either."

"What about Trevor and Dax?" I ask. I look towards the door. "Should we invite them up to eat? Is there enough for all of us?"

"I got them their own," he says with a smile. "They're weird and like to eat in the car or outside. Dax says he starts to feel claustrophobic if he's inside too much. But I see him starting to relax more when he's with you."

"I think it's because he and Betty have a thing for each other," I laugh.

"You think so too?" Kallon says with a start. "I've been thinking that for so long now."

"Oh, one hundred percent they do," I laugh. I grab a takeout container and open it. I look up at Kallon and smile, "Pot stickers?"

"I didn't know what you liked, so I got a little of everything," he says with a shrug.

I smile at him and then go back to the containers. I find the soy sauce on the first try. Using the provided chopsticks, I grab a potsticker and dip it in the sauce. I bite into it and groan. My head rolls to my right shoulder and my eyes close.

"Mmmm, food," I say. I open my eyes and see Kallon has a chopstick with sweet and sour chicken halfway to his mouth but he's frozen. "What?"

"You shouldn't moan like that," he says with a shake of his head and pops the chicken in his mouth.

"It was a groan, not a moan," I say bumping my knee into his.

"There's no difference," Kallon chuckles.

"Yes, there is," I say. "A moan is a longer sound than a groan."

"Whatever you say... but whatever you just did, you shouldn't do that," he says with a grin.

"Why?"

"I'll tell you another time, right now, let's just eat."

"Without groaning or moaning?"

"Preferably, but if you must, go right ahead," he says with a smile and gleam in his eyes.

I shake my head and put my chopsticks down. I grab another container and find pork fried rice. I look in the bag and find a plastic spork. I scoop some rice and eat it, fighting the urge to groan again. It's just so dang good! Kallon and I sit in silence and just eat. He slides a bottle of water in front of me and I nod a thanks, my mouth is full of food so I can't thank him with words.

After I feel full to the brim, I lean back against the cushions. I grab the blanket from the back of my couch and pull it over my legs. A sigh escapes my mouth and I smile over at Kallon.

"Better?" Kallon asks.

"Much," I say. "Thank you, again."

"So, I was going to wait to ask you tomorrow but since I'm here. I'll ask now. My family is coming in for my birthday in a couple of weeks, do you think it would be okay if we portioned off part of the third floor at Rose's for us to have a little family dinner?"

"Kallon, you don't have to ask for things like that. Just tell me what you want for dinner and the day, and we put it on the schedule," I say nudging him with my knee again. I had effectively ignored the electric shock all night until just now, this one demanded my attention. I move my legs away and put my feet under my butt.

"I will never just assume I can do whatever I want, this

restaurant might be half mine but it's all yours."

I laugh and say, "That doesn't even make sense."

"Yes, it does," Kallon says. "I might have bought half of it, but it's yours. I'm not going to step on your toes."

I turn and face him, and my tone is serious when I say, "Kallon, we are fifty-fifty when it comes to Rose's. We make decisions about it together but when it comes to needing a part of the restaurant for a dinner, you don't have to ask me permission."

He smiles at me and says, "I appreciate that. I'll stop by tomorrow and check the schedule to see if the weekend they'll be here will work."

"It should because I don't think we have anything for the third floor scheduled until August."

"Okay," he says with a smile. A yawn escapes me which prompts him to put his bottle of water down. "You going to be okay tonight?"

"Yeah, now that I'm fed—" I say with a laugh "—I think I can sleep now."

"I'll help you clean up," Kallon says and before I can tell him I'll take care of it, he's closing containers and stacking them up.

I help pack some to the fridge and ask, "You don't want to take any of this home?"

"No, that's okay," he says as he looks in my fridge. "It looks like you need it more than me. You only have condiments in here."

I laugh and say, "I don't eat here often enough to keep my fridge stocked. I usually have dinner at Rose's and breakfast downstairs."

"What about lunch?"

"Hmmm, I think today is the first time I've had lunch in a long time," I laugh again. "Recently I'm driving back from the set or on my way to Rose's. I'll sometimes make a meat and cheese plate at Rose's if I need a snack before I have dinner."

"You work so much you don't have time to eat properly," Kallon says in a serious tone as he walks towards the front door.

"I'm figuring that out," I say with a sigh.

Kallon opens the front door and turns, "Are you sure you'll be okay?"

"Yes, Kallon," I say with a smile. "I'm starting to feel like I might have overreacted."

"No, don't do that," he says a little angerly. "Don't let him off the hook. He invited you over for dinner, he should have provided said dinner. And for the other thing..."

My face heats, *I can't believe I told him all of that.* "Forget about that."

"No, just... keep telling him what you want, he'll listen sooner or later," he says as he rubs the back of his neck with his hand, his face turning a little pink.

"Yeah," I say, my face turning redder. "Thanks, for everything."

"Anytime," Kallon says. He gives me a quick hug and says as he pulls away, "Sleep well, Abby."

"I will," I say, halfheartedly. Kallon gives me a smile and then heads down the stairs. When he gets to the bottom, he opens the door, then turns towards me and waves. His smile bigger than before.

"Good night," he says up to me.

"Night," I say, returning his smile.

He walks out of the door and I wait to hear the lock click into place before I shut my door. I go to my bag, that one of the guys put on the kitchen counter and pull my phone out of it. I decide to grab the book too, maybe some reading will help me fall asleep faster. I grab a bottle of water before walking to my room, turning the lights off as I go.

Before crawling into bed, I use the bathroom and brush my teeth. I turn my lights off and switch on the light on my nightstand. I check my alarms on my phone to make sure they're set for the morning when see that I have a missed text from Jason.

Jason: Hey, I'm sorry about tonight. I'm an ass. Can I see you tomorrow?

Me: I'm working at the bakery and then I have the wedding at Rose's. Can I call you when I get home?

Jason: Sure, fine. Good night.

I'm not sure how to take his text, even though he responded quickly, his text seems off. Shaking my head, I plug my phone in and turn my ringer back on. Before putting it down, I set a timer for two hours. I pick up the book and start reading.

Before I know it, the timer's going off. I've read past chapter seventeen and I can't believe what I've read. The couple had been driving, on their way to dinner, when the female character had decided to give the guy a blowjob. They called it a broady, a blowjob on the road. He started to get handsy with her and it got to where they couldn't handle it. So, he pulled off on a side dirt road and they finished off in the back of her little SUV with the rear door wide open, and they just banged one out real quick.

I can't imagine a place where I'd feel comfortable having sex in a car. There are just too many people walking around New York for someone not to see it happening. But the thought of having sex somewhere other than a bed or couch has me intrigued.

The thought of not being able to wait until I got home to have my guy, makes me think about how I feel about Jason. We had waited until we were out of high school before we lost our virginities to each other. There was maybe a good three months where we couldn't keep our hands off each other but then Jason went off to college and I started at ICE. We still enjoyed each other when we got together but it felt like the heat had already died out. There weren't any moments where it felt like I had to have him right then and there or I might combust.

I put the book down and turn the light off. I roll over and wrap the blanket around myself. I close my eyes and will myself to fall asleep. But my brain won't shut off.

Am I just holding on to Jason and our relationship because it's familiar and safe? I love him but am I in love with him? Is the spark gone? And if so, can it be found again? Am I holding on to the future of us because it's something we've talked so much about but have never taken the steps towards that future? Is it weird that we don't live together after so many years of being together?

Deciding that forcing myself to sleep isn't going to

work, I grab my phone and sit up in bed. It's 10:37pm. I decide
to text Kayla and see if she's awake.

> **Me:** Hey K, you awake?
>
> **Kayla:** Sure am. Just going over my to do list for the wedding again.
> What's up?
>
> **Me:** Can't sleep. How's that going?
>
> **Kayla:** I can see why people elope. This wedding planning stuff sucks.
> Don't get me wrong, I want to marry Peter more than anything in the world!
> But if one more person tries to tell me I should do something this way or that
> way, after I've already decided on something? My head might explode.
>
> **Me:** People are actually saying that to you?
>
> **Kayla:** Yes. It's mainly about the colors I picked. I've heard, "They're
> more fall wedding colors than early summer wedding colors," so many times,
> I've lost count. I've bitten my tongue so much on A snarky reply that I think I
> have a permanent canker sore.
>
> **Me:** Your colors are beautiful. I'm sorry people have been causing you
> stress.
>
> **Kayla:** It's okay, I think my facial expressions have been telling people
> to back off lately. Peter says I'm going to have RBF for the rest of my life now.
> Hahaha
>
> **Me:** As long as it's telling people to keep their unwanted opinions to
> themselves, I'm all for RBF's.
>
> **Kayla:** How's it going with Jason? How's being back together going?
>
> **Me:** It's been a little weird and rocky, but I think we'll be okay. Maybe.
>
> **Kayla:** Maybe?

I finally tell her about the sex we've been having and
had that first night we got back together and then about the
disaster that was tonight. The three little dots showing that
she's replying, seems to be blinking at me forever. But then
she finally replies.

Kayla: Are you freaking kidding me? >:-@ He actually expected you to cook tonight? Does he not have a considerate bone in his body? Of course, he doesn't. He doesn't even try to get you to O before he does. I can't believe he's so self-centered that he can't see that you've never had an O with him, like ever. Abs, that sucks. I mean, really, that really sucks!

Me: I know but I think the not O'ing is my fault. I've never told him I haven't and I haven't been very vocal about what I need or want to get there, until recently.

Kayla: Ok, that's fair but... come one. He expected you to cook?After he invited you over? Even Peter says that's some low dickhead shit right there.

Me: You told Peter?!?!?!

Kayla: Just about the dinner stuff. Chill. I won't tell him about your sex life. Hahaha

Me: Thanks.

Kayla: So, what are you going to do?

Me: Talk to Jason and see if we can figure it out, I guess.

Kayla: You don't sound so sure.

Me: I guess I'm not.

Kayla: :-(I'm sorry.

Me: It's okay. And hey, we don't need to be talking about my depressing love life right now. You're getting married to your best friend!

Kayla: I KNOW! I can't believe it. Well, I can! Peter and I have been talking about this for so long now, I'm just so glad it's happening.

I take a second to think about her text. They have been talking about getting married for a long time now, that it never crossed my mind that they wouldn't be together forever. They had decided to wait until they were settled into their jobs after college, so that way they weren't having to juggle a new job and wedding stuff. It has me thinking about Jason and me and how we've talked about it in theory but never actually planned for when it would happen. Maybe it's time to have that talk, a serious talk about it this time.

Me: I'm so excited for you and Peter.

Kayla: Hey, I'm going to get off here. We have some meetings in the morning. Can I text you later?

Me: Absolutely. Love ya, K.

Kayla: Love you too, Abs, night.

It's 11:03pm. I click my phone screen off and put it back down. I scrunch down into my blanket again and breath slowly, willing myself to sleep. But sleep doesn't come. At this rate, my night of getting some good sleep has turned into a night of no sleep. *Why can't I just shut my brain off as easily as I can turn my phone off?*

CHAPTER 24

ARROOOOGAHHH**ARROOOOGAHHH** ARROOOOGAHHH**

I reach over and hit my phone to turn the alarm off. I sink back into my bed and fall back to sleep.

ARROOOOGAHHH**ARROOOOGAHHH** ARROOOOGAHHH**

"Ugh!" I roll over and grab my phone. It's 3:45am. I shoot out of bed. "No, no, no!" I look at my alarms and see that I turned them all off in my sleep. My 3:45am alarm is my, 'Need to make my way downstairs,' alarm.

I run to my bathroom and burn my retinas as I turn on the lights. My hair looks ridiculous. I turn on the water and get my hairbrush wet. I rip my hair out of my low, now messy bun, and brush it out quickly. I braid it fast and grab a face wipe and wipe yesterday's eye make-up off. All the crying I did has helped take most of it off already. I add some mascara and eyeliner, looking a little better. I grab a washcloth and do a quick armpit rinse and then add some deodorant.

I rush to my closet and grab some Rose Bud's work clothes, fresh undies, and bra, and socks and hurry to my bed. I throw everything on my bed and strip down bare. Once I'm dressed, I grab my phone and the book off the nightstand and go to the kitchen.

I grab a bottle of water and throw the book in my bag, putting my phone in my pocket. I hurry to the back door and practically run down the stairs. The clock in the bakery's kitchen says it's 3:58am.

I run to the front and turn on the light for behind the counter and turn on the ovens and proofer to warm them up. I go back into the kitchen and into the cooler to grab things to start prepping for the day when I see the cupcakes for the wedding tonight. I freeze.

"Shhhhhit," I say, closing my eyes. I'd forgotten about making the bridal cake. "Shit, shit, shit!"

As panic starts to set in, I look around and take in the rest of the cooler. I see that Betty didn't listen to me yesterday and stayed. Everything that we need for today, is already prepped, we just have to bake it all. I feel a bubble of another sob about to erupt from me, but I knock it down.

"Knock it off, Abby, we don't need to cry again," I say to myself. Man, my emotions have been all over the place. I haven't cried this much in a long time.

I shake myself out of my emotional moment while I pull trays of scones and other pastries out of the cooler and head to the front. I put them on the rack and head back for a couple more trays. My third trip, the ovens and proofer are ready. I slide in some trays of pastries that don't need to rise into the oven and set the timer. Then I head back to the cooler for the trays of cinnamon rolls to get them in the proofer so they can start to rise.

As I wait for the first batch of goodies to come out of the oven, I whip up some icing and take it to the front. A minute later, the time on the over goes off. I take the trays out and set them on the racks to cool before I put some icing on them. I put some more trays in the oven and check the cinnamon rolls to see that they're just about ready.

I go to the cooler and grab fruit to start making the stuff for smoothies. I'm just dumping the first mixture into the dispenser when I hear the side door unlock. I look over and see Betty and Maggie walking in, the later looking half asleep.

"Morning," I say. "Maggie, you can head upstairs, the couch or the guest room is calling your name."

"Thaaa—" she yawns mid-word "—nk you."

I pat her shoulder as she walks by.

"Did you sleep well?" Betty asks.

"Not even a little bit," I say. I tell her about the fiasco that was last night.

"Oh, Abby, I'm so sorry," she says, giving me a hug.

"It's okay," I say with a small smile. "I'm going to talk to Jason tonight after the wedding. Which by the way, thank you for not listening to me yesterday. You saved my butt."

She smiles and asks, "Whys that?"

"I was so upset last night that I completely forgot to make the cake for Syble and Chris. Once I get things finished for the morning, do you mind if I work on it?"

"Abby, you're my boss. You keep forgetting you don't

have to ask me permission to do anything. If you tell me I'm running the shop by myself today, I'm all for it. You do whatever you need to do," she says with a big smile and gives me a tight hug. "In fact, why don't you go get started on it now and I can finish up things for here. Then you can go take a nap before you need to leave for Rose's."

"You know, for once, I'm not going to argue with you," I say with a laugh. "Thank you."

Betty shoos me towards the back. I'm laughing as I walk into the kitchen, my spirits are lighter than they've been in the last eight hours. I plug the mixer in and start gathering the ingredients I need to make the cake. While the mixer is doing its thing, I get the ingredients for my frosting and get it started.

Once I've poured the batter into four medium round pans, and the rest of the batter is poured into my large muffin pan to make two cupcakes— I always make an extra cake just in case something happens to the first one and two cupcakes are for taste testing when I'm finished — I go out front to see if an oven is open for me to use. There's one open so I put them all in and set the time.

"Here you go, Sweets," Betty says as she hands me a coffee and a blueberry scone.

"You are my savior," I say smiling at her. I take a sip and it's heaven sent. As I walk back to the back, I take a bite of the scone. *Mmmm so good!*

While I wait for the cakes to bake, I pull out the cupcakes and start frosting them. The bride wanted the frosting to look like a white flower sitting on top. I am once again thankful she went with white frosting. It makes decorating so much easier.

I've got the cupcakes frosted and boxed when I hear the timer going off for my cakes. I walk out and check to see if they're finished baking, they need just another minute or two. I go finish putting the boxes of cupcakes back in the cooler and check the cakes again.

"Perfect," I say, smiling at the cakes. I pull two out and take them to the back, coming back for the next two. I look over and see the Trio are sitting by the window. I put the cakes in the back by the other ones to cool off and walk back out to the front.

"Frank, Bill, Henry," I say as I walk up to my favorite gentlemen. "Good morning!"

"Oh, sweet Abby," Henry says with a big smile. "We were just talking about when we'd get to see you again."

"Your ears must be on fire," Bill says with a gruff laugh.

I touch my ears with my fingers and then pull them away quickly, pretending they are in fact hot. "Ouch, they are!"

The old men laugh, and Bill asks, "How's the catering gig going?"

"It's going great! It makes life a little hectic, but Betty and Maggie have been such a big help," I say just as Betty walks up with another carafe of coffee.

"We sure love Betty and that sweet Maggie, but we miss seeing you around," Frank says, patting my hand softly.

"I've missed you guys as well," I say turning my hand over and giving his hand a gentle squeeze.

The doorbells above the door jingles as the door opens and Randy walks in with a smile on his face.

"Good morning," I say to him. "Fancy seeing you here."

"I could say the same to you," he says with a laugh.

"The usual?" Betty asks as she makes her way to the counter.

"Yes, please," Randy says with another laugh.

I look out front, daylight starting to fill the morning, and I see Trevor standing next to Dax at my car. *My car? When did I start thinking of it as my car and not Kallon's?* I shake my head, tell my trio to have a good morning, and walk to the counter, following Randy.

I help Betty get his order ready, but I make an extra coffee for Dax and grab a cinnamon roll for him.

"Which one is for Trevor?" I ask.

Randy points at the small black coffee— the exact same one I made for Dax— and he says, "That one."

"Of course, it is," I say with a laugh. "Does Trevor have something to eat?"

"No, he usually just asks for a coffee," Randy says with a shrug.

I grab another cinnamon roll, put it in a to-go box, and stack it on top of Dax's. I put their coffees in a separate cup carrier than the one Randy will be taking and walk to the front. Frank jumps up and holds the door open for me.

"Thanks, Frank," I say sweetly. He just nods at me as I walk out.

Dax jumps from leaning against the car and comes towards me. He takes the two boxes from me and says, "Morning, Miss Rose."

I pretend to glare at him but say, "Good morning, Dax. Morning, Trevor."

Trevor nods at me but when I hand him a coffee he says in his deep, gruff voice, "Oh, thank you."

"I didn't know what you might like to eat so I brought you a cinnamon roll, they're Dax's favorite," I say to Trevor and then turn to Dax and shoot him a smile. "I figured you might like it since you both drink the same coffee."

"That was not necessary but thank you," Trevor says with a nod.

"You've got to eat something, keep your energy up and wits about you," I say with a small laugh.

"I could say the same to you," Dax says with a knowing look.

"I'm working on it," I say and then shrug. I turn and nod my head towards the door, and say to Trevor, "I need to get back in to finish some wedding cakes. Tell your boss I say good morning when you see him."

"Will do, Miss Rose," Trevor says with another nod of his head.

"Dax, come on in once you're done out here," I say as I walk to the door. Dax gives a noncommittal sound, so I say, "Bring your book in and grab a table. It'll be more comfortable than sitting in the car or standing by it."

He doesn't answer and when I reach the door, Randy is walking out.

I hold the door open for him and he says, "Thanks Miss Rose, see you tomorrow."

"Bye Randy," I say.

I walk in, wave at my Trio, and make my way towards the counter. I smile at Betty as she's wiping down the counter and I head to the back. I take the next hour decorating the cake the way the bride wanted it decorated. I hurry and frost the second cake and then I put them into their own box, nice and secure, then they're put it in the cooler. I finish off by frosting the two large cupcakes and put one on a plate, and box the other.

"Betty?" I holler loud enough that she can hear me.

She comes back and says, "Yeah?"

"It's cake testing time, you wanna try it with me?"

"Heck yeah, I do," she says excitedly.

I grab a knife and cut one of the cupcakes in half and offer a side to Betty. She hands me a fork and we both scoop some up and put it in our mouths.

"Mmmmerrr goodness," Betty says with her mouth full. She swallows and says, "If I ever get married, this is what I want my cake to taste like."

"It's good," I say, taking another bite. "Did Dax come inside?"

"Yeah, he's sitting in the corner up front. Reading a book?" Betty says in a questioning tone.

"He reads," I answer, wiggling my eyebrows at her. "Big man prefers to read while he waits to drive and protect."

Betty's face turns a light shade of pink but all she says is, "Hmmm."

"Hmmm is right," I say laughing. I point around and say, "I need to cleanup back here, do some office work, and then I'll be up to help you."

"Okay," she says. "I have a couple orders due to show up in about fifteen minutes, I'll get them started."

I watch her walk through the doors towards the front before I start cleaning up. After I've put all the ingredients away and washed all the dishes, I go to my desk and check the mail that's come in. I sit at my desk and check my email to see if we've gotten any orders from our website.

The website order idea was Betty's. She said we could get our name out there to businesses that might not know we're here. She wasn't wrong. I made a rule that we must have a couple days' notice to do an order that has more than two drinks and two food items. We've gotten a good amount of business from the website and they have turned out to be standing orders. I see we have an order for Monday for a business down the street. They're wanting coffees and scones for their Monday morning meeting.

I've also noticed that more people have been coming in during our lunch hours on Saturday's and Sunday's. People are starting to love our wraps and sandwiches. I've been tossing around the idea to make soups to add to the lunch menu, but I'll have to wait for the cooler months to roll around again before I make them.

After I've gone through the mail and finish some online banking, I organize my desk to get it back to its normal state. I pull my phone out of my pocket and see it's after 7am. I check my list of things to get done for the wedding and see the food prep is all marked off now that I've finished the cake and cupcakes. I'll double check when I go into the restaurant this afternoon. I need to call Bridget and see how things are going there this morning.

I go to my contacts 'Favorites List' and tap Bridget's name. As I wait for her to answer, I check my list one more time. It's all marked off. We should be good.

"Morning, Abby," Bridget answers with forced

cheerfulness.

"Bridget? What's the matter?"

"Nothing," her voice is a little too high pitched.

"Ummm, there's something wrong, I can hear it in your voice. What's wrong?"

"It's nothing, honestly."

"Bridget, please tell me," I plead, my anxiety starting to flare up.

"Nothing is wrong on our end. It's just... The groom showed up hungover and the bride is pissed. She's not speaking to him and to save our dishes, I had to send him to the other side of the reception area to decorate with some of the bridesmaids. I've tried talking to Syble, but she keeps ranting about how she asked him to do one thing and it was to not be hungover today. I don't know what to do."

I think really fast and say, "Okay, here's what you do. Go into my office and in my fridge by my desk, grab a couple Gatorades. In my top desk drawer, find my Midol bottle and get two pills out. Then, you'll want to go into the kitchen and get some of the chips that we use for our appetizers. Have him drink one of the bottles of Gatorade and take the Midol. Then have him eat the chips. I'm going to send over a bagel from the deli down the street. I'm hoping by the time it gets there, the drink and Midol will have kicked in enough that Chris won't fight you on eating it. How are the other groomsmen?"

"They're about the same as Chris."

"Okay, scratch getting two pills and the two drinks. Take enough drinks for all the guys to have one but take the whole bottle of Midol. It's a new one, so there should be enough for them all to take two. Have them all eat some chips and I'll have bagels made for them all. I'm going to get a breakfast box put together for the bride and bridesmaids, so they have something to eat as well. I bet Syble is upset, not only because she has every right, but because she hasn't eaten anything yet, on top of wedding day jitters. I'll stop and get the bagels and then I'll be right there."

"*Thank you, Abby,*" Bridget says, sounding relieved. Poor girl doesn't do drama well, I should have asked one of the hostesses to help her out this morning.

I hang up and call in the order of bagels and tell the girl taking my order that I'll be there shortly. I walk to the front and turn to Betty with a grimace.

"I need to run to Rose's. The groom showed up hungover and the bride is really upset. I'm going to box up some goodies for her and her gal pals and stop to get some bagels for the guys. Are you good with holding down the fort?" I ask her.

"Absolutely," she says as she grabs a big to-go box. "What are we sending?"

"A little of everything. I thought I'd take a carafe of coffee and some creamer for them too," I say, walking over to the coffees.

"The one on the left just finished brewing. Take it and I'll get another one going," Betty says over her shoulder as she fills the box up.

"Dax?" I holler just loud enough for him to hear me. He looks up and I nod at him to come to me.

"What can I do for you Miss Abby?" he asks.

"Do you mind going into the cooler and getting the box

that has the to-go creamers in it and putting a handful of each flavor into this bag?" I ask as I hand him a large pastry bag.

"Sure," he says as he takes it and disappears to the back.

I put the coffee carafe on the counter and hurry to the back. I grab a box that we haven't broken down yet and bring it to the front. I put it on the counter and add some cups, lids, and straws to it, as well as some napkins. Dax walks in and hands me the bag of creamers.

"Thank you," I say. "You ready to go for a drive?"

"Always," he says with a smile.

"Great, I need to stop by the little bagel shop down the road from Rose's and then I need to go there," I say as I pick the box of supplies up. Betty places the box of pastries on the top.

"I'll get the coffee," Dax says, reaching for the carafe.

We make our way to the front, but a thought hits me.

"I should take the cake and cupcakes now," I say.

"I'll start bringing them out," Betty says from behind us. I turn and see her turning and walking back towards the kitchen.

"How big is the trunk in the car?" I ask Dax as we get to the door.

"It's pretty roomy," he says, holding the door open for me.

We get to the car and Dax opens the trunk for me and I look inside. I put the box in but then point to the back seat for Dax.

"Let's put the coffee up there so I can hold it, so it doesn't topple over on our drive."

"Where do you want these?" Betty asks.

"Cupcakes in the trunk, but I want to hold the cake boxes, or at least one of them. The other can ride upfront with Dax," I say.

Dax heads into the bakery as I help Betty put the boxes into the trunk. We turn and see Dax walking out with a couple cupcake boxes. Betty hurries in as I take a box from Dax. He patiently waits as I arrange the boxes. Betty comes out with the last of the cupcakes.

"Dax, just bring one cake box out at a time, please?" I ask.

"You got it," he says with a nod.

I put the last of the cupcake boxes in the trunk and as I'm shutting the door, Dax walks out with a cake box. Betty runs back in to grab the other one. I open the lid of the box Dax is holding and see it's the second cake I frosted. It's just as nice as the first but a touch different from what the bride wanted. She won't notice but I do. I open the front passenger door and have Dax set the box onto the seat.

"Think you can keep it from flying to the floor or into the door?" I ask half-jokingly.

Dax looks at me with an eyebrow raised, and says, "I'll try my best, Miss Rose."

Betty comes out with the last box, but she also has my bag slung over her shoulder.

"Oh Betty, thank you," I say. I would have left without it.

"No problem," she says with a smile. "Let me know if I can help any other way."

"Will do, thank you," I say as I sit down in the back of

the car, buckle up, and reach my arms out for the cake box.

She hands it to me and then she puts my bag down at my feet. I turn and put the box in the middle of the seat and then scoot my bag over to the middle of the floor. I grab the carafe of coffee and put it between my feet so I can hold it in place with my knees. Then I put the cake box back on my lap.

"All set?" Betty asks. I nod and smile at her. She laughs and says, "Have fun."

"Thanks," I say with a roll of my eyes.

She shuts the door and steps back onto the sidewalk. Dax says something to her and whatever he said, has Betty blushing and ducking her head to the side, stepping closer to the door. I see Dax wave at her as he gets to his door and I look over at Betty to see her waving back at him.

Dax hops in and we're off into traffic. I lean my head back and enjoy the hum of the car as it drives through the city. I don't let myself fall asleep, that would be disastrous for the cake and the coffee. I look at my watch and see it takes us about twenty-five minutes to get to the deli. Luckily it's only five minutes from the restaurant.

Dax pulls up to the deli and I ask, "Do you mind running in and picking up the bagel order for me?"

"Sure thing," Dax says. He unbuckles and jumps out of the rig, running inside. They must have had the order ready because he's back in less than five minutes. He puts the bag next to the cake box and eases back into traffic.

"If you park in the back, we can go in and get a cart or two, to use to take everything into the kitchen," I suggest. Dax just nods and pulls the car down the ally and into the back parking area.

Dax gets out and comes around to open my door. I hand him the box, grab my bag, and then I maneuver myself out without knocking the coffee over. I grab the carafe and we walk to the kitchen entrance door. I enter my code to get in and the door beeps open. We walk in and I point to a table for Dax to put the cake there, I put the coffee down next to it. I hurry to my office and put my bag on my desk.

I walk to one of the station chef's tables and pull the cart out that fits underneath it perfectly. I point to the other table and say, "There's another one under there. Let's take two out so we don't hurt any of the cupcakes by stacking too many on top of each other. The boxes are strong but not that strong."

Without saying a word, Dax walks to the table and grabs the cart. I go to the service door and open it and we wheel our carts out and down the ramp. We get to the car and load all the boxes up quickly. Dax goes to the front and grabs the cake box and the bag of bagels.

When we get inside, I check all the cupcakes and cakes and see that they all made it here without so much as a smoosh to the frosting. We put them back on the carts and then put them in the cooler. I grab the bagel bag and put it on top of the pastry box and nod at the carafe of coffee.

"Mind bringing that up?" I ask.

"Don't mind at all."

I walk over to the elevator and hit the up button. It dings open and we get in, and I push the button for the third floor. It doesn't take long before the doors open and we're walking out. I hear music blaring and I'm shocked to see how the bridal party, friends, and family have transformed the area.

We sectioned it off so that no one will see the reception area until after the ceremony, in a dramatic reveal of removing the partitions. Staff will come in and move the chairs out of the ceremony area, that will transform into the dance floor. The DJ has set up behind a smaller partition that will also be removed.

The ceremony side has been decorated in just some white chiffon curtain paneling and a little bit of eucalyptus garland. There are twinkle lights strung up along the two permanent walls.

The reception side is decorated with a lot more eucalyptus garlands, fake tea candles that are in glass jars, and more twinkle lights. It's absolutely beautiful in the simplest of ways.

I look around and see Syble working on putting the names out onto the tables, but she keeps shooting death stares over into the far corner of the room. I look over and see Chris sitting with a bunch of the guys, their filling little bags with something.

Out of nowhere, Bridget is beside me, "Oh, thank goodness you're here."

"Did you give the guys the stuff?" I ask, smiling at her. Hoping she can relax a little now.

"I did but I don't know if it's helping at all," she says and she then bites her fingernails. That's her tell that she's stressed.

"Why don't you go to my office and hangout in there, I can take it from here," I say as I rub her shoulder.

"Thank you," she mouths and hurries from the room.

I look up at Dax and he looks at me like he'd rather be anywhere but here right now. I shrug and try not to burst out laughing. I start walking towards Syble and when I'm a few feet away, I say her name cheerfully.

"Syble," I give her a big smile when she looks at me. "Happy wedding day!"

She looks like she's about to say something negative but then she sees that I'm carrying something. Her eyes go big, and she smiles, "Good morning! What's this?"

"Coffee and goodies," I say with a laugh. I put the box I'm carrying down on a table closest to Syble that doesn't have any name placement cards on it yet. Dax follows suit and puts the carafe down. He steps off to the side and lets me unpack everything. I put the cups next to the carafe, along with the lids and straws. Then I pull out the box of goodies and with a flourish, I say, "And these are for you and your helpers."

"Oh goodness, those look delicious," Syble says with a sigh. She takes a cinnamon scone and takes half of it in her mouth.

"Coffee and creamers," I point to the carafe and creamers that I set out.

"You didn't have to do this," she says timidly.

"I heard you were having a rough morning. I thought I'd try to help," I say with a smile.

"You could say that again," she says as she shoots a glare at Chris.

"I've got just the thing for that as well," I say, holding up the bag with bagels in it.

"More?" she asks. "Bridget said you'd given her tips on

how to help the idiots."

"This should push them back over the edge to being sober," I laugh.

I walk over to Chris and all his groomsmen. One of the guys hits his arm and when Chris looks at him, the guy nods in my direction. Chris jumps up and walks towards me.

"Hey, thanks for the Gatorade, chips, and... er, whatever those pills were. We feel almost normal," he says with a shocked expression.

"They were Midol, completely legal," I say and then laugh at his reaction. "They're not just for periods."

He gawks at me and stammers out, "Well damn."

"These are for you guys as well," I say, holding up the bag. "There's coffee over there but I'd give Syble a couple minutes to finish eating and having her first cup before you go over there."

"I've totally messed up, haven't I?" he asks, shaking his head.

"Not totally but you might want to think of a way to make it up to her," I say with a shrug.

It seems as if a lightbulb goes off in his head because he looks at me and beams. He asks, "Is the suite still available?"

"It is, but as we talked about before, it costs extra," I say.

"That's okay, I'll pay whatever. I know she wanted it, but it wasn't in our wedding budget. I hadn't figured out what to give her for our wedding present, this will be it. And hopefully it'll get me out of the doghouse," he says with a small smile.

"Well, let's go see if it works," I say, pointing towards

Syble.

He opens the bag he's now holding and grabs a bagel out and then tosses the bag to one of the guys. Chris takes a huge bite and eats it as he practically runs to Syble. I see him shove the rest in his mouth just before he gets to her. The girl that was sitting next to Syble taps her shoulder and then points to Chris. Syble turns, crosses her arms, and leans back in her chair. She has a 'What the hell do you want,' look on her face.

I walk over to them slowly, letting him have the moment to tell Syble what he's done. Just as I'm getting to them, she squeals and leaps up into him. She throws her arms around his neck and hugs him tightly.

"Really?" Syble asks. "Are you serious?"

"Yeah, babe. It's my gift to you," he says holding her tight.

She leans her head in and kisses him sweetly but then pulls away and says, "You aren't completely off the hook for this morning."

"I'll make it up to you this evening," he says with a wink. She giggles and her face turns pink. I try not to look like I just heard that last part when I walk up to them.

"We all good?" I ask.

"Yes," Chris and Syble say together.

"Good," I say. "I'm going to go check the suite and let you guys get back to this. Bridget and I will be in my office if you need anything else."

"Thank you, Abby," Syble says wholeheartedly.

I smile and then remember, "Oh, I have the cake and cupcakes down in the kitchen if you'd like to look at them before you leave. I also have a cupcake for you to test, to make sure it's what you were thinking you wanted," I say.

"Oh, that would be wonderful," she says. Chris gives her a quick kiss and then walks back to his corner. "I'll be down as soon as I'm finished here."

"Sounds good," I say. I wave to her and the girls around her and look at Dax, tilting my head towards the elevator.

"Crisis averted?" he asks.

"For now," I say with a laugh.

We make our way down to the first floor and go to the office. Bridget is sitting at one of the desks with her head down, she looks to be asleep. I motion for Dax to take the other desk, but he points behind him and then does a motion with his hands like they're a book. I nod and smile at him. I watch as he goes back out to the kitchen and hear the back door open and close.

I move the mouse for my computer and as I wait for the screen to turn on, I pull my phone out of my pocket to see if I have any missed calls or text. I have zero. I turn my ringer off so that it'll vibrate in my pocket, which I'm more likely to feel than to hear the ringer.

My computer screen comes on and I delve into my office work for Rose's.

CHAPTER 25

I lean back in my chair, put my arms up and over my head, and stretch my back. The night is finally over. The wedding went off without a hitch. Syble loved her cake. I ended up giving them the second one for their one-year anniversary cake, something she forgot about.

Bridget told me there were a couple concerts in town that must have drawn quite a few people to them because the rest of the restaurant was busy but not swamped like we had anticipated. It didn't bother us one bit.

Still leaning back, I pull my left arm forward so I can see my watch. It's after 2am. I sit forward and see Royce lounging on the couch. He looks half asleep.

"Why don't you take off?" I ask, startling him. We've been sitting in silence for a good fifteen minutes.

"I can wait until it's time to close up," he says with a yawn.

"Meaning, you're waiting for Bridget?" I ask with a smirk.

"Maybe," he says doggedly. "Why don't you take off? I can lock up."

Ignoring his question, I ask, "How are things going with you two?"

"Really well," he says with a big grin. "Honestly, Abs, I've never felt this way before."

"Eeeee," I squeal. "I'm so happy for you!"

I see him blush, but he doesn't say anything. I look over at Dax and see him dutifully reading his book, acting as if he didn't just hear our conversation. I'm sure that's part of his job description. He hears everything but doesn't let on that he does.

I reach into my pocket to pull out my phone. I need to call or text Jason to let him know I'm finally done with the wedding. The guests have all left. I just need to wait for the last of the Rose's customers to leave. I pull out my phone and see I have ten texts, three missed calls, and two voicemails, all from Jason, except one text from Betty.

"Shit," I mumble under my breath.

I open the texts from Betty first.

Betty: Hey Sweets. Take tomorrow off. You're going to be exhausted. You didn't get your nap this afternoon. Mags and I have the bakery covered. I know I can't order you around but, I'm ordering you to please take tomorrow off and sleep. Don't worry about texting me back. I'll send Maggie up with breakfast in the morning, sometime around 10. She's to report back to me and if I hear you are out of bed or at least not comfy cozy on your couch, there will be hell to pay. ;-)

I smile at her text and then look at Jason's texts.

Jason: Hey, babe. It's 8. You done with the wedding yet?

No, you ding dong, I told you it wasn't starting until 6

o'clock. I think to myself.

    Jason: Babe? Hello?
    Jason: Okay, I'll try calling you.
    Jason: I tried calling but you didn't answer. You must be busy with the wedding. Call me back.

    Yeah, because it didn't start until 6 o'clock.

    Jason: Babe, it's 9:17. When does that wedding get over?
    Jason: Hello?! Seriously? It's 10:33. How long is that shit show going to go for? I need me some Abby ass. Call. Me.

    Shit show? If we ever get married, he better not refer to our wedding like that.

    Jason: Fcking hill, Abi. I thought we was going 2 talk 2nite. R u
        still mad @me?
    Jason: Fuckit, I try calling again.
    Jason: Ignore the VM. I love u. I talk 2 u 2morrow.

    By the time I'm done reading, my heart is racing. *He's drinking again and he's plastered.* I don't listen to his last text and open the first voicemail.

    "Hellllllooooo pretty-sexy lady! You off work yet? My diiiick needs you—" pause with a laugh "—Hello? Abbsy? Are you there?—" another pause "—Of course you aren't. You're never around when I need to fuck. There are plenty of girls here that would—" hiccup "—love to ride me. I could take any—" hiccup "—one of them home. Hell—" hiccup "— I could take multiple home. That's something you'd never —" belch "—do, uh? Or

would you? Is that something you'd be down for? —" a longer pause with voices and laughter in the background "—Fuck it. Bye."

Tears start to fill my eyes. I listen to the next voicemail.

"Shit Abbsy, I'm soooorry. I just miss ew. I didn't mean—" belch *"—anything I said. I'm gonna take a cab home. I shouldn't have come out with Deven and Shane. I'm sorry. Love you."*

I hang up and look down at my phone. I tap his name to call him. As the phone rings, I look to see that the last time he called was almost two and half hours ago. He might be passed out by now.

"Hello?" a female voice says on the other end. I look at my phone to make sure I called the right number. Yup, it says Jason. The female voice says again, *"Hello?"*

"Hello, who's this?" I ask.

"You called, who's this?" she asks snarkily.

"This is Abby, Jason's girlfriend, who is this?" I ask, my anger rising.

There's a long pause and then a shuffle on the other line and then I hear Jason's sleepy, but still a little drunk, voice, *"Hey baby, I didn't think I'd hear from you tonight."*

"Who is that woman that answered your phone?" I demand.

"It's—" there's a pause and then he continues *"—Lorrie. She and Shane came back to my place. Ummm... they were too drunk to drive home... Aaand too cheap to pay for a cab all*

the way back to their place. My place was a lot closer," he says quickly.

My mind instantly senses a lie. "That was Lorrie? It didn't sound like her?"

"Have you talked to her on the phone before?" he asks.

"Well, no, but why did she answer your phone?"

There's a pause and then he answers, *"I left it out on the counter, she heard it ringing when she went out for water and answered it. She brought it to me when you said it was you."*

"She didn't see my name on the caller ID?"

It's quiet again before he answers. He says, *"I don't have your name as your caller ID."*

"What is it?" I ask. It's quiet again. "Jason, what is it?"

"Don't be mad but it's Sexy Cakes."

I roll my eyes and ask, "Where's Shane?"

"Passed out in the guestroom."

"She's not one of the many girls you could have taken home tonight?"

There's another pause and then Jason's says, *"What? No, what are you talking about?"*

"You seriously don't remember the voicemail you left me?"

"No babe, I don't, I'm sorry. I made a mistake and went out with Shane and Deven and their wives. We got carried away. We came back to my place and I passed out. I swear. There are no other girls here."

I don't say anything, I just sit and listen. I still feel like he's lying to me.

"Come over and see for yourself," he finally says.

"Jason, I'm not going to do that. I'm going to go home

and go to bed. It's been a long and stressful day. I'll just talk to you tomorrow."

"Are you sure?"

"Yeah, I'll call you tomorrow."

"Okay, love you babe. Bye."

He hangs up once again without waiting for me to say anything. I toss the phone down on my desk and put my hands over my face. I know Dax and Royce heard the whole conversation, at least my side of it, I can feel them looking at me.

"Don't say it," I say to them both.

"Say what?" Royce asks.

I drop my hands and look at him and shake my head. I look over at Dax and see he's looking at his book, but his eyes aren't moving.

"I'm going to go check out front and see if all the customers have left yet," I say and storm out.

I walk into the bar and see no customers. I walk to the bar and sit down.

Cammy walks over to me and asks, "Want a drink?"

"No thanks," I say. "Are all the customers gone?"

"The last table is in Brennah's section. They are just finishing up their last drinks. Bren already cashed 'em out, and she gave them the ten-minute warning," Cammy says as she pulls a tray of steaming hot glasses out of their dishwasher.

"Sounds good," I say. I stand and say, "I'll be in my office. Let me know when they're gone, would ya?"

"Yeah, I can do that," she says with a smile.

I walk back into the kitchen and see it's sparkling

clean. Anyone walking in that doesn't work here, would have no idea we served a wedding of two hundred guests and our restaurant was at eighty-five percent capacity all night. That's about one hundred and eighty people, steadily, from 5 o'clock to about 9:30pm. I'm tired. My staff is tired. We all just want to go home and go to bed.

I walk into my office and see Royce sitting up, playing a game on his phone.

"What's Bridget doing?" I ask.

"She wanted to do inventory so she could make sure to put in the order tonight, so she doesn't have to come in tomorrow," Royce says without looking up from his phone.

"Good thinking," I say. I then yawn and ask, "You okay if I take you up on the offer for you to hangout and lock up once everyone's gone?"

"Thought you'd never ask," Royce says with a laugh as he looks up from his phone. "Go home. We're good here."

"Thank you," I say. I take my jacket off and toss it in the hamper. I grab my bag off the hanger, I'd actually hung it up today. I look at Dax who stands and stretches, "You ready?"

"Whenever you are," he says.

"Night, Royce. Good job today," I say as I start to walk out the door.

"You too, boss," he replies with a smile.

I shake my head and walk into the kitchen. I lead Dax and I out the back door and out to the car. Dax opens my door and I slide in. Exhaustion taking it's hold over me. I buckle myself before I lean my head back and I'm asleep before we leave the parking lot.

◆ ◆ ◆

I hear my name being called with what feels like hours have passed. I try to roll over in bed and find I'm restrained. I jolt out of bed and see that I'm still in the car. Dax is standing beside me with my door open and his hand is outstretched, like he'd been patting or shaking me awake.

"Holy crap," I say, running a hand down my face. "How long was I out for?"

"Just the twenty-five-minute drive here," Dax says with a chuckle. "You were really out of it."

"Yeah, I was," I say. I unbuckle and grab my bag that fell to the floor at some point and scoot out of the car.

"I was about to pack you upstairs if you didn't wake up soon," Dax says with a smile.

I laugh and say, "Well, luckily you don't have to do that."

He gives me an exasperated look.

"Good night, Dax," I say, patting his arm. I start to walk but he falls into step with me.

I look at him expectantly and he says, "I'm walking you to your door."

"I don't have the energy to argue with you," I say with a yawn.

"Then don't," he says. He takes my hand and he puts it inside his arm. I hold on to his large bicep and let him lead me around the side of the building too my door. I enter my code and Dax opens the door for me. "You going to be okay with those stairs?"

I laugh and say, "Yes."

"Alright, up you go then," he says. He steps inside but holds the door open with his foot. I turn and see him watching me.

"You're going to watch me climb the stairs?"

"I'm going to watch until that door closes behind you."

I roll my eyes and start my ascent. I laugh and say over my shoulder, "Such an overprotective brother."

"Better than an overbearing babysitter," he retorts and then laughs.

I throw my head back and laugh so hard I double over. *I think I'm nearing my hysteria stage of exhaustion.* I practically crawl the last couple of stairs and use the doorknob to pull myself up. I'm laughing so hard, I can't stand. I enter the code and turn towards Dax. I see he's taken a couple steps up.

"I wasn't going to fall," I say, laughing again.

"I'm not so sure about that," he says, eyeing me closely. "Get in and go to sleep. I'll see you in a few hours."

"No, you won't," I giggle out. I laugh hard again and say, "I've been ordered to take the day off and sleep until at least 10am."

Dax laughs too and says, "Who has pull enough to make you listen to them?"

"Beeeeetty," I say as I wink at him. *I feel drunk.* I laugh at my thought and then at his expression. "I'm sure she has some pull over you too."

Dax stands up straight and walks down the stairs backwards, "Good night, Abby. Get some rest. I'll be here tomorrow if you need me."

I shake my head at him, but I say, "Night, Dax, the big man, Wilson."

Dax chuckles and shakes his head as he watches me step inside. I let the door shut but I don't move until I hear the door at the bottom shut. I open my door and hear the bottom door's lock click into place, Dax nowhere in sight. I shut my door again and listen to the automatic lock slide into place like always.

I toss my bag on my coffee table, where it lands with a loud thud. I walk straight to my room, toss my phone on my bed, and then beeline it to the bathroom. After I answer Nature's call, I brush my teeth embarrassingly too fast, strip down to my undies, grab a t-shirt and shorts, and crawl into bed.

I'm aware enough that I reach for my phone and plug it in. As soon as my head hits the pillow, I'm out again.

I stir at the smell of fresh coffee and cinnamon rolls. I open one eye and see Maggie putting a cup and plate down next to my bed.

"I'm sorry, Abby, I didn't mean to wake you," Maggie says apologetically.

"You didn't. The amazing smell of coffee and cinnamon roll did," I say, groggily. I ask, "What time is it?"

"A little after 10am," she says with a smile.

"Oh," I say. "Thank you for breakfast."

"You're welcome. I'll be back in a couple of hours with lunch."

"Thanks," I say as I roll over and pull my blanket back around me and my head. Sleep, my favorite friend, finds me instantly.

◆ ◆ ◆

"Check her, see if she's okay," I hear someone whisper. I feel a hand on my neck.

"She's okay," I say with a horse laugh. I clear my throat and roll onto my back. I open my eyes and see Dax and Betty standing over me. I look at them skeptically and ask, "What's the matter?"

"It's a little after 3pm," Betty says with concern. "You didn't wake up when Maggie brought lunch up. She said you hadn't touched breakfast either. We came up to check on you after we closed the shop. You were still asleep, but you didn't wake up to my shouts or prodding."

"I told her we could give you another hour to wake up before we physically made you wake up, at least long enough to tell us you were fine and to go to hell," Dax says with a laugh. Betty swats his arm but he just grins at her.

"You guys have been hanging out in my apartment for an hour?" I ask, stunned.

"Yeah," Betty says. "Kallon said that if you didn't wake up soon, he'd get a doctor friend of his to come look at you."

"Kallon was here?" I ask, quickly sitting up in bed.

"No, he'd called to check in on you because you weren't

answering your phone," Dax says.

I stretch across my bed, I'd ended up clear on the other side, where I never sleep, and I pull my phone to me. I have quite a few missed calls, some texts, and a couple voicemails. Varying from Kallon, my parents, Kayla, and Jason. I groan and lean back.

"I feel like I could sleep for days," I say, closing my eyes.

"Because it's finally caught up to you," Betty says with so much attitude that I open my eyes. I see her standing with her arms crossed over her chest now. She takes a breath, drops her hands to her sides, and says tenderly, "You're doing too much. You're not eating enough and definitely not getting enough sleep."

"I know," I say in a small voice. "I made a decision last night after the wedding was over."

"What's that?" Betty asks.

I drop my eyes to my hands, that are still holding my phone, and say in a defeated tone, "I'm going to step down from Head Chef. At least until the movie set gig is over."

"Abby," Betty says to get my attention back on her. "It's okay to let go of something. It's not permanent. You'll still be at Rose's but in not such a demanding way. I think this is a good thing."

"I know. I do too. I just feel..." I trail off and lean my head back. "I just feel like I have failed."

I see Dax and Betty share a look. Dax nods and leaves the room. I close my eyes but then I feel my bed sag and look up to see Betty sitting down beside me.

"You haven't failed at anything, Abby," Betty says. "Rose's is doing fantastic. You've been telling me about all the weddings and other events that you have on the calendar. You are full on days that you used to say were your slowest days. Rose Bud's has never been this busy either and the catering gig has been another blessing. You are doing an amazing job. You just can't keep doing it all by yourself."

"I—"

Betty interrupts me by gently saying, "I know what you're going to say. You've had help. And you're right, you have. But only enough for you to say you've had help. You give just enough that you can say, Betty did this, or Royce did that, but in the end, it's not enough."

"It's going to take me awhile to get used to giving up Head Chef," I say. "It's what I went to school for."

"Is it though?" Betty asks.

"Yes, of course," I say.

"I know you wanted to be a Head Chef like your dad, but you also wanted to be a baker. Which you are and a damn good one. Not to mention you have the managerial and time management skills of your mother. You set your goals and you achieved them," Betty says, reaching over and grabbing my hand with hers. "It might be time to set some new goals."

"I know you're right," I say sadly.

"If giving up the Head Chef position is too hard right now, what about this idea? Cook Fridays and Saturdays and let Royce do Tuesdays, Wednesdays, and Thursdays, be manager/owner those nights. Take Sunday's completely off from everything, let that day be your true rejuvenation day."

"That would only leave me here at the bakery on Saturday's, I can't do that to you," I say sternly.

"Am I doing a bad job running the shop for you?"

"What?" I ask horrified that she'd make that conclusion. "Not at all. You've been amazing."

Betty smiles and is quiet for a minute, thinking. Her eyes light up and she says, "Okay, how about this option? Give me and Maggie tomorrow at the movie set and if it goes well, and Stephanie has a positive report for you about how I handled things, what if I keep Mondays and Fridays?"

"You cater the movie set on Monday's and Friday's?" I ask, thinking hard about it.

"Yes," she says excitedly. "Think about it. By me doing those days, it gives you Monday's, Friday's, and Saturday's to be here at the shop where you can see the regulars that have been missing you these last few weeks. When you're in management mode at Rose's, you can mingle around, checking on customers, and then office work when it's not your day to cook. When you have to be up at 1:30am or 1:45am to get things going for the movie set, all you have to worry about those days is the movie set and office work at Rose's. You won't be on your feet for essentially twenty hours a day if you do it this way."

"That's not a bad idea. I know that being manager is important too. It's just hard to think of switching into that role so soon after my parents retired," I say, sitting up. Thinking out loud, I say, "So, I'd work here Monday, Friday, and Saturday. The catering job Tuesday's, Wednesday's, and Thursday's. And at Rose's, I'd just cook Friday's and Saturday's while being management Tuesday's, Wednesday's, and Thursday's?"

"Yes," she says smiling. "And taking Sunday's off to do nothing but what you did today or at least something you want to do."

"I think that could work," I say smiling. "I'll talk to Kallon about it and if he agrees, I'll talk to Royce."

"Kallon will think anything's a great idea if it means you taking some time off and resting," Betty laughs. "And remember, it's not forever, Abs. Tell Royce it's just until after the catering gig is up and then you'll take back on the role or even just a couple more days. Or who knows, you might enjoy being the manager and fulltime baker."

I smile at her and squeeze her hand, and say, "I'm so glad you're my friend, to help me talk out stuff like this, thank you."

"You've always been there for me, I finally get to be here for you," she says with a warm smile.

"Thank you."

"I left some soup and a sandwich in the fridge. You should get up soon and eat something. Maggie and I are going to take off, but we'll be back in the morning to help with catering stuff," Betty says as she stands up. "It was fairly slow today, so we worked on all the prep stuff, it's all ready for the morning."

"Thank you, Betty. I'll eat something after I check these messages," I say as I shake my phone in my hand. I pull my blankets back, stand next to her and I laugh a little when I add, "I need to let them all know I'm alive."

"That's a good idea," she says as she starts walking out of my room.

We walk out into the living room where I see Maggie on the couch reading and Dax sitting in the comfy chair, doing something on his phone.

"Maggie, we're going home, sweety," Betty says to her daughter.

"Okay," Maggie says as she stands up. "Bye, Abby."

"Bye, Mags. Thanks for checking on me today," I smile at her and she smiles back.

"Bye," Betty says to me. She turns to Dax and says, "Bye, Dax."

"Thanks, Betty, bye," I say.

"Bye," Dax says with a wave.

I watch Betty and Maggie leave and then turn to Dax. He's staring at me with concern.

"What?" I ask.

He shrugs and says, "Nothing. Just making sure you're not going to fall asleep standing there."

I shoot him a fake glare and then say, "I'm not going to sleep right now. I have some messages and phone calls to return. But you can go home, if you want. I'm not going anywhere."

Dax stares at me for a long moment, thinking, and then he says, "Are you sure?"

"One hundred percent," I say with a yawn. I laugh a little and add, "I'm going to eat something while I reply to these—" I wave my phone at him "—and then go back to bed."

"You'll call me if you need me?"

"Yes," I say.

My tone must have sounded unsure because he says, "Promise me you'll call me."

"I promise I'll call you if I need my big brother," I laugh.

"That'll work," he says as he stands up. "I'll be back

around 2. Have a good afternoon, Miss Abby."

"Just Abby, Dax."

"You're lucky you're even getting Abby."

I roll my eyes, shake my head, and laugh. As I sit on the couch and pull the blanket over my lap, I say, "Thanks Dax, I'll see you in the morning."

He walks to the door and waves as he walks out. I pull my phone closer and open my text messages. Jason is the last person to text me, so I look at his seven texts.

Jason: Good morning.

Jason: You must be busy, text me or call me when you have a break.

Jason: I tried calling the shop, but no one answered, you guys must be busy.

Jason: It's 11, are you ignoring my text and calls or just busy? Call me.

Jason: I know I messed up last night, but this is stupid, call me.

Jason: Betty finally answered and told me you took the day off to rest. So, you can't answer a text or phone call from me. I know you're pissed at me but fuck, Abby, we can at least talk about it.

Jason: Just... fucking call me when you want to talk.

Shaking my head, I send him a quick reply.

Me: Jason, I've been working so much that I just slept for like 12ish hours. I just woke up. I'll call you in a minute.

I close out of his message history and go to Kallon's.

Kallon: Hey, Abby. Hope you're having a good day. I was wondering if I could come over later this evening to talk to you about something. Nothing serious. Just a business meeting I'd like to have at Rose Bud's next weekend.

Kallon: Hey, are you okay? I haven't heard from you, which is fine, it's just that you normally answer back pretty quickly. Dax said you've been sleeping all day. Just text me back to let me know you're okay, please.

I smile and send him a reply.

Me: Hey, I'm alive. I just slept the day away, literally. Yeah, you can come over. I'm about to reheat some soup and a sandwich for lunch. Come over anytime.

The three dots appear instantly and then his reply is here.

Kallon: I am so relieved to hear from you. From what Dax was saying, how concerned he and Betty were, I was on my way there. Is it okay if I come over now? I'll stop and get food from down the street. Burgers sound ok?"

Me: Yeah, come on by and yes, burgers sound amazing. Thanks.

Kallon: See you soon.

Next is my mom.

Mom: Hey, sweety. Just checking in to see how your week was and to see if you're good with a good old fashion BBQ for dinner tomorrow. Your dad decided to get himself an early Father's Day gift. I told him he needed to wait but he insisted. There goes our idea on what to get him. So be thinking of something else.

Me: Mom, a BBQ sounds great. Tell Dad he's in trouble. He knows the family rule about buying ourselves gifts before holidays and birthdays. Maybe we can get him hooked up with some BBQ essentials. Like a bib that says something about being the best BBQ'er in the world or something like that. We can talk more tomorrow while he's out on the patio.

Kayla is last.

Kayla: Hey bestie, how's your day? I need to be better about calling or texting you. This wedding has been all consuming.

Me: Oh, don't worry about it. We have one of those friendships that will stand the test of time. We can go weeks, months even, without talking but as soon as we pick up the phone or hit that send button, it's like no time has passed at all. Love you girl, don't stress yourself about me. I'm here, always.

I look down at my clothes and see that I'm in my t-shirt and shorts. *Shit! Dax saw me in this and my boobs are floppin' all over the place!* My face heats. His face didn't show signs of noticing anything but I sure as hell am not going to be walking around braless with Kallon freaking Keller in my apartment.

I hurry to my room and change quickly. I put undies and a bra on and throw on a different pair of shorts. I decide to go with a hoodie but put a tank top on underneath. I quickly use the bathroom and then throw my hear into a messy bun on top of my head. I'm not worried about my makeup but wipe yesterday's off.

I walk back into the living room and head for the kitchen. I open the fridge and see that Betty had left a soda pop next to the soup for me. I grab it and crack it open, welcoming the fizzy goodness. I stand in the middle of the kitchen, letting the caffeine fill my veins.

I walk back over to the couch and grab my phone to check my missed calls. I see that I have one missed call each from my parents, two from Kallon, and four from Jason. My parents left one voicemail each, Kallon left two, and Jason, he left three.

"Hey babe, it's Jason. Call me when you have a second."

"Abbigail, it's Mom. If you're up for BBQ tomorrow, just bring dessert, we've got everything else covered."

"Buds, it's Dad. Mom thinks you're going to be upset that I bought myself a new BBQ'er. Please don't me mad, I couldn't wait. K, love you."

"Babe, it's Jason. Please call me back."

"Morning Abby, I wasn't sure if you got my text. Call me when you have a second, thanks, bye. Oh, this is Kallon. K, bye."

"Are you seriously going to ignore me all day. Call me back. It's Jason, you know, your boyfriend."

"Hey Abby, it's Kallon again. Dax and Betty have me worried. Call me back as soon as you get this, so I know you're alive. K, bye."

I open my contacts and hit Jason's name.

"Hey... babe," he says out of breath.

"Hey, what chya up to?"

"Oh... ummm... just working out," he says while taking deep breaths.

I sit quietly for a minute, waiting for him to say something, but it seems like he's waiting for me. So, I prompt, "About last night..."

"Yeah, about that. I'm sorry. I know I messed up and it'll never happen again. I promise."

"Jason, you said you'd never drink again."

"Oh!" he says sounding startled. *"Yeah, I know. Drinking, yeah, sorry. I know. I'm a work in progress."*

"And about what you said in your voicemails?"

"I know, it was dick-head things to say. I'm sorry."

"We should probably be having this conversation in person, but—" I take a deep breath "—do you truly feel that way? That you could have taken any of those girls home?"

"I wouldn't do that."

"But you wanted to?" I ask. It's too quiet for too long on his end, for my liking, so I add, "Jason, did you want to?"

"No, babe, no," he says too quickly. *"Listen, can I come over later so we can talk about this. You're right, we should be having this conversation in person."*

"Yeah, that's fine, but Kallon is coming over to talk about something to do with business. Why don't you come over around 6?"

It's quiet for a second and then Jason says in a slightly angry tone, *"Why can't I come over now?"*

"Because Kallon and I are going to be talking business. After your slip up with Deven and Shane, I don't think Kallon can trust you with anything to do with his business ideas."

"That's low, Abby."

"But is it really, Jason? Can you honestly tell me that if you hear him say something juicy, you won't have the strongest urge to tell your buddies?"

"I told you I won't. I've learned my lesson."

"What about the next time you slip up and drink again?"

It's quiet again and then he says, *"I guess I have to prove myself some more to you before you trust me again."*

"Prove some more? Jason, the first chance you got, you went out drinking with Deven and Shane."

"Last night wasn't the firs—" he trails off when he

realizes what he's saying.

"You've drank before last night, since you promised me you were done drinking?"

"Like I said, babe, I'm a work in progress."

"How hard are you working?"

"Hard enough."

ZZZZZZZZZZZZZTTTTT

The buzzer for the door goes off, which comes at the perfect time because Jason is starting to upset me.

"Jason, I'll talk to you later. Please don't come until 6 o'clock or later."

"Sure, whatever you want. Bye."

Before I can say bye, he hangs up.

"Gah!" I holler as I toss my phone to the couch. I get up and walk over to the door. I push the intercom button and ask, "Hello?"

"Hey, it's me, Kallon," Kallon's voice says through the speaker.

"Come on up," I say. I hit the button to unlock the bottom door. I open the top one and watch Kallon walk through the door and jog up the stairs. He gets about halfway up before he looks up.

He's startled to a stop and almost falls back. He stammers out, "Holy shit! I didn't know you were standing there."

As he starts to walk back up, I say with a laugh, "Sorry, I thought I'd get at least this door for you since you've got your hands full."

He's carrying three to-go containers and a cup carrier with two large soda pops and has a black folder in his armpit. When he gets to the step below me, I reach out and take the sodas from him.

"Thanks," he says with a smile. "And, hi."

"Hi," I say back with another laugh. I step to the side and motion for him to come in. I shut the door behind him and he waits for me to lead the way. I take us to the kitchen and put the drinks on the counter. He puts the food on the counter and looks around.

"Where's Dax?" he asks.

"I sent him home. I have no plans to leave and I promised him I'd call if I decided I needed to go somewhere," I answer.

"He must be tired if he listened to you," Kallon says with a chuckle.

"My hours have been crazy lately, which means his have been too. I, uh, need to run something by you about that."

"His hours?" he asks confused.

"No, mine."

"Oookaaaay," he says, drawing out the word.

"Let's get food and go sit on the couch. I'm still really tired and feel like getting comfy."

"Sounds good to me," he says as he opens the to-go containers. "I wasn't sure what burger you'd want so I got a cheeseburger, a bacon cheeseburger, and a double decker, which is a double bacon cheeseburger. I got all curly fries because they're the best from that joint."

"They look good," I say with a smile. I haven't had

curly fries in a long time. I look up at Kallon and ask, "Which one do you want?"

"I'll eat which ever one you don't want."

"What about the one left over?"

"I'll run in down to Trevor. He didn't want anything when I ordered but he'll eat it anyways."

"Okay, umm... well, the bacon cheeseburger sounds good," I say, a little uncertain.

"Here you go," he says as he hands me the container with the bacon cheeseburger. He grabs a soda out of the carrier and hands it to me and says, "It's Sprite. I wasn't sure if you drink it all the time or if you got it at the game because of the beer's effect on you."

"It's great, thank you," I say sincerely. Waiting for him to pick up his food and drink, I lead us to the living room. Kallon sits down on the couch and puts his black folder on the table. I put my stuff down and go back to the fridge and get condiments.

Once I get back, I hurry and straighten the magazines and other random stuff on the table. I sit on the couch, a couch cushion away from Kallon and wait for him to finish with the condiments. After he puts ketchup and mustard on his burger, I add it to mine. We sit in silence for a second, eating the deliciousness he brought.

Kallon takes a drink from his soda and then prompts by asking, "So, before we talk about my business thing, I'm curious about what you want to talk to me about with your hours."

I tell him about what Betty, and I talked about, and then ask, "What do you think about that?"

"I think it's a great idea," he says with a huge grin. "I think giving yourself a full day off is the best thing about it."

"I've never needed a full day off but, after sleeping most of today away, I think it's needed now," I say, sounding a little defeated.

"You're running three businesses, of course you need a day off," he says with his smile getting bigger.

"You don't think it seems like I'm half-assing any of it? By splitting my time up between the three of them?" I ask.

Kallon looks taken aback and answers with, "Absolutely not. You give so much of yourself to these businesses, that you feel like taking one day off is too much. If anything, you could do with some 'half-assing'—" he rolls his eyes as he uses air quotes "—more often. But knowing your work ethic, you'd never do that."

"I just don't want people to think that I've lost my mojo or something like that," I say, voicing my concern.

"To hell with what people think, Abby," he says. He looks at me straight in the eyes and says, "I'm serious. Don't worry about what anyone is going to say. Your health is more important than keeping up with what you think anyone is going to say about you. I don't know anyone who works as hard as you do and I'm not just saying that."

"Okay, thank you! I'll text Steph and let her know," I say, smiling for the first time since I started talking to him about it. I take a bite of my burger and say once I've swallowed, "So, what's your business talk about?"

"In a couple of weeks, I'd like to have my meeting with my agent and lawyer down at Rose Bud's. I've been offered a role in a movie, but I need to talk to them about it first," he says and then takes a bite of his burger.

"Yeah, that would be fine," I take a bite and I get sauce all over my face. I stand and say, "Ooop, I'm going to get us some napkins."

As I walk into the kitchen, Kallon says, "I brought the script I was sent. I was hoping you'd read it and tell me what you think of it."

"Oh, for sure, I'd love to," I say excitedly. I go into my pantry and grab a new roll of paper towels. "What's it about?"

Kallon doesn't say anything, so I ask again, "What's the movie about?"

I walk through the kitchen and into the living room, wiping my face and carrying the roll of paper towels. I look up and see Kallon holding a black folder open in his hands. His eyes are wide open in a shocked look and his cheeks are pink.

I freeze.

CHAPTER 26

I can't stop my eyes from darting from the black folder in Kallon's hands to his face. I try to take a step but I'm completely frozen. I watch him turn a page and then another. I watch as his Adam's apple dips low in his throat and bounces back up.

I finally find my voice and praying it's not what I think it is, I ask, "What... what are you looking at?"

Kallon doesn't respond right away and as if he's been shocked, he closes the folder quickly. He holds it tightly between his hands and says, "I'm sorry. I thought it was my folder."

He looks at the table and moves some magazines around and finds a scarily similar folder and holds it up. He still hasn't looked up at me.

My eyes go big, and I say in a whisper, "Oh... Oh my gosh... Those were my... You saw my... Me in..."

"Ummm..." is all Kallon says as he finally looks up at me as he gets a sheepish grin on his face. His eyes travel from my face down to my feet and then they shoot up to my face like he didn't mean to do it. "I'm sorry, I didn't know what they were."

Finally able to walk, I stumble to the couch, and I sink down and tuck my legs to my chest. I cover my face with my hands, I can feel it flaming hot. I mummer out, "Oh no."

"Abby, I'm so sorry. Had I known your folder was sitting here, I would have made sure to keep mine next to me. I didn't mean to look," he says quickly. He slides over and puts his hand on my back. "Please don't be mad."

"I'm not mad," I say against my hands. "I'm embarrassed beyond belief. No one was supposed to see those, except for... but now... you of all people have seen them."

"Except for... Jason?" Kallon asks.

"Yes, but he's not getting them now. Not after all we've been through lately," I say as I pull my hands away. I look up at Kallon and when he sees me looking, he grins at me. My face gets redder, and I say, "Stop looking at me like that."

"Like what?" he asks with a laugh.

"Like you've seen me naked," I say as I grab the folder out of his hands.

"Nearly, but not all the way," he says with a flirty wink. He laughs and says, "Now we're even."

"Umm what?" I ask.

"You've seen the movies I've played in and Friday on set, I was in a towel with a modesty cover on, but you didn't know that because of the towel. For all I know, you thought I was standing there naked with just a towel from keeping all of my manhood from being on display. You've seen more of my naked body than I've seen of you. You're not wearing much clothing in these, but you're still covered up," he says with a laugh as he points at the folder in my hands.

"It's hardly the same thing!" I exclaim. "And in some, the clothes are see through."

He opens the one still in his hands and he bites his bottom lip, raises an eyebrow, grins a devilishly handsome grin, and looks at me, "Wrong folder."

"Ahhh!" I toss the folder I'm holding on the table and reach for the one in Kallon's hand. He holds it up over his head, I lean into him to get to it. "Kallon, give it back!"

"Who's going to get it now? If you aren't giving it to Jason," he says with a chuckle. His breath tickles my neck. I lean away, breathing fast.

"No one, I'm burning them," I say harshly. My face feels so hot, I must be three shades redder.

"You will not," he says shocked. "I'll keep them if you're going to do that."

"Like hell you will," I say, reaching up quickly, I grab it from him.

"They're too good for you to burn," he says honestly. "Save them."

Now I'm embarrassed for a whole different reason. *Kallon Keller thinks my boudoir pictures are good?* The question floats through my head before I can stop it. I shake my head and tuck the folder behind my back and pick up my food container where I left it.

"Let's change the subject, please," I say before I take a bite of my burger.

"Fine," Kallon says with a chuckle. He reaches out and grabs the folder closest to him. He hands it to me and says, "Here's the movie description and some of the lines of the character they want me to have, tell me what you think."

I wipe my hands on my paper towel, put my food back down, and grab the folder. We sit in silence as I read it. I eat a couple fries and drink my drink as I go through the whole folder. When I'm finished, I put it down, and think.

"So…" Kallon prompts after a few quiet minutes. I can tell he was trying to give me time to process but also wants my opinion.

"Well, it's a lovely story. I don't remember you ever doing a rom-com before," I say. "Am I forgetting a movie you've done in this genre?"

"This will be my first romantic comedy, yes," he says with a smile. "Which is why I am interested in it. I need to step out of my comfort zone and expand my talents."

"Expand your talents?" I ask in a teasing tone and laugh.

"Yes, expand my talents," he says in a teasing tone back. "I've got action down and I like to think I have the romantic skills down, but I need to work on being funny."

"I'm sure you'll do great. I think this part was written with you in mind," I say as I go over the lines again.

"You think so?" Kallon asks before he takes the last bite of his burger.

"I do," I say with a smile. "You should definitely do it. Well, if your agent and lawyer say it's a good deal or whatever."

"Thank you. Your opinion means a lot to me," Kallon says with a smile.

We sit in silence for the next little while and finish eating our food. Sitting quietly with Kallon has never felt awkward or weird. His presence is calming, it feels nice. After I've eaten, I gather up our containers and take them into the kitchen and throw them away. When I come back in and sit down, Kallon turns to me.

"Have you talked to Kayla recently? How's her wedding planning coming along?" he asks.

"Yeah, I have," I say happily. "I know Kayla and Peter are ready for it to just be over and done with it when the time comes, so my goal is to be there for her. They aren't hiring a wedding coordinator, so I'll take on the responsibility as the maid of honor to make sure we're on schedule the day of and make sure the guys don't get too carried away with their shenanigans."

"Does she have an idea for a timeline?"

"The ceremony will start at 4, which will be short and sweet. There will be refreshments and appetizers for guests to enjoy while we're doing pictures and then dinner... the reception will start at 5:30."

"Sounds like a good timeline," Kallon says with a nod.

I laugh and say, "Have you been to many weddings?"

"Just my brother's," he says with a laugh of his own. "You?"

"My brother's too," I say in agreement. "I was a bride's maid for that one, so my duties were limited. Seeing what my sister-in-law, Mary, went through with her maid of honor not helping with much and didn't help keep things going and how stressful that was for her, I told myself I'd do all I could do for Kayla for her wedding. A lot of it is just talking her down from a spiral she's worked herself into from one thing or another. The last one was flowers. Even being so far away,

I was able to help her. I'm just glad she knows she can call me about anything and that I'm here for her."

"She's lucky to have you," Kallon says sincerely.

I shake my head and say, "I'm the lucky one."

My phone goes off, so I grab it off the table. I see a notification from Jason.

"Sorry, it's Jason," I say.

"No worries," Kallon replies with a smile.

Jason: Hey, something's come up. Is it ok if I come over later? Like around 8?

As I inhale through my nose, my nostrils flair. *It's not a big deal,* I think to myself. *He's still wanting to come over. He's not totally blowing you off.*

Me: Yeah, that's fine. Just remember I have to get up really early, like before 2am.

Jason: So fucking all night is out of the question? Haha We could pull an all-nighter. We haven't done that in a long time.

Me: Jason...

Jason: I'm kidding. I know you have an early morning, I'll respect that, or try to.

Me: Thanks....

Jason: Abby, I'm trying. Really, I am. It's just hard (lol) when I want you so bad, all the time.

Me: Then why are you coming out 2 hours later. If you "want" me so bad, wouldn't you be asking to come over sooner?

Jason: You told me not to until 6. Something else has come up that I need to take care of at that time. But if you're saying we can have sex, I'll push the other thing to 8 and cum (haha :-P) over first.

I roll my eyes and think. I don't know when the thought of being physical with Jason, my boyfriend, the man I love... or thought I loved... became such a chore. Something that feels forced. It used to be we couldn't keep our hands off each other. We'd sneak away from parties and go to my place early just to have some alone time. Now... I don't know if it's because I just feel so exhausted, that the thought of having sex with him makes me feel even more tired, not excited like it used to make me feel. I shake my head and decide that instead of dreading it, if I change my thought process, maybe I'll start enjoying it again. Maybe I'll get excited about it again.

> **Me:** I'm not saying we won't have sex. ;-) but do what you need to do.
> **Jason:** I'll be there at 6. :-P

I put my phone down and grab my drink. Trying to be flirty with him didn't really help my excitement level but maybe I need to keep trying.

"Everything okay?" Kallon asks.

"Oh, yeah, it's fine," I say with a smile that I can feel is forced.

"You just look... I don't know, a little upset maybe?"

"I'm not really upset. Jason was trying to rearrange when he was going to come over this evening, but he's decided to come over at 6 like we'd talked about earlier."

"Everything going okay with him?"

"I think so... He says he's trying. He slipped up and drank last night and said some things and then—" I was going to tell him about the phone call and the strange woman who answered but I change my mind "—he let slip that he's drank a couple other times with his friends."

"Drinking is a hard habit to kick, especially if you're friends aren't on board with your sobriety," Kallon says.

I tell Kallon the fear I've been subconsciously having since Jason told me he'd stop drinking, "I know. But I have a feeling Jason might choose his friends and drinking over me."

"He'd be a fool to do that," Kallon says, turning towards me. "He's a lucky man to have you as his girlfriend and if he can't see that, you deserve better."

I smile a small smile at him, but I don't say anything.

"Well, I better go," Kallon says suddenly. He's looking at his watch. "You've got a couple hours before Jason is supposed to be here, that's enough time for a short nap."

I laugh and say, "Maybe a shower first."

Kallon's cheeks go a little pink as his eyes roam from my face down to my lap and then back up to me. He's eyebrows raise just enough for it to be noticeable, and he says as he stands up slowly, "If you don't give him those photos, save them for another time."

My eyes about bulge out of my head when he winks at me. I shake my head as I feel my face heating up again, "Please forget you saw those."

Kallon reaches down for his folder, places both hands on the table and looks at me from under his long, dark lashes. He says in a whisper, "They were good pictures. They'll be hard to forget."

"Kallon," I say in a pleading voice.

He chuckles and stands up and walks towards my front door. "Bye Abby, see you on set in the morning."

He waves over his shoulder but stops at the door and turns to me.

I'm shaking my head and laughing, "You're going to tease me about this all the time, aren't you?"

"Not all the time," he says with a laugh and another wink.

"Great," I say with a laugh. "Goodbye, Kallon."

He smiles a devilishly sexy smile and says, "Bye, Abby."

He opens the door and walks out. I stand and tell myself that my racing heart is from the teasing and embarrassment of him seeing the pictures. I grab the folder off the table and go to my room. I put the folder in a box that I have in the corner of my closet. It's my, 'I'm not sure I need this still but I'm going to save it,' box and it's almost full. I'm going to have to go through it to remind myself what's in there, but not right now. I close my closet door and get some fresh clothes from my dresser and go to the bathroom.

"A hot shower will feel nice," I say to myself.

I'm sitting on the couch, reading, when I hear the buzzer for the door. I look at my watch and see that it's a little after 6 o'clock. I've been reading for an hour and time flew. I hop up and go to the intercom.

"Hello?" I ask.

"Hey, babe, it's me," Jason's voice comes from the

speaker.

I push the button to unlock the bottom door and say, "Come on up."

I hear running up the stairs and open the door just as Jason gets to it. He wraps his arms around my waist and lifts me up, pulling me to him, using his hands to wrap my legs around his waist. My heart flutters and feels like it drops to my stomach from the quick motion. He spins us, shuts the door with his foot, and then presses me against the door. And then his mouth is on mine.

"God, I've missed you," Jason moans out as his lips pull away from mine and then he starts to kiss hurriedly down my neck.

He pushes himself into me, to hold me against the door, so he can use one of his hands to slide up my shirt and roughly grabs my left breast. He pulls on the cup of my bra, trying to get it down so his hand can touch skin. His other hand goes to my ass and squeezes.

"Baby, I need you now," he says as his hand on my ass slides forward and tries to move my shorts and undies to the side. He's pulling my bra some more, which doesn't feel the greatest.

"Jason... Jason," I say urgently. "Slow down a little. You're hurting my shoulders pulling on my bra like that."

"Sorry," he mumbles into my mouth as he plasters his mouth to it. His tongue is all but down my throat. I use my tongue to try to push his out a little, he moans at the tongue wrestling happening. He moves his hand from my breast and puts it to my ass. His other hand is still trying to find its way to my center, but the way he has me against the door and his body pressed against me, it's making it difficult for him to move my clothes.

"Jason, please," I beg.

A sound that's between a moan and growl comes from deep in Jason's throat. He pulls me away from the door and walks us to the couch. He practically jumps us onto it and then he's all over me.

"I've got you baby, I'll make you feel good, don't worry," he says as he kisses down my neck to my chest. So fast, he pulls my shirt up and over my head, but only enough so that my chest is uncovered, it's still under my back. I go to move my hands, to pull my shirt all the way off but Jason grabs my wrists with one hand and holds them over my head. "I said I got you."

"Jason please," I say again, wiggling underneath him. Realizing that he's mistaken my plea as a plea of desire and need for him now, and not as the plea to slow down and take it easy like I meant it to be. I say, to clarify, "Just... slow down a little."

"I can't... I need you... I want you now... I... can't stand it," he says almost painfully as he reaches behind me and unclasps my bra. Instead of releasing my hands and letting me take my shirt and bra off, he just pushes my bra up under my chin. His mouth goes to my left nipple, and he pulls it into his mouth, sucking vigorously. He thrusts his hips into me, grinding hard. He pulls his mouth off me and says, "I need this shit off."

He reaches down with his hand that isn't holding my wrists and fast as lightning, he pulls my shorts and undies down to my ankles. I use my feet to quickly kick them off, so they don't end up tangled at my feet like my shirt and bra at my neck.

"Jason," I say just as he kisses me. I pull away and look at him. "Why are you in such a hurry? We have time. Slow down, please."

"I can't, baby. It hurts how much I need this release," he says with a grunt, and I can feel how hard he is against me. I then watch as he quickly shimmies his pants and underwear down. He settles between my legs and as he takes my nipple into his mouth, my eyes closing on the surprisingly good feeling that comes over me but, before I can say anything, he thrusts into me, hard.

"Ugh," I grunt out in a little pain, the good feeling short lived. I wasn't expecting him to go so deep, so hard, so fast.

"Yeah, baby, you like that?" he asks as he pulls out and does it again. I'm about to tell him no, that it actually hurts, but then his mouth is on mine and his tongue is once again close to choking me. I feel a rumble against my mouth as he moans out, "Mmmmmm."

I try to pull my mouth away from him, but he just pushes his mouth harder into mine and drives himself deeper and harder into me. I moan again, trying to make it sound as pained as I feel. I try to pull my hands away from his, but he holds on tighter.

As soon as it started, it seems to be over. Two more thrusts and then Jason is pressing his face into my neck, groaning out his pleasure.

"Fuuuuuuuuuuuuucking shiiiiiit baaaaabe," he groans. He does another two quick pumps, goes to my nipples, and sucks them each hard, once. He pulls out and then thrusts back in hard, one more time.

"Ugh," I groan.

"Yeah baby, that was good, huh?" Jason says. He kisses me across my chest, up my neck, and then surprisingly, gives me a sweet, soft kiss on my lips. My lips that feel a little swollen and slightly sore now.

"Actually, it hurt," I say pulling my hands from his and this time he lets me go. I put them on his shoulders and push him off me.

"What do you mean?" he asks, surprised.

"I was telling you to slow down, but you weren't listening to me. Then you went too hard, too fast, I wasn't ready," I say sitting up. He reaches over to the coffee table and grabs a paper towel and uses it to take the condom off that he put on at some point. It all happened so fast. I'm surprised to know that he at least did that.

"Oh," he says as he wraps the condom up in the paper towel. He reaches down and pulls his underwear up. I see they only made it down to his ankles, along with his pants. He pulls those up now too. As he's buttoning them up and buckling his belt, I strap my bra back on and pull my shirt down.

"Oh?" I ask. "That's all you have to say?"

"I'm sorry, I thought your moans and groans were because you were enjoying yourself. You didn't say it hurt."

"You were practically choking me with your tongue, I didn't have a chance to tell you it hurt. And then you finished and... well, here we are."

"So, you didn't enjoy any of it?" he asks.

"No, I didn't," I say honestly.

"That's too bad, it was good for me," he says with a laugh and a wink.

"I'm glad for you," I say sarcastically as I stand and put my undies and shorts back on.

He pulls me to him and sits on the couch, with me on his lap. "I'm sorry baby, next time will be just for you."

He kisses me on the neck and runs one of his hands over my breasts. I pull away and sit on the other side of the couch.

"I'm not in the mood," I say, annoyed.

"I can get you in the mood," he says as he starts to crawl over to me.

"I'd rather talk for now," I say as I put my foot out to stop him.

"Ugh... fine," Jason says, now sounding annoyed himself.

"What?" I ask. "You got your orgasm. Can't we talk now?"

"Sure," he says as he adjusts himself and sits back. I can see he has another hard-on. He rubs himself a little and asks in what I think is his seductive tone, "Can we have round two after we talk?"

"Jason, seriously?" I ask.

"Most girls would feel proud that they could make their man want them as bad as I want you," he says as he grabs himself. "Look what you do to me!"

"Please?" I beg.

"Okay, okay," he says surprisingly sweet. "We can talk."

We sit silently for a minute, and not in the comfortable silence like I sat with Kallon. This silence feels awkward and uncomfortable.

"So," I start to say. "About last night."

"I'm sorry," Jason says quickly. "It won't happen again, I swear. It was an accident. I was feeling lonely and then the guys called and said they were going out. They invited me and I wanted company, so I went. Before I knew it, I was drinking. It won't happen again."

"It's not an accident if you do it on purpose," I say, starting to get upset. I take a breath to calm myself, and say, "You know that they won't ever be on board with you being sober, right?"

"I can handle it," he says with a grunt.

"It doesn't sound like you can. You said you've drank before last night and you were out with them," I say.

"Well, what am I supposed to do? They're my friends and they invite me out. You've been so busy with work and that's great and all, but we haven't been out in a long time."

"You can always come to Rose's and hangout there while I work. You used to do that all the time. You can sit in the bar and have a nonalcoholic drink or hangout in the office. Plus, I'm stepping way from being Head Chef until the catering job is over."

"What a loser I'd look like asking for a nonalcoholic drink in the bar," Jason says as he rolls his eyes.

"Who cares what people might think?" I ask him, my tone getting hot. "It's what would be best for you."

"Best for me because you say it's the best for me."

"Are you saying you don't think you have a drinking problem? Because I'm pretty sure you're the one who said you did, when you told me you'd stop drinking."

"Well, maybe I think it's not so much a drinking problem but an amount problem. Maybe I drink too much, too fast. Maybe having one or two, throughout the night wouldn't be a bad thing to try."

"If you feel like you have to have a drink to get through the night, or an event, or to have fun, don't you think that's a good sign you have a problem?" I ask earnestly.

"Shane and Deven don't think I have a problem," Jason says, sounding more like a little kid than an adult.

"Do Shane and Deven have your best interest at heart, or do they not want to lose their drinking buddy? Someone to split the bill with?" I ask, really annoyed now.

"They care about me. They care about my happiness," Jason answers defensively. "They don't think my behavior is just my fault."

"I'm sorry, what? Are you saying they think your drinking and the way you act when you're drunk is my fault?" I ask, dumbfounded.

He looks like he's rethinking what he was going to say. He clears his throat and says, "They think that if you spent more time with me, with us, and not working, that maybe I wouldn't act the way I do sometimes."

I'm speechless. I look around my living room and take a minute to think. *Are Shane and Deven right? Has Jason's behavior lately been because I haven't been present in our relationship?*

I can't help but feel like maybe they are right. I look at Jason and say, "Jason, maybe they're a little right. But your behavior isn't just my fault. You need to take responsibility for it too. Maybe I haven't been giving enough of myself and attention to our relationship in the last couple of weeks. But I also know that it's not just recently that you've been acting weird and pulling away. It's been going on for a while now. Our relationship has been strained… has been changing for over a year now. Ever since—"

"—your pregnancy scare," Jason interrupts, finishing what I was going to say. "I know. I realize that."

"Why do you think that is?" I ask, ignoring how he said 'your' instead of 'our'. I know why it is for me, but I want to know why he thinks it's changed.

"I don't know," he says.

"Yes, you do," I say. I reach over and grab his hand. He looks at our hands and then up at me. "Just tell me."

"It freaked me out," he says, tears filling his eyes. Looking into his eyes and hearing his voice, I finally see and feel the Jason I fell in love with. "I wasn't ready for it and the thought of becoming a father scared the hell out of me. I felt selfish for the thoughts I had about it and then breaking your trust by telling the guys and other people at the office… I knew it'd get back to you that I spilled the beans, but I didn't care, I just couldn't handle waiting to find out. And then the relief I felt when you told me the test said negative and then when you started your period, it made me feel so good that I almost felt guilty."

"I was scared too," I say. "I wasn't, and I'm still not, ready to be a mom. I think the scare opened our eyes to the fact we aren't ready for that step in our relationship. But Jason, we have to do better at communicating. I know I've said it before, but I need you to talk to me. I know you need the physical part of our relationship to feel like I'm in this relationship, but I need you to talk to me and I need you to hear me when I talk to you. I need you to take the time to answer my calls or texts. I need to know you're thinking of me and our relationship when you go out with your friends, that you're putting our relationship and what we need, first... Ahead of what you feel like your friends need from you."

"You say you know that I need the physical part... the sex... but how many times have I called, asking if I can come over but you've been too busy or you say that it's too late, that you have to get up early?"

"I know, it's happened a couple of times and I'm sorry. I'm trying to figure things out and I think stepping back from Head Chef will help. I can leave Rose's a little earlier on slower nights and if things go well tomorrow, I won't be doing all the days at the movie set. I'm trying to rearrange things so I can give us more time too. But I can't be the only one that is trying, Jason, you have to put in the work also."

"Like how?" he asks, sounding like the new Jason, annoyed and frustrated that he's being asked to do something.

I take a deep breath, calming my instant annoyance with his reaction. I say, "By being a little understanding that my schedule is a little crazy right now. If there's a night that I have to stay late at Rose's because we're busy or because we have an event going on, then it's probably not a good night to come over. I am the owner and manager of the restaurant now and that means more responsibilities. The catering job won't last forever and Rose Bud's... Betty has been amazing and has basically taken charge of it. Which is great, but it wasn't my intention for that to happen. I have to juggle my jobs and our relationship right now. I need your help and understanding that there might be days, and nights, that I might just be too tired to do anything but sleep, and you getting cranky with me for not getting some ass, doesn't help anything."

Jason puts his head back against the couch cushion and closes his eyes. He takes a deep breath and says, "Okay, I can do that. I'll work on being more understanding."

"Why do you sound like that's so hard to do?" I ask, honestly wondering why his tone sounds like being understanding is the hardest thing in the world.

"I just need to adjust that I'm not the center of your world anymore," he says, looking at me finally.

"I'm sorry you feel that way," I say with tears in my eyes now. "I love you and you're the only guy I want to be with. I'm sorry work has become so consuming, but it won't last forever."

"I know it won't and I don't want you to give up your dreams and goals, but I need to feel like I'm in those dreams and goals as well," he says as he reaches for my hand. I squeeze it. He pulls my hand, which pulls me towards him, and kisses my hand softly. He looks up at me and winks and asks, "So round two?"

I pull my hand away and say, "We aren't done talking."

"We aren't?"

"No," I say. I take another calming breath, building my bravery, and ask, "That woman last night who answered your phone—" Jason stiffens and his eyes dart from my face to the coffee table "—was that really Deven's wife?"

I didn't want to test him, but I still have a feeling he's lying to me. I'm hoping with how open we've been with each other the last few minutes, no matter what he tells me, I hope he'll be honest.

"Ummm yeah," Jason says, he looks at the coffee table one more time and then turns and stares at me. He thinks for a minute and adds, "They stayed the night. My place was closer than theirs."

"Oh, I thought you said last night it was Lorrie and Shane that stayed?" I ask.

"Who did you just ask stayed? Didn't you say Shane?" he asks instead of answering me.

"No, I said Deven."

"Oh, no it was Shane and Lorrie," Jason says a little hurriedly.

"Jason now is the time to tell me if something happened," I say, a little pleading in my tone.

"Nothing happened, I swear," Jason says, scooting towards me, reaching for both of my hands. "Other than me drinking when I shouldn't have been."

"Are you sure?" I ask, my lie antennas are pinging.

"Yeah, I'm sure," he says and then he kisses my hands.

"Okay," I say, not fully believing him. But I tell myself I need to trust him. If he says it was Lorrie who answered, then it was, and I need to believe him.

"So, if we aren't going to have sex again, maybe I should go so you can get to sleep," Jason says, kissing my hands again and then letting them go.

I pull them back into my lap and say, "I don't think so, it honestly really did hurt."

"I'm sorry about that," Jason says sincerely. "I'll do better next time. What's your schedule this week?"

"Tomorrow I'll be in the bakery. Tuesday-Thursday I'll be doing the catering gig and starting on just doing the manager side of things those days too."

I grab the paper towels, tear one off and wrap it around the used one from earlier. I take the roll and the garbage into the kitchen. After I've thrown the garbage away and put the roll on the paper towel holder, I get a glass of water. As I walk back into the living room, Jason is standing and tucking his shirt into his pants.

"Your leaving?" I ask.

"I think we've talked enough for one night and you made it clear we aren't having sex again, so yeah, I think it's time for me to go," Jason says, sounding like his new self again. He walks to me and wraps his arms around me to give me a hug. He bends and kisses me on the cheek and then turns towards the door. "I'll come over tomorrow after I get off work."

"So that's it?" I ask, my feelings hurt. "You got laid. Stuck it out long enough to talk a little and now you're leaving?"

"What more is there?" Jason asks as he gets to the door.

I can feel my face turn into a look of surprise, with my mouth hanging open. As I close it and my eyes, I shake my head. I say in a small voice, "I guess nothing."

"K, night. See you tomorrow," Jason says, not at all sensing how upset I am. He again, doesn't wait for me to say bye, he just opens the door and leaves before he's finished saying 'tomorrow."

Feeling slightly dazed and confused, I grab my phone off the table, turn the lights off and go to my room. I plug my phone in and look at my watch when I take it off and see it's only 7:34pm. I feel emotionally and mentally drained. I can't figure out how we went from talking so well, to me feeling like Jason didn't hear a single thing I said to him. How could it have felt like my old Jason was back, just for the new Jason to appear with whiplash speed?

I remember I need to send Steph a text, so I grab my phone again.

Me: Hi Steph. I'm going to send Betty and Maggie tomorrow. If it goes well, they'll be doing Mondays and Fridays. Let me know if that'll work.

She replies instantly.

Stephanie: Sounds good to me. See you Tuesday. :-)

I put my phone down and ask myself, as my thoughts go back to Jason, "What am I going to do?"

I pull my blankets around me. That question repeats it's self over and over in my head as I fall asleep.

CHAPTER 27

BEEPBEEP**BEEP**

BEEPBEEP**BEEP**

BEEPBEEP**BEEP**

I roll over and hit my phone. My alarm goes off loudly in my ears. I roll back onto my back and keep my eyes closed. I had a pretty restful sleep. After the evening I had with Jason, I didn't think I'd sleep as well as I did. I must have been extremely exhausted still.

I reach to my side, grab my phone off my nightstand, and pull my phone to me. I see that it's 12:30am.

"Crap," I say to myself and sit up quickly. "I have so much stuff to get done."

I jump out of bed and rush to the bathroom. Just as I'm turning on the water for a very speedy shower, I remember that Betty had told me she and Maggie had gotten all the prep done. I hang my head and laugh a little. I also remind myself that Betty and Maggie are taking the catering side of things today. My five hours of sleep really got me confused.

I still take a quick shower and make it downstairs by 1am. I start getting the fruit out for the fruit bowls and smoothies. After everything's out, I get the smoothie stuff going. I put the smoothie mixture in the cooler and just as I'm scooping the fruit into the bowls, I hear the ding of my security cameras telling me that someone is at the side door. I look and see Betty and Maggie. I look at my watch and see it's almost 1:30am.

When I hear the side door open, I holler out, "Good morning my amazing friends!"

"Abby?" I hear Betty ask, confused.

Just as she comes through the doors into the kitchen, I laugh and say, "Who else would it be?"

"You should be sleeping. You don't have to be down here until at least 4:30," Betty says.

"No, I'm helping get things going for you guys. If I'm feeling tired after you guys leave, I'll go back up for an hour or two before I need to open up the shop," I say as I continue scooping fruit into the bowls. "The smoothies are done. We just need to finish this—" I wave at the fruit "—and make the frosting for the pastries. Then start loading stuff up."

"Sounds good," Betty says.

"Umm Abby?" Maggie says from the doorway leading to the front. "Would it be okay if I practice making coffees for you and Mom?"

"Sure!" I say excitedly. "Have you been practicing while you've been here?"

"No, Mom said I needed to ask you first," she says with a smile. "But I've been watching her every time she makes one."

"That's good," I say.

"What would you like?" Maggie asks excitedly.

"I'd like a large, iced, chocolate toffee, one shot please," I say, laughing as she bounces up and down on the balls of her feet.

"Okay," she says, mouthing my order to herself. "Mom, do you want your usual?"

"Yes please," Betty says as she finishes adding the ingredients for the frosting into a mixing bowl.

"Can I make myself a drink?" she asks both Betty and me. I answer with a shrug and a nod towards Betty.

"I don't want you to get used to drinking coffee. It's not a habit you need to have yet, but yes, I think one today would be fine," Betty says. As Maggie claps with glee and bounces out of the kitchen, Betty adds, "Maggie Lynn, come back please."

When Maggie walks back in, she looks a little taken aback. Her mom never uses her middle name unless she's in trouble.

"Yes?" Maggie asks uncertainly.

"You can have a small one. You're already hyper enough as it is, you don't need a huge caffeine boost, so put half a shot in yours and the rest in mine. I wouldn't mind having a shot and a half this morning," Betty says with her eyebrows raised at her daughter.

"Okay!" Maggie says, back to her bouncy excited self.

"You alright?" I ask. "You don't usually have so much caffeine."

"Oh, I'm fine, I just don't want her having a full shot.

Who knows what havoc she'd spread around the movie set if she was hopped up on caffeine and her already hyper self."

"If we could bottle her enthusiasm and energy, we wouldn't need the caffeine either," I say with a laugh.

"That's for sure," Betty says with a laugh of her own.

After Betty is done with the icing, she helps me finish the fruit bowls. We run down to the basement and grab some boxes. We'd been putting them away every Friday after coming back from the studio so that they weren't in our way. When we come into the kitchen, Maggie is standing by my desk with three to-go cups sitting on top of it.

"How did it go?" I ask.

She shrugs and is trying to hide a smile, "I don't know, you tell me."

She hands me my cup and then she hands her mom, hers. We say, "Cheers," tap cups, and take our first sips. If I didn't know Maggie made it, I would have guessed a well-seasoned barista made it.

"Maggie, this is delicious!" I exclaim.

"Really?" she asks sincerely. "You're not just saying that?"

"It's really good! I'd tell you otherwise. True honesty is the best way to improve," I say with a huge smile. "This is really good."

"Thank you," she beams. She looks at Betty and asks, "Mom?"

"I'm sorry Abby, but this is the best coffee I've ever had," Betty says looking at her cup and then at Maggie. "How did you do it?"

"Just like you and Abby," Maggie says with her cheeks

turning a little pink.

"No, you did something different," I say as I take another drink. "Maggie, would you like to make some coffees when you're here?"

"For real?" she asks, completely surprised.

"Yes," I say. "We'll get you your food handlers' card so you're legit and then you can start making coffees."

"Thank you, Abby," Maggie says as she flings her arms around my neck.

"There's some children labor laws that we have to go over, but I think we can make it so you're getting some time at the machines," I say with a laugh, as I pat her back. She pulls away and I see that her smile is lighting up her entire face.

My computer dings, telling me that someone else is at the side door. I look and see Dax standing there, looking up at the camera.

"Shoot, I forgot to tell him about my change in schedule," I say as I put my hands to my face. I turn to Maggie, and I ask her, "Will you go let in Dax?"

She bounces to the door, but stops before she goes through, turns, and asks, "Can I make him a drink if he hasn't had anything yet?"

"Sure," I say. "But he's not as exciting as we are, he usually just has black coffee."

"Maybe I can talk him into trying something else today," she says as she runs through the doors.

"If anyone can, it's her," Betty says with a laugh.

"And you," I say in a whisper and hip bump her.

"Oh, don't get started," Betty whispers back. "He's not

interested in me like that."

"How do you know?" I whisper back hurriedly. Knowing Dax, we don't have a lot of time before he's back here.

"He hasn't made a move or anything," she says, sounding hurried like me.

"Have you made it clear you're interested?" I ask. I then go to the doors and peak through and see Dax talking to Maggie in front of the counter.

"I think so," she says.

"Give him time," I say as I turn around and help finish boxing stuff up. "Don't lose hope."

Just as we're putting the last of the stuff in the boxes, Dax walks through holding a cup.

"Good morning," he says to us.

"Morning," I say with a smile.

"Morning, Dax," Betty says with an even bigger smile.

"Maggie make you something?" I ask.

"Yeah, but I couldn't tell you what it is. She talked me into something new, she rambled off a long name," he takes a tentative sip and then his eyes go big. "What in the world?"

Betty and I laugh as he takes a bigger drink from his cup.

"Good?" Betty asks.

"Better than good," Dax says with a chuckle. "This is way better than black coffee."

Betty and I laugh again. I say, "Took a twelve-year-old to get you to try something new. I should feel offended."

Dax laughs and then pushes the door open and steps halfway into the front and says to Maggie, "What did you call this again, Mags?"

He steps aside and lets her walk into the kitchen. She answers him with, "It's a large, double shot, extra hot, no foam, caramel mocha latte, but I made it with chocolate milk instead of regular milk."

"What made you think to make that for him?" Betty asks, looking as shocked as I feel.

"I don't know," Maggie shrugs. Then she adds, "He likes black coffee so I thought the chocolate milk would calm the caramel down enough it wasn't super overpowering. The two chocolates might make it taste just good enough."

"Genius," I say, stunned.

"You can make this for me anytime you like," Dax says, tipping the cup towards her before taking another sip. "Seriously, I think you've ruined coffee for me. I'm going to be one of 'those' people now."

Betty laughs and says, "One of 'those' people?"

"Yeah, when it takes longer to say their order than it does to make," Dax laughs.

We all laugh, and I say, "Welcome to the club."

"Thanks," he rumbles out. He looks around and sees everything is boxed up. "Everything ready to be loaded into the van?"

I stop laughing instantly, remembering I forgot to tell him about my new schedule.

"It is, but Dax, I forgot to tell you last night. I'm not going to the studio today. Betty and Maggie are going, to see how it goes, with me still in town in case something happens. I'm sorry I forgot to tell you last night. You got up so early for nothing," I say. Then I have a thought. I look at Betty and asks, "Unless you want him to drive you guys?"

"Oh, no, that's okay. I don't mind driving," Betty says. "Plus, you need him here for you."

"I'm not going anywhere today," I say.

"You never know," Betty says with a shrug. She looks at Dax and says with a smile, "I got it."

"Okay, well take the credit card to fuel the van back up on your way back," I say. I pull the top drawer in my desk open and pull out a card holder wallet and hand it to Betty. I always leave the card in it, so I always know where it's at and it doesn't get lost.

"Will do," Betty says as she puts the little wallet in her pocket.

We all grab boxes and start loading the van up. Once it's loaded, I look at my watch and see it's 3:30am.

I turn to Dax, Maggie, and Betty and say, "I think we have this down. Perfect timing."

"Yeah, we do," Betty says.

I high five them all and then hug Betty. I say, "You've got this and thank you for helping me figure out my options yesterday."

"Anytime," she says as she hugs me back tightly. She lets go and turns to Maggie, "Ready kiddo?"

"Yup," she says with even more bounce in her step.

"You sure you only had half a shot in your drink?" I ask kiddingly.

"Yes," Maggie says. "I'm just so excited to go back to set."

"Well, be careful," I say, giving her and Betty a look.

"We will," Maggie says and then she heads to the back

door. "Bye Abby, bye Dax."

"Bye kid," Dax says.

"Bye," I say with a laugh as she heads out the door.

"I'll text or call if there's any problems," Betty says.

"I won't hear from you until you're back," I say with enthusiasm.

"Bye," she says with a laugh and a wave to me and Dax.

"Bye," we say at the same time.

Betty goes out the door and I turn to Dax and smile.

"So, what chya gonna do now?" I ask him.

"Hangout outside I guess," he says as he takes another sip of his drink.

"No, why don't you go home?" I suggest.

"Nope, I'm on duty. I'm here if you need me," he says as he heads for the doors to go out front.

"At least come up to my condo and rest until I need to come back down here at 4:30," I say. "And then you can sit at one of the comfy tables. You don't need to sit in the car all day."

"I don't mind."

"I do," I say. I turn and head for the stairs. I open the door and turn towards him and wave, "Come on, big man."

He chuckles and starts to walk towards me rather than away. I head up the stairs and I don't turn around until I get to the door. I open it and turn, seeing Dax right behind me. I let him in and then lock the door behind us.

"Take the couch, I'll lay in the chair," I say as I walk into the living room. I put my coffee down on the table and pull the blanket off the back of the big chair and wrap it around myself before I curl into a ball in the oversized chair.

"Thanks," Dax says. He looks more relaxed than I've ever seen him. He even takes his shoes off and lies all the way down.

I pull my phone out of my pocket and make sure I have an alarm set for 4:20am. I put it on the armrest beside where my head will be and then lay my head down and close my eyes.

◆ ◆ ◆

The morning is flying by. When I check the clock on the register, I see it's already 10:37am. I look at my phone for the first time and see I have no missed calls or texts from anyone. I didn't check it all morning, knowing that I'd feel or hear it if it went off. But not hearing from anyone, it started to make me feel a little antsy. I told myself I couldn't check it until after 10:30.

No news is good news, I kept telling myself all morning.

The morning had been just what I needed. I reconnected with all of my regulars. My gentlemen trio were so excited to see me this morning. I apologized to them for not being here more often and told them how I had changed my schedule around so I could see them.

I also got to see how many more regulars we'd gotten in the last couple of weeks. A lot of them were from word of mouth from people at the studio telling their friends and family about how amazing Rose Bud's coffee and pastries were.

A little while later, as I'm cleaning up after making a

sandwich for someone, I feel my phone vibrate in my pocket. I pull it out and see a text from Betty.

Betty: Just fueling up. There was a wreck just before the bridge, took us a little bit to get through but we're on our way back now. Should be there in about 20-30 minutes. It went great today.
Me: Perfect! Thank you!

I look up and see Dax looking at me from his seat he's been occupying all morning. I wave him over and he comes up quickly. I smile at him and say, "That was Betty. They should be back in about thirty minutes."

"It's a little later than normal, did she have trouble?" he asks, sounding concerned.

"There was a wreck just before the bridge, it took some time to get past it. She said it went well today," I say with my smile getting bigger.

"That's great news," Dax says with a big smile of his own.

The next twenty minutes goes by quickly and then I hear the beep from the kitchen. I finish ringing up a customer who found a couple books and then holler for Dax.

"Dax!" I say just loud enough for him to hear me but quite a few people sitting closer to the counter turn and look too. I smile and wave at them, mouthing an apology. When Dax gets back to me, I say, "They're back."

We turn and go through the doors, just as Betty and Maggie are putting boxes down on the counters.

"It was so fun today," Maggie says excitedly. Dax waves a hello as he heads out to the van to bring in more stuff.

"She got everyone's autograph," Betty says with a smile. "Kallon made sure she met everyone today."

"Kallon is so nice. He let us hangout in his dressing room and watch tv in there again."

"He's a very nice man," I agree.

"How did it go here?" Betty asks.

"Great," I say. "Just got through the lunch rush. And that book order I've been waiting for finally came in. I got all the barcodes scanned in and got them shelved between customers. I think I've already sold four from the shipment."

"Oh, thank goodness! I was starting to wonder if we were ever going to get them," Betty says as she starts to pull stuff out of the boxes. I hear the ding of the bell we leave on the counter for customers to get our attention if we're in the back.

"I want to hear all about how the set went today," I say to Betty as I walk to the front.

"I'll be up there as soon as we have everything put away," she says with a smile.

I walk through the doors and take the order of the customer at the counter. As I'm finishing making his sandwiches, Betty comes through the doors and rings him up for me.

"Maggie went to go lie down upstairs, is that okay?" Betty asks after she hands the customer his bag and receipt.

"Absolutely," I say. And then I add, "In fact, why don't you go rest as well?"

"I'm actually not tired," Betty says earnestly. "I feel great."

"Okay but know you can go up at any time if you start

to feel like you need a rest," I offer.

"Thank you."

As we work side by side together for the next hour or so, Betty tells me about the morning on the movie set. She told me about how all the set crew and actors were all very kind and appreciative to the spread we put out. She said that quite a few people said they were finally eating on set again, whereas before they always picked something up on the way to work.

We're just cleaning after a large lunch to-go order was called in when I feel my phone vibrate in my pocket. I look and see it's text from Jason.

Jason: Hi babe, how was the movie set today?

Me: I didn't go to the set today, Betty went instead. I rearranged my schedule, remember?

Jason: Oh that's right. So how was the morning at RB?

Me: It went great. How's your day going?

Jason: Swamped. Going to be in meetings all day. I had a minute so I thought I'd see how you were doing.

Me: Aww, thanks for that.

Jason: What do you have planned for after work?

Me: I'll probably head to my parents' house early. It's dinner night. Dad's BBQing. Do you want to come with me? You haven't made it to Monday night dinner in a long time.

Jason: Sorry babe, I wish but I can't tonight. Meetings w/new clients, today is the only day that worked for them.

Me: K

Jason: So probably not going to be up for me to come over when you get home?

I roll my eyes. It always goes there with him. I'm

starting to wonder if he has another addiction, not just drinking.

> **Me:** I guess it just depends on when I get home from Mom and Dad's.
> **Jason:** What would be too late?
> **Me:** Probably 8.
> **Jason:** Shit babe, that's still early.
> **Me:** It's not when I need to be up by 12:30am.

It takes a minute for him to reply. More than a minute, I have time to ring a customer up and cash them out before my phone vibrates on the counter.

> **Jason:** You're right. Ok, well if you get home before 8, let me know.
> **Me:** K
> **Jason:** Hope to see you later.
> **Me:** Me too.

I didn't know what else to say because I'm not really hoping I'll see him later. I know that sounds bad, but I was so drained after seeing him last night. I need another night of a couple of hours of good sleep. I really need to talk to someone about how I'm feeling towards him, maybe they can help me figure out what's wrong with me.

My phone vibrates again, I look down, expecting a text from Jason but I see Kallon's name on my screen.

> **Kallon:** Hey, just wanted to let you know Betty did great today.
> **Me:** I knew she would but thanks for letting me know. :-D How's your day going so far?
> **Kallon:** Kind of weird. I had started to get used to seeing you in the

mornings. :-D

    Me: Hahaha Sorry. Looks like you'll have to get used to Betty's and Maggie's happy faces on Mondays and Fridays from now on.

    Kallon: They sure are chipper in the mornings, aren't they?

    Me: Yes and Betty swears she doesn't have any coffee until she gets to the shop. I don't know if I believe her. haha

    Kallon: I wish I could wake up and be that happy.

    Me: Me too.

    Kallon: I don't think I've ever seen you grumpy. Maybe a little tired but not unhappy.

    Me: I have my mornings.

    Kallon: How did today go at the bakery?

    Me: So good. It was really nice to reconnect with my customers.

    Kallon: I'm glad to hear that. What do you have planned for after work?

    Me: Nothing really. It's dinner night at my parents' house so I might go over there a little early.

    Kallon: I was thinking of checking out the Farmer's Market to see what they have and to see if there's anything we can get for Rose's, you wanna come with me for an hour or so? We won't cut into your family time, promise.

I think for a minute and decide why not. Jason said he's in meetings all day, so I won't miss out on doing anything with him.

    Me: Sure, I'll go.

    Kallon: Sweet. I'll have Trevor drop me off at Rose Bud's around 3.

    Me: Sounds good.

    Kallon: See you in a bit.

"What's that smile for?" Betty asks.

"Jason texted to see how I was doing," I say. I then add, "And then Kallon texted to tell me how great you guys did this morning and then invited me to go to the Farmer's Market."

"Oh, that'll be nice," she says. "How's Jason going to like that?"

"There's nothing for him to dislike about it. He's in meetings all day. Plus, Kallon and I are going to look for things for Rose's. He's never been to the Farmer's Market. I'll show him the booth where we get the seafood. It'll be good for him to see that side of the restaurant," I say.

"Just be careful. Jason has been acting especially jealous when it comes to Kallon," Betty says as she cleans up around the sandwich making area.

"I've noticed that too. He's brought up that I spend time with Kallon but not him. I've told him that I ask him to do things with me but he's always busy, always in a meeting of some sort. Even today, I told him we could do something after work, before I go to my parents. I even asked him if he wanted to go to their house with me, and he said no, he has an important meeting. I'm not hanging out with Kallon to spite Jason or make him mad and definitely not doing it to make him jealous. I'm hanging out with Kallon because he's my friend—" I don't think the customers are close enough to hear me but just to be on the safe side, I continue with a whisper, "—and business partner."

"I know that... you know that... but when guys feel threatened, they get possessive and sometimes dangerous," Betty says.

"I'll talk with Jason about it again the next time we're together," I say to reassure her.

Betty smiles and goes back to cleaning. I look at my

watch and see it's nearly closing time. I grab a rag and go out to the tables and start to clean the ones that no one is sitting at, putting chairs on top of the tables as I go. I straighten the bookshelves and end tables, wiping those down as well. When I pass Dax, I fill him in on what Kallon said about being dropped off around 3 o'clock and our planned trip to the Farmer's Market.

Soon all the customers have left and I'm turning the open sign to close. Betty is sweeping so I go into the back and get the mop water ready. When I come back out, I see Dax washing the windows and front door glass.

"Dax, you don't need to do that," I say with a laugh.

"I need to do something," he says as he sprays the window cleaner on the upper part of the door.

"I'm going to put you on the payroll with all you do around here," I say with an eyebrow raised.

"You will not," he states turning to look at me with a glare. "I'm already getting paid to sit here, the least I can do is help out."

"You'll be driving us soon enough," I say, reminding him about the Farmer's Market trip.

"Well, until then, I can help around here. My ass was getting sore from all the sitting I was doing anyways," Dax says as he wiggles his rear at me. I laugh and as I turn, I see Betty staring in Dax's direction.

I cock my head and raise an eyebrow at her. She catches me looking at her staring at him and her face blushes. She smiles sheepishly and returns to her sweeping. I go to grab the mop, but Maggie walks out from the kitchen.

"Can I mop?" Maggie asks.

"Sure," I say. "I'll go in the back and do the books."

Maggie happily grabs the mop out of my hand and starts to mop where her mom had already swept. I grab the receipts and cash drawer from the register and head to the back. Once I'm to my desk, I get out my book to record today's card and cash payments. It doesn't take long before I'm finished with that, so I grab the bills that are due in a couple weeks and decide to pay them now.

While I'm doing my work, I think about what Betty had said about Jason being jealous. Maybe a quick call to him wouldn't be a bad idea, just to let him know where I'm going. I grab my phone out of my pocket and hit his name in my contacts.

As I wait for the call to connect, I finish putting the last check into the envelope with the bill and seal it. The call never rang, it goes straight to his voicemail. *He must have turned his phone off for the meetings today.* I think to myself as I listen to his voicemail greeting.

"Hey, it's me, call me when you have a second," I say. "Love ya, bye."

Deciding to send him a text, I open our text history and send a quick message.

Me: Hey, just wanted to let you know I'm going to the Farmer's Market after work with Charles**. I'm going to show him where we get out seafood. Call me when you have a second. :-*

I put my phone back in my pocket and organize the things on my desk. I head out to the front and as I'm walking through the doors, the front door opens causing the bell to ding. I look over and see Kallon walking in. He's wearing a black t-shirt, jeans, and a baseball cap.

"Afternoon Betty," he says to her as she locks the door behind him. He looks over at Maggie and smiles, "Maggie, good to see you again."

"Hi," she says happily.

Kallon looks over at me and his smile grows larger, "Hi Abby, good to see you."

"Hi, good to see you too," I say with a smile back. "How was the set today?"

"Good as always," he smiles. "We're moving along at a pretty decent speed. It might not take as long to shoot as they thought."

"Oh, that's nice," I say with a laugh.

Kallon looks around and asks, "Anything I can do to help?"

"I think we were just finishing up," I say as I check the front coolers are still on and make sure everything else is turned off.

"I'll go pull the car around," Dax says. He walks to the side door but before he leaves, he turns and says to Betty, "Have a good rest of your afternoon, Betty."

Betty's smile is contagious, I can feel my own smile widening at her happiness. I look at Kallon and raise my eyebrows at him but all he does is smile.

"Betty," I say as I clear my throat and look back at her. "I'll see you tomorrow. I was able to prep for the movie set while I was prepping stuff for here. Have a good evening off."

"Thanks Abby," she says happily. She looks at me and

Kallon and adds, "Have a good afternoon."

"Bye, Betty," Kallon says. "Bye, Maggie."

Maggie waves and then follows her mom out the side door. I smile at Kallon and walk towards the back. I hear him following me.

"I just need to turn lights off and make sure the doors are all locked," I say over my shoulder.

"Sounds good," Kallon replies.

"Are you excited to go to the Market?" I ask as I check the back door and the door leading up to my apartment.

"I am," he says with an excited tone. "I can't believe I've never been before."

"It's a lot of fun and Mondays are a good day to go," I say with a laugh. "Everything is fresh and if there are any new vendors, today is the day to visit their booths."

"I'm glad it worked out that we could both go," he says as I take my apron off and hang it up and then turn towards him after turning off the lights in the kitchen.

"Me too," I say. "I haven't been able to go the last couple of weeks, what with how busy I've been. Royce has been going to get our order of seafood. It'll be fun to surprise him."

"Will Jason be joining us?" Kallon asks.

"No, he has a meeting. It's a pretty important one. They got some new clients and today is the only day they could meet," I say as I hit the lights behind the counter to turn them all off except for one directly overhead.

"Is he still pretty mad about the fine?"

"He actually hasn't brought it up. I'm hoping it's a sign he's truly accepted responsibility for his actions," I answer.

"How are things with you and him?" Kallon asks as we

walk to the side door. He opens it and holds it for me to walk out.

"Thanks," I say as I pass him. "We're… okay. We're not in the best place but we aren't in a horrible place either. It's hard to explain."

As we walk toward the street, where we can see Dax standing by the parked car, Kallon says, "I'm here if you need to talk."

"With your unbiased opinion about him?" I ask.

"I can be unbiased and it's hard to have a true opinion of him when I've hardly spent time with him. All I really know is what you've told me and what I've seen the handful of times I have been around him."

"That's true," I say. We get to the car and Dax opens the door for me. I pat his arm and say, "Thank you."

I slide all the way over and start to buckle my seatbelt as Kallon is getting in. Dax shuts the door and makes his way around the car. As he gets in, Kallon turns towards me.

"Honest, Abby, I'm here if you want to talk. I've been told I'm a good listener," he says with a sweet smile.

"Can you be a mutual advisor and not side with me if you think that maybe I'm not being fair?"

"Sort of like the devil's advocate?"

"I guess just don't take my side because we're friends and business partners. Try to see Jason's side?"

"I can do that," he says. He puffs out his chest and adds, "I'm a dude, it's not hard to get inside a guy's mind when you are one."

"I don't think it's hard for anyone to do that, whether you're a guy or not," I laugh.

"Touché," he laughs.

I spend the drive to the Farmer's Market telling Kallon everything I've been feeling about Jason's and my relationship. When Dax pulls into a parking spot, I look around and see that we've arrived.

"I've been talking nonstop for twenty-five minutes," I say as I put my hand over my mouth.

Kallon laughs and gets out of the car as Dax opens my door. Kallon walks around the side and joins me and Dax as we start to walk to the main entrance of the Market.

"Okay, Devil's Advocate, what's your opinion?" I ask Kallon.

"I can see how Jason might feel a little neglected. You have been burning the candle on both ends," he answers. He must see my face fall because he continues with, "But, you're not the only one who has been putting work before the relationship. And I'm not saying this next thing because I want to make you feel better or because we are friends. I'm saying this because it's true. You have been working so hard, but you have been trying to make an effort with him. You said you asked him to do something today and he said no. You asked him to go to dinner with you and he said no. And instead of canceling his business plans, he's just not going. He wants you to adjust your work schedule to accommodate him and his schedule, but he's not willing to do the same for you."

"Don't you think he's wanting me to prove to him that I'm in this relationship? That by me making time for him will show him that?" I ask.

"Why can't you both do that?" he counter asks. "Why

does it have to fall on you? Have you always changed plans on him? Do you cancel at the last minute? Do you forget important dates? Plans?"

"No," I say quietly. I step up to a booth that's selling roasted almonds and buy a bag. Once I've paid, I turn back towards Kallon and Dax and shrug. "I see what you're saying. I just don't know how to get Jason to see it too. I can keep trying to make plans with him."

We start walking but neither of us say anything for a while. We get to the seafood section of the booths and I spot two familiar people standing at the booth where Rose's gets their seafood products.

"Royce! Bridget!" I holler. I turn and smile at Kallon and Dax and then hurry to the other two.

"Abby?" Royce asks, turning in shock. "What are you doing here?"

"Have the afternoon off so I'm showing Kallon where we get our seafood. I thought I'd see you here," I answer him and then I smile at Bridget. "Good to see you."

"You too," she says with a smile and then her face turns a pink as she looks over at Royce. "We... It was—"

"Don't worry, she knows," Royce says as he loads the last package into the cart he has and grabs Bridget's hand.

"You do?" she looks at me in shock.

"I do," I say. "And as long as it doesn't interfere with work, it's all good."

I see her relax and her smile widens, "Thank you."

"We better get these back to the restaurant," Royce says. "It was good to see you."

I look over and see Kallon nod at him. He waves bye

as Royce and Bridget leave. I walk up to the booth and point out everything that we get for Rose's. The owner has a little cooking station set up and offers us a shish kabob of huge shrimp and vegetables.

We make our way through the booths, stopping here and there to look at things that are being made or to sample foods that have been prepared. We're walking towards a booth I've been raving about having the best ice cream, when Dax stops and steps in front of us. He turns and looks at me and then at Kallon.

"What's the matter?" Kallon and I ask at the same time.

Dax looks down at me and says quickly, "Maybe we should go back for some more of that popcorn you like."

I look down at the full bag still in my hands and say, "I think I have enough."

Dax looks at Kallon with a pleading look and then ever so slightly, he tilts his head to the side and behind him. I think the gesture was meant for Kallon, but it has me peaking around Dax's back. I can't believe what I see.

CHAPTER 28

Jason is walking towards us with his arm around some tall, skinny red head. She looks familiar for some reason. She's eating ice cream and offers it to Jason, and he takes a bite. She takes a bite and gets some on her upper lip. Jason leans over and licks it off. They stop and share a deep, passionate kiss. He wraps his hands around her back, they slide down to her ass, and he squeezes.

I hear ringing in my ears. My heart is racing so fast, it feels like it's thudding against my ribcage. Someone is pulling my arm but I'm not budging. All I can do is stand here and watch Jason make out with someone in the middle of the Farmer's Market.

"Abby," I hear my name being called but I can barely hear it through the ringing. Another set of hands are on my other arm and their trying to pull me away. I pull my arms free and finally find my feet. I start walking towards Jason and his red head.

They don't notice me, so I get within an arm's length away before I stop walking. They finally pull apart and Jason looks down at me. At first, it's as if he doesn't recognize me and then shock and confusion hit his face.

"Abbbby?" he stammers out.

I haven't found my voice yet. I just look between Jason and the red head. She's looking between Jason and me and she looks like she's been caught as well. *So, she knows who I am.*

"Abby?" Jason says again. "What are you doing here?"

I feel two big forms come up behind me. I look over my shoulder and see Kallon and Dax standing with their arms crossed over their chests. I look back at Jason and then at his... friend. I raise my hands, palms up in a 'what's this' gesture.

Jason looks at the red head and then back at me and stammers out, "She's... we're..."

"What—" I try to say but it sounds like I'm choking on something. I clear my throat and try again. "What are you doing here?"

"I—" Jason starts but I interrupt.

"You said you had a meeting that you were going to be at all day. You said you couldn't do anything with me because of that meeting and you couldn't come to family dinner because of it too," I say in a monotone voice. My brain is still trying to catch up to what it just saw and comprehend what's happening.

"I—" Jason again starts to say.

"You lied to me so you could come here with her?" I ask. I don't look at the girl.

Jason looks at Dax and Kallon and then his surprised look turns into a sneer, "You came here with them... with him."

"I called you and sent you a text about what I was doing. Your phone was off," I say, my voice still no louder than normal volume.

Jason grabs his phone out of his pocket and pushes a button. I hear some notifications ding and when he looks at me, he looks slightly embarrassed. I start to shake my head.

"We're just friends," he says with a pleading tone.

"Friends don't make out in the middle of a public place. Friends don't touch friends like you're touching her," I say. I see his hand is touching the top part of her ass and her lower back. He moves it quickly up by her shoulder blades. I go to walk by them and when I almost bump into her, I freeze. I take a step back and look at her with my head slightly tilted to the side. "You're... You're the girl from the elevator."

"I... You..." she mumbles out, shaking her head. Her voice has me stepping back further. I bump into Dax and Kallon.

I'm hit with realization. I can't believe it.

"You... you answered... his phone the other night," I stammer out. I look at her shocked face and she looks at Jason with a look that's asking him what she should do. I look at him and he looks terrified. "Have you... Was she at your place before I came over for dinner the other night?"

"She... I... it's..." Jason stammers out.

"She was, wasn't she? You weren't running around picking up when you called to see how long I'd be, you were finishing up with her and making sure she was out before I got there!" I say, my voice starting to rise. "And the other night, she answered your phone. You've been cheating on me?"

I say the last part in a whisper because I can't believe it.

"I... It's been... Abby please," Jason pleads, he reaches for my hand while he's still touching her.

I step away from his hand, Dax and Kallon allowing me to step back. I raise my hands to should height, shake my head, and say, "Don't touch me. I can't believe you. How long?"

I think back to the times I've called, and he's been out of breath, and he said he was working out. I feel bile rise up in my throat.

"Almost two years," the red head says in a small voice. Jason looks at her with a look that has her bowing her head and shutting her mouth.

I take a step back again, almost tripping over one of the guys' shoes. One of them catches me, I look over and see Dax's hands on me.

"Two... years..." I stammer out in a whisper. Then I raise my voice, "TWO YEARS!"

"Abby let's talk about this," Jason says, stepping towards me.

I step back again and say, "I don't have anything else I need to hear from you and we're over Jason, for good. I'm leaving. Don't. Follow. Me."

"Abby please," Jason says.

Dax steps up to block his path to me and growls out, "Miss Rose says to leave her alone."

"Move," Jason growls back.

I reach forward and grab Dax's upper arm and turn him towards me, "Please Dax, I want to leave."

"Abby, please, I want to talk to you," Jason says. He

reaches around and grabs my arm and pulls me towards him.

Now both Kallon and Dax step up but it's Kallon who says, in the scariest voice I've ever heard, "Take. Your hands. Off her. Now."

Jason lets me go and I step back. I grab both Dax and Kallon by the arms and pull them away. They both put a hand to my back and usher me through the crowd. Luckily, there aren't a ton of people staring, so we didn't cause a huge scene.

"Abby, please!" I hear Jason yell as we walk away.

I'm led back to the car in a daze. Dax opens the door and I slide in without really knowing what I'm doing.

"Abby?" Kallon asks quietly. I don't respond. He reaches over and pulls my seatbelt across my lap and chest and buckles me in. The thoughtfulness behind that action breaks the walls inside me that were holding my tears at bay.

"I.. he.." I blubber out. I put my hands over my face and bawl into them. I feel Kallon slide over and he pulls me to him.

"Shhh, Abby, it's going to be okay," he says.

Dax pulls out from the parking spot and starts to drive us away from the Farmer's Market. I lean away from Kallon and take a calming breath.

"I just... I knew we were having problems. I knew we were drifting apart but I never, in my wildest dreams, thought he'd cheat on me. And two years?" I almost scream. I take some more calming breaths. "When we had our pregnancy scare, he was seeing her too. I wonder if that's why he was so freaked out. Worried he'd gotten me pregnant and it might mess up the sweet set up he had for himself."

My phone starts to ring and buzz in my pocket, I pull

it out and see Jason is calling. I hit the decline button. His name pops up again after a voicemail notification appears, so I answer.

"I don't want to talk to you!" I scream into my phone and then hang up. He calls again. I let it go to voicemail and turn my ringer and the vibration off.

"Should I have seen this coming? Was I so oblivious to our relationship that I didn't know he was cheating?" I ask. I turn to Kallon and see he's raking a hand through his hair. "Should I have?"

"No," he says quickly. "The only thing you thought was fishy was the girl who answered the other night. His explanation was a good one, it was believable. But for him to have hidden this for two years, that's on him. Don't blame yourself for not knowing."

"If I would have been around his place more often, maybe there were signs that I wasn't seeing," I offer.

"Don't do this to yourself," Kallon says. "You can't blame yourself for something he chose to do."

"You know he's going to blame it on me anyways," I say.

"That's because he's a narcissist," Dax says from the front.

I inhale deeply and when I exhale, I let it fill my cheeks. I close my eyes and shake my head. I lean my head back against the head rest and breathe. I roll my head to the side and open my eyes back up to look at Kallon.

"I just can't believe this," I say. A tear rolls down my cheek. I reach up and wipe it away.

"I know, Abby. I'm so sorry," he says. He puts his arm

around me and pulls me towards him again. "What can I do to help?"

"Nothing," I say.

"We could go back and beat him to a pulp," Dax suggests.

I feel Kallon chuckle beside me, and he says, "That's an option."

"No, it's not. No one is going to fight," I say sternly.

"I mean, we could," Dax says again.

"Daaax," I say, drawing out his name. I then laugh and say, "Thank you."

I see him nod his head and he continues driving. I lean away from Kallon and wipe my face with my hands.

"Where do you want me to take you?" Dax asks.

"To my parents," I say. "I'll break the news to them, we'll have dinner, and then I'll go home."

"Okay," Dax says.

The rest of the drive to my parents' house is quiet. I stare out the side window and watch the city pass by. When we pull up to their house, I look over at Kallon.

"Do you want to stay for dinner? I'm sure they'd love to see you," I say with a small smile.

"No, that's okay, thank you though," Kallon says. "I'm meeting with my agent tonight."

"Okay, if you change your mind, we'll be here," I say, pointing to my parents' house.

"Thanks," he says with a nod.

Dax gets out and opens my door for me. He says, "I'm going to take Mr. Keller home and then I'll be back."

"Thanks Dax," I say as I touch his arm as I walk past

him.

The next hour is spent telling my parents about me and Jason. They had a lot of questions, some I had answers to, some I didn't. Patty didn't look to upset that things were over between us. He was never really that nice to her, which should have been my first clue he wasn't right for me. The time after that while we ate was me telling them about my new schedule. About how I rearranged things to give me more time with Jason but now, I'll use it to sleep or do something more than just work.

"Dad this chicken is so good!" I say as I take another bite of the third or fourth drumstick I've eaten.

"That new BBQ'er sure is nice," he says with agreement. "Thanks for not being upset about me buying it."

"It's okay," I say around the meat in my mouth. I swallow and say, "It's worth it if the food that comes off of it taste this good."

"Thanks Buds," he says with a smile.

After I finish my plate of food, I say, "I'm going to have to get going."

"Are you sure honey?" Mom asks.

"Yeah, I have an early morning, or night, however you want to look at it," I say with a laugh.

"Do you want to take some food home?" Mom asks. "Your dad made enough to feed a crowd."

"No, thank you," I say. "I don't really have time to eat at home much lately."

"I was excited to use the BBQ'er," Dad says, which makes us all laugh. He looks at me and says, "It sounds like your new schedule will give you more time to eat."

"It will but not much. I'm afraid it'd go bad in my fridge before I'd get to it," I say, giving him a hug. I look out the window and see Dax standing by the car.

"Maybe Dax wants a plate to take home?" Patty asks as she carries a plate out from the kitchen.

"I bet he does," I say with a smile. She walks out with me after I give Mom a hug goodbye.

"Dax, I brought this for you," Patty says with a smile.

"Oh, Patty," Dax says taking the plate from her. "The first two plates were delicious. This one will come in handy when I get home. Thank you."

She smiles at him, gives me a hug, and says, "I'm sorry you are sad. But Jason was not a nice man. You will find a nice man that will not make you sad."

"Thanks Patty," I say, hugging her tightly. "Good night."

"Night," she says as she waves to me and Dax. She then hurries to the door where Mom and Dad are still standing. They wave as they go inside.

"Thank you for being so kind to her," I say as I get into the car. Dax closes my door and gets into his driver's seat.

"She's easy to like," he says with a genuine smile. "How did the evening go?"

"Awful but good," I answer. "Mom kept asking if I saw it coming but she'd answer herself by saying that of course I didn't see it coming. Dad called him an asshole, but he said he didn't want to say anything more incase Jason and I get back together."

"Is that an option?" Dax asks.

"No," I say. "He cheated on me and lied for a couple of

years and who knows what else. How could I ever trust him again?"

"I'm sorry this happened," Dax says. I look at him through the rearview mirror. "You don't deserve to be treated like that. To be so disrespected."

"I guess it's better to find out now than ten years from now if we got married," I say with a sigh.

"Would you have married him?"

"I probably would have said yes if he asked, but I would have been worried. Our relationship was so rocky these last few months. I thought it was just from working so much, but I now know it's because he was wanting to spend time with his other girlfriend."

I look at my watch and see that it's 7:46pm. I yawn and put my head back against my headrest and look out the window. I sit up when I feel the car slowing down and look over to see we're back at Rose Bud's.

Dax gets out and walks around to the side of the car and opens the door. I slide across the seat and get out. Dax shuts the door and offers me his arm. I slide my hand around the back of his, hold on to his bicep, and let him walk us to the side of my building. I don't argue with him walking me to my door, it feels nice.

He reaches for the door and waits for me to enter my code. He opens it when we hear it unlock. I pat him on the arm and step inside.

"Have a good night, Miss Rose," he says giving me a nod.

"Good night, Dax," I say waving at him.

I walk up the stairs and wave once I have the door

open. I step inside and I'm greeted with a surprise. And not a good one.

A special thank you to my Beta readers. I really appreciate all the time and support you all have given me through the process of writing "Rose's" and "Rose Bud's". It's been another long road, but with your encouragement and enthusiasm throughout it all, I was able to keep moving forward. Thank you, THANK YOU, THANK YOU for once again being in my corner and coming along this journey with me!

Logan Nedrow
Stephanie Mays
Jane Wisdom
Lacey Warner
Danielle Martin
Nina Stephens
Melissa Kendall